Praise for Elizabeth Jane Howard

'She is one of those novelists who shows, through her work, what the novel is for . . . She helps us to do the necessary thing – open our eyes and our hearts'
Hilary Mantel

'Magnificent, addictive . . . deeply enjoyable, beautifully written' *The Times*

'Elegantly constructed and intelligently and wittily written . . . remarkable' *Daily Telegraph*

'A compelling storyteller, shrewd and accurate in human observation, with a fine ear for dialogue and an evident pleasure in the English language and landscape' *Guardian*

'Howard is such an astute observer of human behaviour. She conveys volumes with tiny, brilliant touches . . . This is Howard's true magic: her humanity transcends the individual' *Sunday Times*

'Love and relationships are the abiding themes of Howard's novels . . . [this is] a novel about constants – loyalty, kindness, compassion – and like the best of its characters, never less than heart-warming and wise' *Observer*

'A dazzling historical ꞏrald

'A lyrical read full of ꞏharp emotional intelligence eted'

ꞏview

00 2934288 X

FALLING

Elizabeth Jane Howard was the author of fifteen highly acclaimed novels. The Cazalet Chronicles – *The Light Years, Marking Time, Confusion* and *Casting Off* – have become established as modern classics and have been adapted for a major BBC television series and most recently for BBC Radio 4. In 2002 Macmillan published Elizabeth Jane Howard's autobiography, *Slipstream*. In that same year she was awarded a CBE in the Queen's Birthday Honours List. She died in January 2014, following the publication of the fifth Cazalet novel, *All Change*.

FALLING

ELIZABETH
JANE HOWARD

PICADOR

First published 1999 by Macmillan

This paperback edition published 2015 by Picador
an imprint of Pan Macmillan
20 New Wharf Road, London N1 9RR
Associated companies throughout the world
www.panmacmillan.com

ISBN 978-1-4472-7239-7

1 3 5 7 9 8 6 4 2

A CIP catalogue record for this book is available from the British Library.

Typeset by Palimpsest Book Production Ltd, Falkirk, Stirlingshire
Printed and bound by CPI Group (UK) Ltd, Croydon, CR0 4YY

For my daughter
Nicola

ACKNOWLEDGEMENTS

I want to thank Sybille Bedford, my friend, Jane Wood, my editor, and Elliott Starks, my son-in-law, for their – different, but essential – support.

ACKNOWLEDGEMENTS

1

HENRY

She has left me. This last, most terrible blow has knocked me out. I don't seem able to think about it for long enough to gain the slightest inkling of *why* this has happened. She was in love with me – I'm sure of that – or was she simply sexually infatuated? My experience of women – considerable, for I am, after all, over sixty – had, I presumed, taught me a good deal about how extraordinarily different they are from most men. I except myself here as I feel I have always had an intuitive understanding of the comparatively few women I've been in love with, have known them often better than they've known themselves. I now think that one reason why I've found it difficult to get on with my own sex has been that what I've learned of them has been largely through women. It has been through their confidences, and sometimes simply their responses, that I realized long ago how so many of them are mistreated, that that enchanting early awareness of their sexuality and romantic inclination is all too often nipped in the bud. Thus are bred the ice maidens, the termagants, the nymphos, the drab domestic servitors and the hysterically sentimental matriarchs. I blame men for these sad consequences, much as other people blame parents for the delinquent child.

It has been my good fortune, and naturally my pleasure, to undo and heal some of this damage; indeed,

1

I can honestly say that my greatest joy has come from pleasing a woman – in teaching her to inhabit her own body with pleasure and pride. This cannot be achieved by mere sexual prowess; I have no way of, and indeed no interest in, measuring my own against that of any other man. It comes from that mixture of affection, cherishing and *loving* that cannot be assumed, but once present needs constant expression. Women need not only to be loved; they need to be told so. I believe George Eliot has something to say about that.

But knowing what I do, how has it happened that she has gone? Why? What can have possessed her to do anything so destructive of her happiness? Not to mention my own: I have as much – some would say more – to lose by her defection. It took many months to find her, time and ingenuity to effect a meeting, and then many more months and a quantity of letters to assure and reassure her of my eligibility. I must confess that when I started the whole thing, I was very uncertain of success, regarded her as something of a challenge, but I have a romantic as well as an adventurous nature, and at the time had little or nothing to lose. In the course of a very few months I had lost both my job and my wife, and while these losses were more tiresome than tragic their coincidence was, financially at least, most unfortunate. I was reduced at a stroke to isolation and penury.

I have lived for two years now in a small cabin-cruiser lent by a couple who were going to live abroad and who wanted me to sell it for them. I have my state pension, for some time supplemented by money that I had salted away from the joint bank account with Hazel. I was glad to be shot of *her* with her cold prying nature, her controlling ways and her carping at everything I did or didn't do. She had a steady and well-paid job, which fortunately occupied her so thoroughly that for the last few years of our marriage we did not have to spend very much time together. But her resentment at my failure to earn as much money as she, and more, the fact that she was of no importance to me, manifested itself in spasmodic outbursts of bitterness and anger, and my indifference to her congealed to something very like hatred. The boat was a relief. I could stay in bed in the mornings as long as I pleased, eat what I wanted when I felt like it, read all night if I was so inclined, and have my papers undisturbed. Very few people came to see the boat, and it was easy to put them off buying it. I would fill the bilges before they came and explain that I had spent the morning pumping them out, which had become a daily occurrence. No doubt if the boat was taken out of the water, repairs to her hull could be made, but who knew what else might then be found? My frankness was commended and that was invariably the end of that. I had no compunction about this; the owners already had a house to live in when they returned, which would not be for another year. I was content. I am never bored, and when I felt the need for company I could always go to the village pub.

Once a week I would take a bus to the public library to return and collect books. For the past year I've been making a study of women novelists, both nineteenth- and twentieth-century authors. Another fascinating light thrown upon the relations between the sexes is often contained in their novels.

But towards the end of my first year in the boat, the future began to loom, as I realized that the present situation had a finite ending. True, there would one day be a divorce from which I might expect some money: the flat that Hazel and I had bought was in my name and she would eventually get a handsome pension from the people she worked for. But this money, in turn, while it would not provide me with enough to live on, might affect the amount I could expect from the state. I would have to do something.

My first attempt led to nothing at all. I began with my local pub, the only place where, apart from shop people, I had any social contact, though that had been of the most casual order. The customers were mostly men, and on the occasions that they were accompanied by a woman she proved always to be a wife or a girlfriend – the wives looking variously like people I was glad not to have had as a mother, and the girlfriends so jealously partnered that it would have been folly to approach them. I did consider the landlady, an ample widow in her late forties, but there was something both mechanical and common about her responses that put me off. I never saw any woman there who was capable of inspiring a spark of romance, and I am someone who cannot function without that. I would have to go further afield than the small village a quarter of a mile up the towpath from my boat.

Over the years I have come to understand that while one should always look out for opportunity, it was equally important to determine what kind of opportunity it was worth looking out for. What I now sought was a woman about ten years younger than myself: anything younger and one would be faced with having to endure their menopause, and the thirty-year-old and younger tended to want more bedtime than I at my age felt willing to provide, or worse, to want children which I have taken the means to make impossible. This may sound cold-blooded: it is not. If you have a temperament as whole-hearted, as passionately absorbed in the object of affection as I know mine to be, a certain caution at the outset repays itself.

The woman I sought proved, after many nights of cogitation, to be someone who had survived the elementary fences and was facing the last straight home in solitude. No longer in her prime, she would have at least to *have been* possessed of some beauty – to have the air of past romance, like the classical folly in a great park, past its original use and now surrounded by an aura of neglect. I could carry this analogy much further: the ivy of her experience that had been slowly strangling her for years would be gently stripped from her by my experienced touch, et cetera.

She should have *had* her marriage and her children and have slaked all commonplace ambition in those directions. It would be an added bonus if she had achieved something in her own right, had some profession or career: I've always found success aphrodisiac. She must like men and have been disappointed by them. I should not in the least object to her liking women as well – indeed, for a week or two I indulged the fantasy of finding a woman already in love with another woman, and my completing the trio. However, I am able to be realistic, and recognized the improbability of hitting such a sexual jackpot. But I did, of course, fantasize about her appearance, and lived in my mind with a small, full-breasted woman with tiny hands and feet and short, very thick, reddish-gold hair, bobbed to a point at the back of her neck. This was all very well, but imagining such a creature brought me no nearer to finding her.

On one of my visits to the library, it occurred to me

ELIZABETH JANE HOWARD

that I should look at the personal columns where people advertise their requirements for a partner. It was interesting how similar the advertisements were. All the women seemed to want a non-smoker with a sense of humour interested in the arts and aged between thirty-five and fifty. They were also usually keen on being sent a photograph. I smoke, but am able to lay off it when necessary, and in any case have had to cut down considerably owing to lack of funds. I have a sense of humour, although for a good deal of my life this does not seem to have been appreciated by most of the women with whom I have been connected. I cannot honestly say that I'm interested in all the arts – pictures, for instance, do not make much impression upon me. Whoever it was would have to make do with a mild enjoyment of music and my considerable knowledge of fiction, and although I had accumulated a collection of photographs of myself, including a few as a child, none of them were more recent than ten years ago. Still, if fifty was the top age limit, one of the more recent pictures should do.

I chose one of these in which I'm leaning against a large tree, wearing an open-necked shirt and smiling at the photographer. My hair, which has always been satisfactorily thick and curly, is ruffled by the wind and has all its original colour – a dark brown that is almost black. I look confident, kind and – dare I say it? – sexy. While copies of this picture were being made (I did not expect to strike lucky first time), I began drafting the letter that I would send with them. As my hair has graduated inexorably from pepper and salt to a decent grey, I would have to account for this. It was not difficult. I decided that I should have been recently widowed – not from Hazel, who no stretch of my imagination could render a romantic figure, but from somebody far younger and more lovable than she had ever been. Suddenly the girl at Jane Eyre's terrible school came to mind – the clever, patient Helen Burns who died, you may remember, from tuberculosis after months of starvation, abuse and general neglect. Helen should be my dead wife whom I had nurtured until her end.

Once I had decided this, thoughts flowed from it in all directions. Helen Burns had been an orphan and so was my Helen. Her life had been difficult and lonely until she met me, when all had changed for her. With me, she flowered. My love for her, my care and ceaseless vigilance of her peace and happiness changed her whole being and what remained of her tragically short life. The bitterness of discovering her illness was terrible. I remember reading that Rex Harrison had concealed the gravity of her disease from Kay Kendall, that she had died without ever knowing that he had married her because he knew that she was to die. So would I conceal the same knowledge from my Helen. It was a short step from this to my having married her with the awful knowledge of her failing health.

I have to say that for a couple of weeks I forgot the reason for my writing this account, so fascinated did I become by making it for its own sake. I wept for Helen as, in the story of her dying, she came more and more alive to me. At the end of two weeks – when I collected the prints of the photograph – there was nothing I did not know about her and I had covered over seventy pages. When I read them through (of course I knew that they could not be a letter to anyone), I realized not only how much I loved her, but how much I had gained from the experience. It was clear to me, first, that I had never loved anyone as I loved Helen, and second, that in order to fulfil and ennoble the deepest part of my nature, I *needed* such a love. I set to work on the letter with renewed enthusiasm.

Apart from the fact that my instinct told me that the letter should be short, I had the problem of how to present myself in the best possible light without appearing in any way smug. The seventy pages were full of my tenderness, my cherishing and my courage in facing the steadily approaching end. The best way of presenting this must be through the expression of my great love. But it might not be wise to give the impression of *too* great a love, or the recipients of the letters might feel that they had no hope of taking Helen's place, and none of us like the notion of being second best. I could, of course, place Helen's death much earlier in my life, but this meant that I could not send the photograph and claim that my hair had turned grey from grief, which had been my intention. No, it would all have to be in the last ten years, but I could have recovered from it – enough to know that I sought a comparable life with a new partner. The answer, of course, was to make clear my *capacity* for love in general, rather than dwell upon Helen, but in the end I settled for a simple statement of my marriage, her illness and death.

The months of that winter passed. To begin with, I sent out one letter at a time, but the answers, when they came, were uniformly so disappointing (and sometimes there was no answer at all) that I took to writing about three a week, and sending them off by the same post. Twice I went to London to meet women whose replies had seemed hopeful and endured two separate hours drinking tea in the Charing Cross Hotel.

The first woman, a widow, kept asking impertinent questions about my past career with a barely concealed view to discovering my means. When I said that I had retired, she accused me of insincerity about my age, which I had never told her in the first place. It was clear to me in the first five minutes that we would have nothing going for each other. But feeling it would be rude to say so, I stuck it out until she made some remark about my not seeming to have much of the ambition she liked in a man, but she supposed that at my age I must make do with some hobby. Her look of patronising indulgence filled me with rage. I said that I had probably one of the finest collections of pornography in the country, and that I specialized in bums rather than breasts (both of hers were outsize). She left me at once, to pay for the tea – ridiculously expensive – and get the bus home.

The second woman seemed at first sight more promising: she was younger, better-looking and becomingly nervous, but she had a tiresome laugh that punctuated everything either of us said. She seemed to have lived all her life with a mother who had demanded all her spare time – she worked as a dental nurse – and who had disapproved of any boyfriends. Her mother had recently died, and she had been left the house. She was in some ways pathetic, but she did not attract or inspire me, and our meeting ended with my saying I had to catch my bus and would write to her. 'You won't, though, will you?' she said, and then just as I was beginning to feel sorry for her, she laughed again.

Going back to the boat, I felt that the whole notion of finding someone in this manner was hopeless, and I knew that I deserved something better than the kind of woman who placed advertisements for friendship or marriage.

I wrote no more letters; instead I concentrated upon my Helen, proliferating the happy times we had had, adding innumerable small touches to her appearance and behaviour until she was more real and more dear to me than any woman I had known.

So I passed my second autumn on the boat. I had finished George Eliot by the time the winter set in, and was casting about in the library for a new subject. I ended up by taking one novel each by Iris Murdoch, Virginia Woolf, Ouida and Elinor Glyn – an odd bag you might say, but I like to cast my net as widely as possible, and I'm no intellectual snob. I mention this particular trip to the library only because it was on that evening that, walking back from the village, I noticed the cottage. It was not that I had never seen it before; it had always been an unremarkable part of the landscape of the familiar walk from boat to village and gave every sign of being uninhabited. Now I observed the cottage because there were lights on; I could see that one of the rooms had red walls, which made a rosy glow in the grey autumn dusk, and the contrast between this picture-postcard cosiness and my damp and generally cheerless abode impressed me. If my life had not been so studded with misfortune, *I* could have owned such a place – more modest than my original ambitions had dictated, but better by far than my present lot.

That evening, while I consumed what was left of a tinned steak and kidney pudding, I did find myself sinking into a depression, which began with a résumé of my present condition: in my sixties, living on the state, homeless, or shortly to become so (the owners had written to say that they were returning sooner than expected), and without a lover, let alone a companion of any kind. How had I come to this? When I thought back to my youth and remembered how easy it had been to get any girl who interested me interested in me, it seemed extraordinary that I should end up alone. Women of all ages had succumbed to my attentions. If I had married Daphne, might things have been different? Or perhaps if I had *not* married Hazel success might have shone. But it had never done that for more than a few weeks, or perhaps months. I could not understand why, when I possessed a talent that from my observation of them was given to few men, I should not have landed myself with all the emotional and other security so necessary to someone of my nature. It was true that, years ago, in the Daphne days, I had had hopes and dreams far beyond any that I might entertain now. I was, though I say it myself, extremely good-looking. I was bright. My English teacher at school told me that I should try for university; she thought, if I worked, I had a good chance of a scholarship. But Daphne had intervened, followed – mercifully as it turned out – by the war. It was really my father who persuaded, or rather bullied, me into learning his trade but to me there has always been something menial about being a gardener, which no quantity of upper-class, middle-aged ladies in green wellingtons can dispel. However much they yap on about old-fashioned shrub roses and white gardens, I know that someone else does the double digging, the muck-spreading, the hedge-cutting, the seed-thinning, the potting-up and other countless tasks that are made wearisome by their repetition. My father 'put me through it', to use his phrase, and this meant that I did all those things. It used to take me ages to get my hands clean enough to meet Daphne.

I remember coming back that evening into the saloon from the galley where I had gone to make a cup of instant coffee and wondering idly what Daphne – or, indeed, any of the others – would think if they saw how I lived now, and at once it was as though I was viewing the scene before me through other, actually critical eyes. It's true that I have never been much of a one for domestic life (the man who cannot find some woman to clear up and generally administer to him has hardly the right to call himself a man) but really, in this particular case of the boat, I had let things go rather too far. I had fallen into the habit of waiting to do the washing-up until there was not a clean crock left. Anyone who has had to water a boat then boil any they want hot will understand this point. But that autumn I had taken to eating off bits of the *Sunday Times* when I had run out of plates, or rinsing one mug whose pottery was heavily stained with tannin, and otherwise drinking straight from cans. The place was a litter of paper, crumbs and minor congealed spill-ages of anything from Guinness to strawberry jam. The small carpet was filthy; the windows clouded with paraffin fumes and condensation. The oil lamps were dull with the greasy black that results from untrimmed wicks. The galley was in a revolting state. In fact, the only bits of the boat that I had kept clean were the toilet and basin (I have never been able to endure squalor in those areas). My books were covered in a scum of untouched dust. I knew, because every time I returned to the boat and unlocked the saloon doors it assailed me, that the place smelt of paraffin, damp, unwashed clothes and tobacco. If I *did* find anybody, I thought, it would have to be on her ground rather than mine. That I can rise above almost any mater-ial circumstances does not mean that I should expect

others to do the same. It is not even a question of prior-
ities: for me love has always been the single most important
influence in my life.

And now I have lost it – again! It is strange how one's
mind shies away from unbearable reality into past, quite
trivial detail; into small pointless pieces of reminiscence
or speculation of what might have been if some minor
aspect of a situation had been different – anything, I
suppose, to protect oneself from more than a second's
endurance of pain as fresh as it is relentless. I know that
in the end the freshness will fade. If pictures of her slip
across my inner vision with that soundless poignancy
that makes one want to cry out, their recurrence (it is
curious how repetition is the chief habit of memory) will
degenerate into a familiar ache. At the moment, however,
the loss of her is too new for me even to contemplate the
idea that it may diminish. Worse – and how I recognize
this! – I do not *want* it to: I clutch at my pain as the last
straw of feeling I may ever possess before the Ice Age of
a vegetable senility sets in, such as I have seen so often
in a vacant gaze, a trickle of mucus generated from mum-
bling jaws, the pointless fidgeting of veined and liver-
spotted hands that smooth non-existent hair or shabby
clothes. Old age has become something that I dread – far
more than death.

I can remember that when I was young, a boy, old age
was something that I regarded with a kind of incredulous
boredom. It could have nothing to do with me because
I was never going to be like that. My horizon then
extended merely to my becoming dashingly adult, past
the age when people could call me boy and boss me
about. It is strange how, when we are very young, we
equate growing up with freedom; we think that having

escaped parental bondage we shall live thereafter exactly as we please. The business of having to earn one's living has not impinged. But when we have to start doing *that*, old age shifts from its distance and settles nearer: at least it was so for me. And since then it has loomed, edged ever nearer, usually – as in that game that the girls at school were so fond of called Grandmother's Steps – when I was not looking. Shortly before I left Hazel I remember waking early – I had tried to turn over in bed and the pain had woken me – looking at my watch and realising that I couldn't see what time it was without my specs. Then I understood that at last old age had succeeded in creeping up on me, had woken me with a tap on the shoulder. *I* was old; in good nick, but indisputably old.

All that day to counteract panic I added up my assets: nothing wrong with my heart or blood pressure; memory not quite what it had been, but still pretty good. My hair was now a steel grey but there was plenty of it. My teeth, apart from a small bridge, were my own, and the use of spectacles for reading was no indictment. And in spite of failing to make much of bed with Hazel (it does take two to tango, and Hazel was no dancer of anything) there was nothing wrong with my equipment in that department either. But anyone meeting me for the first time would dub me old. They might *say* I was elderly – a kind of genteel pastel version of ageing – but what they would mean was that I seemed to them old.

I knew from experience that I could talk myself past this damning view. Wells was right when he said it did not matter to a woman what a man looked like as long as he could talk. And, I would add to that, listen. Yet whichever way I looked at it, I had not all that much time in which to design a new and delightful life for myself. Give me the woman and I would fall in love with her, but even I could not do this without an object for my affection.

These thoughts came back to me on that dank evening. I remember it in so much detail because it was the last evening I was to spend in that way. When I had drunk my coffee and smoked a cigarette – the last in my pack – wishing I had the cash for some vodka, I boiled a kettle and washed up for as long as the water lasted. This only made everything else look worse, so I boiled another kettleful and set to work upon the rest of the galley. It was four in the morning before I had finished and I fell on to my bunk without a thought for Helen, or indeed anyone else.

I slept late; the heavy white mist that makes the canal look as though it is smoking had almost dispersed. Condensation had dampened the outside of my sleeping-bag, and I lay for a few minutes contemplating the familiar, boring and uncomfortable interval there must be between getting out of a warm bunk and sitting in the saloon with a scalding cup of tea. The thought of another winter in the boat was not cheering. While I was pulling on my jeans and oiled-wool jersey the evil thought occurred to me that I *could*, actually, smarten up the boat and make a real effort to sell her as mine. Then I could scarper with the money and start somewhere else. Naturally I did not pursue this idea: I am by nature rather more honest than most, but it is sometimes amusing to consider notions that are so out of one's behavioural orbit as to be fantastic.

I have nothing against fantasy *per se*. Indeed, it seems to me one of the most harmless ways of enriching one's life. I can always remember as a child the shock of teachers or parents accusing me of 'day-dreaming', as though this was some kind of offence. However, this particular morning – an ordinary, humdrum, end-of-Indian-summer Saturday morning – required me to be dully practical. I had to water the boat. This involved hauling it about a hundred yards the other side of the first bridge, to the lock cottage whose owner had a hose that reached to my water tank. I had also to do some shopping for food, and to fetch my laundry from the woman in the village. I made a shopping list of the usual things: eggs, bacon, sausages, corned beef, potatoes, onions and carrots, a large loaf, tomatoes, milk and a jar of Nescafé. I also needed more cleaning materials; it looked like more than one trip.

I noticed as I passed the cottage that the curtains were drawn in the upstairs windows and that there was no sign of life. I also observed that the garden, what I could see of it, was a total wilderness filled with sodden hay, nettles blackened by the frost, old man's beard, thistles and even ragwort. Then at the far side of the cottage, past the hedge that surrounded its garden, I noticed the most beautiful car I had ever seen. It was a two-seater, drop-head Mercedes, probably over twenty years old, its black canvas roof set off by the metallic green-grey bodywork. It was a car that could only belong, I felt, to a rich romantic, a Gatsbyish car made for the privileged few. I could not help giving it a closer look. It was in excellent condition; its long sleek lines polished, its chrome trim gleaming. Inside it had a walnut dashboard and black leather upholstery. Whoever owned that car was not short of a bob or two. It was probably some film director or pop star, I thought: country cottages and expensive cars were all part of their equipment, and the state of the garden was just what one would expect from some *nouveau riche* townie. For the rest of the walk I indulged myself with straightforward envy. It was not so much that I wanted particularly to *own* a car like that Mercedes, but that I wanted to be in a position to *choose* whether I owned one. The worst thing about poverty was the lack of choice. I imagined myself having to choose whether I would have either the cottage *or* the car – even that was a choice wildly beyond my present means.

While I was shopping I asked who lived in the cottage near the canal bridge. A lady from London – just moved in – a Mrs Redfearn. I asked if there was a Mr Redfearn, but that was not known. Looking back, I realize that even then I was considering the possibility of Mrs Redfearn as I then thought of her. If there *was* a Mr Redfearn I would go no further. Experience has taught me that there is very little point in pursuing women who are seriously, or even socially, married. You have to battle with their better natures – always the dullest part of them – and there is the danger that the husband will cotton on at the wrong moment. In any case there are quite enough women on their own to make pointless the pursuit of those already spoken for. I suppose when I was far younger, I did not understand this: the presence of a husband made romance more exciting and, of course, there were women, although with one exception I hardly encountered them, whose position in life made reckless effort worthwhile. Poor Charley, I thought: poor rich Charley! It was extraordinary how relatives' interference was invariably destructive. But in Charley's case they thought of nothing but money, which was why, I suppose, they had so much of it, and they were prepared to pretend that the drunken sod to whom she was married was a better bet than I could ever be. Anyway, after that débâcle, I avoided married women.

As I trudged back to the boat with the first consignment of shopping I saw that the car had gone. On the other hand, there was smoke rising from the chimney, so presumably Mrs Redfearn had simply gone out to lunch. Or *they* had gone out. I had suddenly an intense desire to walk through the jungle garden up to the cottage and see what I could of the inside. If there was anyone in the cottage and they accosted me, I would say I had come to enquire whether they needed a gardener. The sitting room did actually have red walls and clashing pink curtains. There were two very large sofas and, in the middle of the floor, several tea chests that seemed to be full of books. I noted also a number of very large cushions with bits of glass in their embroidery. A fire smoked reluctantly on an enormous hearth but there was no sign of anyone.

I moved past the sitting room and the front door to the side where the kitchen must be. If I could see cups or mugs lying about, I might have some idea of how many people had had breakfast.

The kitchen had windows front and back, was two rooms knocked into one. It had, apart from the usual kitchen things, a round pine table on which the remains of breakfast for one still lay. Of course, all that told me was that Mrs Redfearn had come here alone; for all I knew she might be fetching him from the station at this minute. Somehow (and this is *not* hindsight, I do remember the feeling very clearly) I had the intuition that she lived alone, was either divorced or a widow.

I remember so well the curious prickling that comes

after that little shot in the dark when one *knows* a small piece of something without the slightest reason for knowing it. For a split second, I knew that Mrs Redfearn was going to be of paramount importance in my life. I need look no further: here she was going to be.

In the middle of these discoveries, I heard the car return. I had just time to get back down the path and outside the gate before she appeared round the corner of the hedge. She was tall, wearing a long raincoat and boots, and a man's black felt hat set rather far back on her head. She was carrying shopping-bags and stopped a moment when she saw me.

'What can I do for you?'

'I thought there might be something I could do for *you.*'

'Oh?' She had reached the gate and we were face to face. Her eyes were grey and she looked wary. I launched into my garden bit.

'I suppose I do,' she said. 'I hadn't got round to thinking about it. Let me just go and dump these.'

As she walked into the cottage, I heard the telephone ring, and after a few minutes she reappeared and asked if I could come back in the afternoon at about three.

I agreed to that, reflecting as I went about my domestic chores that most, if not all, women are addicted to the telephone. At that point I wanted to find something ordinary about her to still some of the violent surging of excitement that seeing her had engendered. It may seem extraordinary to an outsider, but I had only to look on her face to find it beautiful. I have a theory about this, because it is something I have found several times in my life and when I have told the woman concerned she has always questioned – and in some cases totally misunderstood – me. It has something to do with looking for the first time at someone with *no* preconceived notion, picture, image, whatever you want to call it, of them at all. I can, if I choose, look at a new face and experience a sense of complete discovery and at the same time recognition. Then I *know* them – for the duration of my looking – and so, inevitably, I love what I see and know. One woman argued that this could only be true if I was predisposed to love them anyway, to which I simply replied that something did not have to be true with everyone to be true with some. I certainly don't love everybody, but I also *see* very few people and those who I see I love, or have loved.

And now Mrs Redfearn had joined the club.

Another thing about this kind of seeing is that it imprints itself indelibly on my mind. With all the pictures that I have of her now, I can at any time shut out the present and conjure that first sight – when I was within two or three feet of her and our eyes met. I knew that she was sizing me up, or trying to do so, but there was something more to her look than wary appraisal – a wildness, a fear, a familiarity with disappointment, these things so instant and glancing that most people would never have caught anything of them, but after a lifetime of passionate interest in the nuances of response I am finely tuned; nothing of the kind escapes me. I think I knew then that more of her life had been endurance than enjoyment.

I observed other things . . . I estimated her to be in her mid-fifties: her complexion was pale and clear but it was inscribed with myriad tiny lines, round her eyes, round her mouth, and deeper marks between her eyebrows that had in turn the narrow arched symmetry often seen in Elizabethan portraits. I could go on like

Shakespeare: item, one nose of a shape known as aquiline; item, one mouth – or pair of lips – small, also pale and rather prim excepting when she smiled. But I am anticipating: she had not yet smiled at me, nor had she taken off her hat.

Naturally I got to know all kinds of details, physical and other, but nothing I subsequently learned altered or belied my first impression.

I went back to the cottage at three. It was still, not a breath of wind, and the chilly sunlight made every leaf in the hedgerow and on the towpath livid. From the bridge, I could see her slated roof; the road sloped steadily downhill from the bridge to the village nearly a mile away. I could not see any smoke from the chimney, and for a moment I thought that perhaps she was not there. Then I thought, no, people from London were not used to open fires. I would offer to relight it for her.

I was right about the fire. She had taken off her mac, but she was wearing a black, roll-necked jersey that looked like cashmere and over it a jacket of thick wool embroidered with poppies.

'Oh – hello. Thanks for coming back. Sorry about the telephone, only it was long distance and I didn't want to have to ring them. What do you think you could do about the garden, then?'

'I haven't looked at it yet. I thought that was something we should do together.'

I felt rather than saw her glance at me and then she said, 'Oh, well, it can't be much colder out than it is here.'

We walked out into the middle of the overgrown path.

'I've only just bought this place.' She sounded doubtful, as though this might have been a mistake.

'It's this jungle round it,' I said. 'Cottages need their

setting and that means their garden, however small. Think of *Lark Rise*. Cottages always have a garden. In the mind's eye.'

'What?'

'Flora Thompson's book. *Lark Rise to Candleford*. Village life at the turn of the century. Very different from now.'

'Oh, yes. Yes, I did read it – years ago.' Again I felt her looking at me – and looking away. 'I was wondering why on earth I *did* buy it.'

'I know you were.'

Another covert glance, and then she said distinctly, 'Of course, I would need a price for doing the whole thing.'

I sensed that reading her mind – understanding her – would only make her shy like a nervous horse.

'I just want a few rough measurements, and then we can discuss what you would like indoors. If you like.'

'The fire's gone out and I've run out of firelighters.'

'I don't need them.'

She said nothing to this, but held one end of the tape while I measured and wrote down the dimensions on the back of an envelope with Charley's gold pen, which I was pretty sure she would notice. Nothing was said, however, until we had finished (the measurements were hardly extensive or difficult) and she had led the way back into the cottage. I said, 'I apologize if I was pushy just now, but I'm one of those people who leap at any chance to light a proper fire.'

'Go ahead. There's some newspaper and sticks in that basket.'

'And logs?' There seemed to be only one lying about – far too large, like a great rafter.

'I think in the back of the garage. And there is a wheelbarrow, because I found one full of logs outside the back door.'

'Right, I'll get them.'

All the time I was collecting the logs and wheeling them cottagewards, I thought about her voice. I hesitate to use the word girlish, but it was high and very clear. Somehow it was a shock coming from her, instantly making me imagine her much younger and more vulnerable than her present appearance implied. But it was a very pretty voice, ageless, and charming to me.

I must say here that I am very sensitive to voices – to pitch, to timbre, to accent. I can imitate other people, including myself in earlier days; having adapted my way of speaking considerably. For the last twenty years of his life my own father would not have recognized me on the telephone. At any rate, I was fortunate that she had a voice that could charm me. At that point I wanted, was determined, to be charmed. I was also nervous – at this stage a very small thing could jeopardize the enterprise entirely. This was also a time (which, of course, I knew from past experience) when getting Mrs Redfearn to take an interest in me was a challenge, an adventure, more of an exciting game than an affair of the heart. So the first aim must be to encourage one thing to lead to another.

I returned with the logs and set about the fire. She offered me a cup of tea; I accepted. I asked if she had paper on which I could draw her garden for her. I sensed that formality reassured her. I spent longer than I needed sitting back on my heels watching the fire, and then watching her as she went to and fro from the kitchen for the tea and some shelf paper, which was all she had, she said, for me to draw on. She put the tea-tray on to one of the glass-embroidered cushions. 'Haven't got a table for here,' she said. 'Got to get one.'

The firelight made the room feel warmer at once. Outside dusk coloured the sky and I knew that there was going to be a frost. I noticed the sky because she was drawing the curtains, 'to keep the warmth in'.

Eventually we were each sitting on a sofa opposite one another, and she offered me a cigarette. I had to get up to light hers for her.

'Do you always wear a hat?'

'Of course not. I forgot it.' She pulled it off and tilted her face for the light.

She had the most amazing hair of a kind I'd never seen before in my life. It was dark, brindled with pure white, and sprang richly from her head in small curls that, if her hair had been longer, would have been ringlets. But the most unusual thing about it was its fineness. It looked like gossamer or the hair of a fairy and must have made anyone seeing it for the first time want to touch it.

She asked me to switch on the lamp that stood by my sofa, which was good because the light from the new fire was romantic but unrevealing. She poured the tea into two striped mugs and started to talk about her garden. She had always loved the idea of having one, but knew next to nothing about gardening. She didn't want anything elaborate. 'You made me feel rather nervous when you said you wanted to draw a design – I can't afford to spend thousands of pounds on it, you know.'

'Of course not. It was more for me to find out what you want.'

'I told you, I know so little about it that I don't even know what I like.'

'Like art critics, you mean? They never seem to me to have the faintest notion of what they actually like.'

She threw back her head and gave a little shout of laughter.

'What on earth made you think of that?'

'I read.'

'I wasn't laughing at you. It's just so true.'

'Does the truth make you laugh?'

'Very much, sometimes. Why not?'

'Isn't the truth important to you, then?'

She gave me a look that was both incomprehensible and daunting, and threw her cigarette into the fire. 'I'm not much in the market for philosophical forays. We're meant to be talking about my garden.'

'Right.' I became at once professional. I know enough about gardens to know that I don't know nearly enough, but I still know more than most people or, with many of them, have been able to give the impression that I do.

So I plunged into things like aspect, soil tests, high or low maintenance, the pros and cons of deciduous or ever-green foliage . . .

'Look,' she said in the middle of my spiel, 'all I want is a simple, nice cottage garden. You know, roses growing up the walls and lavender and those tall flowers with long spikes that people used to embroider on tea cosies – holly-hocks! Them. I don't want anything grand or elaborate. I shan't be here much for the next few months anyway.'

This was bad news.

'Were you thinking of it as a summer place, then?'

'Not particularly. Just somewhere I can bolt to when I'm free.'

When she said this, I had the distinct impression that she did not expect this to be often, and as the implications of this began to sink in I wondered whether I had made the wrong choice in Mrs Redfearn. Then she said, 'I suppose you don't happen to know somebody round here who could look after the place for me – the garden, I mean – while I'm away?'

'I might. I'll think,' I said.

'Are you going to do a drawing?'

'I don't think there's any need. You've been very clear about what you want. Of course it would be nice if you could choose about the planting. When are you going away?'

'Oh – on Monday. I'll be leaving here tomorrow evening.'

It's amazing how fast and how much one can think in a split second. I thought, It's no go, there's not enough time, if I agree to do the garden I'm keeping my options open, if I do the garden for her I could make her spend quite a lot of tomorrow with me, find out more about her, she'll be back, you don't buy a cottage and then *never* live in it, I think she does like me in a wary sort of way and that's a start. Anyway, there's nothing to be lost by going all out for the hours that are left. Limitations – of any kind – are simply a challenge. You used to enjoy them, remember? I got to my feet so that I could look down at her.

'I'll do your garden for you – dig it and plant it and then keep it tidy. But I'll need some tools, a fork and so on. Perhaps if we went to the local garden centre we could get them and you'd have a chance to pick out a few plants – and bulbs, it's not too late for them.'

'I've got an awful lot to do tomorrow. The book-unpacking and the kitchen things.'

'I happen to be entirely free tomorrow, and there's

26

hardly anything I like better than getting a look at other people's books.' Then, because I sensed at once that I had gone too far (and whenever I recognize this I also know that it is essential to seem utterly unaware of it), I added, 'I know it's always embarrassing to talk about money, but I charge four pounds an hour – for the gardening, of course, not for getting tools et cetera.'

'How do I know how many hours are involved?'

'Well, I reckon it would take me about a week to clear the garden and replant, and then I suppose half a day, say four hours a week, less in winter and possibly more in the spring and summer. That's the dicey part of it. If you are away, you would have to trust me to put down my hours.' I let myself smile fleetingly at the very idea of dishonesty, before saying, 'I could, of course, produce some quite splendid references if required.'

'By splendid, I take it you mean snobbish.'

'That's it.'

'Don't bother. You're on.'

She was on her feet now, and walking me to the door.

'What time would you like me to come tomorrow?'

'About ten?'

'Fine. Thank you for the tea.'

I walked down the weedy path to the gate and when I turned she was in the process of shutting the front door – as though she had been watching me but did not want me to see.

A fairly conventional encounter, that; nothing remarkable had been said by either of us; nothing, or nothing very much, had happened. It had been studiedly impersonal, we had not even exchanged names.

That evening I ran and reran the events of the day. I have a good memory, particularly for dialogue, and remembering exactly what someone has said can often spark perceptions that I had been unaware of at the time. Not only do the words recall the voice, they recall the eyes, the posture, the whole set of the body (body language is, I believe, the modern term for it), thus providing a quantity of retrospective information. And that was what I was after, what, given the short time available, I desperately needed. One cannot expect to be successful in pursuit of a shadow or ghost. Her going away so soon (and for how lóng?) made speed and accuracy of the essence. Her going was a blow; on the other hand her appearance had been a delightful shock.

Every now and then, during that evening and night, I would stop all thoughts and plan to recapture her face as I first saw it, the wary grey eyes that were shaped, I could recollect, like horizontal diamonds from a pack of cards. Far into the night, as I was wondering what shape they would become when she smiled, I realized that she hadn't. She had laughed when I had made the remark about art critics, but then she'd thrown back her head and, anyway, I'd thought she was laughing at me and when that happens I can't think or observe anything at all. But she said she hadn't been, and she had not smiled once. Was she deeply, chronically unhappy? Or had she simply never experienced carefree pleasure (true of far more women than is generally known)? Who was Mr Redfearn? I had a strong feeling that, alive or dead, he was not with her. None the less, it was one of the first things I must find out. The second was what she was going away for, and for how long. And, come to that, where?

I finally slept, with several possible but, of course, no

certain answers to these questions; the one thing that I knew was that I was on the brink of what I prayed would turn out to be the adventure of my life.

2

DAISY

She had meant to leave for London early in the afternoon but that had proved impossible. Originally, before Carter had called, she had meant to stay at least until the Monday morning. Six o'clock – she looked at her watch – six *thirty* on a Sunday evening guaranteed the worst weekend traffic, and when she *did* get back at whatever time it was, she would have to pack and write notes for the daily and leave messages on people's answering-machines and do all the things that had to be done before going away, in this case for an unknown amount of time. Thank God she had a garage for the car, she thought, as she eased herself into it. She had parked in front of the cottage to load up, although in the end there had been remarkably little to load: just her clothes and her typewriter and briefcase of papers. Now she looked back at the cottage to check that she had turned off all the lights. It was dark – a vaguely darker silhouette against a sky lit by a murky moon. And I turned off the water, she thought, and doused the fire and shut all the windows. She had reached a stage of fatigue where she wanted to go back and see that she had locked the door, but the difficulty of wrenching the key in the lock was so recent that she knew it would be dotty. Now. Up the hill, over the canal bridge and then first turning left. After that it was plain sailing for about fifteen miles to the M40. She threw her hat into the back and turned over her Glenn Gould tape – the partitas this time. Seatbelt, a cigarette and she was off.

The Mercedes' headlights made the trees and hedge-rows look like some unearthly ballet set; it was well equipped in this as in all things. I do love my car, she thought. I shall actually miss it. But when she came back, there it would faithfully be; it would not have sought another owner, nor crashed itself. In these ways it was definitely more reliable than husbands.

As she approached the bridge, she saw that someone was sitting on the right-hand parapet. A man. He kissed his hand to her as she passed – an elegant and romantic gesture of the kind more read about than experienced. It had been Mr Kent, she realized. How odd that he should be there just as she went by. Had he been trying to stop her? No, he had merely been saying farewell in a rather unmere sort of way, and he'd said something about living in a boat temporarily on the canal. There was nothing odd about his being there. On his way back from the village pub most likely. He had offered to stay and help her pack the car and shut up the cottage, but after the whole morning and a late sandwich lunch with him she'd had enough – wanted to be on her own in this new place that was now hers.

But he had been helpful, especially with the books. If she had known that they were going to send for her *and* expect her to hang on right through the picture, she would not have had the books sent down at all. But, given that she'd got them there, it had seemed better to unpack them, although if the cottage was left to itself long enough, damp would prevail. Perhaps it had been mad to take on a second place – particularly somewhere completely strange to her, where she knew nobody and had no ready-made contacts that would enable her to find someone to look after it when she was away. But she'd wanted the cottage to be away from everyone she knew; had not wanted that crowded, frenetic weekend society experienced from staying with friends in their weekend places – drinks, lunches, drinks, dinners. She had wanted somewhere quiet, where she was unknown and unnoticed and could work and sleep and read in peace. Anthony had offered to come down with her to help her settle in, but she had refused. And so she had ended up by allowing a total stranger to help her. It had been odd, coming back from her first visit to the village shop to find him apparently hanging about – almost as though he was waiting for her. She had felt a vague sense of alarm at the sight of him, but it turned out that he was simply wanting a job in the garden (useful and reassuring); on the other hand, she had later realized, he hardly had the voice of a genuine jobbing gardener. This had struck her after he had made that really rather surprising remark about art critics, then asked a series of questions that were unexpected and – although it was hard to say how – impertinent.

But long before then she had implicitly engaged him by asking him to come back in the afternoon. If the call from America had not come a few seconds after she had encountered him, she might well not have asked him back – might not have engaged him at all? Well, if he turned out to be too chatty and generally time-consuming, she could always tell him to go away, say that she wanted to do the garden herself, anything. That problem, if it was one, was far away; she expected to be stuck in Los Angeles for at least two months, possibly three. A peevish way of putting it.

She started to enumerate all the possible advantages. She would escape a good deal of the English winter. She would be able to go to New York and Mexico for short breaks. Money would not be a problem for at least two years. She liked working with George. And finally, but by no means of lesser significance, it would be an enormous relief to be somewhere where she *knew* she would not bump into Jason and Marietta, which during this autumn had seemed to happen with a regularity that she would have liked to call monotonous, except that it left her gasping inwardly with pain. And rage, she reminded herself – hang on to the rage, whatever you do.

But even after twelve years, ten of them divorced from him, her grief and . . . not shock but the memory of shock was there, and humiliation, wounded pride and subsequent anger had always to be deliberately invoked. But not now, she thought, you're getting away from all that. And really you're away from it anyway; you don't have to worry about how to divide your time between work and love; you can dress to please yourself; you can read in bed all night if you want to; you can skip meals, spend too much money on your car, buy a cottage on impulse – in short, please yourself. Pleasure was all very well, but I don't *enchant* or *delight* myself, I need someone else to do that – or, rather, would need, if I wasn't too old for it. Work is the thing at my age, and jolly lucky to have it. But she didn't want to start thinking about that now.

In order not to have to try too hard, not to think about it, she pressed the play button for the tape. Bach streamed into the car and into her; passion and logic locked together to the enhancement of each – an aspect more noticeable in him than in any other composer she could think of.

She could see the motorway ahead and hoped that the partitas would last out.

She had thought that the drive from North Oxfordshire plus all the things she had to do when she got home would have tired her enough to make her want to sleep, but they hadn't. She had had a hot bath, hoping that it would release some of the nervous tension she felt at the immediate prospect of the trip, but it had not. Now she lay on her back in the dark trying to bore herself to sleep. She went through her lists; the messages left on her answering-machine, what she had done about them; she couldn't ring Katya because she went to bed long before eleven thirty, so she had left a long message explaining what was going on and saying she'd call from the States. Other messages, too boring to enumerate even if one was aiming at tedium, had taken a good deal of time. Then there were notes for the caretaker of the flats and her Portuguese lady who cleaned for her. Then the packing. She decided to take with her all three drafts of the play as well as the film script – all of them likely to contain alternative scenes that they might think they wanted her to write. It would save time if she had already written them, and spirit, since they never used their own sugges- tions once they had seen them in the flesh, as it were. She wasn't going to think about any of that. She thought about Katya; she spent a lot of her life doing that, and worrying about her fruitlessly, ineffectively and, she suspected from Katya's point of view, irritatingly. She had had Katya when she was twenty-three, married to Stach and called Mrs Varensky. It had been after she had realized that Stach drank far too much, and before she had known that he slept with other – several other – women. The drink she had excused on the grounds that after his frightful battle and subsequent crash-landing in the Spitfire, he had suffered an injury to his spine that left him in continuous and sometimes agonising pain. Drink, while it did not alleviate the pain much, did alleviate what he felt about it. It certainly alleviated what he felt about what *she* felt about his infidelity. 'I shall not *leave* you,' he would reiterate, as though that was the only thing she could legitimately mind. 'I shall always be a family man.' And he had looked at her with his pale green eyes snapping with sardonic self-mockery. She had been crying that first time, and he wiped her face caressingly with two fingers, licked them and twitched his nostrils with a kind of delicate distaste. 'Just how I imagine the Dead Sea.' He had managed, she had thought afterwards, to have a new woman exactly when she had become resigned to the one before.

He had been delighted by the birth of Katya, who was named after his mother – shot by the Russians for harbouring a Jew only weeks before the end of the war in Europe. Whenever Katya cried, he picked her up and walked her up and down, crooning to her in Polish, exclaiming upon unknown – to Daisy – family resemblances and predicting a fairytale future of health, wealth and happiness for his daughter. 'The eyes are like my sister's!' His sister had been raped by five Russian soldiers and had died years later in an asylum. Whenever, even now, she thought about Stach's family, or rather lack of it, since all of them one way or another had been destroyed, she felt a rush of protective love for him. The Poles had really been sold down the river at Yalta, their heroism, hardship in no way recompensed, and she felt it was up to her to try and make it up to him. Katya was all his family now, and then, in those early weeks of their daughter's life, she had thought that perhaps all would become well – that love would find a way. But it gradually became clear that hers certainly would not and that his – if it existed beyond physical adventure – would always be distracted. This situation was compounded by the fact that Stach earned money only spasmodically and was likely to have parted with most of it before it reached her. It was then that she had started to look for work that she could do at home and sometimes found it. She read plays for a new company that had started, and when Katya was old enough to go to nursery school she cleaned the house of a film director and his French wife. In the evenings, when usually Stach was out, she wrote a novel about a young woman who married a foreigner and had a small baby. Nobody wanted to publish the novel. One editor did actually offer to see her, and she went to the office trembling with hope. After waiting in a passage that contained the switchboard and its operator, she was fetched by a tired-looking man who conducted her to what seemed like an enlarged cupboard that contained two chairs and a table with an unsteady mountain of type-scripts. When they were both seated, he offered her a cigarette and plunged straight in.

'Is this your first novel?'

'Yes.'

'Well, a jolly good start anyway.' He cleared his throat. 'You did say in your letter that you wanted an opinion?'

'Yes, I did.'

'Well, you have a very good ear for dialogue. Really excellent.'

There was a pause, so long that she said, 'But nothing else much?'

'I wouldn't say that, exactly. It's more to do with – I

mean, take your heroine's husband. He's a bit of a caricature of a foreigner, isn't he? I mean, just because he's Polish it doesn't follow that he'd get drunk and sing in the street or keep *on* having all those affairs with girls. I mean, she wouldn't stay with him, would she, if he was as awful as that?'

She gave a small, acquiescent shrug: 'I suppose not.' Not in a novel, anyway, she thought on the bus home as she grappled unavailingly with the chasm between art and life. The point was not whether she had drawn a good likeness in her portrait of Stach (who *was*, she knew, an almost operatic character), it was that she had not made him seem credible. But other thoughts came out of that meeting. Why *did* she stay with Stach if he was, as Mr Milnethorpe had suggested, as awful as that? At first she shied away from consideration of this uncomfortable question, but it returned at odd and unexpected intervals, trapping her each time into some negative admission. One, she didn't stay with him because she loved him; two, she didn't stay because of Katya; three, she didn't stay because of money. She didn't stay because any of it was fun, and she most certainly didn't stay in order to prevent her family from saying they had told her so. Marriage to Stach had brought all the social isolation, domestic responsibility and lack of freedom associated so often with the state, but without the attendant compensating joys of chronic intimacy, companionship and, of course, a regular sex life. None of these did she have.

After many essays into work with some glamour attached to it (he was, after all, a war hero) he had settled for the last two years into driving cabs or cars for various companies. Every now and then he slipped up, drank too much too near a job and got sacked. But most of the time he had a remarkable discipline about his drinking, which he explained he had learned from flying. You did not drink before you took a plane up, but you made up for it at other times. But sitting in cabs was extremely hard on his back, and this was another reason why he had to lay off. This did not necessarily mean that she saw more of him; it was then that he conducted his affairs.

She remembered now, as she lay in the dark, the first time that she had experimented with the idea of leaving him. It had been after she had reread her novel and decided that there was nothing she wanted to do to it. I might as well put it in the dustbin, she had thought, get on with something else. That had been the moment. Yes, why *not* get on with something else? And now for something completely different . . . Such thoughts had at first to be disowned but this did not get rid of them. She agonized over his probable despair and helplessness: he could not sew on a button or boil an egg – in spite, she thought, beginning to laugh at herself, of being in close proximity for nearly twelve years with someone who was constantly doing such things . . . Oh, really! But the end, when it came, was sudden and painless. He announced one evening that he was going to be away for a couple of weeks and she told him not to come back. He had stared at her in silence then said, 'Whatever you like, of course.' As he was stuffing the shirts she had ironed into a bag, he had said, 'I understand you are jealous. I cannot blame you for it. But with me, as you know, these things do not last long. It will all change and be better, you will see.'

From this she gathered that he did not believe that she meant what she said. It had been in July, and she had taken Katya out of school a week early and gone to her aunt's house in Brighton. From there she had written him a letter addressed to the flat reiterating her decision to leave him. She would not try to prevent him from seeing Katya; she did not wish to return to the flat except to collect the rest of her and Katya's clothes, and from now on he was financially responsible for it. Her aunt, an antique dealer who lived in a small, elegant Regency house filled with exquisite furniture, seemed neutral about these arrangements.

And then Stach suddenly appeared and said, enough of this nonsense, he had come to take them home. It was August, early evening; not quite the end of a stifling day that now threatened thunder, and she and Aunt Jess, having washed salad and deadheaded the petunias, were just settling down to a bottle of white wine in the pretty garden when the doorbell rang.

'She's forgotten her key again. All right, Daisy, I'll get her.' Aunt Jess adored Katya and thought that she was often too hard on her. She heard a man's voice and recognized that it was Stach's, and then he was in the room making his announcement.

When she did not immediately answer, her aunt said, 'Has it occurred to you that she may not want to do that?'

'Everything occurs to me, but I do not always take notice.'

She realized then that he had been drinking – not a great deal, she guessed, but enough to face them with bravado.

'Well, I don't want to. I wrote to you about it and said what I meant.'

He stared at her for a moment, then said histrionically, 'And what about my daughter? What about my child? You *cannot* be so heartless as to take her away from me.'

'I said I wouldn't stop you seeing her, but she will live with me.'

'I wish to see her. I wish to ask *her* about that.'

'Stach, you can't. You've no right to upset her with ideas like that when you know perfectly well that it wouldn't be practical for you to look after her.'

She was getting sucked into familiar black holes of conflict and unreason.

She remembered again how grateful she had been for Aunt Jess's presence and the knowledge that her support was unequivocal. It wasn't that she always thought I was right about things, she just loved me. She recalled trying to explain what this had meant to her – several times and to different people – after Jess had died, and she had discovered what a lonely business mourning could be if there was nobody who had known the person, and how trying to talk about it to strangers simply made her miss her aunt more.

It would never go, she thought, as she sat up in bed to turn off the light. She had read, or someone had said to her, that grief diminished with time, but this was not her experience. Her sense of loss had remained life-sized and as fresh as it had been nearly twenty years ago. After Jess died she had no family left, no home where she had been and could in some sort still be the child. She was in the front line, with Katya but nobody else. Her parents had both died in a car accident when she was not quite three – she could not honestly remember them. It had been Jess Langrish, her father's sister, who had taken her on. She would get up and go into the kitchen and make tea. At her age it did not matter whether one slept a great deal or not.

She was nearly as old now, she thought, as Jess had

been when she died of cancer aged sixty-four. She was sixty, a grandmother – Katya had married a doctor and lived in the West Country – and she earned a surprising (to her) amount of money. Now, she could easily have afforded to keep Jess's house, which had been left to her with its contents, but the legacy had coincided with Katya starting at university, and debts, due to being more or less out of work for the previous year as she had been spending as much time as possible with Jess, ultimately nursing her. At the time she had told herself that perhaps it was as well that the house had to go: it contained so much of Jess and her life with Jess that she might have found that she could not bear the place without her. She kept some of the contents – the furniture, pictures, china, things she had remembered all her life – and when Katya married she gave some of them to her.

She had made tea and smoked a cigarette and her watch said half past three. Why did insomnia always seem to ally itself to pain and fear and grief? Why could she not lie in the dark revelling in joyful or at least pleasant bits of the past? The answer or answers to that were neither reassuring nor complimentary to her nature. Her life seemed to have been composed more of difficulty than ease, more of pain than pleasure, and while her losses were permanent – she did not wish either Stach or Jason back in her life and Jess was inexorably gone – her gains seemed always to be temporary. But she knew, or had glimpsed, that this sense of having been short-changed went with a kind of greed that demanded of anything good that it should persist before it could be appreciated. The only good memories she had were when she had lived entirely in their present, which became timeless if you were really in it.

She was back in bed and as she lay down she remembered climbing into Jess's bed after a nightmare, and feeling Jess's bony but wonderfully comforting arms round her and her voice, full of endearments that were inexpressibly soothing, as she made her tell everything about the bad dream until it became puny and meaningless. Then, 'Would you like a hot drink, pet?' Aunt Jess would say, and she would say yes, and while Jess was away making it she would lie reiterating all the blissful affection: the words, 'My pet, my little Daisy, my best girl, I love you, all right, don't you worry about that. I won't let a single sea serpent into the house, they'd soon find they'd come to the wrong place, they would.' Kisses, hugs, strokings. 'Your little feet are like ice!' 'Blow your nose, my sweetheart, you'll feel better if you can breathe properly.' 'I won't be long. You lie there and think what you'd like to do on your birthday.' She had been going to be seven, and happy then. And, of course, there had been other times when she was growing up – particularly the wonderful first week in Brighton where Aunt Jess moved them when she was eleven. 'Better schools for you, pet, and a very good place for my trade.' And the sea! The idea of living near the sea seemed a fantastic luxury. They had moved at the beginning of the Easter holidays. By noon the movers had dumped everything in the house, drunk tea provided by Aunt Jess, pocketed their tips and left them standing in the kitchen that was littered with tea chests, muddy footprints on the black-and-white-check lino (it had been raining) and screws of grey newspaper from the mugs that they had unpacked for the tea.

'What do we do now?'

She remembered so clearly the way Aunt Jess had

opened her mouth to say something then shut it; the way her expression had changed when their eyes met and then her saying, 'I think before we do anything else we should go and see the sea, don't you agree?' Oh, she *did*! She wanted to see it every day – to make the most of the marvellous chance. It had stopped raining, but the streets were shiny and glistening in the sunlight. They had walked to the end of their road and turned right into a wider street that descended quite steeply towards the cloudy green-grey sea at the bottom. When they reached the front they went down some steps that led to the beach.

'Shall we bathe?'

'It will be too cold, pet, but you can paddle if you like. I'm going to settle here for a bit.' And she sat, with her back against a breakwater, and smoothed her sensible tweed skirt over her knees.

The sea had been deeply cold: it seemed at once to go straight through her skin into her bones, although she could not go far into the water because the beach shelved so steeply and the waves surged in different shapes and sizes. There was a lovely smell, which wasn't exactly fish, or exactly salt or even seaweed but a bit of all three. Then, quite suddenly, the sun went in and it seemed darker and another shower poured down. She went back to her aunt then as fast as she could, and put her wet bare feet into her shoes without the socks and they started back up the steps. They were looking up the street they had come down, and at the top and a little to the left was a rainbow. 'It's pointing to our house,' Aunt Jess had said, and she felt as though she had been stabbed with tremendous happiness, with joy, as though God had said, 'What a good thing you have come to live here.' She watched until the rainbow had dissolved, but by then they were nearly home. Aunt Jess stopped at a fish and chip shop and bought them their lunch. Later in her life, after she had grown up, she would sometimes buy fish and chips simply to remind herself of that blissful first day.

So there had been good times, of course there had, but as she grew older the good times seemed to become tied to the subsequent bad ones with shorter and shorter links. And now she could not recall her early days with Jason without pain, because every time she thought of him – the first time she saw him at a drinks party on someone's boat at Chelsea, for instance – that last awful evening when she had made him come round for a drink and *tell* her to her face that he was leaving, came back and engulfed all other remembrance of him.

They had married three months after meeting, flouting all caution, advice from friends and, for her at least, one or two very faint internal messages of warning. She was forty-five, and he was seven years younger, although he had an appearance – not unlike Rupert Brooke – that had an agelessly heroic quality about it and which made him look even younger. They had married in a register office and were given a small lunch party at Prunier by Jason's agent. Katya was a witness, unsmiling, withdrawn. She had not wanted to come to the lunch; it was only when Daisy had said, 'Don't, if you really don't want to, but I shall miss you awfully,' that Katya had relented. Nothing that Jason said to her dissolved Katya's hostility, and yet, Daisy thought now, it hadn't been because she was close to her father and resented this remarriage on his behalf. She hardly ever saw Stach and spoke of him as though he was some sort of emotional outpost in her life – a boundary that she had neither time nor inclination to reach. But she had always been against Jason, and he, early sensing that she was impervious to his charm, wasted no more of it upon her. Katya had been twenty-two when Daisy had married Jason and this had accelerated her flight from home and her mother. They had been painfully estranged until Katya's sudden marriage to Edwin.

It was while she was away that Jason's career moved from being successful to his becoming a star. He played the grownup Pip in a six-part drama for television of *Great Expectations*, and at the end of the six weeks of its showing people recognized him in the street. He was interviewed and photographed and asked to appear on chat shows, and offers, mostly within the range of down-right horrible to bizarre, began to flow in. He had been most sweetly excited by his success, very much including her in it. It was true that she had adapted the book, but apart from one, quite idle, suggestion that it might be worth auditioning him (they were looking for a new face to play Pip), she had no hand in his getting the part. He liked to say afterwards that it had been her great influence, which initially had made her cross because she felt strongly about nepotism in any shape or form. He had teased her out of this. 'The point, my darling girl, is that I wouldn't have got it if I'd been absolutely *no good*. So graft doesn't come into it. You just got me the chance.' Other chances came – not through her – but they agreed that they should be turned down, although as the winter slowly warmed and lightened to spring, he became fidgety and anxious.

'Perhaps I won't get a decent offer. Perhaps one has to take some of these awful jobs while one is waiting.'

'Only if we couldn't eat. We eat,' she reminded him. 'Anyway – think of them! That fatuous notion of producing

Lear with a thirty-year-old Lear suffering from Alzheimer's. What happens to the daughters, for God's sake?'

'They were to be his sisters.'

'But *why*?'

'Oh, I agree. *Why*?'

'You haven't carried spears in respectable productions for years to have to do that.'

'Nor been various characters' best friend. Have you noticed how *dull* best friends always are in plays? I suppose it started with Celia in *As You Like It*, and went on to Horatio.'

'He's not so bad.'

They were lying in bed on a Sunday morning.

'Anyway, you were never Celia,' she said, shifting luxuriously so that her head lay in the crook of his shoulder. They had made love earlier and her limbs felt becalmed.

'Yes, I was, at my school. We did a play every year and they kept on casting me in the women's parts. It was being blond that did it. They had a Dickensian idea of heroines.'

'You,' he said later, 'would never have done. Apart from being the wrong colour, your hair is like a sort of royal bird's nest. How about me making some hot chocolate?'

'Yes, please.'

Happiness, comfort and joy: remembering now, she had to recognize that the good time had lasted for nearly two years. It had not been so fleeting as afterwards she had imagined. For the whole of the rest of that year and most of the next she had been so happy with him that nothing else had seemed to matter at all.

She loved his even, sanguine temperament, his physical beauty, his jokes, his imitations of people and animals, his clowning mime, all thrown off with spontaneous ease, his charming, light, true singing voice, his greed about chocolate, anything chocolate, his passion for every kind of game and his determination to win every one that he played. In company he treated her with tenderness and courtesy; alone, he would tease her, take her off and then, in the midst of these games, drop it all to declare his love and the degree of it for her. 'For *you*, my amazing beauty, I think you were made for me. Nobody has ever come so near to being everything I want in the ways that you are. Think if you'd never gone to that party, I might never have found you. Wouldn't that be sad?' He would elaborate on this theme: 'Or you might have been on your way to the party when you were waylaid by some be-witching chap who carried you off to some handy lair or other while I was stuck on that boat knocking back warmer and warmer gin and tonics (do you remember how quick-ly they ran out of ice at that party?). And all I would get would be the headlines, "Ravishing Playwright Carried Off by Wealthy Plutocrat." At least the pictures of you don't look painfully like you. So I wouldn't have abso-lutely known what I was missing.' Every time he indulged these fantasies, *she* imagined what it would have been like *not* to have met him, *not* to have fallen in love with him. She would have been slogging along, working fairly hard, being her own personal staff, with the exception of Anna – secretary, cook, housekeeper, accountant – much as she did now. She would have taken comfort from and sometimes refuge in various friends: there are always some people who quite enjoy an unattached free person who is more likely to be available to them. She would give herself small treats like massage – the only way of getting touched – or buying expensive clothes like her lovely poppy jacket. She would treat herself to an opera or a gardenia in a pot, or a bottle of good scent. Once she had tried a winter weekend break in Venice by herself, but in spite of (she thought) strenuous and thoughtful efforts to enjoy herself, she had not succeeded. It had been beautiful and bitterly cold and she had felt loneliness in a general manner and on a scale hitherto unknown to her. 'I can't go on like this!' 'For the rest of my life?' Getting back to her silent, empty flat had actually been a relief. It was full of her things, her life, was hers. Here, it seemed to say, she could be allowed choice and chance. People wrote her letters, rang her up here. But the fantasy of a life without Jason had been all very well; she need only imagine it when she chose to; it simply pointed up the wondrous relief of life *with* him.

There had been two years of unalloyed happiness. And then, suddenly, there had been his contract with Paramount, and Marietta. They seemed to happen at the same time, but afterwards she realized that Marietta must have occurred some time before the contract. They had been to a party after a first night and across the room she saw this small, birdlike creature in a mini-dress of dark red velvet, arriving on the arm of a fat, bearded man whose face seemed vaguely familiar. She noticed the girl because she was looking at her; there, for a second, they held each other's gaze, then the girl put up a small white hand and patted the man's beard, laughing at him. She had turned to Jason.

'Who is that?'

'Who?'

'That girl. Over there. She was looking at us.'

'Was she? Oh – that's Marietta Reed. Friend of Bernard's. Didn't you meet her at that Boat Race lunch?'

She was deflected. 'That's Bernard? Good Lord, when did he grow that beard?'

'He grew it for Falstaff. He's had it for ages. You can't have been at his lunch.'

'I had an abscess on a tooth, you remember? You went without me. And then you stayed so long and I was famished and there was nothing to eat in the flat.'

He was about to reply when Bernard was upon them: delighted to see her – to see both of them. Been on tour and they were opening in London next week – oh, this was Marietta Reed. She'd been in Ireland making a picture. There – introductions made. His beard tickled like a fir tree.

Marietta said, 'How do you do?' She had the slightly common vowel sounds of the truly upper class.

'Very well, thank you,' Jason was saying. 'This is Daisy, my wife.'

'Oh, yes. I recognized you. I thought *Great Expectations* was stunning.'

She was tiny. Everything about her seemed miniature, except her eyes, which were huge and velvet and the colour of bitter chocolate.

She remembered that Bernard had suggested they have supper together, and Jason had refused. 'Rather be with you,' he'd said; the sort of thing he said so often that she had almost stopped hearing him. They went to their local Indian restaurant and talked about the Hollywood offer. Initially, he was to go over to make one picture with the studio reserving a fairly open-ended option. 'I won't have to *live* there, will I?' he had said. He always seemed to expect her to have the answers to that sort of thing.

'I shouldn't think so. Not unless they keep on and *on*

wanting you to do things for them. Which they probably will.'

There was a pause, then he said, 'I'll miss you, darling. Horribly.'

'I could come out and join you.'

'Oh, no, I don't think so. I think I've got to find my feet first.'

In retrospect, that evening was full of minute warning signals, and she had observed none of them.

'After all,' he said, 'I shan't be there long. And if I'm not with you, you'll get stuck in with the play.'

Hours later: 'I distract you, don't I?'

They were home, naked and in bed, and he lay propped on one elbow, his free hand caressing the back of her neck.

'No, no. You don't at all.'

'Oh, *don't* I?' His hand slid round from her neck to her left breast, and instantly her whole body was alerted.

'Have I – inadvertently – started a small bush fire?'

She could not answer. She ached for him and blushed to ache – something that had never happened to her with Stach. With Jason, he had only to reach out and touch her and she would start to tremble, and the frequency and familiarity that marriage had engendered had simply refined and accelerated the process. The knowledge, that evening, that he was about to go away, be out of reach for weeks at least, only sharpened her nervous excitement to a point where she felt it could be assuaged.

The night before he left for America they went to the Ritz. He arranged it – it had been his idea and he had wanted it to be a surprise. He had chosen well: a beautiful room, a bowl of yellow roses and a bottle of champagne; nectarines in a silver dish and autumn evening sun filtering through the muslin curtains that shrouded them from the park. The setting for a honeymoon night, she had thought, but they had been married for two and a half years, and just as she was thinking that there was something contrived about the scene, he had said, 'A touch of unreality is what I was aiming at. Very good for one, don't you agree?'

She watched him, intent upon opening the champagne, the usual lock of silky yellow hair falling across his cheek-bone, his beautiful hands untwisting the wire over the cork and easing it out of the bottle with momentous care . . . out! He was pouring it into the flutes, bringing hers to her. He looked so beautiful, so much all of a piece that she felt momentarily overwhelmed that something so dazzling existed and, more, that she knew him and he loved her, that tears rushed to her eyes.

'Daisy! Darling!'

'It's all right – perfectly all right.'

'I know what it is.'

She looked up into his eyes, the colour of woodsmoke, bent so tenderly upon her.

'Do you really?'

'Listen. Either it will be six weeks like they said, or if it turns out to be longer, you'll join me.'

He did not even ask her if he was right about the tears. She raised her glass. 'Here's to the star.'

They both drank and then he tilted the glass towards her. 'And here's to *my* star.'

They finished the champagne, and went down to dinner, and she saw how – it seemed to her – every woman in the room noticed him, and then her and then him again, although he seemed unaware of any of it. It hadn't always been like this, but she supposed that from now onwards there would be more and more of it.

He ordered all her favourite food and an extremely expensive bottle of claret, which they had with grouse after the vodka with their blinis: far more than they usually drank, but somehow the evening never took off. It was as though each of them was waiting for whatever was happening to be over – there was a railway-station air to the dinner.

Back in their room, the sight of her artistically laid-out nightdress on the turned-down bed made her long to be at home, in their rather grotty, dark little flat that they were always going to move from when they had the money. Tomorrow night she would be back there – sleeping alone. Indeed, they might already have spent their last night there together, it having been agreed that she should find a new place for them while he was away. The flat had been hers before she met Jason, but it now seemed completely to be *theirs* – she hated to think of it without him. She began to dread being alone there, but then, there he was, arms round her, asking her what was the matter, no, he knew that something was, what was it, tell him, if she loved him she could tell him anything.

'Of course I love you. I don't know. I just *dread* you going. I mean, it somehow feels worse than I know it is.'

'Six weeks,' he repeated. There was no longer any if about it, it *was* six weeks. He soothed and consoled, made love and slept. She lay awake for a long time trying to keep her head above the rising tide of misgivings, un-named, unknown, but there.

What she never afterwards understood was how he had been feeling that evening. Sometimes she thought that he had simply been assuaging any guilt he had by spending every penny he then possessed upon her. Sometimes she thought that he had been truly divided – sometimes that he had wanted to go to the States to escape temptation in the form of Marietta. (She could not think that for long, as she discovered fairly quickly that Marietta had also gone to Hollywood.) She had begun by thinking simply that the parting was hard for both of them, but naturally less hard for him because he was the one going to new realms.

He rang her when he got there, the evening after his first day in the studio.

'Just camera tests,' he had said, 'and they've cut my hair and I've done five interviews for TV and the trade papers. Oh, and then they took me out to the most fantastic Chinese meal. Now I'm going to zonk out. I've got a couple of days off and I feel as though I could sleep for a week.' Then he asked about her. 'Did you take Sykes to the vet?'

'Yes. He's got an abscess due to that awful ginger cat attacking him.'

'He's a bit of a wimp, isn't he?'

'I don't see that not wanting to attack other people makes one a wimp.'

'I see I'm speaking of the cat you love. I suppose the moment my back is turned you've let him back into your bed?'

'He just sort of seemed to be there. I hadn't the heart . . . !'

'No. I expect in your shoes I'd do the same.'

'The licence only applies to cats,' she reminded him.

'The trouble is that while I don't think the hotel would turn a hair if I imported a girl, they'd almost certainly veto any cat.'

That sort of talk went on until she heard him yawn and told him to go to sleep and much love was exchanged.

After that he called her every other day. What was evening for him was morning for her and she was usually drinking her China tea in bed when he called. She worked in the mornings and looked for the new place to live in the afternoons. It was neither a good nor a bad time – more a kind of limbo. She had finished the first draft of her play – a contemporary version of Orpheus rescuing Eurydice with the name part, she hoped, for Jason.

The weeks dragged by. She did not at first notice that he spoke to her after longer intervals until she thought she had found exactly the right flat for them and waited for two days for him to call, to no avail. So she called him at his hotel, but he wasn't there, which seemed odd at six in the morning (his time). Then, because she had to say yes or no to the flat or risk losing it, she called the studios to leave a message for him. When, the following morning, he did not respond, she tried the hotel again. This time she asked if he was staying there or away. He was away. She decided to take the flat, only to find that someone had offered more for it; she had the choice of upping her bid or getting out, and chose to lose the flat. When he called the following morning, she discovered that she felt angry with him, and he, who'd opened warily with, 'They tell me you've been trying to get hold of me,' became cold and defensive. 'Surely you can decide about a *flat* without me.'

'Next time I will.'

'*Good!*'

There was a silence. Then, she said, 'Well, how is every-thing?'

'All right. We're behind schedule.'

'Much?'

'I don't know.'

Another silence – they frightened her. 'I miss you. Shall I come and join you?'

'Better not. I keep awful hours and I'm knackered at the end of the day. Don't worry about me, darling. You just get on with—' And then the line went dead. She waited a minute and dialled his hotel. He wasn't there. He must have called her from the studios, she thought, as she waited for him to call back. But she heard no more from him. She spent the rest of the day, of that week, clearing out the cupboards in the flat, so that the move, when it happened, would be easier. In the middle of one darkening afternoon the telephone rang, but it wasn't him, it was her agent, Anna Blackstone.

'Just wondered how you were getting on.'

'I've finished the first draft.'

'Good. Do you want me to see it?'

'As a matter of fact, I sent it to you this morning.'

'Right.'

'It's only the first draft.'

'Why don't we have dinner at the weekend? Then I'll have read it.'

'Fine. Where shall we go?'

'Come to my place. It'll be quieter.' There was a pause, and then she added, 'Unless you want to come earlier?'

'Saturday would be fine.'

It *was* fine. For the rest of the week when she was not worrying about why he had not called, she looked forward to her evening alone with Anna, whose company *à deux* she realized she had been missing for a long time. She had become so used to doing everything with Jason that except for the odd lunch – usually in crowded restaurants where Anna seemed to know everybody – she had not spent time alone with her since before her marriage, and seeing her with other people, even Jason, or perhaps especially Jason, was not at all the same.

One of the things she loved about Anna, she thought, as she lay in her bath after the day's clearing up, was her sameness. Ever since she had known her, Anna had had her iron-grey hair cut short with a rather fierce fringe, had always worn black trousers and a black cotton high-necked sweater or, in summer, a white collarless shirt. She had always seemed neither old nor young, neither fat nor thin; she had a husky voice that many found seductive, but she had never been seen or known to pair up with anyone. Her face had a workaday, rather homespun appearance, except for her eyes, which occasionally gave the lie to her being simple or homespun. She was a brilliant negotiator and, even more valuable from Daisy's point of view, a good positive critic, thoroughly at home with incomplete work. And her flat would be comfortingly the same.

She lived on the top floor of a house in Bedford Square that consisted of three rooms, a tiny kitchen and a bathroom on the half-landing below. It had no heating, except for two ancient gas fires, and draughts skidded in through the beautiful windows and came to a screeching halt as they struck one's face. Books stacked in both directions lurched on cheap, once-white painted bookshelves – occasionally one of these collapsed under the strain and its occupants were then stacked on the floor. A landscape mirror hung over the mantelpiece, so badly foxed that, as Anna had once said, one looked like somebody from a Le Fanu short story in it. All these things came to mind as she climbed the elegant staircase. The rest of the house was always dark and quiet at night as it was entirely taken up by offices of various kinds.

Anna stood in the open doorway, smiling and with a drink in her hand.

'Is that for me?'

'It's for you to try. If you like it, I'll make you one.'

She sipped it: it was the most marvellous colour.

'Campari and red Cinzano?'

'And gin. It's a negroni. I've got rather keen on them.'

'I'd rather have a glass of wine. No, I won't – I'd like a negroni.'

'I do admire the speed with which you change your mind, no mucking about. Come in. The smell of food is a stew. I always think one feels better about cooking smells if you know what they are.'

Daisy sank gratefully onto a stool before the fire.

When Anna had given her her drink, and they had both found their packs of cigarettes and lit up, she felt Anna's sharp appraising eye upon her and said quickly, 'How's the literary world?'

'Underpaid, undersexed and absolutely *everywhere*.'

'What do you mean, "everywhere"?'

'I mean that you need to have a rather serious, confidential lunch, and you pick what you think is a nice quiet place and, lo and behold, there are at least three lots of people who've had exactly the same idea.'

'You all listen to each other.'

'No – but every now and then you hear things. And *they* hear things. It's not evil, it's tiresome.'

Again she felt Anna's eye upon her but before she could attempt a second deflection, Anna said, 'Would you rather we ate, and then talked about the play?'

'I think I would.'

'So, I'll just say what an interesting and difficult idea it is and how much I admire you for tackling it.'

'But?'

'No buts now. No buts at all, really. I just want to know one or two things. Enough. I daresay we can find *something* else to talk about while we eat.'

Anna came back with the tray of food and together they laid the small round table. Anna served the stew, and Daisy poured the wine.

Then she found herself saying, 'I'm a bit worried about Jason.'

'Oh? In what way?'

'Well, he suddenly seems to have become elusive – I mean when I call he's never there, and he has stopped calling me with any regularity. I haven't heard from him for six days now.' She looked at Anna, willing her to be breezy and dismissive, but she said nothing.

'He thought it would only be six weeks, and then at least he would get back for a break, but it's been more than that and he hasn't even *mentioned* coming. I suggested my going there—'

'And what did he say?'

'Better not, he said. He said he was working flat out and too tired or something. I don't know what's going on.'

There was a long, uncomfortable silence. Then Anna reached across the table and held her hand. 'I've got to tell you something – not good. I hate it, but I can't *not* tell you.'

'What is it? What?'

'Jason was in Paris last weekend.'

'In Paris? In *Paris*? How on earth do you know? What do you mean anyway?' But already she had begun to know. Indeed, as she recounted the telephoning – and the subsequent lack of it – since he had been gone, it seemed so clear that he had come to an end with her that she could not see why his being seen in Paris without her was in the least a shock.

She said something of the sort to Anna, who replied, 'But a shock isn't always something that you weren't expecting. It's often more a secret dread coming out.' After a minute, she asked, 'What else is there?'

So then the rest of it got told – Marietta, the girl she had met at the party, whom Jason had met at the earlier party. 'She thinks you know,' Anna said. 'She thinks Jason has told you. It was because I was sure he hadn't that I had to tell you. She thinks she's going to marry him, you see.'

'I expect she's right,' Daisy had said dully.

But Marietta had been a shock of the most straightforward kind. When, as she had done then, and ceaselessly, she tried to see how and when things had started to go wrong, she could find nothing – no indication, not the faintest clue, except his saying that he did not want her to join him in L.A. Then, when she thought that, *everything* he had said that last evening seemed to be full of hidden meaning. His refusal to dine with Bernard and Marietta, the way in which he had said that he would miss her terribly . . . But always she came back to Marietta being a shock. If she could have thought they were happy, had *been* so happy, and – not all but some of the time – he was engaged with Marietta, how could she ever discern about anything? How could she feel that she had ever been, could ever be, enough for one other person?

That evening had been the beginning of the desert. Anna had been a real friend, letting her talk, weep, rage, struggle with comprehension and acceptance. She had made her stay the night with her, had supplied a sleeping pill with some whisky and a hot-water bottle. She resolved to cry quietly as the spare room was a mere slip partitioned off from Anna's room and she did not want to keep her awake, but in fact she fell into exhausted sleep as soon as her feet got warm. Then there had been the next day all waiting to be got through somehow.

She had gone back to her flat and found a letter from him, postmarked New York. 'Darling Daisy, This is the most difficult letter I've ever had to write in my life', it began. It went on to describe his struggle (agonising, according to him, but unsuccessful) not to fall in love with Marietta; the pain that they had both endured at the thought of hurting her (Marietta was the sort of person who would naturally feel that), and the conclusion that he had finally reached that there was no other way for them but to be together. There was then a lengthy description of his feelings for Marietta and hers for him. The letter ended with his pledge of eternal friendship.

She read the letter four or five times: in spite of the night with Anna, she found it at first impossible to take in. How could *anybody* – how could *he* be writing a letter like that? The pain of its matter was only equalled by the crassness of its manner. So she should be sorry for him having to write such a difficult letter! He had hardly ever written her letters of any kind, she realized; only occasional, loving, funny little notes. Perhaps, she thought, as she blinked away the scorching tears, perhaps he had found *them* difficult to write as well. For what was happening as she read and reread the awkward string of clichés was that not only did they destroy the future, they were annihilating the past. If he could feel as he said he felt now, he must have been lying about what he felt for her during their two-year *affair* – she would not call it marriage. No, he had wanted her and, unknown and penniless, marriage must have seemed a good deal. Now he wanted someone else more and he no longer needed either her money or her help. Why should *she* want to know anything about his feelings for Marietta? She read the letter again, trying to find some other reason in it that accounted for his no longer loving her, but she could find nothing.

She tried to recognize that he must always – in some sort – have been acting a part (lying) and was choked with bitterness, but when she tried to believe that he had once loved her, that some of the things he had said, some parts of their time together had been truly felt and meant, grief submerged her utterly and she cried till her throat ached.

About a month later, his agent rang her. He began by saying how sorry he was 'about the whole business', and she heard herself agreeing that it had been – was – a pity. Then he said that Jason wondered whether she had had his letter. Oh, yes, she had received it. She did not say that she now knew it by heart. Ah. Well, Jason had been a little worried, because he hadn't had any reply. She said nothing, waited. He *was* a bit anxious to know how she felt about a divorce. Of course, he could get one anyway in time, but he was rather keen to get on with it – tidy everything up sort of thing.

There was nothing about divorce in his letter, she said. She was beginning to feel a cold anger at having to talk about any of it with someone she hardly knew (cold anger made a nice change). He was talking again, as though he didn't believe her but was making allowances – extraordinary, Jason had sworn . . .

'If he wants to talk about divorce, he can do it face to face. Tell him that. Tell him I don't want any more letters or other people telling me what he wants.' And she rang off.

All very fine, but she soon discovered that she had simply manufactured an unbearable suspense for herself. *Would* he turn up? She realized from the rest of his behaviour that he would find it very difficult to face her. On the other hand, she suspected that his, or possibly, oh, yes, *Marietta*'s desire to get married would force him to come. Her feelings for him were by then so grievous that she was entirely divided about what she wanted. She knew that there was no future for her with him; she felt a miserable contempt for his moral cowardice (among other things); and she loved him more than she had ever loved anyone in her life.

The days – once she had willed herself to get up – were not so bad: she could cram them with action. She decided to move just to get away from the place where she had lived with him, so she had to start flat-hunting again and force herself to care where she lived. She packed up his clothes and a few other possessions to send round to his agent. There were surprisingly few of the latter: half a dozen paperbacks, some scripts, his squash racquet, an expensive camera and an album half-full of pictures of them. Their married life in half a small book. If she packed this last in the case, he would surely throw it away. It was not, she told herself, that she wanted the album; she simply didn't want it to be destroyed. Why not? Given the situation, why on earth not?

She had been kneeling on the floor because she had

pushed all these things into the bottom drawer of the chest. Now she sat, with her back against the end of the bed, to go through the album for the last time. Then she would either pack it up with everything else for him, or destroy it herself.

The pictures were pretty evenly divided between ones of them separately, with a few taken of both of them by a friend or passer-by. There were four to a page, and he had written below each one: 'Avignon', 'The ferry to Le Havre', 'Kensington Gardens', 'Siena' and so on. She stared at each picture of him, trying to see past his holiday happiness, his astonishing good looks – so much more endearing because he seemed hardly aware of them, his apparent glowing affection for her . . . but he was an actor, she reminded herself: he may never have been more than sexually enthralled – if even that. He may just have been fascinated by *her* infatuation. She may have been no more than an adoring audience of one. The trouble about betrayal was partly the terrible difficulty of knowing when it had begun. It was like liars who destroyed the currency of any words: once you knew that they had lied about anything, you had no way of knowing that there had ever been any truth, or if there had, where it had ended. She realized drearily that she was crying again, crying and hating him. What was the point of keeping the pathetic little book, and why should she give him the privilege of destroying it? No doubt, as soon as he got back his camera, he would start a new album with Marietta. She thought for a moment of destroying the camera (it had been her first birthday present to him) but the idea quickly disappeared: she had no heart for spite or destruction. She wrapped the camera in bubble-wrap and put it in the case. The album went into the drawer where she kept her underclothes, buried under a pile of nightdresses – just for the present, she had told herself, until I move, until I've made up my mind . . .

He *did* turn up in the end. With almost no warning – rang rather late the night before and asked if he could come at six o'clock the following evening.

Nights had been pretty bad ever since Anna had told her about him – even with sleeping pills she would wake suddenly at three or four in the morning, become instantly and entirely awake, craving him, body and mind. She would lie, staring into the dark above where his imagined face looked down upon her. She would touch her breasts with his imagined, well-remembered hands, repeat his endearments that surrounded her name – and then, just as she seemed to have conjured him up, he was gone and she was saturated with his absence, all the fires hissed out by a tidal wave of reality. She was staring into the dark and there was no one there. But when she woke the night before he came she at once remembered that he was arriving at six o'clock – a mere eleven and a half hours away. The thought that if he came, if they talked face to face, he might not want to leave her, kept up a kind of impish nagging – why not? It had been known to happen: many husbands had abandoned a mistress for their wives and not for reasons of guilt! – rather, that the more serious affection had been recognized. It was not impossible. Not *absolutely* impossible, but very unlikely, she thought, trying to shred the hope.

He was nearly a quarter of an hour late, and apologized profusely: 'Really sorry – I got hung up on the phone and then the traffic was awful.' He dumped a brand new briefcase on the hall table and walked past her in the

narrow passage and she smelt a citrus aftershave – nothing
like his old one.

'I've given up milk,' he said, when she began pouring the coffee, 'on a low-fat diet.' He was tanned and all
his clothes were new. She watched him glance round the
familiar room. He had not, so far, met her eye.

'You wanted to see me,' he eventually began.

'I think it was you who wanted to see me.' She had lit
her cigarette with a tolerably steady hand while he told
her that he had given up smoking. His blond silken hair
had been bleached and streaked, which gave him an oddly
theatrical appearance.

'Daisy, you know I'm really sorry about what has
happened.'

'Surely not!'

'For you, I mean.'

It was easy – and pointless – to make him flounder.
She felt like Eurydice. He would not look at her, but all
hope had died and it would make no difference whether
he looked at her or not.

'. . . but I could probably ante up something. A few
thousand if that would help.'

She stared at him in a silence so long that eventually
he did meet her eye.

'I'm sorry I can't make it more, but you *have* got the
flat.'

I had the flat before I even met you, she thought, but
stopped herself saying so: she would not be drawn into
a squalid little argument about money.

'I don't want any money, thank you!' She stubbed out
her cigarette. 'Or compensation, I suppose you might call
it. I assume you came here because you want a divorce.'

'Well – yes, it would be—'

'Right.' She wanted him to go now – as quickly as possible. 'I'll find a lawyer and get in touch through your agent.'

'You are being awfully good about all this. I'm really—' He had got up from his chair and she could feel his relief: he would go back to wherever he was staying with her, and say, 'My God, it was so *embarrassing*! Thank God it's over.' Things like that.

He had reached the front door, which he opened. A cruising taxi saved him further embarrassment – how do you sign off with someone who has just agreed to divorce you? 'Taxi!' he shouted. It stopped, and blowing her a breezy kiss, he was gone. She shut the door as he got into the cab.

In the silence, impregnated by the citrus scent, her knees buckled and she collapsed in the narrow passage. She wanted to be sick, or faint, become unconscious in some way, anything, but not to cry.

This time it was as though any previous weeping had been a mere suggestion of grief: she was racked by a fit of sobbing that only with sheer physical exhaustion began to subside. She thought of Marianne Dashwood whose sensibility had up until now always provoked her. At least I can remember that sort of thing, can think a bit again . . .

The doorbell rang. It was laundry day. She could open the door and seize the box. Or simply shout through the letterbox to the man to leave it on the doorstep.

But when she did this, it was Jason's voice that answered.

'Terribly sorry, but I left my briefcase.'

She turned back to the hall table. Then she caught sight of her face in the mirror – blotched, swollen, her nose running, her eyes encased in puffy lids that felt scratchy when she blinked. She picked up the case – all shiny leather and gold initials. She could open the door enough to shove it at him, but not wide enough for him to see her.

It didn't work out like that. He had been leaning against the door, so when she opened it, he almost fell into the hall. He took the case, began to explain, apologize. 'Sorry, only it's got two scripts that I have to return without fail today . . . Why – *Daisy*! Whatever's the – oh – darling, oh, my poor love, look at you!' His arms were round her: she was engulfed by his tender concern.

'Oh, do *go*!'

'Can't leave you like this.'

'Yes, you can. Go on. *Go!*'

His arms tightened round her. Then, with one hand, he stroked the hair from her forehead, bent his head and kissed her for a long time – what seemed like the lifetime of their knowing each other, only it was as though they were moving backwards from this painful end to the elysian beginning.

'Hang on. I must get rid of the cab.'

She was trembling.

3

HENRY

Dear Mrs Redfearn,

Just a line to let you know that the garden is getting along nicely. I have more or less cleared the place of brambles, nettles, bindweed, etc., and have seeded a small lawn each side of the path leading up to your gate. If this does not suit, the grass can easily be dug in, but as regards seeding, it was now or wait until next March. Would you have any objection to my ordering some bush roses on your behalf? And perhaps a climber or two for the cottage. Again, if we wait until March (the next possible planting time) you will get far less from them next summer. There is, of course, the school of thought that maintains that one should not allow roses to flower their first year, but I am of a softer persuasion.

I stopped here, and read the letter. The sentence about seeding the grass was clumsy and I changed it. 'But as regards seeding, it has either to be done before the November frosts, or we should have to wait until next March/April, depending upon the weather.'

Thank you for arranging to have my wages sent to me. Your agent, Miss Anna Blackstone, enclosed a postcard with the first payment on which I was to acknowledge its arrival. She seems a very nice and efficient lady. I would never have thought of including an S.A. post-card. If you *do* want me to order roses etc. would you be so very kind as to ask Miss Blackstone to include some money for that? I will, of course, keep a careful account of how the money is spent.

Phew! That was the money bit over. I had thought this to be the stickiest part of the letter but, in fact, the personal note (which I had been looking forward to writing) proved far stickier.

'The cottage seems very empty without you.' 'The place seems simply to be waiting for its owner.' Both managed to be at the same time dull and presumptuous. I was not, you must understand, having trouble with choosing and phrasing what to write in this first letter because I was unused to writing: most of my spare time is spent writing a journal of sorts that contrives to blend reality with my imagination – pronounced unusually powerful by my teacher at primary school when I was seven. No, I was having trouble precisely because I knew the pitfalls – knew how uncertainty represses and distorts communication. I knew that, at times like this, it was necessary to ask myself what it was precisely that I wanted to say – what impression did I want to give and why?

I wanted her to reply to me. To this end, I had asked questions, but I knew that she might well get Miss Blackstone to relay her wishes – they seemed to be in regular touch. So, how could I make sure that *she* would reply? I wanted also that she should like me, should recognize that I am not the usual run. What would make her like me?

Trust. I could clearly recall that the first time our eyes met hers were full of wary defence; she was not accustomed to trusting people. I must disarm her, but so gradually that she would be hardly aware of it. I was beginning to feel really sorry for her: that kind of distrust was nearly always the consequence of some previous, grievous ill-treatment (from a man – they are invariably the culprits). I would protect her from any further crude and brazen attacks while laying siege to her heart. If she had been lied to, betrayed, abandoned, I would make it up to her; she would become the sole object of my affection, my concern and care.

I wrote: 'It may seem extraordinary to you (it does in part to me) but I honestly wish that I knew you better.'

Should I leave it at that? Or was it too faint a signal? I decided to copy out the letter and sign it, letting the last sentence be a postscript.

When I had done this I put a PPS on the next line: 'I've just read this and the last sentence looks rather odd. I've no idea where it came from: please ignore it. H. K.'

This last injunction was, of course, a way of drawing her attention to it. She had been gone now for nearly three weeks and, except for Miss Blackstone's missive, I had heard nothing. Apart from clearing the garden (which was not quite so far forward as I had intimated in my letter), I had not been idle. I had decided to find out as much as possible about Mrs Redfearn. The library yielded very little. A *Writers' Who's Who* (1972) did not list her. I was then introduced by the assistant librarian – a woman of an uncertain age who I knew had a soft spot for me – to the *International Authors' and Writers' Who's Who*. Again, there was nothing. By this time the assistant was by my side and when I exclaimed over the omission, asked me who I was looking for.

'That's not her working name. She was married to that marvellous actor Jason Redfearn – her name's Langrish. Daisy Langrish. I remember the papers were full of their romance; she was years older than him and she wrote that whole series – he played Pip in it, he's stunning. Look under Langrish. Coming, Miss Howarth.'

She was, of course, right.

'Langrish, Daisy Jessica b. Feb 1927 m. 1 Stanislav Varensky, m. 2 Jason Redfearn. Education Roedean and LAMDA.' There followed a quite formidable list of her plays, half a dozen for radio, one or two for the theatre, a large number for TV and four or five film scripts. Her address, given as c/o Anna Blackstone, somewhere in Covent Garden.

I had seen one of the films. It had been about a Walter Mitty-like character living one day of his life simultaneously as his imagination dictated and as it really was. I remember that I had enjoyed it, although in my experience nobody is actually so unconsciously divided. Still, good entertainment was what it was after *and* some of it was very funny. Then I had seen *Great Expectations* when it was repeated one summer, during the last tolerably peaceable weeks with Hazel for whom Jason Redfearn was a number one pin-up. I got quite sick of her going on about him, and as we had long ceased to have any sexual interest in each other this was not jealousy on my part, mere boredom at almost anything she said. I did not realize until some time after I married her that she had few or no interests outside her job – she was a physiotherapist at the local hospital and ran two evening classes a week for expectant mothers, on top of which she was always involving herself in various local enterprises. Some would say that these *were* interests and we had rows about that.

What I meant was that she had no interests compatible with mine. She never read a book, and was always complaining at the way in which she alleged I was wasting my time with them. Enough of her. I really didn't want to write about or even think of her for a single moment. I had far too much to do and to think about.

My days, which used to slow almost to a standstill from lack of incident, now succeeded one another like compartments of a train, linked and smoothly proceeding down the line I had laid out for them.

I would wake in my bunk, stretch out my hand to clear the condensation from the porthole to see what the weather was like. It was nearly the end of October and an Indian summer. Mist rose from the canal, so white and dense that the water itself was concealed, and when I got up and pulled on my jersey and opened the cabin doors the air was sharp and the cockpit wet with heavy dew. I would make tea and eat a bowl of Grape Nuts with the news and weather on the radio, and by the time I had shaved, the silvery-yellow sun was eating the mist, revealing the pewter-coloured canal in the faintly warmer air. Twice a week I went to the village to shop, always stopping at the cottage, where four mornings a week I would do some work in the garden. The cottage contrived to look both snug and forlorn, and as the days went by my urge to get inside it became an obsession. It started by my digging one day when it began to rain, and I thought of getting in simply for shelter, but of course the front door was securely locked, the back door likewise and all the windows were shut. I trudged back to the boat and got sodden – hadn't brought my mac. Thoroughly bad-tempered, I realized that my plan to clean the whole place up had gone by the board – I had done nothing since my meeting with Daisy (as I now thought of her). But I had no heart for the drudgery involved: it took quite enough time to get food, make it, clear it up and get my socks washed, etc. I sat that day eating the last piece of a pork pie and thinking how I could get into the cottage.

I could break in. This, while perfectly possible, presented difficulties. As I was fairly sure that no keys had been left in it, I would have to go on breaking in, and if I left a window open or glass broken from the first essay, others might have the same idea. I could write to Daisy with some reason for it being necessary for me to get into the place and ask for a key. But what reason could I give? And would she not suspect me of being unduly pushy, presumptuous or worse? Unable to solve this, I fell back upon counting the advantages of getting into the place. There would be countless books to read, running water (I could even have the luxury of a bath, a fire, room to move around) but, most of all, it would give me the chance of finding out more about Daisy. That was the point. The creature comforts were completely unimportant compared to that.

Evenings without alcohol in the boat were long, and accustomed as I had been to writing my account of Helen, I found myself wanting to write, but not in the least wanting to continue with that. It was literally the end of a chapter. I hoped, of course, that at some point Daisy would want to know something about me, but I had had no reply from her about the roses and therefore had to find legitimate reasons for writing a second letter. This left me at a loss, until the idea of writing not *to* but *for* her occurred.

Where to start?

The beginning for me was when my mother died – or,

rather, just afterwards. I was five and a half. I can, of course, remember many things before the turning-point, that grey November afternoon when my father came down the stairs to the kitchen where I was playing, and picked me up to set on his knee before telling me that Mammy was gone.

I remember wondering what he meant. She'd been upstairs, in bed, ill, for days and days, and I'd been in the kitchen all the afternoon.

'I didn't see her go,' I said.

'Passed *away*, boy!' He sighed. 'Well, never mind. You'll find out soon enough.'

After that, a woman from the village came in and spent a long time upstairs while my father had gone to fetch the doctor.

I had got back down on the floor to spin my tin lids, but somehow I didn't want to go on doing that. I didn't want to play. I wanted to eat. It was past my tea-time and meals for the last two weeks had been strange and un-satisfactory. Even baked beans, which I liked, were always cold. I got up and went to the little larder at the end of the kitchen. Nothing much there. I took a half-empty pot of strawberry jam and found a slice of bread in the bin. My mother had always spread my bread for me – with marge and then jam and never enough of the latter. I took the pot and tipped it – like a sandcastle – on to the bread and it came out easily, a red, glistening mound overlap-ping the crusts. I bent over it and licked it and the jam went on to my chin as well. I stuck two fingers into it and groped for a whole strawberry, which was delicious. I kneaded the jam into the bread so that when the top was finished the bread would taste good. Licking it off my fingers was a good slow way of eating jam, and it was much nicer eating without people telling you all the time how to do it. A few bits dropped on to my clothes and some were too far away to lick off and my hair got in the way but it stayed back if I stroked it with my hand.

It was nearly dark. The kitchen was always dark anyway as it had very small windows – we lived in the Lodge at the gates of the east drive of the Big House. I could have climbed on a chair to turn on the light, but I never minded the dark.

I remember all this so clearly because it was just before the woman came down from upstairs and told me my mother was dead. I knew what dead meant because of rabbits, and birds in the winter. It meant she wasn't going to move or do anything for me any more.

'Poor little mite. I'll stay till your dad comes back,' she said. She switched on the light. 'Whatever have you been *up* to? You're a right mess and no mistake.' She tried to pick me up.

I sat on the floor holding the jammy bread with both hands.

'Dad said I could have it. It's mine.'

She dislodged one of my hands and I hit her.

'Go away. I don't want you.' She was stronger than me, and she lifted me off the floor still clutching the bread and sat me on the draining-board. She smelt horrid – years later I recognized the smell of Jeyes Fluid and whenever I smell that I think of her. She filled the sink with water and when she wrenched the bread away from me I began to howl. Her fat fingers were unbuttoning my clothes, pulling the shirt off my shoulders, dragging down my shorts, peeling off my vest. I tried to bite her, and she slapped the side of my face as she hoisted me up again and plunged me into the sink.

'You'll not get the better of *me*, you monkey,' she said, and turned on the tap so that the cold water poured over my head.

My father came back with the doctor and they went upstairs.

'I'm washing the boy,' she said. My father cast a look at me and I could see he didn't mind what she was doing to me. I felt suddenly that I didn't mind either. I didn't count, with anyone. It was then that I think I must have realized for the first time that my father didn't care about me – had no love for me at all. The only person who had cared was my mother, and she had left me. I sat, shivering, unresisting in the sink while the woman fetched a towel and my pyjamas, lifted me back on to the draining-board, dried me a bit and clothed me again. My lack of resistance softened her.

'Stop crying now. You're a big boy. Big boys don't cry.'

She began to wipe my face quite painfully with a cloth that smelt like her and I thought I would be sick. But just then the doctor came downstairs followed by my father.

'And how's the little fellow?'

'*He's* recovering fine.' The bitterness in my father's tone was apparent. The doctor laid a hand on my shoulder and said, 'It's a sad business to die so young. I'll let Mr Lark know and he'll be here tomorrow morning.' He shook my father by the hand and went.

'Would you like me to get something hot for your tea?'

My father shook his head and muttered something about his glasshouses having to be shut down for the night. 'I've left them too long as it is, and I don't trust that boy,' he said, and taking his torch from the place where it hung on the wall, he too went. 'You might put the boy to bed if you please, Mrs Greenwich,' he said, over his shoulder.

She did. She lifted me off the draining-board and herded me up the steep narrow stairs. I slept in the small room to the right at the top. The door to my parents' bedroom was closed.

'Do you want to go to the toilet?'

I shook my head. If I did, I would go by myself – not with her.

'Into bed with you, then, like a good boy, and perhaps I'll give you a kiss.'

To avoid this, I scrambled into bed and pulled the eiderdown right over my head. She clicked her teeth.

'Have it your own way, then,' she said. I heard her shut my door and the sound of her going downstairs. I listened while she made up the range and tramped about below. I wanted her to *go* – off on her bicycle on to the dark road – and never come back.

At last I heard her having two goes at shutting the latch on the back door and jumped out of bed to watch from the window. In a minute, she was gone – no sign even of her bicycle light. I could see from the chinks in the floor that she had left the light on in the kitchen, but it was pitch silent.

This – when I had the fever – was the time of the evening when my mother used to read to me. Now that she was dead there would be no one, since I knew that my father would not take the trouble. My mother had been a schoolteacher, and she knew a lot of books. She had been teaching me to read, but I had liked it best when she did the reading. Now I would have to learn by myself to read the rest of her books. Suddenly I found I was wondering what dead people looked like. They might just look as though they were asleep. Or not?

The window was open in her room and it was very cold. There was a candle burning on the chest of drawers by the bed. My mother lay on her back very straight with her long brown hair brushed out on the pillow. There were two pennies placed over her eyes and they spoiled her face – it meant I couldn't see it properly. I leaned over her and took the pennies off her eyelids and – quite slowly – one eye opened. It seemed like pale blue glass and did not look at me at all. There was a faint smell of Mrs Greenwich in the room. I put out my hand again, and pushed my mother's face; she did not feel nice – too cold for her softness. She lay there looking far more peaceful than she usually did, especially since I'd been ill when she was constantly with me, and she'd always looked worried – or perhaps she was afraid because my father shouted at her to leave me alone and see to him. Once he came into my room and hit her on the side of her face and the mark went red and then darker. There was no mark now and her face looked more like a picture than a person. I knew she was taking no notice of me because she was dead, but it still felt all wrong. She once said, 'You mustn't be selfish – like your father,' but *she* was the selfish one, leaving me just like that before I could even *read*. 'Reading is the most important thing for you to learn in your life,' she had said, and she kept saying it at every lesson. I've never forgotten that. It was what made me teach myself to read. I used the stories she had read so often I knew them by heart, and so I could look up words I couldn't understand or pronounce. I could read before I was six.

Anyway, she'd left me, and I left her, and the reason I

remember that evening so well is that it was the first time that I realized that I was on my own in life: nobody was going to care for me better than I could care for myself.

I was right about my father. He regarded me at best as a duty, at worst as a nuisance. Quite soon after the funeral, he engaged Mrs Greenwich to come in, clean and generally housekeep. She was supposed to come only three times a week, in the mornings when I was at school, but she was soon there more often, and after a few months – March, it was – she took to coming in most evenings to give my father and me our tea. There was much more to eat and the kitchen was always warm because she never let the stove go out, but I did not like her. One evening at tea after she had tried to talk to me and got nothing back, she turned to my father. 'He's the spitting image of you to look at, isn't he? Pity he hasn't your nature.'

My father was sitting at the table with his shirtsleeves rolled up. He was packing tobacco into his pipe and did not reply for a moment. Then he glanced at me with utter indifference before he said, 'He bin troubling you, then?'

'Oh, no! He couldn't trouble *me*,' and she, too, looked at me – with power in her eye. 'I only meant he's backward in coming forward, if you know what I mean.' I remember that phrase with particular clarity because I *didn't* know what it meant.

As the evenings became lighter, she would accompany my father on his evening visit to the glasshouses and they would be out for more and more hours. I didn't care. When they had gone, I would go through the larder picking at anything that took my fancy. I was careful how I took things, leaving the carcass, or loaf, or sugar bowl looking undisturbed. Then I would carry my spoils up to my room and read while I ate. I had my mother's box of books under my bed – having dragged it there when my father was at work. I only took out one book at a time, as I didn't want my father to know that I had taken the box, although, looking back on it, I don't think he would have cared if I had. To begin with I read and reread the children's books that my mother had read me and some that she hadn't got to. They were heavy, old-fashioned books with many illustrations that I enjoyed. *Children of the New Forest*, *Treasure Island*, *Five Children and It*, *Black Beauty* were some of them. I can't remember the order in which I read them, but by the time I was eight I was reading Dickens, Somerset Maugham and Mrs Henry Wood. I understood only half of what I read, but that didn't spoil the stories for me at all. In fact, it made them last longer, because each time I went back to a book, I understood more. By then my father had married Mrs Greenwich and she was called Mrs Kent by the teachers at school, and whenever it was fine enough I got away from the Lodge and spent my free time roaming the park, which seemed enormous, and the woods round it, and sometimes the gardens where my father worked as head gardener. There was an orchard, a nut wood, a big kitchen garden and the famous glasshouses – seven of them, ranging from cool to almost tropical. I left the flower gardens alone, because they were in sight of the Big House and I didn't want to get caught by my father or anyone else.

When she was first married, Mrs Greenwich – as I always thought of her – made some efforts to be friendly to me, but she soon gave that up. I could not bear her to touch me, always remembering the humiliation of her tearing off my clothes and putting me in the sink. I think she must have realized that my father had no feelings for me and that therefore she would not gain favour with him by making up to me. I did not make friends with the boys at school as I hated the games they played and their tree-climbing, their fights and dares with each other to jump off walls or knock on people's doors and run away.

I had my own games and – to begin with, indeed for some years – I did not need anyone to play with me. Looking back, it is hard to remember precisely when the main game, as I called it, began, but it certainly did not start until I had visited the house, and *that* happened when I was about eight.

My father came home unexpectedly in the middle of the afternoon or, rather, he was brought back in a cart. He'd hurt his leg in some accident with a ladder and could not put his foot to the ground. Somebody up at the · Big House had bound it up for him. I was told to hold the pony's head while the boy and Mrs Greenwich helped him into the kitchen.

'Hal can go for the doctor,' Mrs Greenwich was saying as I came in.

'No need. Her ladyship has called him.' My father was lying on the narrow settee and his face twitched – I thought from pain, but it was a fleeting, secretive smile.

'Undo these,' he said, touching the crêpe bandage beneath his rolled-up trouser leg. 'It doesn't 'arf throb.'

'I can't do that. Not if they did it up at the house—'

'Do it, Milly. Do as I say.'

I was about to slip away, when my father called, 'You!'

I stopped and looked back at him. His face was pale and his usual lock of heavy black hair fell across the side of his forehead. It was the same colour as mine and grew in the same way.

'You go up to the house and ask for Mr Billings and tell him I won't be up tonight. He'll have to stoke and shut down on his own. You could offer to help him. You go round the house to the back door, the one near the stables.'

I had never been allowed into the house and was excited.

'You go straight there and you come straight back,' Mrs Greenwich told me. I always agreed with her and did the opposite, and sometimes this was tiresome because I didn't particularly *want* to do the opposite thing – it had become a point of honour.

It was a mild evening in early spring and the drive was the best part of a mile. It was not a made-up road, and there were weeds and streaks of grass above the ruts. Each side were beech trees that were full of the furry buds that break to sharp tender green so suddenly. It was the kind of thing I noticed about the place long after I had left it; I wasn't noticing or thinking about them *then*, I was thinking about my reception at the house, how I could coax someone to give me some cake and even a drink of lemonade, a luxury only tasted at Sunday-school outings, but likely, I thought, to be drunk every day at the house. It was so large it felt to me like a village, a place rather than one dwelling. It was built on three sides, like an E without the middle bar, and set back from the open side was another courtyard with stables, and coach-house and garages and lofts and places where outdoor staff slept.

You could only see the front of the house from one part of the drive, the rest of it was curves with park or woods each side of the beeches. Eventually there was a fork, and I went left, which led to the back where the stables were.

There were several black-painted doors into the house and I picked the ones at the centre, which were a pair, and turned the big iron door knob to open one. Then I was standing in a stone-floored passage, rather dark with many doors. At the end I could see there was a staircase and I ran towards it. By now I was determined to see as much of the house as possible. The staircase was funny, it went in a corkscrew, and I ran up the shallow stone steps, at the top of which was a door covered with green cloth and what looked like giant drawing-pins stuck in patterns on it. I pushed this open and found myself in an enormous tall square room. It had a large fireplace and was full of doors, and animals' heads sticking out from the walls. I was just about to try one of the doors when out of another one came a girl. She was about my age, wore riding clothes and had two pigtails that stuck out behind her black velvet hat.

'Who are you?'

I was struck dumb. I was afraid if I told her, she would tell me to go away.

She walked up to me and stared steadily. Her face was covered with powdery yellow-brown freckles: it was quite round and not at all pretty, I thought.

'What do you want?'

'I'm looking for Lady Carteret.'

'She's in the morning room. I'll take you if you like.'

'Thank you very much.'

I followed her to the other side of the room, which opened into a smaller room full of furniture and mirrors and pictures.

'Oh! She must have gone to the library.'

We went through another door into a very long room that had windows all down one side and books all over the other. I had never seen so many books in my life; there must have been thousands of them – millions, even, I thought. They were on shelves from floor to ceiling.

'Mummy! Here's a boy to see you. He hasn't got a name.'

At the far end of the room there was a fireplace with logs burning and settees. On one of them lay a woman, with short golden hair like a cap round her head, who wore a lilac dress and a long rope of pearls. Her pointed shoes matched her dress: I had never seen lilac shoes before and they struck me as extraordinary.

'It's Mr Kent's little boy, isn't it? Of course, I'd know you anywhere. Daphne, do go and change out of those hideous riding clothes before tea. Daphne! I mean it.'

'Kent's a stupid name for a person,' she said, as she went. 'Kent is a county in England. That's what it is.'

When she had gone, Lady Carteret sighed and then looked at me as I stood before her. 'Such a little hoyden.'

I kept silent. I didn't know what hoyden meant: I didn't even know for sure whether she meant her daughter or me.

'And how is your father? Has Dr Maclaren been to see him?'

I shook my head.

'But your stepmother is there, and I'm sure she is a tower of strength?'

She *said* but she also sort of asked it and I felt vaguely afraid of some sort of trap.

'I don't know.'

Her face had a lot of different colours to it: blue on the lids of her eyes, dark blue on her eyelashes, white on her face except for pinks on her cheeks and a dark red mouth.

'What is your name?'

'Henry. But I'm called Hal. Usually.'

'And do you want to be a gardener, like your father?'

'I want to read books.'

She arched her very thin eyebrows, reached for a gold cigarette case and a cigarette and fitted it into a long green and gold holder.

'Have you read all *your* books?'

She had lit her cigarette and blew out a gust of blue smoke. 'I'll tell you a secret. No. I haven't read a quarter of them. Some of them are unreadable anyway.'

'How do you mean?'

'Oh – sermons and histories of battles and fearfully dull journals of people travelling about and staying just as dull as if they'd stayed at home. And then, of course, there are some quite well-known novels but the printing is old and all the Ss are Fs.'

'Could I see? One of them?'

She uncrossed her ankles and sat up. Her stockings were silvery grey. 'Why not?'

She showed me a book in two volumes called *The History of Tom Jones,* and it was true, the letters were different and made it look a bit like a secret language.

'I could read this,' I said.

'All right. You may borrow it, one volume at a time.'

'Could I really?'

'If you promise to be very careful with it.'

'I promise.'

She put a hand lightly on my head to push the lock of hair back. 'I'm sure you keep all your promises. But you came to see me about something. Didn't you?'

ELIZABETH JANE HOWARD

'To tell Mr Billings that my father won't be in tonight, he'll have to stoke and shut down on his own.'

'But surely you were meant to tell Mr Billings that – not me.'

'I was looking for him when the girl found me. Honestly. I didn't know where to find him.'

She walked to the fireplace and pulled an embroidered rope. 'Harker will find him for you.' When she left me there was a lovely waft of spicy smell. A man in dark clothes came into the room.

'Take this boy to Mr Billings, Harker, would you? And ask Mrs Tarrant to give him a nice slice of plum cake. And I've lent him the book. Goodbye, Hal. When you've finished that volume you may come and collect the second.'

'Thank you ever so much—'

'M'lady,' the man called Harker prompted.

'Your lady,' I said. He smiled in a superior way and I wanted to kick him but I didn't want Lady Carteret to think I was a kicking sort of boy.

Mrs Tarrant was sitting in front of a large coal fire in a dark green room in the basement where I had come in. A portly man wearing an apron sat eating hot buttered toast at the table, on which was a splendid tea. Harker repeated Lady Carteret's message about a nice slice of cake.

'Large,' I said. The sight of all the food made me feel ravenous.

'Her ladyship said nice,' he said.

'Nice means large,' I said. We glared at each other.

'I'll cut it myself.' Mrs Tarrant looked at me over her steel spectacles and I felt she was on my side. 'You're certainly like your father,' she said. 'Do you want to eat it here, or take it home with you?'

'Take it home.'

'If you please.'

'Please.' I kept my eyes on her when I said it, and saw her soften. It was interesting seeing how people changed depending on how you looked at them.

The cake was wrapped in a piece of greaseproof paper. I was offered a glass of milk, but I've never liked milk so I said my stepmother didn't want me to have any. This was a mistake, because Mrs Tarrant immediately filled an enormous glass.

'You drink it down, dearie,' she said, in tones so much on my side that they sounded positively ferocious.

'Poor mite,' I heard her saying as I left the room; 'losing his mother like that! And that Mrs Greenwich I wouldn't wish on anyone's child.'

I walked out of the house and on to the drive in the dusk with my spoils. As soon as I was out of sight of the house, I remembered I'd forgotten to give the message. Who cares? I would eat the cake – perhaps not all of it, but enough so that the rest would go in my pocket without a bulge.

There was a lot to think about. I went over the whole time with Lady Carteret. Was I going to be a gardener like my father? Not on your life. I was going to be somebody who *employed* gardeners like my father – who employed dozens of people, like the Carterets, and lived in a House, as opposed to a poky little Lodge. Even Mrs Tarrant's sitting room was twice the size of our kitchen.

I found a place with a fallen tree to sit on while I ate the cake, which was black with raisins and currants and had a hot treacle taste that went up my nose: the best cake I'd ever had in my life. How would I get a house like that? It must cost a lot of money. How would I get the money? I thought of Lady Carteret. Her husband had been an invalid since the war, and spent much of his time in bed or a wheelchair. He'd been like that ever since I could remember and the only time I ever saw him was the occasion when he came to the school to give prizes. How had *he* got any money if he was such an invalid? Perhaps Lady Carteret was the rich person. Perhaps it was really her house and he was simply living in it because they were married. And then a really brilliant thought came to me. If Sir Carteret (even in a wheelchair) could marry Lady Carteret and live in such a grand manner for the rest of his life, why didn't I marry Daphne and do the like? Obviously this couldn't happen for several years: even if Sir Carteret died from being so weak and never walking anywhere, Lady Carteret, who in any case looked younger, would probably live for quite a long time. But once Daphne and I were married we could make her happier than she had ever been. 'You are the perfect son,' she would say, 'there is no one I would rather have living in my Big House. Daphne is a very lucky girl.' This brought me up short. Daphne, with her pigtails and round freckled face, was hardly the golden-haired beauty I had in mind as a wife. I decided to leave her out of the game until she got prettier.

But that was when I started the game – about my whole life when I was grown-up, living in the house and being master of the estate with dozens, possibly hundreds, of servants, with horses and carriages and motor-cars, and perhaps a small private zeppelin. There would be grooms and gamekeepers and butlers (but not Harker) and gardeners (but I would retire my father to a little house by the sea). There would be cooks and maids for all the indoor work and a nurse for Lady Carteret and fireworks at least once a month, and boating parties on the lake, and I might even start a private zoo, and there would be balls to which everyone else who owned a large house would come, and dance to an enormous band, eat ices in summer and drink punch in winter, and girls would get engaged to men in evening dress. I was able to furnish the game from information gained from the books in my mother's box, and later, books lent me from Lady Carteret's (or my) library. For she was in this respect as good as her word. I returned the first volume of *Tom Jones* within the week and was allowed the second. On the next occasion that I met her, she asked if all was well at home. I looked at her blankly, wondering what on earth she meant.

'I mean,' she said quite gently, 'is your stepmother kind to you?'

Oh – *that*. I gazed mournfully at Lady Carteret and thought of Mrs Greenwich and in no time a couple of tears were rolling down my face. After that, Lady Carteret positively encouraged me to come to the house and borrow books. She never referred to my stepmother again, but she gave me a florin on my birthday and another one when it was Christmas.

I kept my visits to the house very quiet at home and for a long time, probably more than a year – I had an instinct that neither my father nor Mrs Greenwich would like the idea, although I was not clear what kind of objections they would make if they knew. By then, I never wanted them to know anything about me and as they were neither of them interested enough in me to be curious, it was easy to keep my secret life – my books and stories and visits to the house, and rare meetings with Lady

Carteret (she was often nowhere to be seen) – completely secret. So sure was I at one point of their lack of interest in me that one term I played truant from school on the days that we had lessons I hated. This came abruptly to an end one summer evening when I came back from what amounted to a whole day in and around the Big House instead of being at school. I was met at the kitchen door of the Lodge by my father, his shirtsleeves rolled up and a look in his eye that I knew meant he was very angry.

'You're found out, you lazy monkey. Come here.'

'I haven't done nothing.' I was frightened and I heard myself whining and knew it would make him angrier.

'The one thing I won't have you grow up to be is a liar. If I have to lam it out of you I won't have that.'

He had seized me by my shirt collar and now dragged me into the kitchen.

'Take off your trews. Look sharp!'

When my shorts were round my ankles he pushed me down over one of the kitchen chairs and beat me with a leather strap. I'd shut my eyes, but the first stinging blow made me shout with pain and at the same time I saw *her* – Mrs G – standing in her bulging flowered overall, arms folded over her huge bosoms (that's what I called them in those days). My eyes moved further up her body, past her double chin to her mouth. It was smiling. I knew without looking that it was watching me that was making her smile. I clenched my teeth and shut my eyes again and stopped any noise coming out of me, and I was full of hatred for her that was louder and harder than the beating. I hated them both: my father for beating me in front of her, and her for being there. But I was also really afraid that someone from the house had told my father about me, not that I had ever gone there, but how often, and even while he was beating me I was struggling to find a convincing story that would appease him.

'That'll teach you never to play truant and lie to us no more. If I catch you at it again, there'll be twice the bill to pay. You can go to your room now and you won't get no tea.'

I lurched past them – it hurt to walk – and climbed the stairs as fast as I could without running.

I fell asleep in the cabin writing that – woke in the small hours, stiff and cramped from my head being on the table. I woke because I was cold. Outside the cabin there was a sharp hard frost and a windless silence. I climbed into my bunk fully clothed and fell asleep again as I remembered how, after that hiding, I hadn't been able to sit down without pain for a week. I woke early next morning – from the cold again. The stove was out because I'd run out of coal. I hadn't cleaned the galley for weeks or taken clothes to be washed or stocked up on tinned soups and sardines – in fact, I'd been so obsessed with my past and anxious about my future that the present, my day-to-day existence, was in danger of being suffocated. I made a pot of strong tea and a bowl of instant porridge, and while consuming these, I read what I had written the night before.

It is an odd sensation to read about oneself. I cannot imagine what it must be like to read a biography, or even a short biographical piece written by an outsider. I suppose it can never be entirely satisfactory, since one expects character to be gilded somewhat by the written word. Or perhaps the written word is more potent – a homeopathic analogy – simply by being set down, whereas speech has all the diffusion of spontaneity and immediate audience, and therefore all writing has to be reduced, the currency of words deflated, in order that the reader should be able to stomach them.

What I chiefly noticed about my childhood reminiscences was what I had left out. Some incidents, of course, were hardly of a nature to appeal to Daisy – my early interest in girls, for instance, which had led to the unfortunate adventure in Park Wood where I had enticed little Mary Cotting and made her take off all her clothes. If I recounted the adventure at all to any woman, I should dwell upon Mary's long golden hair, her damp rosy mouth and her large, round blue eyes. I should not refer to her round, ash-white bottom and the damp rosiness contained therein, any more than I should make note of the trail of oyster-coloured snot that seemed always to inhabit one nostril, nor would I wish to recall the way in which she whined when she tried to blackmail me. I got the better of her there, frightened her so badly that she never said a word.

I had also left out the sense of despair, of being trapped, that I had endured for so long in the dark little Lodge that was crowded by two people who, I felt, would rather I had never been born. I cannot recollect one moment when my father offered me any word or gesture of affection, when he showed the slightest interest in anything that I did; his anger about my truancy was the only time he mentioned my school life.

Perhaps I should not have left this out of the account: women like to feel that they are pioneering with their affections for a man; if he is already sated with love, or sex, or affection from others, she is less involved. I suppose this is the same philosophy that drives men to seek and prize virgins: theirs is the first imprint upon the driven snow; they cannot be compared with anyone else. I have never felt like that. Encountering a virgin I have naturally always tried to do my best for her, but I would not seek them out.

I do not now know when I gave up the slightest attempt to win my father's attention, but I'm aware that for some years my efforts became more oblique, the signals put out fainter, and almost certainly in a language foreign to him. He clothed and fed me – or, rather, Mrs G did that, but with his money. He was not a demonstrative man: even with Mrs G he evinced no particular feeling, although sometimes in the night, when I must have been thought asleep, I would hear the springs of the iron bedstead creak and, if I opened my door (which I did the first time from curiosity), the heavings and shiftings that accompanied their coupling. I loathed Mrs G in a thorough, straightforward fashion. I hated the sight as well as the smell of her. I hated her for always being there. I knew perfectly well that she disliked me back, but was too dishonest to say so and I despised her for that. If my father prized honesty so dearly, I thought, why did he put up with this fat, craven liar?

But there were other things that I had left out of this first account, and I think this was because they were curiously difficult to convey. My secret life in and about the Big House had become so much the major part of my life that in trying to impart it to a stranger, I didn't know where to begin. I imagine that the Brontë family would have felt much the same about the Gondals.

In the four years that followed my first visit, I managed – through enterprise, subterfuge and sheer pieces of luck – to see the greater part of the house, and got to know a great deal about how life was conducted there.

This meant that I actually saw what a grand bedroom looked like and my initial untutored notion of sleeping on a low, flat divan upon a golden throne had to be modi-fied. Nor did the bathrooms contain marble declivities filled with asses' milk and spattered with rose petals that I had read about in my mother's copies of Ouida: they were, in fact, rather disappointing with dark green lino, steep baths with corroded claw feet and a basin with taps of brass rather than gold. 'That's the one the guests use on this floor,' Daphne said.

I had realized early that making friends with her was the only way I could see any of the upper floor (I never got to the attics). I had to work hard on Daphne to get her to show me anything, apart from the stables and her pony. This meant spending hours in a small field beset with juvenile jumps and watching her endlessly going over them; it was very boring. When the weather was bad I had to spend dreary afternoons helping her to clean her tack and admiring the rosettes she had won in local gymkhanas. She offered to teach me to ride, but I declined, and as there was only one pony and she wanted to ride it she did not press me. But one day she actually said she liked me. 'You are the only person who really wants to see me riding. That's why.'

And then one day in the summer holidays I found her sobbing in her pony's loose-box.

'They're sending me to a boarding-school! Next term. Oh, Hal! What shall I *do*?'

I couldn't understand why she was so upset.

'You can't have ponies at boarding-school. I shall be away weeks and weeks without him. Mummy's taking Papa to the South of France for the winter and Miss Poulter is going to live in Broadstairs and there simply won't be anyone in the house!'

'Do you mean Mrs Tarrant and all of them—'

'Of course there'll be servants. I meant people.'

I remember staring at her. 'Aren't I a person?'

She looked at me consideringly, but she went a dark pink. 'Actually, you are. You're different from the others.'

'I'm not your servant. I'm not anyone's servant.'

'No need to get in a bate.'

'What's that?'

'You see? If you weren't a servant's child, you'd know that. Anyway, none of this is the point. The point is they're making me leave poor Blackie with only Fletcher to look after him.' Her round face crumpled and she started crying again.

In the four years since I had first seen her, she had remained almost exactly the same, except for being several sizes larger. Her pigtails were long enough now for me to pretend they were reins and drive her about the field. For some reason she liked this, and I enjoyed the sensation of mastery and the fact that I could hurt her if I chose, by suddenly tugging on the reins until she gasped with pain. She was too fat, and she cried at almost anything, and got hiccups that wouldn't stop, and bit her nails and got heat bumps in summer and chilblains in winter, both unsightly in their different ways. I found her deeply unattractive and this sometimes made me bully her, but she had an unexpected sweetness of nature that always confounded me. 'It's all right, I know you didn't mean it,' she would say, as she sniffed or wiped her eyes with the back of her hand or her flaming face resolved to its usual high colour.

'The thing is I wanted to ask you a really important favour.'

'What?'

'Would you look after Blackie for me? It would only mean seeing him twice a day and, you know, giving him carrots and sugar and talking to him and seeing that his feet are all right and stopping Mr Fletcher from trace-clipping him. Would you? I'd be ever so grateful.'

'What would you do?'

'How do you mean?'

'To show your gratitude. What would you do?'

She thought for a moment. 'You can have half my pocket money for the whole term. I get sixpence a week, so it would be quite a lot. How's that?'

'Well, I might do it if you also promise to show me the whole upstairs of the house.'

'Oh, *that* again! You've seen most of it. I can't think why you find it so interesting.'

'I haven't seen your father's apartment.'

'*Apartment!* It's only a bedroom and dressing room and bathroom and small study. And room for the nurse when she stays. What's interesting about any of that?'

'It interests me.'

'All right. I'll take you. As soon as they've gone to France.'

But, of course, it turned out that she was going to school *before* they left. She was too honest not to tell me this and when I said all right, no deal, she offered me three-quarters of her pocket money. 'I have to keep a bit or the other girls will laugh at me, which they will anyway.' She was never far from tears these days. 'Oh, Hal! Please just say you will look after him and I'll do anything you want in the Christmas holidays.'

But I stuck to seeing her father's rooms as part of the bargain. As they would one day be mine, it was only natural that I should want to take a serious look at them. We quarrelled and I avoided her for nearly a week. I knew she would mind this because she seemed to have no friends, excepting two cousins who came for a fortnight once a year. She admired them deeply and was terrified of them, but their visits, much looked forward to, were always a disappointment. I knew that if I kept out of her way she would seek me out, and she did.

In summer, or whenever it was warm enough, I used to spend much of my time up a particular tree at the edge of the wood overlooking the park. If I climbed high up in it, I could see a long way: the kitchen gardens, the glasshouses winking and glittering in the sunlight, the blue face of the clock set in its small tower on the stable block, one end of the lake and the paddock where Daphne schooled, as she put it, her pony. But lower down the tree was a broad branch that slanted upwards at just the right angle for my back, and here I used to read for hours. I heard her coming from some way off, there was nothing of either stealth or grace about her movements.

'Hal! Where are you? Hal! I bet you're up that tree as usual.'

How did she know that this was my special tree? I'd never told her. The idea that she had been following me about irritated me. I did not answer her. Then, suddenly, when I looked down, there she was, immediately below me, staring straight up into my face.

'Go away. This is my tree.'

'It isn't. All the trees belong to Papa.'

'They won't when he's dead.'

'How horrible you are. He's not going to die. That's

why Mummy is taking him to the South of France for the winter. To get him better.'

There was a silence. 'I was going to tell you something very nice, but I'm not sure if I will now.'

She would; I knew she would. All the same, I made an effort. 'I didn't mean to be beastly about your father. I keep forgetting that he's different from mine and you mind about him.'

Her face cleared. 'That's all right. I know you have an awful time at home, with your stepmother and – everything.'

'How do you know?' I had never told her.

'Mummy said,' she answered carelessly. 'She says your father is an excellent gardener, but an unfeeling man.'

'What else did she say?'

'Nothing. I can't remember anything. Do you want me to tell you the nice news?'

'If you want to.'

'Mummy is taking Papa out to lunch next Sunday. And the nurse has got the day off.'

'Oh!'

'So it will be all right now about Blackie, won't it?'

'You bet.'

Memory is the most fascinating unreliable business. It is not only what one forgets (and certainly for me, large pieces of my life are lost in the fog of boredom that was their chief characteristic) it is how *much* one remembers of any particular incident. I can remember that conversation in the wood with Daphne with remarkable clarity but, curiously, the impression that her father's rooms made upon me is vague. I know that I was disappointed in them: they seemed gloomy and austere rather than opulent and mysterious, which I had imagined them to be before I saw them. And yet I had longed to see these particular rooms, and conversations with Daphne nearly always bored me.

I thought about this as I trudged along the icy towpath to the bridge, where I had last seen Daisy in her car – a flash, pale face, no hat, tip of cigarette glowing in the dark, gone almost before I could show that I had seen her – and then down the winding road that led past the cottage to the village. I was taking all my dirty washing to Mrs Patel's small supermarket where she also did laundry and dry cleaning. It was the day on which I collected my money from the post office, and while there I picked up any post. I had the usual dull list of necessities to buy (again at Mrs Patel's), and then I had the possibility of an hour or two in the pub, where I could either eat and drink moderately, or drink more and give up the idea of food. Perhaps there would be a letter, or at least a postcard, from Daisy, although the chances of this seemed slimmer as the weeks went by and she did not answer my suggestion that I should buy roses for her garden. I decided that if there was nothing – either from Daisy or Miss Blackstone – I would put my plan of getting into the cottage into operation. I had been waiting for a hard frost and here it was. I had not, at this point, determined upon more than gaining access with a view to discovering more about Daisy. My excuse, if anyone noticed that I had broken in, was that the pipes had frozen and I was concerned about flooding when the frost broke. The cottage was so isolated that it seemed unlikely that anyone *would* notice, and I wondered why I had been so cautious for so long.

There *was* a letter, from Miss Blackstone, simply saying that Miss Langrish authorized me to buy what roses I thought necessary. It was clear that she was not going to write to me herself.

By the time I got back to the cottage there had been a short but heavy hailstorm and it was bitterly cold with the promise of more frost. I chose a window at the back of the cottage, which proved to be quite easy to force, and through the gap I was able to undo the latch on the larger casement window.

The cottage was also cold and had that faintly mossy smell associated with damp. The cold was of a different order. There was something still and settled about it, as though it had been infecting the air ever since she had left.

The kitchen was tidy, some crockery left to drain by the sink, a crate of what turned out to be kitchen utensils still unpacked. The larder had fungi growing out of the wall near the floor.

The living room was much as I remembered. The fire had been doused judging by the clogged ash, and a dead bird lay uneasily upon the half-burned logs. Ah. Of course, it was not dead: it had fallen down the chimney. I had seen it desperately trying to get out – what could I do but break in to rescue it?

The books that we had unpacked were ranged along the low shelves on the wall opposite the windows. I went to feel them: they, too, were damp. I decided to light the fire and eat the sandwich I had bought from Mrs Patel when the room was warmer. In fact, a fire should be lit at least once a week, I thought, as I cleared up the bird and put paper and two firelighters in the hearth. But even before I lit the fire I wanted to explore the floor above.

At this point I still had the irrational notion that I might be disturbed and, if that happened, was afraid there would not be a second chance to see everything.

I have no idea what I expected to discover. The narrow, rather steep stairs reminded me of the Lodge except that on a half-landing was a small bathroom, a luxury unknown in my childhood. A few more stairs and there were three bedrooms to the right and left of them. One was slightly larger than the others and had windows in two aspects. This was clearly her room, since it contained more furniture and a dressing-gown hung on the door hook. The walls were white and the floor was covered with rush matting; the bed had a patchwork quilt upon it in various shades of crimson, pink and red. There was a chest of drawers but it contained almost nothing: some woolly socks, a navy-blue jersey of the kind that originated with fishermen, and in one of the two top drawers two silk scarves. I picked one out to smell it and caught the faintest whiff of cloves.

The other bedroom had nothing in it of interest. I went back to her room to inspect the dressing-gown. It was a dark red of some woollen stuff – a man's dressing-gown. Round the neck were some strands of her fairy hair. I scraped the collar with my nail to collect one hair, which, when freed, immediately sprang into a corkscrew. I put it between the leaves of my pension book and went down to light the fire.

That first time in the cottage, I did nothing but warm myself, eat my sandwich and browse through the books we had unpacked. They were mostly plays – a formidable collection, it seemed to me. They were not a form of literature that I had ever explored. They ranged from Euripides to the present day. There were a lot of foreign plays, mostly in translation: Molière, Ibsen, Chekhov, Schiller – names I had heard of but neither seen nor read. I noticed a good many Irish names – O'Neill, Dunsaney, Synge, O'Casey, Wilde, Shaw (I knew about the last two). There were many unknowns: I remember Henry Arthur Jones for instance, because it seemed such an uninspiring name for a playwright, and A. A. Milne, who I only knew as the author of *Winnie the Pooh* – a book that Daphne had shown me so many years ago. They were not arranged in alphabetical order, rather in some sort of chronology. By the time I got to Coward, Maugham, Sherriff, Barrie, Albee, Miller, Bolt and Rattigan, it was too dark to read anything. I left the way I came, having doused the fire, and walked back to the boat by moonlight in a hard frost.

Dear Miss Langrish,

I do apologize for addressing you wrongly in my last letter. I was beginning to be afraid that you had not received it because of this, but today I got a note from Miss Blackstone saying that I may order the roses. I wish I knew what colours you prefer, as once one has planted a rose it is there for a very long time. The more I think of this, the more I feel I should give you some information about them first, in order that you may have what you would really like. I shall start with red, as on the whole they have the strongest scent. Guinée is the blackest of the reds: she rambles in a rather loose manner, but her appearance and scent make her worthwhile. Étoile de Hollande is another good rose that will climb if required. Of the old-fashioned shrub roses, I would recommend Charles de Mills and Arthur de Sansal. The latter is prone to mildew though wonderfully scented. Rose de Rescht is a fuchsia red with a good scent and copious flowering.

If you like the old-fashioned ramblers – the sort that would look good up your apple tree – then Kiftsgate, the Seagull or Paul's Himalayan Musk would suit. They have only one flowering, but are a marvellous sight during that time and fast growers. Of the striped roses, Ferdinand Pichard is my favourite, but Camaieux is also lovely.

I went on through the whites to the apricots and yellows for a page or two.

So you will see that there is much choice, and it seems a pity that it should not be yours.

It has become extremely cold with heavy frosts at night and I cannot help worrying that your pipes may freeze and damage be done to the property. If you would like and if Miss Blackstone has a key, I could go in once a week, light a fire to help keep down the damp and generally see that all is in order. I don't want to be presumptuous, but it can be dangerous to leave a place quite empty and uncared-for in the sort of winter that it promises to be. But of course you may have made other plans. I expect you are very busy, but if you simply sent me a list of the roses you would prefer, I should feel better about ordering them. I do hope you understand. I have had so much to do with gardens all my life that planting is a serious matter to me.

Yours sincerely,

Henry Kent

ELIZABETH JANE HOWARD

Days passed and I continued my account of early life.
I left a bit of a gap, because for several years after that
conversation with Daphne before she went to school
nothing much happened to me except that after I reached
fourteen and had passed my school certificate, the teacher
of my form came to see my father one evening to suggest
that I might continue my education. My father sent me
upstairs while they talked, but by lying on the floor and
putting my ear to the gap between the floorboards I could
hear a certain amount of it.

'. . . the kind of boy who does not try at all at subjects
that don't interest him, but when they do, he shows
considerable promise. He's a bright lad, Mr Kent, and it
seems a pity that he should not go on to learn more. Get
a better job when he's grown if he does.' I heard my father
ask what I *was* any good at as he had not noticed that I
seemed to be good at anything. English – I wrote good
essays and seemed interested in literature generally, had
read a lot for a boy of my age . . . I heard my father snort
at this: he did not even bother to reply. There was a silence.
Then I heard the sound of a chair scraping. My father
said, 'Thank you, Mr Wakefield, for your trouble. But the
boy has a job to go to, so there's no need to worry about
his future.' Footsteps and the sound of the door being
shut.

What job? I wondered. I had not particularly wanted
to continue my schooling. I didn't get on with the other
pupils and a lot of it was boring, but the fact that my
father didn't want me to, made me think again. I also had
a fair idea that I wouldn't want to do whatever job he
had in mind for me, although, of course, it might entail
leaving home, something that I had begun to want a good
deal.

During these years, my fantasy – I suppose you would have to call it – about living as the master of the house in the park had dwindled, largely, I think, for lack of nourishment. After she began going to boarding-school, I saw almost nothing of Daphne. She brought school-friends back for the holidays and had no time for me. She had graduated from the fat pony to horses, and went riding with these friends, played tennis with them, and, on the few occasions when I encountered her, was dis-tinctly cool. Her parents spent more and more time abroad, and the house was often closed down: linen blinds on the windows and fewer servants. There was a new butler, who was unwilling to allow me access to the library. As Lady Carteret was away on the occasion when he refused to allow me in, there was nothing I could do, and pride and a feeling of resentment prevented me from persisting. I had learned to use the travelling library that came to the village once a month and that had to do. I acquired odd bits of money from poaching and bought a second-hand bicycle, which enabled me to take the rabbits or pheasants to the neighbouring market town where I could flog them to a stall that sold such provender. I constructed a sort of game larder in the woods where I could store what I caught and this became my chief enter-prise when I was not at school or doing chores for my stepmother or reading. As I grew taller and older, she ceased bullying me – even attempted some sort of rapprochement to which I responded with a bland indif-ference.

I got caught out about the poaching very soon after Mr Wakefield paid his visit. It was just before the end of my last term at school, and the gamekeeper who caught me went to my father and told him I'd be up before the magistrates for it. My father was furious. It seemed that I had let down the family, by which he meant himself and the family he worked for, the Carterets. He bawled me out, but I was too big – nearly as tall as him by now – to thrash. He must have done some deal with the gamekeeper – who, of course he knew – because he said I would be let off by the magistrates if I was under his eye, to which end I was to be employed as a gardener's boy, under him. The idea of the magistrates so terrified me – I imagined myself in court and going to prison for years and years – that I agreed to this humiliating alternative. So began the long drudgery, of double-digging, wheeling barrowloads of muck to the kitchen garden, watering, hoeing, spraying, cleaning flower-pots after bedding-out, sweeping paths and hedge-clippings, weeding, mowing the narrow strips of lawn that edged the herbaceous borders and clipping the edges afterwards on both sides, raking leaves and gravel – think of any dull garden work and you may be sure that I was ordered to do it.

There were two other gardeners under my father and they got the more interesting jobs, such as layering, taking cuttings, and planting, while I had simply to mix up the compost to my father's recipe of sand, peat and the compost made on the estate and put it in endless rows of small pots for my betters to fill. My humiliation was complete when Lady Carteret, her daughter and some guests came one day to the cool greenhouse where I was disinfecting pots. Lady Carteret said good morning to me, then told her daughter to do the same. 'Good morning, Hal,' Daphne said, in a voice that imitated her mother, and made me realize how patronising they both were.

She, Daphne, looked much the same, a bulky, graceless adolescent, and at that moment I actually hated her.

'He's the head gardener's boy,' she added, to one of the guests. 'His father has worked here all his life.'

'Awfully feudal,' one of the guests said, and someone giggled.

I felt my face and ears going red, looked up and saw Daphne staring at me. When our eyes met, mine smouldering with rage, she began a long painful blush. Then she silently mouthed 'Sorry,' turned away and followed her mother. I thought about this afterwards, but didn't understand why she had changed so suddenly from patronage to apology.

My father worked me hard, for a wage of five shillings a week, which was increased to seven and six after two years. The work and fresh air improved my physique; I graduated from a gawky boy to – I have to say it – a handsome young man. I knew this chiefly because of Lily Palmer.

Lily was three years older than me, which was part of her charm. When you are fifteen, someone of eighteen seems awfully mature and I was flattered by her interest in me. She was the daughter of the pub keeper. We met in the evenings to go for walks, and from the first walk she let me kiss her and touch her ripe, inviting breasts. Quite soon we were frantic for some private shelter where we could explore each other further. It was she who found the deserted barn and led me to it one early spring evening. Half of the roof had gone and the great pair of doors hung crazily upon their broken hinges.

Inside there was the mouldy smell of old hay and a kind of dusty light, which decreased at the end to dusk. She took my hand and when we reached the dusky end she flopped down on to the ground, pulling me with her. It was odd: I remember noticing then that although it seemed that she was in charge of the situation, it was I who possessed the power. She was unbuttoning her mac to reveal a pink satin blouse that also had buttons.

'You can take it off, if you like,' she said.

'Get out of that mac, then,' I said, and she did, bundled it into a pillow and lay back with her arms behind her head and I saw her breasts move as she did so.

'Have you ever done it before?'

I shook my head. My mouth was dry.

'Go on, then,' she said. She had a fringe of dark brown hair nearly hiding her eyes, which were also dark brown and fixed upon my face with an expression that, at the time, was enigmatic to me. I know now – I knew almost at once – that it meant she wanted me to do anything I liked to her, but could not ask. Some instinct, one of the most useful I have ever possessed, guided me to take my time over everything, undressing her, petting her, exploring her body with my hands and mouth and then fucking her for as long as I could hold out. I could tell by her eager mouth as juicy as a ripe plum, her hard nipples and the warm flood from between her legs that I was doing well. I repeated the performance until we were both temporarily exhausted. She fell asleep at once, her hair damp on her forehead, her mouth slightly open as though she had just finished singing something. I did not look at her for long. We had not said a word throughout the exercise. We seldom said much anyway, and we had neither of us indulged in the sickly hypocrisy of exchanging vows of love. It was, it always was with her, pure, straightforward lust. After that first time, we didn't bother with the walk together, simply met in the barn on her days off – she worked for her father. I discovered that I could drive her into a frenzy by delaying everything just a little more than she expected. Then she would cry and call out my name and beg me to do the next thing. I enormously enjoyed the feeling of power this gave me. I did sometimes wonder where, if at all, love came into it. I had, after all, read a good deal about love, or at least lovers or people who went about saying they were and talking about it, but after some months with Lily, I honestly began to wonder whether it wasn't simply some literary convention, designed in more prudish – say, Victorian – times to conceal the true animal feelings that it was clear to me most people possess. Lovers in books were continually telling each other how beautiful they were, or how good, or whatever; they went in for down-right flattery before declaring their love for the owner of such beauty and virtue. I can honestly say that I never thought Lily good-looking. I have difficulty in recalling her face at all now, and her body was only remarkable to me because it was the first put at my disposal. If this sounds callous, it is not. I'm sure that that is how she thought of me.

The affair came to an end when I was nearly seventeen, because she was going to become engaged to a pig farmer and wanted the use of the barn to be sure that he would be a suitable husband. 'Can't tell till I try, can I?' she said to me, and I, quite relieved to be shot of a situation that was becoming mildly monotonous, agreed.

She married him three months later, and five months after that she had a daughter. I did sometimes wonder whether I or the pig farmer was the father.

Dear Mr Kent,

Thank you for your letter about the roses. They all sound delectable. I think, though, that I prefer the red ones for their fragrance, and the striped ones for their appearance. Will that do? Please order what you think fit and send the bill to Miss Blackstone, who will reimburse you. I have asked her to pay the cottage a visit in order that she can see whether it needs more caretaking or not. I am just off to Mexico for a brief respite as this winter has been a hard one for me in spite of unrelentingly fine weather. Thank you for taking so much trouble over my garden.

Yours sincerely,

Daisy Langrish

I read this first outside the post office, then several times more in the cottage, where I had taken to spending much time. Turning on the water heater had enabled me to have the luxury of regular baths and I had also done a certain amount of cooking as an electric stove was infinitely less trouble than paraffin. I had even spent a night there during a snowstorm. To begin with I simply revelled in the fact that she had written to me at all. I examined her rather elegant, spidery writing, perfectly legible but also pretty to look at as decoration of a page. The news that Miss Blackstone would be coming down – time unspecified – was, however, alarming. I set about clearing up evidence of my occupation: turned off the water heater, cleared up the kitchen and removed the large pile of ash from the sitting-room fireplace. But I felt it was essential to see her when she did come, and I also resolved to write to her about the dead/live bird that I had had to rescue in case I had left any clues to my presence. I decided to send this at once, with a bill for the roses.

It seemed unlikely, since she worked, that Miss Blackstone would appear on a weekday, so I took to gardening – preparing the holes for the new roses with compost and manure – on Saturday mornings. I took my lunch with me and ate it in the freezing garage, and stayed in the garden until it got dark at about four. I did the same on Sundays. It was on the third Saturday that she arrived. I heard her car when I was wiring the wall where I intended to put one of the climbers. This entailed being up a rather rickety ladder discovered in the garage. Some of its steps were missing and it was a hazard. I heard the car stop, the door slam and the gate latch open, and then an extraordinarily husky, seductive voice saying, 'Please don't let me give you a fright.'

What a voice! It conjured voluptuous, tightly corseted women in Wild Western saloon bars, a brandy-sodden voice, a gin-and-too-many-cigarettes voice, the voice of the successful Other Woman in certain romances; you could hardly imagine it speaking from any but a hori-zontal position and then only to men – might I, perhaps? I turned round on the ladder.

'I take it you are Mr Kent. I'm Anna Blackstone.'

I said good morning, and turned to the wall again to climb down the ladder, trying to take in the extraordinary dichotomy of her voice and her appearance. She was dressed entirely in black – trousers, a polo-necked sweater and a windjacket. Her iron-grey hair was cut short with an uncompromising fringe of the sort that always makes me think the owner is hell-bent on either a scene or a seduction. Her figure – so far as I could see – was shape-less, a rectangle drawn from below the neck to above the knees, of the kind a child might make below one of those heads with round eyes and a slice-of-melon mouth. I turned to face her again and she held out her hand. I wiped my own on my trousers before shaking it.

'You got my letter?'

'Yes.'

'I thought I ought to let you know.'

'About the bird?'

'Well – about my breaking in because of the bird.'

She was looking round the garden. 'Where are the roses?'

'They haven't come yet. I was late in ordering them because of not knowing which Miss Langrish would prefer and nurseries lift roses by rotation. They'll come some time this month. I've prepared all the holes, and I was just wiring up for the climber.'

'Ah. Perhaps we'd better go inside. It must be marginally warmer.'

'It's the amount that you'd only notice as you walk in. The moment you're in, it simply seems a different kind of cold.'

She gave me a fleeting, but penetrating glance. 'Does it really?'

I must be pretty careful with her, I thought. She's no fool.

Inside, she said, 'Perhaps it would be a good thing if the fire was lit.'

'Right.' I had laid it, so that was easy.

While I was doing this she was walking round the room, touching the books as I had done.

'It's damp here, isn't it?'

'Well, I'm afraid anywhere left empty would be at this time of year.'

She did not reply, but went upstairs.

I heard her walking about above and then apparently not walking. Just as I was beginning to feel nervous, although I was certain that I had left no trace of myself in either of the bedrooms, I heard her start coming down again. She stopped off at the bathroom; perhaps she was using the lavatory. I thought, good thing I'd turned the water off . . . and then I heard the water flushing. I'd *forgotten*. I had turned it off the first time, but put it on again because using the lavatory here was infinitely better than the antique Elsan in the boat.

I explained the last part of this to her when she came back into the sitting room. I didn't say anything about the Elsan, simply that I had been taken short, as it were during the bird incident. She stood by the fireplace, warming her hands and looking at me thoughtfully during my spiel. Then she said, 'And the electricity? Is that on as well?'

'I don't know.' I knew that I'd turned off the water heater, also knew that in fact it *was* on otherwise, but there seemed no point in saying so.

'I saw a tin of Nescafé in the kitchen. I could do with a hot drink. Would you like the same?'

'Thanks, I would.'

While she was making the coffee, I was thinking how I could gain her trust, even, possibly, some sort of confidence. She was not simply the only link I had – except for one brief letter – with Daisy, but I sensed that she had influence with her. If I could get Miss Blackstone to like me it might lead to a stronger connection. I must somehow get her to see that I was not just a jobbing gardener, that there were other, more interesting parts to me. This was, of course, entirely true; it was a question of which parts would most impress her.

When she returned with two mugs of coffee I had arranged the chairs each side of the fire with a low table between them. She sat in one and I in the other. She pulled a pack of cigarettes out of her coat pocket and offered me one. When I had lit both our fags, she said, 'Have you always been a gardener?'

'Oh, no. I was trained in garden design and I did do it for a while. It was the design that interested me more than the actual maintenance. But since the war people haven't had the staff to keep up really interesting gardens.' There was a pause, and then I added, 'I designed and planted a maze once. I suppose I would have liked to be Repton or Capability Brown, but on the whole they are not wanted any more. People want small, low-maintenance gardens, and there is a limit to what one could do with them. One does not any longer have the opportunities presented to one that Maria Bertram's fiancé had at his disposal.'

I saw from her face that she both caught the allusion and was surprised by it.

I have said nothing about her face, partly because it seemed to me entirely unremarkable, but now our eyes met and I saw that hers – a fine hazel – had a lively, penetrating expression, lighting a countenance that could otherwise only be described as homely.

'Do you know when Miss Langrish will be back?'

'In about another couple of months, I think. Why do you ask?'

'You're her agent. I thought you'd know.'

'I'm also her friend.' There was something, not exactly hostile, but warning, about the way she said it.

'Then you are even more likely to know her movements.'

'Why do you want to know?'

'I should have liked – with your agreement – to get the cottage clean and warm for her when she does come back. You can see from today that it's neglected, it isn't a very welcoming place. I should like to do that for her.'

There was a silence, during which I saw her looking at me thoughtfully. I took the plunge. 'It's not just that. I'm book-struck. Have been all my life. She's the first live writer I've ever met. We spent an afternoon unpacking her books and arranging them. I don't know much about plays, but she has hundreds here. I wouldn't want any cash for looking after things, just the agreement that I could read the plays. The books are getting damp, as I discovered when I came after the bird, and they'll warp in the end. One doesn't get the chance to thank writers for what they do: this feels like mine. Do you see what I mean?'

'I see what you mean. Do you mean what you say?'

'I can't think why I'd say it otherwise. But it's clear you don't trust me—'

'I don't know you, Mr Kent. I don't know anyone who knows you. Usually when people do this kind of thing there are references.'

'I'm afraid I can't help you there. I've been more or less self-employed all my life, and there has never been the occasion for them. You will have to take me on trust, or leave me. Though, come to think of it, what on earth damage you imagine I might do to Miss Langrish or her property is beyond me. However, if you have this Whipsnade view of me—'

'*Whipsnade?*'

'A wild animal – better out of doors at a distance. I take it you have no worries about my doing the garden?'

'That was the arrangement Miss Langrish made with you.'

I was getting nowhere. Worse, I began to be afraid that Miss Blackstone would report back to her client, presenting me in an unfavourable light. I got to my feet and made one last effort. With all the charm I could muster I said, 'Miss Blackstone, I'm sorry. I seem to have made an awful mess of things that I thought were quite simple. I'm a country person, and we find it natural to help one another – no strings attached. But I do see that to someone outside it would sound strange – even suspicious, I suppose. I'm rather given to shooting my mouth off without realising the effect it might have on other people: it's a recurrent fault of mine and I've suffered the consequences quite enough to know better at my age. Have you noticed that curious thing about age? How one never seems to be consistently the same? At one point one is – in my case – sixty-five, and then without warning, a crass eighteen. There I go, talking too much. It comes of living alone and then suddenly meeting two people, both you and Miss Langrish whose work is what interests me more than anything in the world.'

I got to my feet. I had been looking her straight in the face during that speech, pushing my lock of hair – iron-grey – away from my face. I wanted her to notice my hands, which have inspired many people with confidence as they look both shapely and sensitive and *not* your average jobbing gardener's hands. Now I smiled ruefully and said, 'I'll be off. Please don't hold my presumption against me. I'm sure, if you wanted to, you could find somebody in the village – or probably not there as it is a very small one, but in the nearest market town about five miles away, who would be able to give you references and who would look after the place if you think it needs it. I should really like to go on doing the garden as I have it all planned and have become rather attached to it. Is that OK?'

'Of course. Oh, I nearly forgot. Here's a cheque for the roses. I was going to post it if I couldn't find your boat.'

As she handed me the envelope she smiled, which gave her face an amused look.

'No, I won't hold your being bookstruck, or any of what you call your presumptions, against you. I'm sure you understand that one has to be more vigilant with other people's property than one might be with one's own.'

I agreed with this and we shook hands.

Phew! I thought, as I walked back to the boat. I was thankful she hadn't bearded me *there*. It had relapsed again into the usual state of squalor. I spent the rest of the day cleaning things up.

There was not much else to be glad about, I thought rather morosely, as I sat down to my baked beans on toast enlivened by my Saturday can of beer and miniature bottle of Smirnoff. Miss Blackstone would be as formidable an opponent as she clearly was a friend. She was one of those women – a minority, I have discovered – who seem impervious to men, for whom sex has played a minor and probably never heterosexual part of life, and who is consequently quite difficult to charm. Not impossible, of course, there is always a way in to anybody's secret or inner self, but there are people who do not provoke the urge to try. This has less to do with sexual attraction than one might think. It is not even a question of being either beautiful or plain. Indeed there are often more barriers to successful sex with a beautiful woman than with a plain one. Which brings me back to Daphne and the dénouement of that chapter of my life.

I suppose I would have to say that in many ways the *affaire* with Daphne was the most unfortunate of my life and, looking back on it, it is clear to me now that it was doomed from the start. I suppose also that anyone reading this (but I do not wish Daisy to read it – as it stands, at least) would wonder how on earth there was an affair at all. I have said how dull and unattractive I had always found Daphne, but this would be reckoning without that occasional, sudden, complete metamorphosis that can occur in young girls between the ages of fourteen and twenty. Daphne was – like Tennyson's Maud – not seventeen when I next saw her and it is true that at first I literally did not recognize her.

It was a Saturday and one of my days off. I had gone into the local town to buy myself some decent clothes for the rare occasions when I was not working. I had also, since Lily, begun to feel that I must get away from my father, the job he had pushed me into and the suffocating dependence and lack of privacy that were the chief miseries of living at home. I had fifteen pounds in my pocket and spent twelve of them at the gentlemen's outfitters in the high street, emerging in a very short time clad in a navy-blue suit with a pale blue poplin shirt, a dark blue tie with white polka dots, and some black shoes and dark socks. In a brown paper bag I carried a second shirt (white) and two more pairs of socks. I had jettisoned my old clothes at the shop. I felt wonderful – kept looking at myself in shop windows and wondering whether people realized that almost everything I was wearing was brand new. It seems odd now to think I could have bought so much with twelve quid but this was 1936, and money was different. It had taken me a year to save it, after all, but I really enjoyed spending it and spending it so fast.

It was a beautiful early-autumn day and the town was busy with a market set out down the middle of the high street. I decided to walk to the end to see what was on at the cinema, go to a pub and then explore the two second-hand book shops. Half-way down the street was the shop that sold new books and I could not resist going in. I was looking at the stand near the door, which had all the newest publications built in a sort of tower – like giants playing at card houses – when there was a cry of dismay and a whole lot of books fell to the floor on the opposite side of the stand to mine. I went round to help retrieve them and as I straightened up with an armful, a woman's voice shouted, 'Hal!'

There was a pause and then she said again, 'Hal!' and I found myself looking into the round blue eyes of a slender brunette. It was seconds before I recognized Daphne, so changed had she become. The freckles were gone, leaving a milk and rose complexion that reminded me of a certain paeony. She was wearing a bright blue shirt open at the neck and a slim chocolate-brown skirt with a leather belt. The clothes emphasized her neat waist, and her small round breasts. Her hair was cut to shoulder length and was dressed in a style known then as page-boy. She looked elegant, groomed in a way that I came to know later was unusual in English girls. 'I can't say, "fancy seeing you here,"' she said. 'I know you always liked books.'

'That's true enough.' There was a pause. 'You look very well.' I meant it.

'So do you. You look . . .' She stopped and I saw the faintest blush.

'Less like a gardener's boy?'

The blush deepened. 'Hal. You can't imagine how bad I felt about that. It was disgusting of me, I've never stopped feeling ashamed.' She was looking at me with a frank and anxious expression that I remembered and that dissolved years of my pride and resentment.

'Mummy was always on at me for spending so much time with you, and I suppose I was half showing off to her. It doesn't make it any better,' she added quickly, 'I just wanted to explain. We never had any lies between us, did we? You said what you thought, and I said what I thought, and sometimes we didn't agree. That's how people are, isn't it?'

'I expect so.' I hadn't the slightest idea.

'Listen! Couldn't we have lunch together? The Swan does quite good lunches, or are you busy?'

'No. It's my day off. I was thinking of the flicks, if there's anything on worth seeing.'

'I expect there will be. I do love going to the cinema, don't you? I don't mind seeing films that I like again and again. If I give us lunch, will you take us to the film?'

'All right.'

She picked up her bag, well-polished brown leather, and slung it over one shoulder, and with her other hand, took my arm, and marched me out of the shop.

I had never been into the Swan Hotel. It was also a pub, in the sense that it had a saloon and ordinary bar, but somehow its beautiful sign – a golden swan preening – and the loud county voices of those at its entrance had intimidated me. I realized that I had never, in fact, eaten anywhere except at home and at the boarding-house near

Clacton that Mrs Greenwich had insisted upon for an unspeakably dreary summer holiday. Judging by the house's dining room, which I had several times seen when the table was laid – covered, you might say – with silver and glass for dinner, this meal might present difficulties insoluble to a novice. As Daphne led the way down the carpeted passages with sconces in them that illuminated prints of gaudy and improbable birds, I was thinking as fast and as hard as I could. There were three options. The first was simply to let things take their course: if I got it wrong, just laugh my way out of it. The second was to pretend that I knew everything, and when I tripped up (if I did) to brazen it out as my way of doing things. The third was to confess to Daphne that I was a novice at eating in an hotel restaurant and ask her to tell me what to do. By the time we reached the large, rather full dining room, and were being taken to a table by a knowing little snob dressed up to the nines, I had decided upon the third course.

How right I was! Not only did it save me untold embarrassment – who would have thought that you'd have not only different knives and forks but sometimes even two *plates* on which to put different kinds of food? – but it made Daphne even nicer than she had been already. She explained with tact and clarity, and soon I was reaching for my outside knife and fork as one to the manner born. I tripped up over the first course, which was a platter containing six smaller dishes of different, mostly unidentifiable things. I took the dish of sardines, the only one that I felt sure about, but then Daphne explained that one could not take all of everything, we were meant to share. But every time she said anything like that, she gazed into my eyes and said something like, 'Oh, Hal! You can't imagine how glad I am to see you.' Then the faint, enchanting blush would begin at the bottom of her pearly neck and surge upwards, sometimes ebbing slowly away before it reached the crest of her cheekbone, sometimes persisting until it reached her forehead and the roots of her hair.

Once she said, 'You can't imagine how badly I wanted to write to you when I was in Switzerland. How *badly*!' and her eyes filled with immovable tears that stayed, like crystal, in her eyes. I think it was then that I leaned forward, kissed my two fingers and put them – lightly, caressingly – on her mouth. I don't know what made me think of such a thing, I had never done it before, but it suddenly seemed right. These intuitions or certainties or whatever they are have come to me a number of times. I have never been able to *command* them – they simply occur, or they do not, but the effect is always electric. She put her hand over her mouth and closed her eyes for a second and when she opened them they were stars. 'Oh, Hal! Do you . . .' Then she couldn't say any more.

'Yes,' I said. 'You know I do.' I wasn't sure at the time what it was that I was supposed to be sure of, but I guessed that it was right to sound positive.

We turned our attention to the chicken pie that had been cooling on our plates and, perhaps becoming aware that we had been attracting attention from other tables, we set about small talk in what I believe we both thought was a thoroughly sophisticated manner.

'What were you doing in Switzerland?'

'Being finished. You know, learning a bit of another language – in this case, French – and how to make choux pastry and arrange flowers and interview servants and do a proper placement at table. Oh, yes, and dancing, and we played quite a lot of tennis, and walked about with books on our heads to improve our deportment.'

'Did it?' I wasn't going to let on that I had very little idea what on earth she was talking about.

'Of course not. The whole thing was a farce. Except you get to know some girls who you wouldn't otherwise have met. Not at school, I mean.'

'And are you finished now? Whatever that may mean.'

'Supposed to be. The next thing is a Season in London.'

'How is your father?'

'Not well. Much the same, but not the same, if you know what I mean.'

By now we'd reached the pudding. It was called peach Melba and was only quite nice. The waiter came to ask whether we wanted coffee.

'Do you?'

I shook my head. I wanted to get out of the place now.

We didn't go to the cinema, we went for a long walk away out of the town, up steep chalky little lanes that seemed to go on for ever. I kissed her by a stile that began a footpath, and she seemed to melt into my arms.

'Oh, Hal! My darling Hal!'

There was something touching about her inexperience and her passion. When I asked her whether she loved me, she put her arms round the back of my neck.

'Love you? I've always loved you. From the very first time I saw you – in the hall when you came to see my mother.'

'I don't seem to remember you being very loving then,' I said.

'I couldn't have told you. I *looked* so awful – I *knew* exactly how awful. I was afraid you'd laugh at me, like everyone else. But I used to lie and think about you in bed and wish—' She had started to blush.

'What? What did you wish?'

'That you were with me. I used to dream about being grown up and our being married and going riding together and having parties at home—'

Without thinking, I interrupted her. 'I used to dream that sort of thing.'

'*Did* you, darling? Oh, Hal! Isn't that funny and stupid that we both felt the same and never said?'

I agreed that it was. I couldn't – obviously – tell her exactly what my thoughts had been about either her or her house. She was not at all like Lily Palmer. Even on that first day, when we found that the footpath ended by a wood and lay down in its shelter, even then I didn't altogether realize what I was in for. I thought that because she lay down when I asked her to, allowed me to strip off her clothes until she was shivering from the shade and excitement, and she offered me her mouth and all of her silky skin, that she had done it before. It wasn't until I tried to penetrate her that I discovered that she was a virgin. I stopped, but she said, 'Go on. I want you to. I *want* you to.' So I did. I felt bad about hurting her and tried to make it up by a lot of sweet words. I probably said a whole lot of things I shouldn't have, but anything nice I said to her delighted her so much and elicited such a stream of reciprocal endearments and flattery that it was hard to resist.

It was wonderful to be told how beautiful I was, how my nearly black (till then I'd always thought of it as plain black) hair shone and sprang so attractively from the peak on my forehead, how she loved the hardness of my body, the shape of my hands, the colour of my eyes, my – she called it 'chiselled' – mouth. Lily had never commented on my appearance or, indeed, anything at all about me and Mrs Greenwich repeatedly made plain her horror of personal remarks. I discovered that I loved them; could not have enough. There was a kind of security that seemed to come out of such uncritical appreciation. I remember one day her saying I was a prowler, and for a moment I thought she meant like a burglar or something, but not she. She'd meant more like a 'beautiful tiger'.

The first weeks we were both taken up with her love for me. The weather stayed fine and it was easy to find some sheltered spot in the woods round her home. We even accumulated the rough material for a bed of sorts: a groundsheet, a couple of rugs and a cushion, all stowed away between whiles in a canvas camping bag. That was September and the first week of October. It was damp but we were not cold. Daphne took to bringing Thermos flasks filled with soup or hot chocolate. Her parents had gone to the Riviera for the winter, she said, and she was supposed to be going to stay in the flat in London in November. She was to continue having French lessons and was to have clothes made and spend Christmas in Scotland with cousins.

'The ones who used to come and stay with you every year, who you were afraid of?'

'Them, yes. But I'm not afraid of any of them any more. I have a much more exciting time than they do. I bet they'd die if they knew.' The enforced secrecy thrilled her. We had to be particularly careful where the servants in and out of the house were concerned.

I hated all that part of it. It was a nuisance and I felt humiliated by it. It was because of me, I knew, that it had to be secret. If Daphne had been being courted by one of her own kind they would have been complacent.

'Oh, no, they wouldn't. They wouldn't like me drinking hot chocolate under a rug with anybody.'

As October drew to a close, she became much exercised about how we were to meet after she'd gone to London.

At this point I was divided. I enjoyed sex with her, I enjoyed her being so much in love with me, but I was also becoming the tiniest bit bored with the sameness of it all. I had also become preoccupied with how to bring about any public agreement or recognition of our relationship. The idea of marriage recurred regularly, partly because Daphne often spoke of it and always as though it was a certainty – not an immediate one, but none the less certain. I would ask her casually one day whether, when her father died, her mother would be easier to get round.

'Oh, no! My father is the easy one – he lets me have almost everything I want. It's Mummy who is so rigid about everything.

'But never mind,' she said minutes later. 'When I'm twenty-one I can do what I like. And that's less than four years away.'

Four years! It seemed aeons to me. I began to wonder whether I might not, after all, be driven to doing some other work than gardening to earn more money and see the world.

It was more or less while this notion was taking uneasy shape in my mind that she produced her plan that I should apply to my father for a week's holiday and spend it with her in the flat in London.

'I've more or less told Mummy that my friend Penelope

is coming to stay with me – she does French as well – so she'll let me stay there for as long as I like.'

'What will we do about the servants?'

'There aren't any, except when my parents are there. There's just a char who comes in three mornings a week. We'll go out while she's there. Oh, Hal – it will be such *fun*! You'll be able to get a week off, won't you? You said you've hardly ever had any holiday.'

It was easy. I simply told my father that I wanted a week off and that I was going to London where I'd never been. It seems extraordinary nowadays to think I'd lived all that time stuck in one place. It is true that the likes of us didn't travel as people do now, just went away once a year to the seaside. I only ever did that once because I couldn't stand being with Mrs Greenwich and my father all day, and I never had any money to go off on my own. After that one time I preferred having the Lodge to myself for a week and doing exactly as I pleased, although I had to spend the day before they came back cleaning the place up.

London, the idea of it, had always frightened me. I imagined getting hopelessly lost. My idea of the place was perilously poised between palaces and parties for toffs and Dickens's slums and thieves, and I felt it was the latter in which I would become entrapped. Of course I didn't let on any of this to Daphne, simply let her make the arrangements and tried to look calmly enthusiastic. She was to go up first ('We'd better not travel together in case I meet anyone on the train'), and I was to follow the next day. She would meet me at the station and take me to the flat.

It's odd. You'd think my first week in London, my first time of living with a woman, my first real holiday, would be so sharply etched on my memory that I could recall every minute of it. I cannot, now, recall even every day. It was a maze of impressions, embarrassments, a marathon of emotional entanglement that survived, I think, only upon Daphne's unequivocal admiration for everything I did and said and was. London seemed to me a place that could only be enjoyed with a good deal more money than seemed to be available. I had virtually none, and Daphne surprisingly little.

'I only have my dress allowance,' she kept saying, and that didn't seem to run to much more than the odd cinema and eating occasionally in Lyons Corner House, which I enjoyed, but the rest of the time we had to go on boring shopping expeditions for food, which she then made a great fuss about preparing. The flat, in a Victorian mansion block in Knightsbridge, consisted of one long passage with a series of dark rooms leading off it. It was full of furniture, but Daphne's room had a decent bed.

Three of the mornings we had to get up early and she sent me out for three hours while the charwoman cleaned. It was November by now, and the choice for me was either walking about the streets or sitting in a café making baked beans and a cup of tea last as long as possible. After the first morning spent like that, Daphne came with me and we went on a bus to see the Houses of Parliament and Westminster Abbey.

'Let's go home,' she said, quite soon after we'd wandered round the square. 'It's much nicer at home.'

What she meant was it was much nicer in bed. More of that later. We did go to a theatre, but we had to go in cheap seats because I didn't have the right clothes. I didn't have *enough* clothes, either. Two shirts were no good in London where the air was so filthy you needed a clean one every day. Daphne bought me one, and I washed the other two, but neither of us was much of a hand at ironing them. The food shopping was in very grand shops where I always seemed to be bumping into ladies in fur coats or men with tightly furled umbrellas and bowler hats. I felt they all despised me.

But perhaps it was the general feeling of inequality that weighed most upon me. I was poor and Daphne, although she was tiresomely short of ready cash, was rich. I was ill at ease and uncomfortable in London, and she regarded it with familiarity as a place of pleasure. But the worst inequality – I see it now, of course, far more clearly than I did then – was this business of love. Daphne was in love with me. I was the first man in her life, and whatever else she lacked, she was certainly whole-hearted. She not only loved me, she doubted whether anyone had ever loved anyone else more and frequently told me so. Some innate shyness stopped her from enquiring too closely how far her love was reciprocated. I think she felt that enthusiasm in bed was how men expressed their love and there it was easy, and pleasant, not to let her down. It was not difficult to give her pleasure and during that week I learned a great deal, not only about her body but about female responses in general.

For instance, how much reassurance they seem to need about their physical charm, their preoccupation with their breasts – I have not once encountered a woman who tired of attention being paid to *them* – and the need through patience to engender the opposite in a woman: by the end of the week I knew exactly how to make Daphne beg for it. But none of this made me *love* her: in fact, I was conscious of fleeting moments of contempt, dislike and boredom. Looking back on this I can see how much more these feelings disturbed me than I realized at the time. *Then* I simply thought myself incapable of love; *now* I know the very opposite to be the truth.

I think the first week in London was also the first time that I began seriously to consider my future. It came up when we were sitting in the kitchen, drinking Daphne's favourite hot chocolate.

'Darling! I have a confession to make. Only I hope you won't be cross with me!'

She stretched out her small plump hand and touched my wrist. 'You remember we said that we would always tell each other the truth?'

I remembered her saying that *she* would, and nodded.

'Well, I haven't been completely honest about money. To begin with I thought it didn't matter – because who cares about money anyway? – but now I realize that if one is to be truthful it has to be about everything. That's right, isn't it?'

I agreed. I was beginning to feel excited. Perhaps she *was* actually rich and had been testing me.

'Right. Well, the thing is, I haven't just got my dress allowance. Mummy gives me two pounds a week to buy food with as well. Plus I'm allowed to use her account at Fortnum's up to five pounds a month. So really it's much more than my forty-two pounds a year. There. Oh, I'm so glad I told you.' She looked at me anxiously. 'You aren't going to be cross, are you? I'll never do anything like that again.'

For a moment I was completely at a loss, hopes dashed. She wasn't properly rich, simply richer than I was, which made me think bitterly about that. I had been working on her family's estate for four years now. I was no longer a mere gardener's boy but a capable gardener, though hardly meeting my father's knowledge and experience, and my wages were thirty pounds a year, twelve pounds less than the money Daphne was *given* to buy clothes with. And if I stayed where I was, no doubt in the fullness of time (another twenty years or so) I would be earning as much as my father – over sixty pounds a year – because I would have the inherited advantage of a tied cottage, that dark and cramped Lodge we were supposed to be grateful for.

'Oh, Hal! You *look* angry. Please don't be. Let's go to bed.'

'I'm not angry.' It was the easiest thing to say. 'I'm not in the least angry with you,' I said again. 'Hurry up, there's a good girl.' She took far longer than I to get to bed as she spent minutes in the bathroom putting some stuff up herself to stop her getting pregnant. We'd experimented with French letters, but neither of us liked them.

I *was* angry, though. Not with her, but with the general unfairness of life. Why should she be able to do exactly as she pleased, travel, be waited on hand, foot and finger, never expected to do a stitch of work, while I had the prospect of years of toil before me in return for a bare living? But why was I being so fatalistic about my future? Why should it, *need* it, run along the narrow tramlines dictated by my father? It was all very well if I'd been only the average country working-class boy, but I wasn't. Due to my years of reading I knew far more than anyone I had yet met. I was also intelligent enough to know what I did not know, or at least to have some idea of it. These feelings, plus the intuition that occurred easily when I was alone with a woman, added up that night to my being unusually rough with Daphne. She loved it. There is always a touch of masochism in women, if you know how to find it.

It became more and more of a strain being with one person from morning to night. She expected me to talk to her all the time; she never wanted to read or go off on her own to do anything. I think I would have found this difficult with anyone – but at the time I thought it was due to some lack or failing in Daphne. She was not much more than a schoolgirl, and freshness and innocence had to be equated with ignorance and a generally unformed mind. How priggish that sounds as I write it now! At the time I used my intellectual superiority to bolster my lack of confidence in every other direction.

I did try once, casually, to discuss my future with her, but she did not understand me at all; she saw it entirely in terms of herself. 'We'll think of something nice for you,' she would say, snuggling up to me – insinuating herself into my arms. 'In any case, when I'm twenty-one I'll have loads of money and you needn't do anything. Or you could be some sort of director in a bank or in the City like Daddy used to do.' Even I could see that this was a mere child's-eye view of life.

'What about the next four years?' I asked, with little hope of a sensible reply.

'Well, we won't be able to see each other much while I'm doing my Season, because Mummy will be in London with me and there'll be dances and things all the time. But don't worry, I shall never look at anyone but you.'

'And after this Season?'

She shrugged. 'I don't know. We'll think of something. My parents spend nearly all their time abroad, so I can do pretty much as I like.'

The week came to an end and she saw me off at the railway station.

'Come up next weekend.'

'I can't. I don't *get* weekends off. Just one day.'

'Come up for that, then. Oh, do.'

'I'll try.'

'How will you be able to tell me if you can or can't?'

'I'll ring you.'

'When? I must be in for it. When?'

We settled for eight o'clock on Wednesday evening.

Just as the train was leaving, she gave me a pound.

'For your ticket.'

I was on the train then and she was standing on the platform by the window.

'Kiss me.'

She stood on her toes and held up her face. Her mouth was bruised from last night's love-making. As I kissed her I felt the salt of her tears. 'There.'

'Again,' she said, like a child, but the train had started to move. 'Hasn't it been an amazing week?'

'Amazing,' I said. I saw her wipe her face with the back of her hand and she tried to smile. She was walking with the train.

'Goodbye, my most darling Hal.'

'Goodbye, sweetheart.'

She started to run, then gave up. She waved and I knew she had started to cry again. I waved back and sank into my seat. Relief seeped out of me like sweat.

Throughout that winter I tried to make decisions. I went to London to see Daphne. I did a deal with my father, which resulted in my getting a whole weekend once a month; the other visit had to be for the day. My father had mellowed – or weakened: it was the winter when his arthritis began to incapacitate him and he depended more upon my physical strength. I think he must have been in a good deal of pain most of the time, but he never complained – to me, at any rate, though his temper was shortish with Mrs Greenwich. He was only forty-two and he was terrified of losing his job 'On account of the Lodge goes with it, boy.' So was my stepmother, who made efforts to confide in me and also to ask for my help. 'If you were to tell him he should see a doctor, he'd go,' she said. 'He thinks the world of you.'

This seemed to me to be merely a blandishing lie, and I refused to respond to it. She treated me now with all the conciliatory attention that I knew arose from her being a little afraid of me and at the same time finding me attractive (I was, she kept saying, the spitting image of my father). I might look like him, I thought, but I damn well wasn't going to lead a life where I remained hard up and dependent upon the whims of the Carterets. I tried to have a conversation with Daphne about my father's situation. 'But he's the head gardener!' she said. 'They'd never turn him away. Especially now they're selling plants and things. And when he gets too old to work, he'll be able to retire like people do.'

'On what? The Lodge isn't his. It's a tied cottage.'

'What's that?'

'It means that you can only live in it while you work.'

'Oh, darling, I think it's sweet of you to mind about him so much, but of course he'll be all right. He'll have saved money, won't he, all these years?'

I was conscious both of not really minding about my father, and of disliking her for her lack of concern.

She must have noticed the latter, because she put her arms round my neck. 'I know Mummy thinks very highly of him. She'd never turn him out or anything beastly like that. And if she *did*, we could look after him somehow, couldn't we?'

I agreed with this as the quickest way of not talking about it any more.

The next time I saw her was after King Edward had renounced the throne for Mrs Simpson. She was most indignant about that. 'Poor King.'

'He sounds mad to me.'

'I think it's fearfully brave of him. To give everything up for love!' There were actually tears in her eyes.

'It seems extraordinary to me. I bet he'll regret it.'

'Hal! I'd give everything up for you. Absolutely anything!' There was a pause, and then she said, 'But you wouldn't for me, would you? We're not the same about that.'

'I haven't got anything to *give* up.'

'But would you, if you had?' It was the most overt approach she had made to the question of my love for her.

'I don't know, Daph. I haven't thought about it. I've never *had* anything, you see. I'm a member of the working classes – unlike you.' I saw her face, and made another effort. 'It's not the same for a man anyway.'

By now I knew exactly how to change the subject and minutes later she was saying, 'I know you do, really. It's just that men find it harder to talk about it. That's it, isn't it?'

Her parents came home for Christmas, and went with her to Scotland to stay with the cousins. She wrote to me from there and sent the letter to the Lodge, which occasioned repeated attacks of curiosity from my stepmother. I did not read the letter until we had consumed our usual

Christmas dinner of roast chicken, mashed potato and Brussels sprouts, followed by the small, leaden mince pies she always made and third choice from a box of Black Magic with a good strong cup of tea. My father was presented every Christmas with a bottle of sherry and a bottle of Johnnie Walker whisky, the latter not offered to us, although we all had a glass of sherry and there was brown ale with the meal.

Conversation at lunch had been conducted mainly by my stepmother, whose ruminations about the Duke of Windsor bored us both. After lunch, they listened to the King's broadcast on the wireless and I was able to escape to my wretched little room above. Since staying in the flat with Daphne I had become fully aware of how miserably cramped we were, jammed up in bad weather with nowhere to be except the kitchen or in bed. I lay on my bed to read Daphne's letter. There were four pages of dark blue paper with a picture of a castle at the top. She had written on both sides of each page with extra bits down the margins. It was a mixture of Christmas in the castle and declarations of her love.

. . . yesterday there was a wonderful party for everyone of the estate. They all came with their wives and children, and we took it in turns to hand out the presents for the children. They were so sweet – all dressed in their Sunday best. There was a Christmas tree that nearly reached the ceiling of the hall all lit with candles – you can't imagine how pretty. When they had all gone, we had a cold supper and then we – the younger ones – played a marvellous game called Murder. [There followed a detailed account of how you played the game and what happened to her.] I got murdered on a corkscrew staircase with stone steps and I had to lie there for ages, which was rather cold. Oh, darling, I miss you so *madly*. Sometimes I can't sleep for thinking of you and wanting to be with you. I imagine you touching me, kissing me – and everything – and it makes me feel faint . . .

The letter ended with her longing for me to write to her. 'We'll be staying here over the New Year which is the main event in Scotland.' Then, written down the last margin: 'So funny. People eat their porridge standing up and walking about. It's supposed to happen because people used to be afraid of being stabbed in the back! I love you – love, love, love.' And then dozens of Xs.

I read this letter twice, and realized that I was quite unmoved. Love seemed to me an overrated business. But perhaps Daphne didn't love me really – she was simply in love with the idea of having someone to go to bed with. This notion relieved me: it meant that I could continue the affair if there seemed any point in it for me, feeling that after all she was getting what *she* wanted. But it didn't clarify the future at all. I had two problems. How to get away from home, and what to do with myself when I did.

Dear Mr Kent,

I have now been in touch with Miss Langrish about her cottage and in view of the fact that her time abroad has unfortunately been extended, she would like you to go into the cottage once a week, to light a fire and generally see that it is not getting too damp. I enclose a key for this purpose. If you find anything amiss there, please get in touch with me at once and I will deal with it.

Yours sincerely,

Anna Blackstone

The key was encased in bubble-wrap. I read the letter three times on my way back from the village. It was good news in one way, but maddeningly uninformative. Why had her stay been unfortunately extended, and for how long? And where exactly *was* she? If I wrote to her c/o Miss Blackstone how could I know whether the letter was read before it was forwarded? The answer to that was that I couldn't be sure. If I wrote to her, it would have to be in terms that were innocuous to Miss Blackstone, and I felt the time was coming when that would not be the sort of letter I wanted to write.

I thought about all this while I ate a sandwich in front of the fire in the cottage and an idea began to form. For the past weeks I had been reading plays, which was a new experience. They seemed as though they could be read much faster than a novel, but I quickly found that if they were any good this was not true. Plays had to be read more slowly, and with careful attention – preferably at least an act at a time. Reading them made me realize how very little I had had to do with the theatre. Opportunities had been few and inclination timid. Faced with the choice, I had chosen the cinema where, it was true, some plays had been turned into films, but this had very seldom meant that what one saw on the screen had much to do with what one read on the page. I longed to talk to *her* about all of this. Possibly, I thought, it was one way of reaching her: a letter expressing my enthusiasm and ignorance, asking her advice and opinion on what I should read. I must avoid admitting to having already read so much since it would imply illegitimate time spent in her cottage.

It took me several days to write the letter – partly, I suppose, because I was so anxious about sending it. Even if Miss Blackstone did not in some way veto it, it might still be regarded as an impertinence by its recipient who would then have no more to do with me. Make or break, I said to myself, as I wrote draft after draft. Also, the roses arrived, as they so often do, when the frost was at its worst; indeed, I had to contrive a small area where they could be heeled in for several days until we had something of a thaw. I planted them carefully, and covered round them with straw a foot thick, which, of course, the wretched birds disturbed in their hunt for rare food. Cold weather made living in the boat both cheerless and tiring, so I took to spending more time in the cottage, but this in turn meant that the small store of logs was running out and I was forced to spend four or five days with a logman, sawing for him in return for a load.

I spent Christmas day in the cottage; cooked myself a meal – a piece of steak and Brussels sprouts, a small packet of oven-ready chips and a Christmas pudding of the size made for one. I had treated myself to a hot bath and a clean outfit. Ahead of me was a small packet of Dutch cigars with my Nescafé.

Outside it was pouring with rain. I thought I might even spend the night in the cottage. What was *she* doing on this day? I tried to imagine her, in Californian – or perhaps Mexican – sunshine, by somebody's swimming-pool, wearing a white one-piece bathing-suit over her

golden skin, her beautiful hair damp and drying, spring-
ing slowly to life in the hot air. But what company would
she be keeping? I'm too old for hypothetical jealousy: I
furnished her with a kindly woman friend, somebody she
had known for years, like Miss Blackstone. She was wary
of men, I knew that; would not be likely to respond easily
to any bronzed Tarzan. By now I had got through the
steak, and was on my way to the kitchen to collect my
pudding when the telephone rang. It gave me the kind
of shock that makes one nearly drop things and stagger
like someone in a farce. It had never rung before except
that first day in the cottage and I had become unused to
telephones anyway. My first instinct was to let it ring,
which it did. Then I thought it was certainly a wrong
number, and as it continued insistently, I went and
answered it. 'Hello?'

'Daisy?'

'She's not here, I'm afraid.'

'Who is that?'

'I'm just the caretaker.'

'Well, where *is* she? She was due back from the States
a fortnight ago. She's not in her flat. So where *is* she?'

The voice was treble, sounding almost shrill as she
repeated the question.

'Who is that speaking?'

'Her daughter. I had to get *this* number from Directory
Enquiries. Anyway, that's not your business. She never
told *me* about a caretaker. How do I know you're not a
burglar, or a squatter or something?'

I laughed convincingly. 'My name's Henry Kent, and
I'm definitely neither of those things, but thank you for
asking.'

'She *was* in hospital in Mexico. She fell down some

awful Mexican pyramid and broke her left shoulder and her left foot. But she told me she was due back anyway. I'll try the hospital again. They said she'd checked out.'

'Doesn't Miss Blackstone know where she is?'

'Probably, but she doesn't answer her phone – away for Christmas like most people. It's my fault, I didn't call her back when she asked me to. Oh, Lord! It's all my fault!' She sounded almost childishly dramatic, but her distress was evident and she seemed distinctly more friendly.

'I've been wanting to know where she is,' I said. 'There are one or two things here that need her attention. Do you think when you find out, you could call again and give me her address? I could arrange to be here whenever it suited you to call.'

'I could probably help you there. What sort of things? Is the place leaking or falling down or something? She bought it so suddenly she probably didn't have it surveyed.'

'No, the place is quite sound as far as I know. It just gets damp if left to itself. That's why I'm here. Lucky you caught me really. I do hope your mother is all right. I shouldn't think Mexico is a very good country to be ill in.'

'What an extraordinary thing to say! How do you think Mexicans manage?' Then, before I could answer that, she said, 'Why am I talking to you so much anyway?'

'I can't think,' I said. I knew perfectly well why, but she would not like me knowing. Any charm that I possessed needed to be a mutual discovery.

'You've got a rather nice voice, reassuring.'

'What a kind and surprising thing to say, Mrs . . . ?'

'Moreland. Katya Moreland.'

141

ELIZABETH JANE HOWARD

'Well, Mrs Moreland, if you *do* hear from your mother, perhaps you would let me know. I'm usually here between eleven and twelve in the mornings. Just an address that I could write to. I mustn't keep you any longer. I hope you have a wonderful Christmas.'

Ringing off precluded her asking me any more, *why* I wanted to get in touch with her mother. But something told me that Katya Moreland was a much softer touch than Miss Blackstone, and provided she – Katya – didn't consult Miss Blackstone about what I should or should not know of Daisy's whereabouts, I was pretty sure she would tell me.

She did. The following Saturday she rang at half past eleven and gave me the address in Los Angeles. I posted the letter that evening.

4

DAISY

'Are you quite comfortable, Daisy?'

She nodded weakly and smiled. When they went away she shifted so that the weight was completely off her left shoulder, which intensified the cramp in the right one. While she waited for them to tell her that the ambulance was ready to take her to the airport she reflected how much people harped on anything in short supply. Elizabethan poems about the lover's perfumed breath, freedom in places where there wasn't any, truth allowed by politicians and governors to emerge in much the proportions that icebergs were visible, and comfort in hospitals – some relative degree of it was constantly alluded to.

'Quite comfortable' had come to mean for her only that she was not wanting to scream from pain. People had lived for centuries with rotting teeth, lack of any choice about their lives, in various travesties of democracy and only with what truth they could make out of the whole thing for themselves. And pain, like terminal illness and death, was shoved into the background where everyone hoped it belonged and would stay. She started to consider what acceptable degrees of all these things *were* confronted, but then the amazing adaptability or resilience that she had observed patients displaying in both of the hospitals she had been in intervened: it was impossible to gauge other people's pain against one's own. Talk of low thresholds, of courage, of good behaviour or not complaining, of never wanting anything, varied hopelessly from patient to patient, so the word 'relative' wrote the whole thing off as insoluble.

The worst bit had been the fall and lying in scorching sun while various tourists milled helplessly about her. There was not a doctor on the pyramid and several well-meaning people tried to help her to her feet until she fainted. She came to strapped to a stretcher in an ambulance that jolted and blared its way along the road, at a speed that took no account of the potholes. Someone gave her an injection and the pain retreated.

The next thing she remembered was lying on a bed or trolley – something that had been moving anyway – in some passage or anteroom, with a nurse asking her questions in Spanish that she did not seem able to answer satisfactorily. She managed her name and her date of birth, English, on holiday. No, she was not with anyone, she was alone. Where was she staying? She tried to remember the name of the hotel, but could not. '*Amigos, familias,*' the woman repeated, putting her face nearer and speaking loudly as though this would make her understand better and produce them, but the thick lenses on her spectacles made her eyes menacing, and the gold rims glinted intolerably from the fluorescent lights.

Her head was throbbing, her mouth parched. She asked for water, but the woman shook her head, '*Agua niente,*' and went away. Time passed and the pain seeped back – her foot, her leg. It crept up her body, her left side. She tried to collect some saliva in her mouth to swallow and coughed – and felt as though she had been stabbed in the ribs. Her body was covered by a sheet, she could not see it. Tears of shock began, but when she attempted to wipe them away her hand had blood on it. She tried to use her other hand to wipe her face, but that was agonisingly impossible. She began to feel extremely afraid, and to steady herself tried to remember exactly what had happened when she fell.

The steps of the enormous pyramid were extraordinarily steep, she remembered. She had almost crawled up them, using her hands to pull herself up each one. It was very hot, and while she was resting she looked up to see how far there was to go – miles, it looked like; she could not have climbed more than a third of the way. Then she looked down and experienced a moment of terror. The ground looked horribly far away. Tourists arriving looked like dolls milling about toy buses. She could not climb down: even if she sat on a step her feet barely touched the step below: she would have to jump, and there was nothing to hold on to. She felt the onset of vertigo paralysing her. She shut her eyes and willed herself to move and not to look beyond the step below. This worked quite well but when she was four or five steps from the bottom a small gust of wind blew her hat off, and in trying to catch it, she lost her balance and fell. She kept trying to clutch at the stone, to stop herself, but this seemed only to make her fall faster, until the ground below the first step met her with a different kind of force.

When she came round it was to the ordeal of the sun and people with good intentions making things worse. Oh, well, I expect if it had been someone else who fell, I would have been one of them, she thought. The desire to prove that someone is alive, to prod and try to move them, to wipe blood from obvious places, to deliver sustenance (a teenager offered her some bubble-gum), was exhaustingly strong. After she passed out, she did not know what else they had tried to do.

The nurse returned with a doctor, a man in a white coat with a bushy grey moustache who looked extraordinarily like the novelist Marquez.

'What happened to you?'

'I fell down the steps of the pyramid.' Her spirits rose because he spoke English.

'You have no one here with you?'

'No, I am alone.'

He pulled back the sheet and muttered some Spanish imprecation. 'Why was the shoe not cut from her foot?'

There seemed to be no answer to this. She looked down. Her left foot was the colour of black grapes and so swollen that her sandal strap was almost invisible.

That was the beginning of it. She was wheeled away to a small room bright with lights and put on a table.

The doctor bent over her. 'Do not be disturbed. I give you something for the pain while I am cutting.'

After the needle in her arm she waited, trying – as she always had with anaesthetics – to remember the exact moment when she lost consciousness, but she remembered nothing. When she came round, she was in a room with two beds in it, but alone. The empty bed made her feel her isolation, not simply from other patients in the hospital, but from everybody in her life.

She was to spend ten solitary days there. After the evening of the first day the doctor came to tell her that she had broken her left arm so high into her shoulder that it could not be set – must be left to recover on its own. She had also cracked a rib and nothing could be done about that, either. Her left foot was broken in several places; some surgery had been effected, and that, too, would have to heal itself. 'But your face, Señora, that was merely cut and, of course, bruised. There will be no lasting damage there. For all ladies of a certain age the face is important, yes?' By then she had remembered the name of her hotel where she had arrived the previous evening, and asked him to arrange for her luggage and passport to be sent to the hospital. It was then that she realized that her bag – containing some Mexican money and her travellers' cheques – had disappeared, had been left or stolen where she fell.

When her things arrived she at last had books to read. Movement, of any kind, was painful and, oddly, the cracked rib hurt most of all. After three days, she managed to get them to put her in a wheelchair to reach the ward's telephone, and she called the producer with whom she had been working. She got his secretary on a very bad line. Josh was away for a week.

Eventually, but not until after Josh's return from his vacation, she got herself returned to Cedars Sinai Hospital in Los Angeles where they said that a mess had been made of her foot: they would have to operate to remove an ill-placed pin, and she would be unable to walk for some time.

The second hospital, although the nurses spoke English, did not decrease her sense of isolation. She had no friends in Los Angeles, and her producer, although he visited her once or twice, was deeply engaged upon another film. Other people she had been working with – the director of her piece and one or two others she had lunched with in the studio canteen – sent flowers, called her and sent jokey cards wishing her a speedy recovery, all stuff that acquaintances might do, but there was no steady visitor, nobody whom she could look forward to seeing. Her time was spent with physiotherapists, nurses who washed her and brought meals, and the various doctors who monitored her progress.

She tried to work on her script but found it strangely difficult. She could not concentrate, slept badly, and alternated between feeling cut off from people and wishing that she did not want to be. For a time she thought that she was suffering from homesickness, but imagining herself back in London made her feel worse. Her days were passed in painful idleness: she was both bored and sorry for herself, and disliking both these conditions did nothing to dispel them.

She was sixty-one, had failed with both of her marriages, had one daughter whom she felt despised her, had remarkably few friends. Friendship when she had been married to Stach had been out of the question, she never had the time, or energy, for anything but trying to keep their heads above water. And although she had had many friends when she was married to Jason, it had been Jason, she felt, and felt it more now, whom those people had wanted to see. She had been the also-ran of the couple, and it had not occurred to her that that mattered because she had been so happy with him: it had seemed to her then simply the consequence of being half of a marriage. How often she had heard him say, 'I'd adore to see Jonathan but Audrey *is* rather a pill, isn't she?' She wondered now how many and how often people had said that of her and Jason.

'You're a loner,' he'd said to her once, when she had demurred about a holiday with other people. She remembered denying this, and his stroking her arm and saying, 'Of course you are. Brought up alone with your aunt, no parents, you poor darling, and then that prison-like life with ghastly old Stach, and choosing writing for your career – what could be more lonely than that?' Indeed, what? she thought now. She had not particularly wanted to go by herself to Mexico, really it had seemed a sort of challenge. Other people went on holidays by themselves and clearly enjoyed it: why shouldn't she? But that first evening in Mexico City, sitting in a corner of the dark little bar attached to her hotel and drinking margaritas, she had instantly wondered why she had come. After dinner with a book, she had picked up some leaflets about sightseeing at the desk and taken them upstairs. She must concentrate on doing things.

There was a splendid museum, and those amazing pyramids to see that could be reached by bus. She would see and do everything within reach of the city. That evening, as she was undressing, something odd happened. The floor seemed – not exactly to slide or tilt, but to shift temporarily in an uncertain manner, giving her the sudden feeling that it could not be trusted. She stood motionless in the bedroom, and just as she was beginning to think she had either imagined it, or it was the result merely of the high altitude and the tequila she had drunk, it happened again. This time it didn't seem to be just the floor, but more as though the whole building was minutely resettling itself. This was so frightening in a way beyond any of her experience that she rang down to the desk. It was a relief when a soft voice the other end answered.

'Señora?'

'Er, my room seemed to have – a sort of – well, it seemed to *move* – I don't know what—'

'Nothing, Señora. A little tremor – very small.'

'You mean an *earthquake*?'

'It is nothing. You can have no fear. It is a natural thing from time to time.'

Natural! She thanked the man, then said, 'Should I perhaps come down?' She had heard that this was what people did in earthquakes.

'If you wish.'

'It's not necessary?'

'Ah, no, Señora. It is nothing.'

So she had gone to bed.

Well, she had not had the chance to find out whether she could meet the challenge of a holiday by herself. It had lasted less than twenty-four hours; after that she became an accident, a patient, an invalid.

After she had spent a week in the Cedars Sinai, Katya called her. 'I didn't know where you were!' Her voice sounded accusing.

'I'm so sorry, darling. I did write a postcard when I got here, and asked the studio to call you.'

'They did and I was out and they left a message saying you'd fallen off a pyramid but they didn't tell me where you were. I thought you were still in Mexico and then I thought you might be back in England, but there was no reply from your flat so I tried your cottage and a man answered and said he thought you were in America. *He* hadn't got your address either.'

'What man?'

'Your gardener. He was seeing to the damp or something. Anyway, Ma, how are you?'

'Getting on. But my foot seems to take ages to heal. I can hobble about on crutches now, which is nice. How's Edwin?'

'I hardly ever see him. He comes home after the

children are in bed, eats some food and falls asleep over the telly news.'

Her voice warned Daisy that further questions about Edwin were undesirable.

'And the children?'

'Thomas has gone to prep school – awfully homesick, but Edwin insists he should stay, and Caroline wants to learn the *saxophone*.'

'Goodness!'

'She's only six – it seems a ridiculous instrument to me. And it's awfully hard to find a teacher, stuck out in the wilds as we are.' There was a pause, and then she said, 'I do wish you'd *told* me where you were. I've been worrying about you.'

This crumb of comfort (mattering to somebody) contracted to something more like a bit of grit in an oyster (it was entirely her selfish fault that Katya had been worried).

'When are you coming back?'

'As soon as they'll let me. I'll write to you, darling.'

'OK.'

'Will you write back? With your news and things?'

'Oh, Ma, you know I never have any news. It's utterly boring here.'

'I'd just love a letter from you.'

'All right. But you know I was never much of a one for letters.'

'Any old letter will do.' She paused, then added as lightly as she could, 'I'm feeling a bit cut off. Lonely.'

'That makes two of us.' But she sounded placated. 'OK. I'll write.'

After the call, she reflected that Katya had never forgiven her for leaving Stach, for having that fundamental piece of news sprung upon her. She had tried to be gentle and straight about it, but she had clearly not found the right way. Perhaps there was no right way of doing that, any more than there was a right way of being left. She thought of that last time with Jason, when he had come back for his briefcase and she was in the middle of her grief about him. He had been so gentle to her, so comforting and then, when they were in bed, she had wildly thought that Marietta was a bad dream – over and done with. It had been nothing of the kind. Making love to her was his way of saying he was sorry; pity had dominated the scene, pity so unobtrusively administered that she had not recognized it until he had put on his clothes and left. But she had been happy for that last time (barely an hour although it had seemed much longer). How easily she had been taken in!

Two days later, she got a letter forwarded from the studio. The envelope did not have Katya's writing on it – nor Anna's, nor indeed any hand that she recognized.

Dear (I don't know whether to address you as Mrs Redfearn or Miss Langrish),

I thought you might like to know that your garden is planted now – with roses, anyway, and a few bits and pieces that I have acquired from the folks round here. It does not amount to much at present, but it looks as though its hair has been combed – kempt, if that is the right word. Since Miss Blackstone kindly sent a key to the cottage I have been able to light a fire every few days and generally see that frost and damp do no damage. It is as well that I did so, because there was evidence that someone had tried to break in through a back window, although I could find no damage. Caretaking for you has been a great pleasure for me, as my life (for reasons I will not trouble you with) has been rather bleak of late. You know that feeling (or perhaps you don't) when one moves to a new area and has to start one's life all over again. The superficial things settle themselves quite quickly, but the ones that really matter do not. I am very much on my own and not, I think, designed to be so. Enough of that.

I hope you will not mind, but I have been reading some of your books. I have, of course, taken the greatest care of them, but it was such a temptation to someone who lives on a public library and does not always know what to read without a good browse. The sight of your shelves filled with volumes most of which were entirely new to me was too much. I had not, for instance, read any plays at all except for some Shakespeare, and this has been a revelation to me. I realize now that you are a playwright which I did not know when we met (forgive me for not acknowledging your fame), and at first I found plays quite difficult to read. There is so much inference in them that novels are often without, but once I had recognized this, and read them at a different pace, a great deal became clear. Plays seem to make one *see* people as well as hear them, to place them, as it were. How often in novels has one wondered where the hell the characters *are* while they are talking to each other and the moment you start wondering that, the reality or momentum is diminished. Also I see how much more poignantly plays can make a social point than novels seem to manage. This is especially true in reference to women, their status in the world, their rights or the lack of them and how they are treated by society and men in particular. Of course social values have changed since Ibsen's day, but the true position of women, in my view, has not. Lip service is paid. The vote and the divorce becoming acceptable are only the tip of the iceberg.

Oh dear! I fear I may be boring you with this dissertation. The thing is that if we were face to face, I should know what *you* thought about these matters and much else, but we are not.

I have to say this because I have lived long enough to know that withholding is simply another form of dishonesty. When I saw you coming in at the gate of your garden I felt an extraordinary sense of kinship – not precisely that I had always known you (I would not presume to anything so brash), but that I *ought* always to have known you. That first impression has never left me. Forgive this, or ignore it as you will. I have no one to talk to. My present life – quite uncharacteristic of the rest of it – precludes company of any interest at all.

I have a request to make, which I hope you will treat kindly. I should so very much like to read some of *your* plays if that is possible. Do you, by any chance, recollect whether you have any copies of them in the boxes not yet unpacked? (By the way, if you feel that these boxes *should* be unpacked, of course I should be delighted to do it for you. I am fighting the battle of the winter damp here, and possibly whatever is in the boxes would be better for an airing.) What a wordy parenthesis! I fear I am rather given to them. Naturally, you may want to do this for yourself, and the last thing I want is to invade your privacy in *any way*.

This letter has gone on long enough – too long probably. Sorry about that. I have always been a great one for letters and at the moment I have no one to write to.

That is not quite true. The only person I felt I wanted to write to is yourself.

I hope that your work is going well in Hollywood. I imagine you in violent sunshine having parties with all sorts of famous and glamorous people who are your far more intimate friend than,

Yours sincerely,

Henry Kent

5

HENRY

Her first letter to me arrived sooner than I had expected. It was written on the hospital paper and was addressed to the cottage. I did not open it at once, but put it on the kitchen table and sat before it, devouring her writing of my name on the envelope. As I stared at her spidery handwriting, her appearance and her voice returned to me – her pale complexion, her wonderful hair that sprang from her forehead, her rare smile that transformed her mouth and dissolved the wariness in her eyes that sometimes in the last months I had remembered to be grey and sometimes bluer than grey, and then her unexpectedly high, clear voice that sounded so much younger than it was.

I opened the letter, still hearing her voice as I read it. It was short.

Dear Mr Kent,

It was kind of you to write to tell me about the garden. I suppose that as the spring approaches it would be sensible to get some seeds to plant to fill up the beds you have made. I cannot send you the money for them, but if you write to Miss Blackstone she will arrange for the money to buy them. It sounds feeble of me not to send you money from here, but I am still virtually immobile and have not anyone to run errands for me at the moment.

I had a silly accident in Mexico and broke my leg rather badly – or rather my foot which has meant having quite a lot of surgery which I am, with maddening slowness, recovering from.

No, I do not mind you borrowing my books. I am sure you are careful with them from the way you write about what you have read. And I am anyway grateful to you for your care of my new place, about which I often think with longing. Hospital life, even if one can hobble about a bit, contracts one's world in a curiously inexorable manner. I feel I am in danger of becoming institutionalized – cut off from work and, indeed, almost everything else.

So I do understand what you mean when you say that moving to a new area means that only the superficial things become settled. I feel very much on my own here – none of the glamorous parties you imagine for me.

Yes, I think it would be as well to unpack the remaining tea chests. I had thought that I should have done them before now, and as there is no immediate prospect of my being able to do so I should be grateful for your help. There may be some typescripts of plays in there, but I cannot remember now what I packed for the country and what remained in London. If you find any, by all means read them.

You do not mention Chekhov, but I imagine that is because you have not got to him. A treat in store: the best playwright, I think, since Shakespeare. Has to be read several times to get the full impact, as apart from anything else he is a master craftsman and many of his points are very fine.

Thank you for writing. Yours sincerely,

Daisy Langrish

(I prefer to use my professional name as I am divorced.)

That was it. I read the letter again, more slowly, trying to glean her state of mind. Most of it was reserved and practical; she did not reveal herself, except with the phrase 'I feel very much on my own here'. I did not think that she would have written that unless it was severely true. And she was grateful to me for looking after her place of which she 'often thought with longing'. That, too, was promising. And she was to allow me to unpack her tea chests into which I had so far only tentatively burrowed.

The 'silly accident' sounded far more serious than she wished me to think. If her recovery was to be slow, and she was not able to walk or drive, I might eventually have the chance of doing much for her when she did return. By then, through letters, I might have inspired enough confidence in me for her to convalesce in the cottage. This was an intoxicating thought, but it was far ahead, and meanwhile I must somehow encourage her to feel that I was trustworthy. She had not replied to my remarks about how I had felt when I met her, but I sensed that, apart from a natural reserve, she was shy and that great care must be taken or I would frighten her off. That evening I despatched a short note simply to ask her what kind of flowers she would like me to grow from seed – what colours, particularly. I thanked her for her letter, and expressed my concern about her leg. I was hers sincerely.

The following morning as I walked from the boat to the cottage where I now spent most of my time I noticed a small clump of snowdrops growing near the hedge. I picked the most perfect I could find and pressed it between blotting paper weighted by a doorstop she had in the shape of a lion. Then I embarked upon the interesting task of unpacking the tea chests. There were only three of them, and they had been piled in one corner of the sitting room. The first was full of filing cases and folders, the second contained a miscellany of stationery, a portable typewriter and, wrapped in newspaper, some framed photographs, and the third consisted of typescripts of films and television plays. After a quick look at all this, I set about the first case.

I looked at the pictures first. There were only half a dozen of them. The largest was a picture of an elderly woman with shingled hair sitting in a basket chair in a garden. Her mother, I supposed, although she did not seem to resemble Daisy. On the back was written: 'Jess. Brighton, 1938'. Who was Jess? Then there was a much smaller one of a man in plus-fours with his arm round a young woman wearing a cloche hat and a low-waisted dress that utterly concealed her figure. The picture had faded to a brownish yellow. On the back Daisy had put 'Your grandparents: 1928'. The next was a portrait of a very young man in RAF uniform sitting at a table with his forearms resting upon it. The back said: 'Your father: 1942'. When I unwrapped the fourth picture, which was of a very pretty little girl sitting on a pebbly beach and the caption on the back read, 'You, aged four at Brighton', I began to get the point. The pictures were meant for her daughter, Katya Moreland. The remaining two pictures were of Katya grown-up in jeans and a fringed jacket captioned, 'You at my wedding'.

Another one of the same girl arm in arm with a man in a roll-necked jersey with a pipe said, 'You and Edwin 1980'. There was no picture of Daisy at all. This was disappointing. I went back to the grown-up ones of her daughter, to try to detect a likeness, but I could not see it. The one taken at Daisy's wedding (presumably to Jason Redfearn) showed her looking very sulky. She had long dark hair flowing round her shoulders. It looked straight and heavy – utterly unlike her mother's; she had a large mouth, which was compressed, and her expression was almost dramatically hostile. The one with the young man, however, was entirely different. In that, she looked alive: she glowed, and her mouth when she smiled was beguiling; she looked joyful and carefree and extremely attractive. But I was not interested in Katya. I wrapped up the pictures again and placed them on a shelf.

For days I searched through the contents of the chests. The files proved to be almost entirely professional papers, filed under the television companies that she had worked for, but they also contained one or two quite interesting press cuttings that referred to her second marriage. There was one with a picture of both of them standing at the top of a flight of steps, and there was Katya again in the background in her jeans and fringed jacket looking bored. 'Register Office Wedding for Playwright Daisy Langrish and Actor Jason Redfearn'. It was not a good picture, but clear enough to see that she looked serious and he was extraordinarily good-looking. I put this cutting to one side, to study it later when I had fetched my magnifying glass from the boat, and ranged the files upright along the bottom bookshelf.

I left the stationery and typewriter and tackled the chest full of typescripts. There were a lot of them; in the case of television plays sometimes several versions of the same piece. There were also some plays, bound typescripts with their titles and Daisy's name typed on a label in front. I put them aside to read. Would they tell me more about her? They must, I thought, if I had the wit to divine it. It didn't seem possible that people could write fiction without betraying themselves – for better or worse. From the novel reading that I had done this had several times become clear – in spite of my having no particular interest in the authors. With Daisy, it would be different: I would be aware of what she cared about, feared, wanted. I would in some sense *know* her, and this would make letters to her easier to write since I was aiming at intimacy with someone who must regard me – at the moment, certainly – as virtually a stranger.

It was well into February now, and I was finding it more and more difficult to leave the cottage to spend the night in the bleak, neglected boat. I could not keep the fire in all day, and therefore went back to a cramped space that was increasingly dank and cheerless. One night I collected some blankets and a pillow from the spare room and slept in front of the fire, and after that I visited the boat once a day to see that she was not actually sinking, collected my sleeping-bag and kept it in the sitting room. If Miss Blackstone appeared, which seemed unlikely, I could easily say that my sleeping bag had got soaked from a leak in the cabin, and I was drying it out in front of the fire. To this end, I left it handy to put there if needed.

About a week after I sent the letter asking what seeds she would like me to plant, she wrote back.

I should like some blue flowers: delphiniums, corn-flowers, only not the pink ones, and some phlox. I love their peppery smell. Poppies, too, I love, the little deli-cate ones in pale yellows and whites and pink. And nemophila. You may think it strange that I know all these names, but my aunt had a lovely garden when I was a child and I should particularly like to grow the things she loved. Lavender – the dark purple kind and if possible some pinks, those white ones that smell so good, I don't know what they're called. And rock roses. Perhaps not all of these can be grown from seed, but I'm sure you will know, and with those that can't perhaps you would buy me plants? I'm sorry I was so feeble about money: I forgot that I had some English money in my wallet. Here is some for seeds and/or plants. If it is not enough, perhaps you would let me know. Gardens here – when they have them – are full of the sort of plants that people put in their Gothic conservatories. I am so glad that the cottage has not got one of *them*. It seems odd, when I have hardly spent any time in it at *all*, but I really miss the cottage, and especially not seeing it come alive in spring – the garden, I mean.

I wonder if you have started upon Chekhov. I am reading his letters, which are very good and tell me much more about him. I cannot do much *but* read. My film is to go ahead without me, which is frustrating, although watching things go wrong or be rewritten by director or actors can be worse. So I am stuck here. In the evenings I watch old movies of which there is a plentiful supply.

I have been looking at the first letter you wrote, and cannot help wondering *why* you are so much alone since you do not like it. Do you have friends who are simply too far away for visiting? Or family? [This last was crossed out but I managed to decipher it.] Your boat must be rather cold in winter: I hope you warm yourself when you light fires in the cottage. Here, it seems almost a luxury to be cold – to need warm clothes and hot drinks and fires. Really, I should not complain. This hospital is more like a luxury hotel. I have a beautiful room with every imaginable gadget, menus like a restaurant, fresh flowers and bowls of fruit and even a little fridge to keep my fruit juice and water cold. Once a day I hobble up and down the passages with two sticks – I have graduated from crutches but walking is still fairly painful.

Oh, dear, I can't think why I have written so much of what cannot be of the slightest interest to you. There is too much time on my hands or wherever one keeps it.

I forgot foxgloves – white ones. And I think I had already said I like hollyhocks even if they remind other people of tea cosies.

Yours sincerely,
Daisy Langrish

A twenty-pound note was attached to the letter.

Here, unexpectedly soon, were the openings I had been hoping and planning for. The letter told me much: she was lonely, even homesick. She had begun to display interest in me. Her rereading of my first letter and her question about why I was lonely showed that. It would enable me to tell her something of myself, which in turn might lead to her doing the same. I stopped my perusal of the chests and settled down to a letter. It took me all of the rest of that day to write a draft and the next day to edit and copy it out. When it was finished, I read it aloud to myself to see if it sounded as I wished.

Dear Miss Langrish,

First: here is a snowdrop for you. I picked it from a clump under the hedge near the gate. It is one of the perfect surprises one may find when one takes on a new garden.

Thank you for the money for seeds and plants. I don't think it is possible to get seeds of phlox, but I will buy two or three of them and they will increase with time and sometimes seed themselves. The pinks you like are Mrs Sinkins – called, I believe, after the wife of the gardener who bred them. They do have the best scent of all pinks. I will get a few and then we can get more from them with cuttings. Lavender is expensive and if you want a little hedge either side of your front door, we would need a dozen plants. However, I will leave them and buy the seeds first and stretch the money as far as I can.

Your life sounds rather cut off from the world. Perhaps that suits you and you are writing and need the solitary peace. Or are you too ill to write? You make light of your accident, but it must have been serious for you to be incarcerated so long. I wish that there was something I could do for you. I have always been good at looking after people, and alas! at the moment have no candidate. Please bear in mind that when you are able to leave hospital and come home,

I would be able to shop and drive for you and indeed do anything necessary for your convalescence.

Perhaps that is impertinent. I am sure you have dozens of friends who would love to look after you. I want only to say that nobody would take more *care* than I in that context.

You ask me why I am so much alone. It is a long story as indeed it must be with anyone who has lived as long as I have. I suppose a great deal of my life has been a battle against being rejected. My mother died when I was five and a half, and I don't think I have ever got over her death. It was fairly sudden: she had been nursing me with the measles and caught it herself. She then got some chest infection (the cottage we lived in was very damp) and died, I imagine, of pneumonia. My father at once married again – a horrible woman who resented me. I suffered frequent beatings from both of them, father and stepmother, and felt always in the way. I had a little room of my own, and took to reading as my only recourse . . .

Here, I paused for some time. I must not tell her too much at once, and had also to choose most carefully *what* I should tell her. After some thought, I continued:

My father was head gardener of the great house of the neighbourhood, and as I grew up I naturally got to know the child of that house, an only daughter. This story must seem obvious – banal, even – but as we grew up together, the friendship changed and I fell violently in love with Daphne and she with me. For some time this situation was kept entirely secret, but Daphne, who was young and innocent, was determined that her parents should be told in order that they might consent to our marriage. When her father died and she became more insistent, in vain did I try to persuade her that this would be a fatal mistake, and that I must prove myself worthy of her beyond simply working for my father on the estate, which he forced me to do. I must add here that earlier, when the time came for me to leave the village school, the teachers wanted me to try for a scholarship for the local grammar, but my father refused to allow this. So I was, in a sense, imprisoned by my lack of education in a job that I was sure Daphne's parents would not consider fit for the husband of their only daughter.

Of course she told her mother. I discovered this when Lady (I will call her simply 'C' for reasons that you will discover as I write) sent for me, and of course I knew, or thought I knew, why.

I shall never forget that scene. She was lying on a sofa in the library – a room of great magnificence which naturally I had never penetrated – dressed entirely in black with a long string of pearls that she kept touching with her white scarlet-tipped fingers.

It is hard to write this. I realize, Miss Langrish, that what happened in that room is more like a scene from a nineteenth-century melodrama than anything else.

'Daphne has told me that you want to marry her,' she said, after she had not invited me to sit down.

I said that although I loved Daphne, I knew that we must wait.

'It is not, and can never be, a question of waiting.'

'Daphne is prepared to wait. She has told me. Ask her.'

'I have sent Daphne away. It is better that you do not see each other again.'

'Where has she gone?'

'I shall never tell you that. And nobody here knows where she is.'

'You cannot prevent her from writing to me.'

'I am sending you away also. Your father has agreed to it. You will be leaving this week.'

'And supposing I refuse to go?'

'I think that would be most unwise. Your employment here ceases from today and you would need references. I have provided your new employer with those, but would not repeat them to anyone else. You do not seem to understand that your behaviour has been thoroughly underhand. You are in no way a suitable person for my daughter, and you are fortunate that I have taken the trouble to place you elsewhere.'

I could think of nothing to say. My mind – my heart – was reeling from the idea that I would never see Daphne again. I was so shocked, however, by her arrogant assumption that I would do whatever she commanded that I began to feel very angry.

'How dare you treat me in this way? Just because I'm working class, you, who have never done a hand's turn in your life, think you can speak to me and treat me as some sort of inferior animal. I love Daphne – I —' and then to my shame I burst out crying – in front of this woman I loathed. It was too much, and I could not stop. I remembered that I brushed my eyes with my arm and almost blinded by tears, started to leave that enormous room.

And then an extraordinary thing happened.

'Come here,' she said, in a voice so different that I turned to see if there was someone else in the room.

'Come here,' she said again, with such gentleness that I was trapped.

She touched a stool by her sofa and I sat down before her. There was a moment's silence while she regarded me thoughtfully as though she was weighing me up and I sensed that she was going to say something that she found difficult.

'You look so like your father when you are angry.'

I was silent. I had no wish to resemble my father in any way. I also knew that this could not be the reason for her calling me back.

'I understand some of what you must be feeling. You are shocked, you are angry with me, you are hurt and you think I am a snob.'

It was all true and there did not seem to be anything to say. But I refused to be placated by soft talk from her. Nor did I wish to display any more emotion in front of her. I regarded her coldly – I think I shrugged.

'Poor boy.'

'You need not think that telling me you are sorry for me will alter anything. I shall search for Daphne until I find her.'

'I am going to beg you not to do that. *Beg* you.'

'*Why?* Surely you would think even less of me if I did not?'

She smiled then and suddenly took my hand. Her hand was slender and cool. I could have crushed it in mine.

'I see that I am going to have to tell you. But there is one condition. I ask you on no account to repeat any of it to your father.'

That was easy. 'Oh, I don't talk to *him*.'

And then she told me. That Daphne and I were half-siblings – that we shared a father, and that nobody knew this excepting herself, 'and now you,' she finished.

I was staring at her, and saw that she could not meet my eye. 'It sounds like Lady Chatterley.' I said this with an attempt at brutality. She met it coolly.

'Not quite. My husband wanted an heir. Your father married later that year. And I had a daughter.' After a pause, she added, 'There was nothing prolonged about our association.' I thought I detected some faint bitterness.

'Now I think you had better go. There is an envelope on that desk that gives you information about your new position. They expect you two days from now. You will be better placed there than here, since their head gardener is shortly to retire. If you give satisfaction, you might well take his place!'

I took the envelope without further word, and left.

At this point, alarmed by how *much* I had written, I stopped and read it over. On the whole I was pleased. The story had all the improbability of truth. I thought for a moment, then added:

The letter contained directions to a house near Sevenoaks in Kent. The coincidence of the county and my name had some irony. In the envelope was a hundred pounds in five-pound notes. I never saw Daphne again.

Another pause, and then I finished:

Heavens, how much I have gone on! I cannot think what has possessed me to write so much. That is not true. I wanted to tell you what I have never told anyone. [This was perfectly true.] I wanted to *confide* in you and one cannot do that without a deal of trust. How I wish that you would or could trust me!

I crossed this out, but in such a way as to leave it legible with the effort of curiosity. People always read crossed-out lines or words in letters if it is at all possible.

I won't bore you with this story any more. The miseries of disastrous first love must be, I suppose, that one is young and consequently resilient, but at the time, of course, the misery was apparent and the resilience imperceptible. Do we all choose the wrong person when we are young and how much does it teach us? I feel that I know so much more now that I am older, but have no wish to live in the slipstream of my own life. Are these questions you could answer, because I cannot?

I was hers sincerely, Henry K.

I had decided that I would put off reading her plays until I had quite finished with the tea chests. This was partly because I was afraid that I might not like or understand them and would find it difficult to write to her about them, and partly because I was hoping for an answer to the above letter before I wrote again about anything.

So I tackled the most boring chest – the one with the typewriter and stationery. But when I had disposed of them, and was about to discard the chest, I noticed that there was a large envelope tied with dirty white tape lying at the very bottom. The envelope was not sealed and it was simply a matter of untying the tape. There was a treasure trove within. A bundle of letters, a small photograph album and a five-year diary. It was of cracked red leather and was locked, but the strap was badly frayed, and very little persuasion would break it. I began with the letters. Some were in envelopes, some not, and they were in three thin bundles, held together by elastic bands, which in some cases had snapped.

I looked first to see who they were from. The oldest-looking (paper yellowed, ink faded) were from the Jess whose picture I had seen already and who turned out to be an aunt. Apart from two postcards they were undated but clearly written to Daisy when she was a child, in the forties. Jess had a hand whose regularity concealed its illegibility and after struggling with one or two, I put them aside for later. The next bundle was a miscellany. There were letters from her daughter written from school: 'Need I go on trying to play the violin? I am absolutely no good at it and simply loathe the teacher'; 'We've had minced mice and frogspawn twice this week – honestly the food gets worse and worse and Lavinia was sick before she could even get to the lav'; from Edinburgh:

I do wish you would stop worrying about me. I am perfectly able to look after myself. In any case, I am not interested in getting a man, getting married and breeding and all that boring stuff which some people here seem to want. I want to go and *do* something, change things, have a proper career. I am sick

171

and tired of the way men treat women and I shall jolly well see to it that I'm not dependent in *any way* on them. You ought to agree about that, at least, considering your experiences with Papa. It must be a relief to be your age and not have to worry about that sort of thing. Look at Aunt Jess. She's perfectly happy without ever having had a man in her life.

Another one said:

I'm sorry if I sounded too hard and beastly to you. I know you do care about me and I know you miss Jess even more than I do. The trouble with you is that you are *too* trusting and gentle. I think you see things in a kind of romantic haze. But for goodness sake don't try and find a man to take Jess's place. I seem to be the realistic one in our family and it makes me feel quite protective of you even though I can see it makes me sound irritable and tactless. I think it's jolly good that you are taking to writing and it doesn't matter if you don't get famous or rich because soon I shall be earning my living and be able to pay you back. I do realize that you have given up a lot for me. Lizzie and I want to go to India when we've done our finals so I shall start getting holiday jobs to save up.

Finally, a postcard that simply said: 'Oh – all *right* – if you really want me to, I'll come.'

There were two letters from Anna Blackstone but they seemed to be entirely about writing and I left them.

The third bundle was a collection of notes, sometimes only a couple of lines. They all had a daisy drawn at the top and were signed 'devoted', or 'distracted', 'delirious', 'distraught' – and once 'dejected – J'. 'Just to tell you I love you more than yesterday and not as much as tomorrow.' One read: 'P.S. Could you *possibly* collect my dinner jacket from the cleaners?'

> It's so lovely to have moved on from carrying a spear to a torch – for that cat of yours, of course. But I suppose Sykes would *prefer* a spear with a sardine on the end of it. He only loves you because you feed and flatter him, whereas I – I would love you, *shall* love you till you are so old your poor little hands will be too weak to open a tin of Jellymeat Whiskas . . . Tell him that. Tell him you're merely his housekeeper, while *I* am your lover, your husband, your friend, your admirer for life. G. F. Jason.

That was the longest of them, but then, when I turned to the diary and gently pulled the frayed strap until it broke, one letter slid out from its pages. It was on airmail paper and felt as though it had been folded and unfolded many times. The first sentence told me all. 'This is the most difficult letter I've ever had to write in my life,' it began. He was ditching her with a brutality that must have felt worse because it was clearly unconscious. Poor Daisy! It is always interesting to see how people justify painful behaviour by explanations of how hard they find it – in this case how hard he *and* Marietta found it. If it was so hard, why did they do it? I read on. They did it because of the intensity of their love, of which there was much description. How much Daisy must have wanted to know about that! As I read, I recollected that I had seen this

Marietta in a sit-com series on television some years ago: a tiny little creature in a mini-skirt, huge eyes, pointed breasts and beautiful legs. And, of course, far younger than Daisy.

Then I began to wonder what all this can have meant to her; how much she had cared. Remembering two things at once – they cannot *be* at once but it feels like that – I thought of the fact that there seemed to be no letters from her first husband, only one photograph and Katya's allusion to what a time she had had with him, and also the look of wariness in Daisy's face that had been practically the first thing I had noticed about her. Perhaps she did not really like men, was afraid of them or could not respond sexually. None of this would be her *fault* – she might simply have encountered two egocentric boors, an all-too-frequent occurrence for women in my experience. But somehow my instinct was that she *had* cared, had been wounded, had suffered, and still bore the scars.

The diary began shortly before she met Jason, and at the beginning contained mostly notes about her working life, anxieties about Katya when she became so suddenly engaged, and a description of the marriage to which her first husband – the Stach of the photograph – turned up so unexpectedly.

I was astonished how little his presence meant to me [she wrote], amazed at how one cannot even remember the water once it is well and truly under the bridge. He looked exactly the same. I felt nothing at all except for some faint apprehension that he might embarrass Katya when he got drunk at the party afterwards. But she was so radiantly happy – there was a kind of charmed circle of joy round her that kept her safe from smashed glasses and sentimental reminiscence.

But it was her relationship with Jason that I wished to know about, and I turned the pages until I reached her meeting with him. There was one brief note in March '72.

This morning I met a most beautiful young man – an actor, of course. It was on Rodney's boat, one of his Sunday-morning drinks parties. I thought nobody looking like that could actually be good company – too eaten up with vanity and egotism and wanting to be a star. How wrong I was! He told me (when I asked) that he was out of work, but after that said not another word about himself.

A few pages later there was no doubt that she was, had been, violently in love with him. The next two years of the diary contained very little: sometimes a page would be started, but it would stop after a sentence or two. One of the few longer sections gave some explanation of this.

I had made a resolve to record everything – if not every day, at least once a week – but I am too absorbed to write anything more than my work. Here I should need to write about my complete happiness and that is far harder to do than I had thought. I can say and know that it is there, filling all the time and thought and everything that I do with him and without him. I am at once entirely happy in the moment, or whatever size the present is, *and* I never cease to look forward to the future – immediate, going out to dinner with him tonight, or more distant, going to France in September. I look forward to his coming back if he has been out, to being able to remember what we did yesterday, to imagining the next time that we shall make love. It is extraordinary how security and excitement go together; until now I had thought them mutually exclusive. But feeling so sure of my love and his love makes quite ordinary life an adventure.

But I wanted to get to the break-up, and turned the pages quickly until I found it, in March 1975.

Anna told me last night. I am glad it was she. She did not, in any way, allude to her original doubts about him and our marriage. I know that she loves me and that there is some comfort in that, but I am not sensible of it. I am not sensible at all. I feel as though a bomb has been dropped on me – from nowhere, for no reason, but somehow it has failed to kill me. I am still alive with nothing left.

Then later,

How did it happen? Why did he lie to me so much and for so long? Sometimes it is horribly clear now that this would happen – endless signs that anyone else would have noticed, but I did not. How can anyone cause such misery to someone they seemed to love? But perhaps he never did. When we met, he had nothing; he had been painting people's kitchens and getting occasional crowd work. If he once loved me and then for some reason stopped, why could he not tell me? Why leave me to find out how I might? But if he never loved me, that would be an even harder thing to say. Is it that men are essentially different from women? He wanted me and that equated with love, and now he wants somebody else and so that is love too.

On a separate page:

He is an actor – he would naturally be good at a performance.

And further on:

I am nearly forty-eight and he is forty-one. A crude explanation. *She* is in her twenties. I suppose that has much to do with it. Even after his letter I can revile him, and the love and loss just go on as though he had never written it. I simply do not know how to become indifferent.

April.

I have made him agree to come and tell me face to face about it. I don't know exactly why this seems so important to me, but it does. I am utterly divided about it – don't want him to know how much I am unhappy, and then I also want him to know *exactly* how unhappy he has made me. I want him to feel about that – to mind, to *care*. Madness, really. Pride is some sort of corset – it can hold one together, at least in front of him. I shall be quite calm, shall simply ask him what happened to us.

No. Don't ask anything. Make him say what he feels. Leave it at that.

He may not come.

Perhaps – it is just possible – when we meet that all this will go away and we shall be back to our beginning.

He did come, just after I thought he might be going to ditch me about that as well. But he came – and it was awful and when he first went, I thought I was going to die, but of course one doesn't *die*, simply breaks down. And then he came back because he had forgotten his damned briefcase. And for that last hour with him – right until the end – I thought that it had all been some frightful nightmare. I remember trying to say something of the sort to him – saying how much I loved him, and his putting his fingers on my mouth and then kissing me to silence. And then he put on his clothes and left. It had been nothing but pity. Pity!

May.

I did not believe it was possible to be so unhappy. To long for him so unmercifully – to ache for his presence, his voice, his touching me – even though I now know that expediency, lies and pity were all he had to offer. How can I love someone like that? Perhaps I don't.

Perhaps for me, too, it was some form of expediency – perhaps there is no such thing as unrequited love. Perhaps I have to weep and make anguish of this in order not to admit the humiliation of such a failure, am too proud or arrogant to admit to the squalor of simply having been taken in.

July.

I thought that writing about it would help. It doesn't. My mind and heart seem to have seized up. If they are to function at all, if I am to think or feel, it will only be about him. Every ordinary thing is an unbelievable effort. Getting up in the morning (one of the worst), having a bath, making coffee. I sit and make lists of what *should* be done and then can think of no reason for doing any of it.

There was a piece in the paper this morning about a boy who had lost his dog, and it was found poisoned, but he carried it two miles to a vet – it was a half-grown Labrador – and he was nine, and the vet saved it. I cried about that all morning. Anything makes me cry. The dog recovered. What was there to cry about?

August.

Anna agrees that I should move out of this flat. She has been so patient with me. We went for a weekend to a cottage she rented in the country – somewhere new to me where I had never been, in East Anglia. The sun shone all the time, and the cottage had a garden that reminded me of Jess and I told Anna how much

Jess had meant to me, the first time I had been able to tell anyone who seemed to recognize what that had been like. That was the first time since he left when I did not think of him for a whole day. I told her that, and she said, 'Good,' but it didn't seem to me good. I said that if I could forget him so quickly, it must show that I had not really loved him. She asked whether that would matter. It shook me. I said of course it must matter. We had been for a long walk and were sitting at the kitchen table drinking tea. There was a silence. I said, 'Surely you agree with that? Surely you believe in love?'

'Sure. But I don't think that feeling has to be permanent to be real. It is real while it is there. And things change. You have an heroic idea of love; you are romantic about it. It doesn't always bear the weight of ideals. Ideals seldom take the other person into account. Pass the fags, would you?'

'So – you mean I expected too much of him?'

'Possibly. Or too much of yourself.'

I said, 'It's difficult to believe that someone loves you if they lie to you.'

'It certainly is. But Jason didn't *always* lie to you. I'm sure of that. It was not like someone cold-bloodedly deciding to make you for what it was worth to him. That would be intolerable. He made you very happy. And truly I think he would have made a success – become a star – whether you had been there or not. That wasn't the point for him. He loved you – and then he fell in love with someone else.' Somehow from her this did not sound brutal.

I said, 'I see what you mean, and you're probably

right. The fact remains that I don't think I could ever trust anyone again if they said that they loved me.'

She shrugged. 'It's a choice, isn't it? I mean, if one spent one's life worrying about being run over, one would never go out. I don't think that would suit you. You can choose what you learn from experience, like anything else. Or you can choose *not* to learn.' She made a curious snorting sound that was nearly a laugh. 'Look at me. I was knocked over once, and now I never go out.'

Later I asked her if she would tell me about that, and she said, 'Sometime,' which was clearly not to be then.

I am sitting in bed in the cottage writing this. We go home tomorrow, and Anna is taking some time off to help me find a flat. I do love her. That won't change. But it was the first conversation I've had about Jason that didn't make me cry – even afterwards, like now.

For several months of the diary there was nothing very interesting.

I took Anna to see the flat in Blomfield Road this morning. It consists of two top floors of a house that looks on to the Regent's Canal and has two quite large and two smaller rooms plus a kitchen (very small) and a bathroom (adequate). At the back there is a large garden that belongs to the people below, but it is nice to see it. I can only buy a short lease, but Anna was enthusiastic about it and infected me with resolution and some excitement. I can start a new life there.

Some weeks later:

My last night here. It is another kind of end that recalls
the worst one. I shall be living somewhere where he
has never been, that he will never see. Anna is quite
right about making this change of scene, but it is an
uprooting – a tearing of him out of my heart. Sentiment?
I think this is how people often describe unacceptable
feeling in others. When I think of him now – not as
often and not for so long – the pain is still there. I have
become used to a celibate life – that ache only returned
some weeks ago when I saw him across the room at
a film awards party. I saw his head above the crowd
– turned away from me – and felt a sudden thudding
movement in the bottom of my spine, not like Katya
when she moved inside me with those tentative velvety
tappings, more of a single shocking kick that left me
trying to breathe. I wanted him: I would have done
anything to have him. It went: he turned away, someone gave me a drink and then I think he saw me and
he moved out of sight.

No: except for that one time, I have become used
to the idea that nobody will ever kiss or touch or come
into me again. I have *not* become used to the idea that
I shall neither love nor be loved by anyone again in
my life. I think the world must be full of secret suffering
of this kind – like arsenic or malaria it stays in the
body, accumulates or recurs without control. I think
of all the women who have lost men through murder
and war – and my loss seems parochial, petty (even
possibly my own fault?) in comparison. But I know
what their loss is. I know how people allow or allot

you time for mourning, and then want you strapped back into lives more or less like themselves, where different things matter and not so much.

I flipped through the remaining written pages to see whether Jason had been supplanted, but there was no sign of this. Then, mindful of the time when Miss Blackstone had descended upon the cottage without warning, I cleared up the boxes and stowed their contents away so that I could continue with them when I liked. It was March now: a blustering wind and driving clouds. I had to pay my daily visit to the boat. This was becoming more and more of a chore, but there were two good reasons for keeping an eye on it: the owners might possibly return – also without warning – and if and when *she* returned I would have to revert to living there. I locked up the cottage, having carefully surveyed it as a stranger might for signs of my occupation, was satisfied that there were none, and trudged up the lane to the bridge where I could join the towpath.

I could see that there was something wrong with the boat when I was yards away from her. The hatch doors were open, one of them swinging back and forth in the wind. Someone had broken in.

Children, I thought, boys probably. They had eaten some of the stores – biscuit packets, chocolate papers. Drawers and lockers had been opened but I could find little missing excepting my penknife (kept with the cutlery), a torch and a fountain pen that I never used. My papers and books had been left untouched, which was something, indeed the most important thing to me. It occurred to me, however, that if they thought the boat abandoned, they might well be back. There was a padlock for the doors of the saloon, but I had become lazy about using it and the Yale lock had been easy for them to break. I set about repairing this, and setting the shanks for the padlock more securely. It seemed sensible to spend the night there with the lamp on in the cabin, to which end I cleaned out and relit the stove (they had made an attempt to light it and it was choked with charred paper). Then I realized that I had neither my sleeping-bag nor anything much to eat and this meant a trip to the cottage.

It was dark when I set out, the wind had slackened, it was becoming extremely cold and I cursed the interlopers as I trudged along without my boat torch. Perhaps, the next day, I would look at whether mooring on the non-towpath side of the canal would provide me with greater safety. I had become used to the comforts of the cottage and dreaded nights in the damp boat.

When I reached the cottage, another surprise awaited me – a letter from her. I saved it to read when I had collected the sleeping-bag, a tin of corned beef and some potatoes, and what remained of a bottle of whisky that I had treated myself to the previous week.

I waited until I had peeled the potatoes and opened the corned beef before I poured the whisky and sat at the saloon table to read the letter.

Dear Mr Kent,

Thank you for your most interesting letter. What an extraordinary story! I hardly know what to say about it, except that the whole affair must have been so painful for you. You describe the scene with Lady C

so well that I almost felt that I was a witness, as though
– I hope you will forgive me for saying it – I was at a
play. But I can see all too well that it was no play to
you. Just a tragic coincidence which neither you nor
the poor girl can have had any idea of. I suppose I can
only hope that long since you did find someone whom
you could marry or live with and love. The happily-
ever-after theme seems to me to be one of those slick
universal unlikelihoods that deceives us all. It would
be almost a relief to me if you could tell me that you
did find someone. In answer to your question about
whether, when we are young, we all choose the wrong
person, I can only say that I suppose many of us must
do that. I certainly did. How much we are taught by
our mistakes depends, I suppose, on how much we
want to learn from our own experience. I think the
chief trap is that we imagine that we learn from
perceiving other people's, and it is easy to forget that
of necessity we view them from some distance (we
cannot *be* them or *know* precisely how they feel) and
that, what with this middle distance, rose-coloured
spectacles, and the defensive criticism we so often
employ about other people, we cannot learn very much.
We dub them foolish, irresponsible or selfish without
much consideration either of their needs or their ignorance. I *say* all this, but I do not live it. I can criticize
with the best of them. Criticism saves one from trust,
and that, I think, is the hardest thing to have.

I think they are going to let me go quite soon now.
I am having another X-ray next week and then they
will say whether my bones have healed enough for
me to go back to ordinary life – which means coming

home. I shall be very glad of it, and shall come down to the cottage as soon as I am able to drive.

Thank you for the snowdrop. I should have said this before. It was truly a charming thing to do and I keep it. I suppose I shall have missed them entirely, but perhaps there will be daffodils?

My parents died in a car crash when I was three, but I was more fortunate than you since I had a wonderful aunt who cared for me and was as good as two parents. Your childhood sounds entirely bleak. I am so sorry.

I am grateful for having such an experienced gardener as well as such a conscientious housekeeper. Thank you for that.

Yours sincerely,
Daisy Langrish

I read and reread the letter until I almost knew it by heart, so full was it of things I wanted to hear. She had begun to be interested in me, that was clear – she had started to confide in me. And she was likely to return soon. What more could I ask? If all the things that might happen occurred in the right order, it would be easy to deal with them, to respond and give the right impression. If Daisy, as I now thought of her, gave me due notice of her arrival, I could remove any signs of my occupation of the cottage but make it ready for her with a fire, the water heater on, flowers, and the basic foodstuffs, which I could leave upon the kitchen table with a small handwritten note and a carefully itemized bill that would confirm her view of my scrupulousness and honesty. If, on the other hand, she arrived without warning, I might be badly caught out. And supposing, having done that, she elected to pay me a surprise visit on the boat? This seemed unlikely, but I am not given to dismissing the unlikely. In the morning, I must make a serious attempt to moor the boat on the other side of the canal. It would also be wise to clear the place up a bit in case she sent Miss Blackstone to find me – another unwelcome thought. This meant a serious clear-up of my numerous papers, which must be locked away. The interlopers had paid no heed to them, but Miss Blackstone was an observant person, and there were many things I did not want anyone observant to see. I set about this clearing up: over the years I had written a great deal – in exercise books, on loose sheets of paper, and I too, like Daisy, had envelopes that contained photographs connected with my past life. I opened my last can of beer, lit one of my two remaining fags, and tried not to get caught into reading or even looking at the stuff I was stashing away. But in the course of putting things in piles to be secreted in carrier-bags, a photograph of Charley fell out, poor, plain Charley, looking her worst in tight white satin on the arm of the upper-class young bounder who married her. She had given it to me under the mistaken impression that as a bride she had for once been looking pretty, and of course I had reassured her as to that, the words radiant, innocent and glamorous coming easily to my lips. 'Oh, Harry! Do you really think so? It was only because I was all dressed up.' This, like so many of her remarks, was to encourage further reassurance. (God, how bored I used to get with providing that!)

Her parents – my employers – had managed to endow her with all of their least physically appealing characteristics. Her father was a short, barrel-ribbed little man with eyes too close together for comfort and a slack mouth. Her mother had a pear-shaped face with a larger pear shape beneath it and legs like a piano's. Poor old Charley had inherited most of this, plus a mouthful of teeth that though regular were quite simply the wrong size for someone of five foot four. But the other thing her parents had endowed her with was a monstrously large amount of money with the promise – she was an only child – of untold wealth to come. The diamond earrings she wore with the white satin were worth a fortune on their own.

The young bounder, Sigmond Kesler he was called, had naturally married her for her money, which she was singularly slow in discovering since she fell wildly in love with him. 'He was the first man in my life,' she would explain. When I met her, she had been married for three years and was intensely miserable. Sigmond, who seemed only to have bedded her twice during this time, was clearly involved with someone else, although even this did not occur to Charley until well after I was sure of it. 'He works so hard, he's hardly ever home and in the last year his firm keep making him go abroad and of course he can't take me 'cos it's business so I sit all day in this huge house in Bishop's Avenue [which I learned was somewhere in London] with nothing to do but take the dogs out on the Heath. Daddy says people have to work hard if they want to prove themselves and I should be proud of him. I am, of course, but I hardly see him, and he says he gets asthma if we sleep in the same room.'

She used to come home to stay at Lawn Court for weekends and sometimes longer when her husband was abroad. Lawn Court was the place I had got when I was invalided out of the Navy after the war – to my intense relief, I have to say. I have never got on well with other men and being cooped up in, successively, a corvette, an MTB and one of the few Steam Gun Boats had been a nightmare of boredom punctuated by fear. At least in corvettes they had had a cook who had gone through the rudiments of training; in the other two it was a useless rating who had neither the cunning nor the intelligence to get out of the job. I suffered – as many of us did – from seasickness. I was trained as a gunner, and by the time I'd been transferred to the MTB I was pretty handy with an Oerlikon. But when I was moved to the Steam Gun Boat flotilla I was promoted to coxswain. This, I well knew, with the captain and his number one, was the most dangerous job in gun boats since we all aimed to knock out the people on the bridge after torpedoes had lost their surprise value. The advantage to the Steam Gun Boats was that they were silent, whereas you could hear the MTBs from either side, miles away. However, the SGB only needed one bullet in her system of pipes that conducted the steam to become crippled or immobile. I imagine that was why not more of them were built. I copped it in a night action off Newhaven, and after hospital was given a desk job in Weymouth, which only lasted a few weeks before I was demobbed. All this, I realized as I recalled it, was good material for a letter to Daisy, but the question whether I should tell the story of Charley was another matter. I thought about this as I finished the clearing up and finally fell upon my bunk in my clothes, dog tired. At least, I thought before I dropped off, I had made Charley happy for a time; happy in a way she had never been and was never likely to be again.

The next morning I moved the boat. The trouble with the non-towpath side of the canal was that it consisted of very steep slippery banks studded with brambles and overhung by trees. I had the devil of a job hauling myself up and got badly scratched in the process. Going down such a bank in the dark was going to be dangerous and unpleasant. As I walked to the cottage I remembered the narrow-boat moored a quarter of a mile the other side of me. Its owner possessed a very small canoe that he some-times used to go up rivers unnavigable by his boat. He was away – and did not usually make use of his boat until summer. If he came down earlier, I would see smoke coming out of his funnel and could take the boat back apologising and saying I had had an emergency. I un-lashed the canoe from the top of the cabin and paddled my way back up the canal. There were some convenient reeds that grew in a largish clump on the towpath side and I could pretty well conceal the canoe in them; in any case, I would remove the paddles.

Problem number one solved, the next thing was to see to the cottage and remove any signs of undue occupation. This did not take so long as I had feared. I relaid the fire and carried out the old ash that had accumulated to spread over the garden. It was one of those clear blue days that herald spring. Primroses were out and there were some daffodils in her garden. I must remember to tell her that. I washed up a few mugs and plates and tidied up the kitchen. Finally I went upstairs to inspect the rooms there. The bedrooms seemed all right. The bath needed a clean, but by now the urge to write to Daisy was overwhelming me. I must somehow make more headway with intimacy before her return, and, as I came down the stairs, the cottage seemed a far more inviting place to write in than the boat. So I lit the fire I had so carefully laid and settled down before it with a mug of Nescafé. I would write the letter, then take it to the village to post and do my weekly shop for supplies, which were running very low.

Dear Miss Langrish,

Thank you so much for your wonderful letter. What marvellous news that you are better and may come home! You have been away for so long, and in such unfortunate circumstances, that I can easily imagine how much it must mean to feel that you will be free at last. The only time that I have been in hospital for any length of time (after I stopped a bullet on the bridge of a gun boat in 1944) I remember feeling more and more imprisoned.

There are daffodils, 'daffodils, that come before the swallow dares and take the winds of March with beauty'. So much better than Wordsworth, don't you think? At least, I remember that the first time I read that line it brought tears to my eyes. But perhaps you think that men should not cry. In that case I am one of the lesser men.

But back to the spring, March is going out like a lamb – the gales have subsided to zephyry breezes, the hawthorn flowers and willows by the canal have become luminescent with fresh breaking leaf. Primroses and violets are out and the wild cherry (I won't mention Housman, but one can quite see why the spring inspires poets, it is so obviously on the move).

Oh, what pleasure it gives me to write to you! And how much more I want to say than I do say. I do agree with you that we imagine we know, or may even in some sort *become*, other people by perceiving them. I think it is always in moments of grief and loss that we thoroughly recognize that we are essentially alone. The paradox is that I don't believe we are meant to be. We make so many efforts to join others or to become part of something outside ourselves, and when efforts are so universal and continuous, there must be a strong argument for saying that they spring from a natural cause. I see that this isn't altogether clear. By natural, I mean instinctive and self-preserving. Am rather rusty at this sort of thing. I read and try to think, but it is so long since I have had anyone worth talking to.

Thank you for your most understanding comments about my distant love. As you say, the whole thing does sound rather like a play. Coincidence, however, is far more connected to life than art, don't you agree? It always seems to me that writers have to work awfully hard to explain away or rationalize a coincidence to stop the reader from feeling that it is needed as a kind of escape route – a back door in the plot. And yet, everybody experiences them more than once in a lifetime.

You say most kindly that you hope I found someone I could marry and live with and love. I did find such a one, but the happiness was short-lived. Looking back, I suppose that this does not really matter; the important part of any experience is its quality rather than its duration.

I must confess to having fallen in love with somebody who was married. I have to say quickly now that not only was she deeply unhappy when I met her, she had never had a moment's happiness since she married the man her parents had chosen for her because he was extremely rich. Poor Charley! She had always been delicate as a child and afraid of her father, particularly, who always expected more of her than she could achieve. They lived in the country, and he wanted her to ride in horse shows, to excel at tennis and dancing, to be amusing and docile. Above all, he wished her to marry well. Charley was extremely shy; she once told me that she found it very difficult, and sometimes impossible, to enter a room full of people. She suffered badly from asthma and terrible migraines and was thus often unable to do what her parents wished.

She married – when she was just eighteen – chiefly because she wanted to escape her father's tyranny.

Here I stopped to consider. I wanted to avoid any suggestion of 'a scene from a play', as this, like coincidence, could only be effective if rarely employed. Coincidence! Of course – the most economical way of telling my tale as briefly and poignantly as I could manage.

I won't bore you with the details of this distressing saga; merely say that, shortly after her marriage, Charley discovered that her husband regularly visited another woman, and that her function was to be his hostess and the mother of his children. Poor girl – she failed miserably in the former and suffered two miscarriages after which she was advised not to make any further attempts in that direction. She hated being alone in the London house so much that she was reduced to returning to her parents for weekends. That was how we met.

Her husband refused to divorce her. When she told me this, I took the plunge. We eloped – an old-fashioned word but I can think of no other – and for nearly a year we were entirely happy. It was then that I began designing gardens and was, unexpectedly, successful.

I hardly know how to tell you the rest. Browsing through your bookshelf I came upon Margaret Kennedy's *Constant Nymph*, and there was the coincidence! My Charley died exactly as that poor girl did – trying to open a window that had been stuck with paint. I could hardly believe it: that a novelist should have so exactly described what happened to me – or, rather, to my darling Charley. Afterwards they said she had a faulty valve in her heart; that this might have happened at any time. She had always been a fragile, delicate creature, although the asthma and migraines got very much better under my care. She brought out a spring of tenderness and a desire to protect that I did not know I possessed. And I, in turn, was utterly beguiled, entranced by being so loved. But that was the end of it. I wonder now how I should have felt if I had read that novel *before* Charley died. The coincidence would have struck me like a knife to the heart either way, I suppose.

I should tell you that subsequently I did marry – more or less on the rebound I think now. I married a woman who turned out simply to have wanted the status of marriage, who was wrapped up in her career, who never stopped berating me for earning less money than she did. We parted nearly two years ago, after I discovered that she was seeing someone else and had been lying to me about it. There was, is, no tragedy there. I simply made an awful mistake and have certainly paid for it, since she has stripped me of my house, its contents, and what money I had. Money has never been a primary consideration for me, but I must confess to a feeling of dislocation: I knew, after Charley died, that I wanted more than anything in the world to have someone to love and cherish, and I find myself without that blessing. So it is for many people: I would not wish you to think I think myself singular in any way. I think there must be many people in the world who suffer from this loss – secretly and for the whole of their lives. Do you agree with this?

Please, if you can, give me some notice of your return to the cottage. I should so like to get it all warm and comfortable and ready for you. You have had such rotten luck that I should like to do anything in my power to make your return here pleasant.

This letter, when I read it, seems far too full of my affairs. I have confided in you – something I have not done for a very long time. I note what you say about criticism saving one from trust. You may criticize me as much as you please, but I *am* also to be trusted. If I knew more about you, my letters would be less ego-centric. I cannot help my curiosity about you, whether it be impertinent or no. It is entirely well meant. I would never betray you, as I sense you have been betrayed. I must stop before I make you angry.

Yours most sincerely,

Henry K

I was anxious about this letter – particularly after I had posted it. If I had gone too far, she might refuse to have anything more to do with me. I considered the possibility of writing an abject note, asking her to ignore my letter (which, of course, she would not, so in a sense I would have nothing to lose), but in the end I decided against it.

I collected my money, did my shopping and returned to the boat.

The first two weeks of April passed in a humdrum manner. I finished cleaning the boat as much as I could bear, did a certain amount of gardening – but left some of the more arduous jobs so that I would have good reason to be at the cottage when she came – and I read two of her plays. There was no reply to my letter and I began to feel afraid that I had gone too far too quickly. I had kept copies of my letters – did not want to risk slipping up on some detail – and thought about her incessantly. The plays, less than her diaries, of course, *did* tell me more about her, in a way, but I saw that my idea of fiction writers revealing themselves willy-nilly was simplistic. It was difficult to distinguish the self-revelation from the craft or art or diktats of plot and character. But I discerned a kind of romantic disillusionment – a rebound from being a victim to feminism of a militant but shaky nature. And she could be very funny, which somehow I had not bargained for. I only read two plays written for the theatre, because that was all there was; the bulk of the typescripts were drafts of these two works. One of them was about the conflict of the heroine between her career and marriage. What was interesting about it was that she had presented the various choices and then enacted each of them. The consequences of each choice were carried on in the subsequent scene, and in the end she had the tail of the serpent in its mouth. The other was a darker play based on the Orpheus-Eurydice myth but set at the turn of the century. This, although it seemed to have an element of women's rights about it, was at another level about the incompatibility of needs that seemed to haunt any love affair. It was a play about the ultimate absence of trust, and that I found very interesting.

I wrote several notes to Daisy as I grew more and more anxious about her reaction to my letter, but something stopped me from sending them – some sense that if I had put my foot in it, any follow-up would only make it worse.

Then, one morning, as I was taking the opportunity between showers to lay out some pieces of York stone to see if they were enough to make a decent pathway to the front door, I heard a car approaching. It was slowing, and I knew it was coming to the cottage. For a split second I thought it might be Daisy, but if so she was not in her own car. I resisted the temptation to stand up and see what was going on, reckoning that steadily pursuing my job would make the better impression.

The car had stopped, I heard the door slam, and the sound of the latch on the garden gate. Then I stood. I was the caretaker, after all.

It wasn't Daisy.

'You must be Henry Kent,' said a voice I recognized.

'And you are Mrs Moreland.'

'How did you know?'

Looking at her, I would have known anyway from the photographs. A youngish woman with a wealth of dark hair scraped from her forehead and arranged in coils at the back of her head. She had green eyes and a wide mouth that became very attractive when she smiled. 'I recognized your voice from our telephone conversation.'

'I've driven miles. Any chance of a cup of coffee or tea or anything?'

'I believe there is some Nescafé.'

'Oh, good! I'll get it, you needn't bother. I've got a key.'

'The door is open anyway. I've been airing the place. It hasn't got a damp course.'

She walked into the cottage without replying. I wondered how she had got a key.

Then she called, 'Do you want one?'

'Thanks.'

I followed her to the kitchen. My lunch was lying on the table and I saw her looking at it.

'I usually eat in here when I'm gardening. It's either too cold or too wet outside.' I was aching to ask *the* question, but something warned me not to seem too eager. It was not until the kettle had boiled and we were stirring the coffee in our mugs – we had sat at the table to do this – that I said, 'And how is your mother?'

'I don't know exactly. But she called her agent saying that she wanted to come straight down here when she gets back, and Miss Blackstone called me because she couldn't get away to come down here this week and could I have a look at the place and see whether it is feasible for her to come. My ma is not the most practical person. Anna says she's still quite lame, and I want to look at things like the staircase and the bath to see if she can manage. How far is the nearest shop? Because I don't know whether she can drive, and she obviously can't walk far with shopping and stuff. I suppose there are taxis?'

'I could drive her.'

She looked at me appraisingly.

'Go on,' I said. 'Size me up.' I could see that she was doing this, and did not want her to get too serious. 'I'm sixty-five,' I said. 'I'm caretaking a boat on the canal for friends. Just a temporary situation. I walk past this cottage most days on my way to the village. When I saw it was taken I asked your mother if she wanted a gardener. That's

FALLING

all there is to it really. Then when she was away for so
long, she asked if I'd keep the cottage aired for her. I
admire your mother very much – have always been interested in writers, although I can't say I've known many of
them. But reading and gardens have been my life.'

I watched her listening to this, which was easy, since
I always find it better to look people straight in the eye:
they seem to find it reassuring, and I have a better notion
of how I am being received.

She had a very expressive face. I could see questions
forming in her mind only a second before I knew what
they were.

'Yes, I have been married – am in fact in the process
of trying to get a divorce, but my wife, since she is sitting
in my house with my property and money at her disposal,
is in no hurry. Fair enough, I suppose, since she married
me for what I had rather than anything that I am.'

'Oh.' After a moment, she added, 'I'm sorry.'

'Not your problem. I'm perfectly all right. I don't need
much, and the money your mother pays me just about
makes everything work.'

'Were you brought up in the West Country?'

'You've got sharp ears.'

'Where?'

'Wiltshire. Those were the early years. After the war I
got a job in Kent.'

There was a short silence; then, I said, 'I feel as though
I'm being interviewed.'

'If you feel that, you're probably right.' She pushed
back her chair and stood up. 'I'm going to have a look
upstairs.'

I washed up our mugs and, without thinking, lit a
cigarette. Better smoke it outside, I thought. I knew

somehow that she did not smoke. The path was going to turn out nicely. I guessed the stone had been bought for it by the previous owner.

She did not look like, or seem to be at all like, her mother. She had arrived in a duffel jacket but had taken it off in the cottage to reveal a plaid shirt with pockets over each ample breast, and a full skirt that was tightly belted. It was easy to imagine her without any clothes at all – a practice, I must admit, that I have often employed. Apart from any sexual frisson, or otherwise, it can bring insights that are sometimes useful. It was important to get Katya to like me, or to trust me enough to consider me favourably.

'Mr Kent!'

She was sitting on the arm of the sofa rummaging in her shoulder-bag.

'It's really quite nice,' she said, 'but there are one or two things that need doing. I thought if I made a list you could find a builder or a handyman to do it all. Only it needs doing quickly, because she might turn up any time now.'

'Tell me what you want. I could probably do it.'

It turned out that she wanted a rail put in for the staircase. 'It's pretty steep, and she ought to have something to hang on to,' and some similar rail for getting in and out of the bath. 'And I think she ought to have a phone in her bedroom.'

I said I couldn't do the telephone, but the rails would be easy, except that the nearest DIY shop was ten miles away.

'If I took you there, we could buy the stuff today, only we must go now, because I've got a long drive home.'

I said that would be fine. We locked up the cottage and left.

She had an old Volvo, rather battered, the back littered with children's clobber. She was a good driver.

'We didn't measure the staircase.'

'I did.'

'You are very practical, aren't you? I'm most impressed.'

'I'm practical for other people, not particularly for myself. I'm always losing things and forgetting things, stuff like that.'

She made two more remarks about her mother between long intervals of silence.

'My mother needs looking after in that kind of way. And there isn't anyone to do it for her. Except Anna, of course. But Anna only has a certain amount of time for that kind of thing. She *thinks* she's awfully practical and realistic, all that sort of thing, but she isn't really.'

'You sound like a very good daughter.'

'Oh, no!' Then she said, 'I'm better *about* her than I am *to* her.'

She did not seem disposed to talk, so I confined myself to telling her the way.

After we had bought all the rails and screws etc., she said she wanted to go to a supermarket to buy stores for her mother. 'There is a fridge, isn't there? Is it working?'

'I think so.'

She bought a load of stuff – cocoa, tea, a tin of drinking chocolate, 'Ma has always been crazy about chocolate,' butter, packets of salami and ham, eggs and bacon, 'if she doesn't come back in a week you'd better eat them', onions and garlic and tins of tomatoes, sardines and anchovies, packets of spaghetti, and rice and muesli, and honey and morello-cherry jam, 'my father loved it, we always had that when I was a child', loo paper and washing-up stuff and six bottles of red wine, 'she only drinks wine and she doesn't like white', three bars of very dark chocolate and some electric lightbulbs, 'the one in her room by the bed is bust'. Then she bought two egg sandwiches and some oranges. 'I'll have a quick bite before I start for home.' We drove back, unloaded everything and I said I would go to the boat to fetch my tools while she had her lunch.

'You don't have to. You haven't had your lunch.'

So we sat again at the kitchen table, and she made tea and we ate our sandwiches – mine were Spam. She rang to arrange for an extension of the telephone, and I said I would make sure to be at the cottage all of the day that the engineers were supposed to come. By then she was much more at ease with me – curious. She kept asking me questions about what work I had done or did. I told her about being a garden designer.

'But how did you *learn* about gardens?'

'I worked on a big estate when I was a boy. They had everything there. A succession of stove houses, a lake and water garden, high-walled kitchen garden, borders, parterres, orchards, shrubbery, the lot.'

'It sounds like Rackham.'

I was astonished by this. 'How did you know?'

She shrugged. 'Just guessed. There aren't so many places like that left now, are there? Though people say it's become rather run down. And the National Trust didn't want it because the house is really rather grotesque. Simply huge but without any architectural distinction, Edwin says. He's interested in that sort of thing. And then you went to Kent, you said.'

'Yes. Another large place, but the people weren't short of money to keep *that* up.'

'Where was that?'

'Oh – not far from Sevenoaks. It wasn't Knole. I don't think you'd have heard of it. It was much smaller, more ordinary.'

'You said it was large just now.'

'Most places are smaller than Rackham. Isn't it my turn now?'

'For what?'

'To ask questions.'

She looked surprised, then she smiled – a rather conscious, flirting smile. 'Why not? It seems only fair.'

So, over the short time that was left before she went, I did glean a few pieces of information. I learned, for instance, that she didn't like living in the country much, that the annual family holiday to Brittany did not fulfil her desire for travel. I deduced that her marriage was going through a sticky stage, that she felt isolated and generally unsure of what to do with her life.

'In the country there seem only to be occupations – I want a *career*.' Later, she said, 'I'm not creative like my mother, or I could sit at home and *paint* or something. She's awfully lucky to have that. Although,' she added, 'she hasn't been so lucky in other ways.'

'How do you mean?'

'Well, I know he was my father, but I can see now that he can't have been easy to live with. Impossible, really. He's always falling in love with someone and then falling in love with someone else. His last woman was nearly ten years younger than I am. And he drinks far too much and never has any money. His whole life is like a bad part for a good actor, if you know what I mean. I can see now why my mother had to leave him, although I hated her for it at the time.'

'Then she married an actor, didn't she?'

'She sure did. He was a shit, if ever there was one. I always knew he was, but she is so trusting. She thought it was the big romance of her life. As soon as he became a film star, he left her for Marietta Reed – you know, the actress.'

'That must have been hard.'

'It was. She was about fifty when he left, and it seemed like the end of her life. Of course, in a way, it would be – one wouldn't expect to find anyone else at her age.'

'Do you really think that?'

'Not men. Men can always find someone. But women are up against all the much younger women who go for older men.' She looked at me: cynicism suited her pale green eyes. 'I bet you could do it if you wanted to.'

'Eh?'

'Find some sweet young thing and chat her up. It doesn't work the other way round.'

'Cleopatra was much older than Antony.'

'Oh, well. There have to be exceptions.' She said this rather airily, as though they were only there to be dismissed.

Then she said she must leave and I went with her to the car.

'Did she ask you to make this path?'

'No. She asked me to do the garden, and the stone was stacked in the garage. It was obviously meant for a path.'

'Well, you do take trouble.'

'Thank you, ma'am. I aim to please.'

'I should think most of the time you succeed.'

'Will you let me know when your mother will be coming?'

'If she tells *me*. How do I let you know?'

'Supposing I say I'll be at the cottage every morning between eleven and twelve? You could ring me.'

'All right. Thanks for all you're doing. Don't forget the telephone engineers. I don't like to think of her alone here without a phone by her bed.'

'Of course I won't.'

She seemed unsure of how to end our meeting, but after she'd found her car keys she held out her hand. I took it, brought it to within an inch of my lips, and then – meeting her eye – I kissed it.

'Heavens! Rather baroque of you!'

'That's what I am: baroque.'

When I could no longer hear the car, I went back to the kitchen. For a while, I simply sat at the table and thought about Daisy. I thought about the first time that I had seen her – in her raincoat and boots and the man's hat that had concealed her marvellous hair. I relived my initial surge of excitement, the memory of my first searching sight of that Elizabethan face, and the next day lighting the fire for her while she came and went from the kitchen to the fire offering me tea, the tray laid on the embroidered cushion. I remembered her high, clear voice – her taking off her hat. When I had exhausted my memories, I moved on to my imagination. Then she had removed the poppy-embroidered jacket after the fire got going, and now I removed the black high-necked jersey: she held her arms obediently over her head while I peeled it off her. This was the moment when patience and no haste at all invariably paid off. I would not slide the shoulder straps of her camisole or make any attempt to unhook her bra: I would talk gently to her of my admiration for her beauty, I would hold and kiss her hands, I would declare my love, but in tones so protective and tender that she would feel reassured; lust would be concealed by awe and when I told her how I would give my life neither to hurt nor betray her, she would feel treasured and safe and able to respond.

Perhaps I should say here that approaches to women have by the natures of the latter to be different. There are women who need to be teased into wanting; there are women who respond to an almost brutal display of need; there are women who simply want their sexual attraction emphasized: but my Daisy was none of them. Everything that I had read about her, things that Katya had let out this day, the first impression I had had of her, all confirmed that hers was a gentle nature made wild by betrayal. The thought of taming her – of her ultimate surrender – was intensely erotic and I could see that my patience might have to be rewarded by fantasy for an unknown amount of time. What comfort fantasies can be! What safeguards they provide; what intimate power they engender!

Before I set about clearing up the detritus of our lunch, I made some notes of what Katya had told me, and then, as an afterthought what I had told her. Nothing very much. It had been faintly unnerving that she had got on to Rackham so quickly, but I reflected that there could be nothing and nobody left there who would even have heard of me. My father had died some time ago; Daphne would have been married off to some dull swell, and her ladyship would never divulge to anyone what she had actually told me. All the same, it had been foolish to answer Katya Moreland's questions so freely, although it would have looked odd not to have answered them at all.

I worked on the path for a while, then cooked myself a good supper of eggs and bacon. I was sorely tempted by the red wine, but nobody gives anyone five bottles of wine and I could not afford to replace it.

A week, I thought to myself before I slept. It can't be much more than a week.

6

DAISY

2 May

I am here at last. Anna brought me down as I am not able to drive yet. She said that she would stay the weekend and made me promise beforehand that I would not stay on alone if she, Anna, thought that I would not be able to cope. I told her that Katya had said she'd been down and met Mr Kent, who seemed to be most handy and willing. I did not tell Anna that Katya had also said that she thought he was rather an unusual man to be a gardener: 'Very odd, Ma, not like anyone I've ever met before.'

I asked if she had not liked him, and after a moment's silence I said, 'You didn't. *I* don't mind, darling, I was only asking you.'

Then she said, no, it wasn't that at all. She *had* liked him. He was rather charming, she had said, and actually quite bright. 'A bit mysterious, though.'

I was very touched that she had taken the trouble to drive all that way to see the cottage.

When Anna came to fetch me, she brought mail that had been forwarded from the studio and the hospital. Among them was a letter from Mr Kent. I had a momentary urge to open it at once, but desisted. For some reason I did not want to be with anyone else while I read it.

Anna was marvellous – as always. I had laid out

my things to take to the cottage, but my cases had been in a top cupboard above my wardrobe and I simply could not get to them. Just as well. I had left out half a dozen vital necessities – socks for my wellingtons, a winter dressing-gown, more jerseys, and my anorak with a hood. I had become so used to warmth that it was hard to imagine what late spring in a damp cottage might turn out to be.

By the time we had packed and shut up the flat and loaded up the car, I was exhausted. Everything tires me – suddenly – and I find this curiously depressing. It is as though in return for my bones and tendons healing, I leak energy or use it all up on that – I don't know. Anna says anaesthetic takes a great deal out of one and that it can take months to recover. It has certainly played havoc with my sleep. I told the doctor in London all that: Anna made me go and see him; she actually took me although I could perfectly well have got a taxi. She nannies me; I told her it was bad for both of our characters, and she said that it was very good for hers.

The doctor, who had been sent my X-rays, said that the Americans had done a marvellous job, but I couldn't expect to recover from such injuries overnight at my age. I pointed out that it was three months. Anyway, he gave me a prescription for sleeping pills and told me to come back in a month. I may not do that, at least, not until I can drive again.

On the way down, she asked me whether I intended living at the cottage. I wasn't sure; I would spend a summer there and then decide. It will be expensive to have two places; on the other hand I don't want to *live* in London any more.

'It's quite charming, but not very *convenient*,' Anna remarked.

I remembered that she had already seen it, and felt childishly disappointed.

'I think you might find the winters rather lonely.'

I did not say that I found the winters lonely in London. Ever since Jason, I have been extremely bad at meeting people. I loathe large parties and they tend to be what one gets asked to if one is single and no longer young. I did have a few friends who had been mine before I married him, and a couple I liked very much whom I met after he left – but they have gone to live in Australia. The others have married, had children who take up all their time, and then there is Anthony, a really close friend who has fallen in love with a man who can't stand me. There is nothing that makes no difference to friendship. I think everything does – sometimes for the better, sometimes for the worse. But the chief enemy is time, or the lack of it. I have time, too much, and, it seems, more than most of the people I know.

Why on earth am I writing this? Because, I suppose, I'm beginning to feel the itch again; the curious, restless, wasted-time feeling that starts me writing. And this scribbling is a sort of cop-out.

She shut the notebook and put the cap on her pen. They had arrived in time for the picnic lunch that Anna had prepared.

The place had a delightfully lived-in feeling. The tea chests were gone and she noticed at once that their contents had been neatly stacked on the shelves. On the kitchen table was a jam jar filled with primroses.

'Did you tell Mr Kent we were coming?'

'No. I thought it would be rather a good thing not to.'

'You sound as though you don't trust him.'

'I don't trust or distrust him.'

Later, Anna said, 'Katya must have told him that your return was imminent when she came down – and that was about ten days ago.'

When she came down from carrying the bags upstairs, Anna said, 'Did you leave the beds unmade?'

'From the last time? No, I stripped mine. I didn't make the other one.'

'Well, yours has been made. Presumably by Mr Kent.'

'That's thoughtful of him, don't you think?'

'Possibly. A bit intrusive. Gardeners don't make beds as a rule, do they?'

'Oh, Anna! I think he just means to be kind. Don't be against him. I'm sure he means well.'

She noticed that Anna did not answer. She had been about to tell her that she knew more about him than she did, that he wrote interesting letters that revealed him to be someone with an unusual and subtle mind, but she didn't. She did not want to argue – let alone quarrel – with Anna over him, and decided to shut up at least until she had read his forwarded letter.

This she did in her bedroom after they'd eaten, when Anna decreed that she should have a rest. 'I haven't even looked round the garden yet!'

'You can do that when you come down for tea.'

So she lay down on her bed and when Anna had gone downstairs, she read the letter. Again she was struck by his capacity to make her *see* whatever scene he was writing about. When he described his Charley's death, she felt tears hot in her eyes. At least the poor girl must have died happy, and she was touched that he was able to be grateful for the time with her rather than simply lamenting its brevity. She was also struck by his truthful account of his marriage – no sentimentalising or absconding from blame. She liked him from that letter, but she also realized that he was clearly extremely lonely and that he might become – as Anna had said he was – intrusive.

It did also cross her mind that he seemed to be rather disaster prone. But then she reflected that she'd only had two letters with accounts of his life and that there must be much of it that had been happier. He had, and really at her request, given an account of some salient events, and if she were to do the same to anyone, she would have to say that her parents were killed when she was three, that she'd lost her beloved Jess at a time when it seemed she most needed her – after the break-up with Stach and Katya to bring up on her own. (But, of course, she would always have loved and needed her.) Then – Jason. Yes, it would certainly sound disaster prone to an outsider – and, indeed, perhaps it was, although she suspected it was more like the wear and tear that are most people's lot: the most cruel moments blurred and distorted by the repetition of memory, which meant for her that she could not remember exactly how she felt because an element of shock was not there; it too was a memory, no longer an ambush, but the recollection of one.

She put away the letter and began to imagine her life in this cottage after Anna had gone back to London. She would walk every day to strengthen her leg. She would get the cottage really comfortable and pretty. She would read; for her next piece of work she had it in mind to attempt a series of plays about the Brontës, the only play she had read seeming not to be comprehensive enough. And so she must read not only all the novels again but Clement Shorter, Winifred Gérin, Margaret Lane, Mrs Gaskell, etc. She fell asleep in the middle of a mushrooming crowd of biographies.

After tea they made a tour of the garden, which surrounded three sides of the cottage. There had been a shower – single drops sparkled in the grass and the air smelt of moss. There were two clumps of narcissi, forsythia, and a dark red polyanthus against the end wall of the cottage. Roses had been planted and manured, and six small lavender bushes were in place each side of the cottage door. The beds were clear of weeds, and looked orderly and bare. It was clear that Mr Kent had done his job well.

Then it began to rain again and they went in. Anna lit the fire and opened a bottle of wine, and they listened to Chopin mazurkas while the stew was heating in the oven, and she watched the sky fade to an aqueous dusk. Supper was to be by the fire, and while Anna, refusing all help, was getting it, she suddenly realized the extraordinary luxury of lying with the firelight and hearing someone else, this loved and loving friend, making ordinary kitchen noises next door. This was what loneliness was not; or, rather, what much of it was about. It was not necessary – or, for her, necessary any more – to be wrapped in someone's arms: friendship, living with a companion, would be a living contentment. And Anna was also alone.

Before they went to bed, she opened the door to smell

ELIZABETH JANE HOWARD

the garden once more and heard the soft seductive hoot
of an owl.

'Oh, Anna! It really *is* lovely here. I wish you could
live with me.'

'You know I'm a London bird. And, anyway, I have to
work. But I'll come and visit you regularly. Tomorrow
morning we'll make a list of all the things you need and
I'll find out how practical it is for you to be here when
you can't drive.'

'Perhaps Mr Kent could drive me.'

'Driving Miss Daisy, I daresay he can do that as well.'

'As well as what?'

'All the other things he seems to have done.'

But as they parted on the landing, Anna said, 'Mind
you, I can see that this place could be very good for work.
As long as you don't get too lonely.'

Again she thought of saying that she had felt lonely
in London, but did not.

When she opened her bedroom window, she heard the
owl again, and stood waiting for him to hoot, breathing
in the sweet dark air. She looked towards the wood where
the owl must be: the high branches of the trees were black
against a sky that was, as she watched, momentarily illuminated by the appearance of a half-moon emerging from
small scudding clouds, then fitfully obscured by more of
them. She thought for a moment that the blackness of the
wood shifted, but when the moon went out, there was
no way of telling.

Before she slept, it did occur to her to wonder why
she had been so sure that she wanted to buy this particular place. It had been the first that she had seen. It
had not looked especially promising: a smudged black-
and-white photograph photocopied with its ill-typed

details before it. 'Detached period cottage with three-quarters of an acre of garden. Large living room 28ft × 15ft, kitchen and toilet on ground floor. Three bedrooms (one of good size, 16ft × 13ft, with double aspect. Bathroom and toilet on half-landing. Garage; garden shed. Village ½ mile. Nearest market town 10 miles approx. The building has a slate roof. The front facade is of plaster over brick and the other three walls of brick and flint. Mains electricity and water. Open fireplace in living room.' Oh, yes, and 'small larder off kitchen'.

This description, which she did not remember in the right order, contained no sales hype: no 'beautifully presented', no 'wealth of period detail', no 'mature and well-stocked garden'. And yet she had picked it as the first to see and, having seen it, saw no point in looking further. It was an honest, unremarkable little building, but it was all of a piece: had not been corrupted by louvred doors, open risers on the staircase, the dreaded brown windows or nasty little front door with ersatz fanlight. It was on a road, but a minor one and she liked the proximity of the wood, which edged one side of the garden and was clearly a good protection against an east wind.

She had gone straight back to the agent in Banbury and offered the asking price (which Anna told her afterwards was *mad*. 'You could at least have tried to negotiate'). But she had the money saved from two films and had not thought. 'And if I *do* decide to live here, I can sell the flat in London, or perhaps buy a one-room flat and still have something to live on if work goes badly.' She had the inside walls painted, and some bookshelves made for the sitting room, and had pillaged the London flat, bought some stuff at an auction and moved in. She had the bare essentials, but it would be enjoyable to hunt for the right pieces, as much as making a pretty garden would please her. Aunt Jess had taught her to use her eyes in junk shops, and she would learn about gardening from Mr Kent. She began to make lists in her head as she drifted into sleep.

Anna woke her with tea and toast on a tray, saying that she was going on a preliminary exploration of shops. 'I've made a list of what it is plain that you need, although Katya did a pretty good job, and we can always go out later for anything else that occurs to us. You take it easy; the water is hot if you want a bath.' She was lying in the bath when she heard the latch of the front door click and then the door shut. She had not bothered to shut the bathroom door so these sounds were clearly audible. Perhaps Anna had come back because she had forgotten something – her purse or the list.

'Anna?'

There was no reply and she was suddenly unnerved. She got out of the bath and wrapped her towel round her. She could hear someone moving about below. 'Who is it?'

She stood on the landing outside the bathroom looking down the stairs: she was hardly dressed for confronting a marauder. Then she saw him, looking up at her from the bottom of the stairs.

'I do beg your pardon. I didn't realize you were back. I come in most mornings to check that everything is all right.'

Henry Kent. It was odd: she had almost forgotten what he looked like. But seeing him, his appearance seemed oddly familiar – familiar and unremarkable; memorable chiefly for the thick, brindled hair, a lock of which lay across the right side of a forehead that was otherwise enlarged by a receding hairline. He was clearly looking up at her, but with his back to the light she could not see his expression.

'I'm so sorry to disturb you. I've got some seeds in the shed. I'll be watering them and then I'll be off.'

She heard herself saying, 'I'll be down in a few minutes.'

'I should so much like to show you the garden.'

'Yes, all right.'

As she dressed, she was conscious of confused, distant but unusual feelings: some excitement, curiosity and a certain embarrassment. The letters he had written were full of revelations not normally divulged between one stranger and another. And she had replied to them; not, she was sure, with the same intensity of intimacy, but still certainly more than she would have expected. She remembered her conclusion the night before, that he was obviously lonely and that therefore he might become intrusive. It was a fine line, she thought, as her own loneliness obtruded, between being isolated and being thought intrusive. He might, she might, *anyone* might be thought to be that when they were simply making efforts to communicate to another person in order to put an end to their isolation. But supposing I don't *want* to know anything more about him? What happens then? He could be sent away; he could stop being her gardener. It was rather ridiculous to *have* a gardener with such a small garden – particularly if she did decide that she wanted to live here. Then she remembered that Jason used to tease her about getting worked up over meeting strangers. 'You're the most *secretly* shy person I've ever known.' She had asked him what he meant. His reply: 'Oh! You get all uptight and queenly and everyone runs a mile.'

This apparently careless remark had caused her further anxiety, and knowing that Jason had no difficulty in meeting people – never had a second's anxiety about whether he would get on with them or be liked by them – she had begun watching to see how he achieved this. But she learned nothing, or nothing that she felt able to apply to herself. He had only to walk into a room for everyone to become more animated, to gravitate towards him, and his apparent unselfconsciousness about the effect he had on people merely increased it. He was never beset by her doubts – about whether he could think of anything interesting to say, or, she now discovered, if she *did* manage that part of it, whether it would involve her more deeply with the recipient than she felt inclined. She didn't take risks with people; she didn't *go* for it; she wanted both insurances and assurance that an intimacy would have happy consequences. No way to live, she thought now, as she brushed her hair, and ridiculous at my age not to have acquired these essential skills for friendship – which, after all, could exist at varying levels. Wholeheartedness, perfection, was not by any means the only thing to seek. She had had that, after all: she'd had Jess and Jason and Anna. And perhaps with time she'd have Katya as well.

She had thought much about Katya that morning: the rails in her bath, the telephone in her room, the banister down the stairs that she was now gratefully clutching, the stores in the cupboard – all that was Katya.

It was a beautiful, milky morning; still, cloudless, the sun quenching the dew on the lawn, the hedge each side of her garden gate glistening with new leaves, budding may and diamond-encrusted cobwebs. The stone path was slippery, and she had left her stick upstairs. As she turned back to the house to fetch it, he came round the corner from the back. He hastened towards her, almost bustled, and held out his hand and she found herself giving him hers. His hand was damp and she felt that he, too, was nervous.

'It's wonderful to see you,' he said. 'You can't imagine how anxious I have been about you. Such an awful thing to have happen. And here you are – walking without a stick!'

'I'm supposed to use one. I left it upstairs.'

'I'll get it.'

Before she could either stop or thank him, he had gone. She remembered his eyes now – a light hazel; she remembered that he had looked at her in the same way the first time that they had met, and she had felt really *seen* by him, and that the experience had been unnerving.

'Here it is. Oh, and I've made a very rough sort of garden seat in case you get tired walking about.'

'In this enormous garden?'

'Well, if the weather stays fine you might want to be out without being about, mightn't you?'

He was leading the way round the corner of the house.

'It's just a plank with two tree stumps. If I had known you were coming I would have done so many things.'

'I think you've done a lot. The garden is almost unrecognizable. Oh, and thank you for the primroses.'

'I've been putting fresh ones in every day. And your daughter came and we made a few alterations inside to suit you. Did she bring you down?'

'No. Anna brought me. Miss Blackstone. She's gone shopping. I can't drive yet.'

'Will she be staying, then?'

'No. She's got to go back tomorrow night.'

'Well, I can drive you anywhere you want.' There was

a pause. He stood in front of her and then, in a voice that sounded as though it was a joke against himself, he said, 'I have no precious time at all to spend – but of course you know that.'

And then, before she could respond, but she didn't know how on earth *to* respond, there was the sound of Anna returning with the car.

'I'll go and help your friend with the shopping.'

Had he meant that she would recognize the quotation, or had he meant that she would know that he had nothing else to do but look after her? Or perhaps both? It was silly to feel uneasy about someone simply because they were wanting to help. Why should kindness make her feel shy? It doesn't with Anna and nobody could be kinder than she. Then she thought that it probably (and drearily) had something to do with sex: no man had been more than indifferently kind to her for a very long time. And, anyway, it wasn't exactly kindness – attentive was more what he was being.

'It looks as though you're preparing me for a siege,' she said later, as the kitchen slowly filled with carrier-bags and cardboard boxes.

'Well, it seems sensible to stock up. I shan't be able to get down for a few weeks. I was thinking that it might be a good idea for you to get a deep freeze.'

Mr Kent straightened up from dumping a case of wine on the floor.

'Where would you like me to put the garden chairs?'

'I should think straight into the garden. The cushions come off, but I shouldn't think we need do that today. I thought you'd want somewhere to sit outside. I got a small table as well in case you want to work out there. Or eat things.'

'*He* turned up pretty smartly, didn't he?' she added, when he had gone to fetch chairs.

'He says he's been coming in every morning to water seeds.'

'And arrange the flowers.'

'Oh, *Anna*! He means well. And if I do stay here I shall need someone to fetch and carry things for a bit.'

'That's perfectly true. Just don't let him mean well too much.'

He returned to say that everything was now out of the car, and that he would be back in the early evening to put the seed trays back in the shed. 'I'm hardening them off, but there can always be a frost until the end of this month.' He smiled at her and turned to go.

'Thanks for all your help,' Anna called.

'It was a pleasure.'

By mutual unspoken consent, they did not mention Mr Kent for the rest of that day. The sun became deliciously warm; they had lunch in the garden with the new chairs and table. There was even some shade; an oak tree from the wood overhung a corner of the lawn. Anna described the town.

'It's nice. A small market town, but with most of the shops you'll need. There's no fishmonger, but apparently a van comes once a week to the market and has a stall on Fridays. There's a butcher and grocer, and an acceptable small supermarket run by an Asian family with an incredible range of stuff. One rather haughty little delicatessen – the kind that explains sun-dried tomatoes to you – and even a cobbler. A lovely sweetshop with huge jars in the window and a greengrocer with pots of herbs outside. No bookshop, of course. And I don't think you'll get papers delivered.'

'I shan't mind that at all. I can have the *Literary Review* and the *Spectator* sent by post.'

'Yes. And you never really *read* newspapers, do you? There's a bank – two, actually, and a post office and what looks like a promising junk shop. And, of course, there are pubs. I didn't count them, but three or four, and one off-licence where I got the wine. There's a square in the middle where they have the market. Just a pity it's ten miles away, really. The village has nothing but one shop and a pub. Poor old people. What a time they must have – having to find buses to collect their pensions and get meat and things.'

'You have cased the joint.'

'I enjoy it. I love going to new places and having a good look round.'

After lunch, Anna read a manuscript and Daisy slept. After tea, they went for a walk – up the lane to the bridge over the canal. From the bridge the canal stretched north, straight for the half-mile to the village. She remembered driving back that first weekend, and Mr Kent kissing his hand to her. She walked to the other side to look south. But here the canal curved rather sharply with a steep wooded bank on one side, which more or less concealed the towpath on the other. His boat must be on that side since there was nothing to be seen on the straight stretch. Anna suggested that they walk beside the canal, but she said she was tired and they retraced their steps. She was reluctant to encounter him in his boat with Anna or, indeed, to talk about him with her.

The subject did come up on Sunday morning, after Anna had rung to find out about trains.

'I'm sure Mr Kent would take you to the station.'

Anna agreed to this. 'But we ought to find out about local taxis. You might need one.'

'I expect Mr Kent will know. I hope he does come about his seeds or we won't be able to ask him to take you.'

But he had thought of that. He turned up in the morning and asked when Miss Blackstone would want to be taken to the train.

'I'm going to ring up every day to see how you are getting on,' Anna said, as she left. 'And I'll go to the London Library with your list to be sent.' And as she kissed Daisy, she said quietly, 'And don't be proud. Come back if you get too lonely.'

While she was being taken to the station, Daisy wrote her a letter saying all of her grateful acknowledgements of the layers of Anna's affection and friendship. Kindness always made her want to weep.

For the rest of that month – for over three weeks – she settled with increasing enjoyment to her country life. May was providing a beautiful end to the spring; she was astonished by how much she had forgotten, how much she remembered and how much she had never known of the country at that time of the year. The different ways in which trees became green; the suddenness of blossom; cherry, may, lilac, chestnut, bluebells in the wood, celandine everywhere. A peaceful, pleasant rhythm developed. She would wake early to the dawn chorus and sleep again in the ensuing silence, then wake again from the sun streaming through her small casement window. She would make tea in her room and drink it in bed while she read Gérin on the Brontës. Then she would bathe and dress and make coffee and toast. At ten the postman would appear; at eleven Henry. He had become Henry the day after Anna had gone when he had arrived earlier than usual in the morning with the car keys. 'I didn't like to bother you late in the evening with them.' And she had said, 'How thoughtful, thank you, Mr Kent.'

'Oh, please call me Henry. Mr Kent sounds as though you disapprove of me. But perhaps you do.'

'No. Why should I?'

'Well – I was afraid that my last letter to you may have . . . *annoyed* you in some way. Or perhaps you never got it?'

'I did. But not until I came back to England. It was forwarded on to me from the hospital.'

'I see.'

'Why should you think it annoyed me?'

'I thought, as you never answered it – but then you didn't get it. But it has not been mentioned between us, so I couldn't help wondering . . .'

'Oh. I felt so sorry for you about your Charley. Poor girl!'

There was a silence. Then he said, 'You cannot imagine what a relief it was even to write about it to you. My last wife was so jealous that even the mention of Charley's name sent her into a furious sulk. It was only possible to co-exist with her in artificial silence. Not my line at all. You need more wood.'

After that, he became Henry.

Later that week it was decided that they needed more plants for the garden, and he drove her to, not the nearest, he said, but the best nursery garden. He drove rather slowly and with a concentrated attention that precluded talk. It was a hot day and she had asked him to put the roof down. It was wonderfully peaceful simply to watch the country at this stately pace, time to see white cascades of flowering may, the buttercups, the hay meadows, the lilac and tulips in gardens, fields full of large lambs all bathed in soft golden sunlight that she could feel warm on her bare arm. At some point during that drive she experienced the almost forgotten sense of pure happiness – a weightless, contented warmth that permeated her entire being so that there was no room for anything else at all . . .

The nursery was nearly empty of customers. A weekday morning, Henry said, was always the best time. Except for one visit years ago with Jason to buy houseplants from a London nursery, she had never been to one. At first she was disappointed. She had been expecting masses of plants flowering away rather than the rows and beds of plastic pots showing anything from a few sprigs of green to almost nothing visible at all. The trees looked more interesting, and the shrubs certainly had more to show, which made her want them.

'What are we looking for?'

'It depends what you like. Tell me what you like, and we'll find it.'

'A blue flowering tree or shrub.' She couldn't think of what they could possibly be – it was rather a test to see how much he knew.

'*Ceratostigma willmottianum*,' he said instantly. 'A wonderful blue shrub that flowers late summer well into the autumn.'

'And a tree?'

'Well, ceanothus is about the only one, but there are two good varieties, Gloire de Versailles and Trewithen Blue. They might have one of them.'

They found the ceratostigma, but the varieties of ceanothus were not to be had. He fetched a trolley and deflected her to herbaceous plants. She chose phlox in several colours, some white lupins, a white Japanese anemone, some asters – or Michaelmas daisies, as she called them. She began to want everything she saw; his suggestion that they get some thyme and camomile to put between the cracks of the new stone path led to a dozen plants; pratia, dianthus, rock roses, besides the several kinds of thyme. Herbs, she said, she must have herbs for cooking, so mint, dill, sage, parsley, basil and tarragon were bought. But he pinched a leaf of the tarragon and said it was not the French variety and would be no good to her. 'It looks the same,' she said.

'I'll grow you the proper sort from seed.'

'Roses. We haven't bought a single rose.'

'I got you six when you were in America. You'll see.'

But she had found a small standard, covered with pale green buds.

'It's only ten pounds. Do let's get it.'

'It is your garden,' he answered, in tones of such amused benevolence that she turned to look at him. 'I can't help smiling,' he said. 'It is like taking a very nice child to a toyshop.

'I know you are not a child,' he said, before she could, 'and I love your excitement about the garden, I really do. We'll make it the best garden in the county. Of course it's exciting. You can have no idea how exciting it is for *me* to have the prospect of making a good garden again – especially for someone as appreciative as yourself. Miss Langrish,' he added, as an afterthought.

She felt that this was a covert invitation to her to invite him to use her Christian name and sensed a shadow – the faintest warning signal. If she was not on her guard he would somehow worm his way (why had she put it like that?) into an intimacy with her that she most certainly did not want.

She said that they had bought quite enough and that she wished to pay for the plants. 'You can load up the car while I'm doing that.'

On the way home she played a tape of a Haydn quartet to preclude any conversation.

When they got back, he came round, opened the car door for her and handed her her stick. 'I'm sure you've had enough for the day. Would it be satisfactory if I unload the plants, put them on the beds where I think they will look best, and then you can walk round tomorrow and see whether you agree about where I've put them? I'll give them a good watering, so they'll be perfectly all right.'

'Yes, that will do nicely.'

She did feel tired, and her leg and her back ached.

'I don't know,' he said; he seemed subdued. 'I don't want to interfere, but would it be a good thing if I made some tea and you put your feet up?'

She was about to say no, she could do it for herself, but then she thought that he must have a mug as well, in which case it would be easier if he made it and took his into the garden. So she thanked him and went to lie on the sofa under the open window with a book, which would show that she did not want company.

He was good. He made the tea and brought it to her, drawing the low table within her reach.

'I hope you've made yourself a mug to drink while you are dealing with the plants.'

'Thank you. I will.' She looked up and he was still standing there, looking down at her with an expression of such gentle anxiety that she felt touched.

'I'm all right,' she said.

'I am so very sorry to have upset you.'

'You haven't upset me.'

'It won't happen again. I'll let you know when I've finished with the plants in case there is anything you want before I go.'

She fell asleep on the sofa, and when she woke it was dark dusk. She was not cold: a blanket had been carefully laid over her and tucked in over her bare feet, and as she sat up and put on the lamp she saw the piece of paper.

You were sleeping so well that I could not disturb you. I do hope this was right. I must apologize for today. I know you thought me impertinent. The trouble is that I feel most awkward – well, *shy* with you, because I have told you so many intimate details of my life. I think of them sometimes when I am with you, and blush – inwardly, of course. I have noticed as I grow older that although my emotions remain as fresh and as deep as they have ever been, the outward signs of them fade. I no longer change colour, or tremble, but inwardly I'm shaking and red. I am in awe of you for two of the best reasons in the world: your appearance and your work.

Henry

She read the note twice and was still unable to sort out the confusion of feeling that it induced. He was smitten by her (what a horrible way of putting it), he *was* being intrusive; he was an acutely sensitive man with a long track record of being made unhappy and bereft. He was extraordinarily good at expressing himself on paper, although his conversation was unremarkable. The short note was charged with feeling. He was getting old; he was clearly an incurable romantic. There seemed to have been little or nothing going for him (beyond the acrimonious ending of an unsatisfactory marriage) before she came into his life – well, coming into his life was putting it far too strongly: he had turned up just when she needed some help, and because she had been unexpectedly away for so long, communication had perforce been by letter. He was not your run-of-the-mill idea of an odd job man; he was not a run-of-the-mill man at *all*, come to that. She read the last sentence again, 'I am in awe of you for two of the best reasons in the world: your appearance and your work', and could not resist the small frisson of vanity that recurred. It was a long time since anyone had referred to her appearance; indeed, she had ceased to expect anything of the kind, and to have her work mentioned in the same breath was certainly a boost for self-esteem. To be seen in these good lights made a change from her private nervous and usually deprecatory estimation – she was slipping into old age; she was nothing like the writer she had hoped and dreamed she might be . . .

Goodness – how ridiculous this was! It was just as well there was nobody to witness these girlish ruminations – certainly unbecoming in a woman of over sixty. But what was it he had said? 'I have noticed as I have grown older that although my emotions remain as fresh and as deep as they have ever been, the outward signs of them fade.' How true she was finding that was! She could be quietly getting on with or through her life and then the simplest remark could hurtle her back to echoes of the confusion and excitement of being young.

Well, she would be calm about it. It was a small thing;

an oldish man who was palpably lonely attempting to draw her towards him. Perfectly reasonable on his part, and even more reasonable that she should quietly discourage him. If they talked at all, it should be about the garden and books, and if he pushed further, he should go.

When she got off the sofa, she saw that her shoes were neatly arranged at the end of it. The stick lay beside them. He must have put them there, she thought, as she went to the kitchen for something to eat. She felt faintly irritated: echoes of Jess saying, 'You want to be waited on hand and foot,' triggered it. She did not the least want to be beholden to Henry Kent. She made herself a large mug of hot chocolate and took it to bed where she rang Anna and they had a long cosy chat about the Brontës. After she had been enthusing about Gérin's *Anne Brontë*, Anna said, 'Don't you think you're reading the wrong way round?'

'How do you mean? Anne died first.'

'I mean Gaskell and Shorter before you read Gérin?'

'Oh. Yes, it might be better. The snag to that is that the London Library didn't send Gaskell – said it was out. Do you think that means that someone else is doing them?'

'Not necessarily. The other books would probably have been out as well if they were. Anyway, it's unlikely that anyone is wanting to write a play. I'll see if I can find a copy somewhere. Everything else all right with you?'

'Fine. We went to a nursery garden this afternoon. I bought an enormous amount. It was fun.'

'Is Mr Kent proving a good chauffeur? Et cetera?'

'Oh, Anna! There you go – sniping at him. He's quite harmless. And most considerate. I certainly couldn't stay here without him anyway.'

'You know, if you do decide to stay there, you'll probably make friends with the natives.'

'I don't think I—'

'Well, at least one chum or two. Somebody who likes gardening and that you can talk about books with.'

'I'll look out for them.'

'One more thing. Don't count on it at *all*, but there has been a faint flicker of interest in your Orpheus play. I'll keep you posted.'

'Who from?'

'Wait until it's a smouldering interest. Sleep well.' Anna rang off.

As she fell asleep – or just before it, the thought occurred that Henry was somebody who liked gardening and who wanted to talk about books. But somehow she knew that Anna would not consider him to be a suitable chum. Could Anna be a snob? And would *she*, in fact, think of Henry in the way she had been thinking of him, if she did not share this prejudice? Class, like equal opportunities for women, was something it was generally pretended was on the wane, if not actually dissolved. For countless years the innumerable exceptions had been proving the rule. One should take each person as one finds them, she thought – very sleepy now – and that is what I am going to do with Henry Kent.

In the morning, another brilliant day, she thanked him for putting the blanket over her, and for bringing her tea. 'And for the note,' she added, 'which you need not have written. But thanks all the same.'

This was while they were walking round the garden and he was explaining the position of the plants in order that she should agree to him planting them. She noticed that he took his tone from her; was merely practical and made no attempt to talk of anything other than gardening.

She had decided to spend the rest of the day looking through the Orpheus play. Her scripts had all been arranged neatly on the bottom shelf of the long bookcase: they had been laid out on their sides because the shelf was not high enough for them to be upright. Beside them, lying wedged between a box of typing paper and a box containing cartridges of ribbons and correcting tape, was a rather dirty white envelope tied with white tape. She had not remembered packing it – knew that it contained letters – and as she pulled it out saw that her red leather diary had been laid beneath it. When she picked that up, she saw that the frayed strap that had held the lock snap had finally broken. Henry Kent had unpacked these things: she had asked him to, but she had entirely forgotten that she had packed the diary and the envelope. Now she examined them carefully, to see whether either had been tampered with. The envelope seemed intact: the tape, which had faded at the point where the knot had been tied round it, was still tied in exactly the same way. But the diary – the strap was broken, and she could not remember when this had happened. It could easily have occurred when she wedged it into the packing case. She picked it up, and as she opened it the thin piece of airmail paper slipped out. It fell from pages that were the same date as the letter: she remembered putting it there because it had seemed too awful to her to be put with anything else. Even now, the sight of his writing caused pain. She put the letter back in the diary, and carried it with the envelope upstairs where she put it in a drawer under some clothes. Doing this she knew was because she did not want Henry – or anyone else, come to that – reading the contents. She tried to dismiss the uneasy feeling that he might already have done so, but although this seemed unlikely the unease persisted.

He disappeared at lunch-time, so she ate bread and cheese in the garden and read her play.

When he returned in the early evening to water – he had been putting out small plants he had grown from seed – she decided to test him. The sun had gone, it had become very grey and still, and the air was sticky and warm and crowded with minute flies. She made tea and called him (it was now established that he got a cup of coffee in the mornings and tea if he was there later in the day). He came in, she noticed, by the back or kitchen door. He looked very hot.

'I wonder whether you would mind if I washed my face in the sink?'

'Of course not.'

When she had fetched him a towel, she said, 'By the way, when you were unpacking the tea chests, did you by any chance come across a leather diary?'

He had been laving his face under the running tap and now enveloped his head in the towel before replying.

'Diary? No. What sort of diary?'

'Red leather – rather battered. It may have been inside a large envelope full of papers.'

He said at once, 'Oh, well, if it was in an envelope, I wouldn't have seen it, would I? I was particularly careful to see that the chests were empty before I took them out to chop up for kindling. Of course, there was such a mass of papers – scripts and stationery and such – that I might not have noticed a diary when I was putting it all away. If it wasn't in the envelope, I mean. I put all those sort of things on the bottom shelf because it was the only one wide enough to take them flat. Do you want me to have a look for it?'

'No. If it's there, I'll find it.'

After a pause, she said, 'I need to go shopping to-morrow.'

'Right. What time would you like to go?'

'Oh, I should think about ten.'

He had finished drying his face, and now picked up his mug of tea off the table. He began to drink standing. There was a faint but unmistakable feeling of tension. It was almost, she thought, as though she had accused him of losing a diary of which he knew nothing. Usually he sat at the table and asked her if she would mind his having a cigarette.

'I'm sorry if you feel I've lost your diary or papers or whatever,' he said. 'I do assure you that I took the utmost care of all your things.' It was uncanny – the way in which he seemed to know what she was thinking.

'Of course you didn't lose it. It'll turn up. I may even have left it in London. Please don't think I was accusing you or anything like that.'

He smiled then, and took out his packet of Silk Cut and offered it to her.

She refused; she had a headache.

'It's the weather,' he said, looking at her with concern. 'There'll be a thunderstorm tonight and that should clear the air.' A moment later he said, 'You're not afraid of thunder, are you?'

'No.'

'Because if there *is* a storm, I could keep you company till it was over. You could tell me about Chekhov. I would really like to know why you think he is the second greatest playwright in the world. Not because I disagree, I just don't know about playwrights as you must do.'

'Not this evening. I think I'm going to bed early. But you can borrow the plays if you like. They are in three volumes.'

'Thank you.' He finished his tea, rinsed the mug under the tap.

'May I go and get the book?'

'Do.'

'I'll put it in a carrier-bag in case it starts to rain before I get home. Good night. I do hope your headache will go. And thank you for this.' And then he made the same gesture with his fingers to his lips that he had made on the bridge on the evening when she had been driving to London.

He was gone. She heard the garden-gate latch click, then silence.

She went to the front door, which she had propped open to get more air into the cottage. The sky was leaden, there was not a breath of breeze and the birds were silent. It was a relief to be alone. She looked at the garden, so neat and promising now, the lawn mown, the hedge each side of the garden gate freshly trimmed. In the sunniest corner against the cottage, he had made her a herb bed, the mint planted in a large pot stood beside it – he had told her that otherwise it would invade everything. He was a good gardener, an interesting and unfortunate man, but she did not want his misfortunes to prevail in her life. It was, undoubtedly, a piece of luck that somebody so knowledgeable and reliable had turned up; in fact, his presence made it possible for her to live in the cottage in her present state. It was odd how quickly he had divined that she thought he might have done something with her

diary but, then, people of that sort were always touchy
or sensitive about whether those employing them considered them honest. She remembered, years ago, an
extremely nice, hard-working Portuguese woman, who
had cleaned her flat and done her ironing – and indeed
anything else she was asked. When one day Daisy had
exclaimed that she could not find her cheque book and
wondered aloud where on earth it could have got to, the
woman had given her one look, taken off her apron, put
on her coat and hat and left. Two days later she had
received a stiff little note saying that the woman was
unaccustomed to being accused of thieving, and would
therefore not be returning for work. Daisy had gone to
her flat with the money owed, had apologized, explaining
that it had not occurred to her that Maria would take her
cheque book (what use could it be to her?) but that had
proved to make matters worse. So she might take *other*
things. Folded arms, a refusal to take the notes owed and
offered.

Yes, no doubt Henry had a bit of that attitude in him,
and if he was smarting from being dispossessed of his
home – and, she supposed, his local friends – not to speak
of the sense of bitterness and failure that an acrimonious
separation or divorce so often induced, then he was all
the more vulnerable. Well, she was vulnerable in some
ways (although, of course, only until her leg was entirely
healed) and he in others. She made herself an omelette
and a green salad, and opened a bottle of Mâcon, before
she remembered that, with a headache already, drinking
any of it might start a migraine.

The air was so oppressively hot that she had a tepid
bath before going to bed. When she opened her windows
wider for the night, she saw a split-second streak of light-

ning racketing across the sky and counted. The thunder was far away, but the storm had begun. The beginnings of a thunderstorm always reminded her of *Rigoletto* and when she turned on her radio there was the quartet from the last act in full voice. This coincidence was curiously comforting. By the time it was finished the storm was well under way – with lightning that briefly illuminated her room and louder and far more immediate rumblings from the crashing clouds. She fell asleep as the audible, heavy rain began.

She woke early. The rain had stopped, but the sky was not clear: it was as though there was a pause before more thundery weather. The air smelt fresher, but it was still oppressive. She put on a sleeveless denim dress and sandals, and went downstairs and into the garden. The stone of the path glistened and the little plants that had been put between the cracks all looked wonderfully revived by the rain. She went out of the gate. She would walk up the lane as far as the canal bridge, something she had meant to do for several days. They had told her that she must walk every day, and she resolved now to do this before breakfast every morning and then again if she felt like it later. But as the bridge came in sight, the rain began again – unspectacular steady stuff that did not feel like a shower at all, more like the beginning of a downpour. So she turned back, and as she neared the cottage, heard her telephone ringing: an unusual hour for anyone to be calling her – unless it was some calamity.

She opened the gate and began to run up the path, but halfway there, she slipped on the stone and fell, heavily, awkwardly, striking the side of her head as she hit the path. A misty, random thought, Why do I keep falling? and then she could remember nothing. Nothing until someone had taken her in his arms and in a voice full of tender anguish was saying, 'My darling – my dear love, my darling Daisy. What have you done to yourself?'

7

HENRY

It *was* more than a week before she came: a nerve-racking ten days, days when I no longer dared to use the cottage as I had become accustomed to doing. It was certainly out of the question to sleep there, but it was also mildly dangerous to have a bath or cook in the kitchen. I did manage a couple of the former, very late at night when I was careful to use every scrap of the hot water so that there would be no evidence of it having been on if she came the next morning. I would boil a kettle to make tea or coffee, and after a week I began eating up the more perishable supplies that Katya had bought. After all, even if Daisy found out that they had existed, I could truthfully say that Katya had told me to use them before they went bad. But they were uneasy days. I picked primroses in the mornings and set them upon the kitchen table. I went up to her bedroom and cleaned it, and then I made her bed. One morning was spent making tea for the telephone engineer who set up the telephone upstairs for her. I spent afternoons potting up the seeds I had grown, most of which were doing very nicely.

I retied the tape round the envelope containing the letters: it was surprisingly difficult to get the knot into exactly the same position on the tape as it had originally been, but in the end I managed it. I looked carefully at the diary. I had replaced the letter from Jason between the pages where I had found it, but looking closely at the broken leather strap could see the pale leather beneath the red exterior. I solved this by moistening my finger, dipping it in wood-ash from the fireplace and rubbing the pale bits gently until they looked dirty and as though the break had occurred some time ago. Then I wedged the diary beneath the envelope on the bottom bookshelf. I waited faithfully in the cottage for the hour every morning when Katya had said she would call, but she did not.

And then, on a Friday morning, when I had finished with the plants I went into the kitchen to eat my lunch and generally make sure that I had left no signs of occupancy, when I heard a car in the lane. I seized my sandwiches and was out of the back door in a flash without even giving myself time to lock it. I ran behind the garage just in time to see a car disappearing on the road towards the village. It had not been Daisy's car, but it had given me a fright. As I went back to the cottage, to look once more round the kitchen before leaving it and locking up, I wondered *why* it had given me such a fright. Cars went up and down the lane fairly regularly – not often, but several times a day – and I had never bothered about any of them until now. Then I knew, somehow, that her arrival was imminent. I had missed having a cup of tea, and the thought of the boat depressed me – boats get more and more uninviting the less time you spend in them – so I decided to walk to the village pub, have a few drinks and see if the landlord would knock me up something hot: she did lunches at weekends so she would presumably have already cooked something.

240

I didn't spend long at the pub; it was empty when I got there, but the landlady didn't seem particularly pleased to see me. 'Quite a stranger,' she had remarked, without smiling. I explained that I had been working. What had actually been happening was that I had taken to buying my drink and lugging it back to the boat in my rucksack for the simple reason that I preferred drinking alone, and got more value for money that way. Pub shorts were useless to me since I could not afford enough of them. I asked for a barley wine and a cigar, but when I mentioned food she said she didn't have anything but packets of crisps and peanuts. Then two more customers arrived who she was clearly far more pleased to see, so I drank the barley wine and kept the cigar for when I got back to the boat. I knew the two men who had come in by sight, but had no desire to know more than that. I have to admit that my own sex bores me, and their presence precluded my coaxing any real food out of Mrs Wilks. I am not prepared to risk losing out with a woman in front of any man.

But, as I trudged back in no very good frame of mind and got to the cottage, there was the car – her car. It was parked in front of but outside the garage. I walked quickly past, as close to the garden hedge as possible. I did not want to be seen as I was pretty sure she was not alone. Katya would have driven her, I supposed – or possibly (a worse thought) Miss Blackstone. But never mind who she had come with, the point was that the long vigil was over; she was here, and soon whoever it was would go away and I would have her to myself. Life with her was about to begin.

Once I was back at the boat I poured myself a large vodka and lit the cigar. I was no longer in the least hungry, but I wanted to celebrate. Also, now that she was safely back, I had immediately to consider the best course to take with her. Her wariness, her slight wildness (which I found erotic) had none the less to be treated with the utmost sensitivity and care: get things wrong and I could wreck everything. Perversely, I almost wished she had been away longer so that our intimacy could have increased in the comparative safety of letters. Contrary to what most people say, it is possible to undo the written word with more of them. They think the spoken word easier to erase, whereas in reality it is made indelible by the speaker's tone of voice, movement and expression – all capable of a powerful imprint. In writing it was possible to say that one had not *meant* quite what had been written, and to compose some alternative sense that was usually accepted.

I gave myself a second drink and fell upon my bunk just as it began to rain.

I slept until six. The rain had stopped. I was ravenously hungry and ate my lunch-time sandwich with a cup of Nescafé. In the morning, I decided, I would turn up at the usual time and discover that she had arrived. Meanwhile, there were a good many hours to fill. When it was dusk I would go up to the cottage by way of the wood, to see if I could discern whom she had brought with her, possibly catch a glimpse of her – even if she was simply a dark shadow moving about the lit rooms.

This idea proved to be hopelessly frustrating. I could see smoke rising from the chimney and hear music playing – piano mostly – but the hedge was too high and thick to allow a view of the ground-floor windows and I dared not stand at the gate to look in, as the last thing

I wanted was to be caught hanging about by either Katya or Miss Blackstone. If she had been alone . . . but she wasn't. If I wanted to see without being seen, I would have to wait until it was dark.

So I went back to the boat again, finished the vodka (it was only a half-bottle, after all), reread her letters and the notes and pieces of copying I had from her diary until it was dark enough. There was a half-moon, but it was a cloudy night, so that the moonlight was fitful. I worked my way through the wood until I was at its edge, looking on to the garden. Now I could see that the windows upstairs were illuminated. An owl had hooted a few minutes before I reached this point, and just as I was considering imitating him to draw her to the window, there she was opening it and leaning out. She wore a white nightdress, long-sleeved and ruffled at the neck, and her lovely hair was silhouetted against the warm light behind her. The owl hooted again just as the moon came out and I moved further back into the wood, but another cloud came and it was comfortably dark. I watched her until she drew her curtain and retired and almost at once put out her light.

The next morning was set fair – not a cloud in the sky and the sun devouring mist from the canal. I drank some Nescafé, ate a banana and set out. It was ten, earlier than I usually went to the cottage, but I could not bear to wait any longer.

When I reached the cottage, the car had gone: I might have thought that they would go shopping, but it seemed like an awful anticlimax. Then it occurred to me that naturally I would assume that if a car was not there they had not yet arrived, in which case I would follow my usual practice of going into the cottage to see that all was well before I repaired to the shed with the plants.

As soon as I opened the door I was assailed by the delicious scent of rose geranium wafting down the stairs from the open bathroom door. Then I heard her call out.

I did not reply. I wanted her to come out of the bathroom, which I knew she would do if she was met with silence. I stood at the bottom of the stairs – could hear my own heart pounding.

Then, suddenly, there she was, wrapped in a white bath towel, her shoulders bare, her legs bare from below the knees. Her skin, against the whiteness of the towel, was like warm ivory. I could see that she was frightened, and hastened to apologize – to say all the right things that would reassure. I had not realized she was back, came in each day to check that things were all right, more apologies and talk of seeing to the seeds. But when she said she would come down, I ventured to say how much I wanted to show her the garden – safe ground, the garden. She agreed to this.

When she appeared, wearing jeans, a dark red flannel shirt and moccasins, I hastened to approach and shake hands. This gave me the chance to look at her at close quarters for fractionally longer. She had left her stick upstairs, and I went to get it. Her bed was not made, and the nightdress lay across it. It was an antique – the kind that can be found in junk shops. I picked it up to inhale the intoxicating scents of fresh laundry that had enclosed warm flesh, and laid it back carefully before grabbing the stick and rejoining her.

During our short tour of the garden, I learned that Miss Blackstone was leaving on Sunday evening.

Flirting with someone you do not know very well,

or – perhaps I should say in this case – cannot *seem* to know well, is a most delicate procedure. Naturally it depends upon the woman you are trying to court. But however tentative or small the advances may be, they have to be made or there will be no progress. Ideally, they have to be on the edge of presumption and retreat has always to be possible. I tried a little of this when she told me that Miss Blackstone was leaving the next day, when suddenly a most apposite line popped into my head. Before she could respond – sometimes one has a stroke of luck – there were sounds of Miss Blackstone's return and I could escape to help her with the shopping.

There was certainly enough of that. The very large boot of the car was crammed: quantities of carrier-bags, boxes and even furniture. She must have spent hundreds of pounds, because there were several boxes of drink – mostly wine by the look of it, but it emerged that she had bought one bottle each of whisky, vodka and gin. And Miss Blackstone was suggesting a deep freeze. There was never any hesitation about whether any of these things could be afforded; and after a pang of straightforward envy (in order to smoke and drink, I had to live on a pretty rugged diet where food was concerned), I felt considerably comforted. Where money is concerned, a sheep is infinitely preferable to a lamb.

When everything was cleared out of the car I offered to help put things away, but I could see that Miss Blackstone didn't want me hanging about. So I went off to put the seed trays and small plants back into the shed. She said nothing, but Miss Blackstone thanked me. She does not like me, I can sense this, and there is very little

I can do about it except play the humble, faithful retainer with as much subtlety as I can command.

During the drive to the station on the following evening, in spite of my efforts to keep the conversation general and innocuous, she asked me leading questions – six I think. She asked if I was married, and I told her about my separation from Hazel and stalemate about the divorce. She asked what I had been doing before I started working for Miss Langrish, and I said that I had been looking for that sort of work. Later she asked me what I had been doing when I was married. I knew that this was a dangerous question because, in fact, after my marriage I did not do very much (Hazel had inherited twenty-five thousand pounds from her mother and nothing would have induced her to give up her physiotherapist's job, so I had plenty of time on my hands). Given the choice of working or not working, I would opt for the latter, and for about eighteen months I was able to do that. I had explained to Hazel that I had invested the money for her and paid what I had told her was the interest quarterly into our bank account. But I had kept the capital stashed away in a separate account, and it had provided me with a few extras that helped to cushion me from the dreary discovery that, in Hazel, I had definitely picked the wrong woman. Of course, I am perfectly aware that such things are 'not done', but I suspect that this is chiefly for lack of opportunity. Such a lump sum had never come my way. Of course, during that time, I did occasionally get the odd job – small ones, like equipping a conservatory with suitable plants, stocking a garden pond with marginals, water plants and fish – but most of the time I read and, from time to time, went to town and picked myself a trouble-free good time. I told Hazel I was going for a job and usually turned up three days later not having got it.

So – I told Miss Blackstone that I had been writing a book about gardens.

'How interesting! How far have you got?'

Sensing what she would say next, I said that I *had* almost finished it, but that made no difference now as my wife, in a fit of anger after my departure, had destroyed it: '"Put it out with the other rubbish," she said.'

There was a silence after this. Then, when we reached the station, she said, 'I'm sorry about your book. It must have been most distressing for you.'

Her voice sounded different, and far warmer.

Driving back, I felt a sense of exaltation – a heady blend of power and excitement. She was mine now: there was nobody between us; it was simply a question of gaining her confidence and interest. Simple! Far easier thought than done, I was to discover in the ensuing weeks during which I made progress, but so slowly as to be unobservable except in retrospect. If I looked back to her arrival and the first morning, I could see that I had got no further: she now called me by my name, but even that small advance had been resisted at first, and I was not invited to reciprocate. She *had* received my last letter and it had had the desired effect. My description of Charley and her death had touched her, as indeed it had touched me when I wrote of it. But, still, I detected that she was on her guard: any too sudden move would cut the little ground I had gained from under my feet. I concentrated upon being the good, reliable servant.

I arrived every morning punctually at eleven o'clock, by which time she was bathed and dressed for the day and working with her books and papers at the garden table. At the end of the first week I suggested a visit to a nursery garden and she agreed at once. It was a beautiful day and I took her to the furthest nursery that I knew of in order to prolong the outing. I drove slowly for the same reason, but she seemed not to mind that at all. Indeed, I glanced at her – only once – during the drive and saw that she was leaning back in her seat watching the country ahead with a small smile curling her mouth.

She was thrilled by the nursery and wanted to buy everything she saw. I had only to suggest something for her to want all varieties of it. When she fell in love with a standard 'Little White Pet' and almost begged to get it, I could not help smiling; she was behaving like an excited child and before I could stop myself, I said so. But when I backtracked on this, I made matters worse. I called her Miss Langrish in a manner that invited her to grant me more intimacy. I saw her face close; her escape into herself, her formality with me crystallising into what I knew to be some fear. She played music all the way home, lay with her eyes closed, but this time my covert glances showed me the violet smudges beneath them. I had gone too far, and she was anyway tired from the excursion. I had noticed how easily she tired and knew that she was often in some pain, although it was never mentioned and I did not know how much. She said that she was tired and her back hurt, and I said that if she would lie down on the sofa, I would bring her some tea. I knew that I had upset her and was sorry for it and told her so. I brought her the tea and said I would put the plants out in the garden, then see if she wanted anything else before I went.

She was asleep. The sun had gone down, and the air from the window open above her was chill. I fetched a blanket from the spare-room bed upstairs to cover her, but first I shut the window. She lay with one hand clasping the back of her neck, the book she had been reading spine upwards on her breast. I removed it gently. The sofa was low, and I kneeled to arrange the blanket over and round her. She was deeply asleep and did not stir. Her long, slender feet were bare. There was something touching and vulnerable about their position askew on a cushion that made me want to kiss them, although I hesitated, for fear of waking her, but the desire to kiss her for the first time without her knowledge became overwhelming, and I put my mouth to each foot in turn before tucking the blanket round them. Still she did not show any sign of waking and when I was standing again I was able to gaze at her face, so pale and still and dreamless. For the first time I touched her wonderful hair, as soft and light to my touch as I had imagined. I wanted then passionately to leave some message – an apology to allay her fear, a declaration of some kind that might kindle her interest. I sat in the kitchen for minutes before I was able to write exactly what I wanted to say, and then I returned and tucked it into the edge of the blanket under her neck.

Back at the boat, I returned to thoughts about my preoccupation with her – what is it, I wonder, that drives one person to become obsessed by another? For I recognized that in my case this was what it had become. For weeks now, almost everything I had done, and much of what I had thought, had been about Daisy. That evening, for the first time, I considered what exactly it was that I wanted from her. I wanted her to love me, to be dependent upon me, to regard me as the most important person in her life. I knew that courting her, flattering, beguiling, pleasing her and, above all, *talking* to her were the ways into her heart – or any woman's heart, come to that. I also knew that all these seducements were much as the Emperor's new clothes – they were the imaginary cover for sensual satisfaction. If you can please a woman in bed – which happens less often than is commonly supposed – you have her, or at least you are three-quarters of the way there. She will invent the rest of you to suit her romantic excuses, and if you lapse, she will make allowances of the most ingenious and sensitive kind. My indifference to earning money would become merely the unfortunate result of my having a better intelligence than was usual in someone with my upbringing. I had laid the ground for her to be the pioneer so far as understanding me was concerned. My trials, the treatment I had received, the tragedies that had punctuated my life were enough for her to want to be the first person to treat me well. It was clear that she had enough money for both of us and I would never interfere with her work. We could travel together: I could still remember with the utmost clarity the heady experience of staying in hotels with Charley where everything was done for us without my even knowing the cost.

These were some of the thoughts that circled in my mind that evening, and I allowed them full rein because I knew that the next day they must be thrust utterly into the background. I would not succeed unless I focused entirely upon my being in love with Daisy, because to convince her I had to convince myself. You see what an honest creature I am, privy to many thoughts that most people pretend have never entered their heads. I have never thought that the world should be lost for love, rather gained, and there was no reason why she, Daisy, should not be the gainer. I wished her nothing but good and, given that premise, there seemed to be no reason why I should not enjoy the power that I might have over her.

That night I indulged myself in any fantasy that occurred to me or that I could summon, working my way through the well-worn film of my sexual triumphs over women hitherto ignorant of or impervious to their own sensuality. Daphne and Charley both appeared here, but mastery over either of them no longer excited me and I had to substitute. Not Daisy: I could not bring myself to do that; my fantasies of her were still of a more general kind (a touch of superstition, I suppose), but even the lightest touch of my imagination where Daisy was concerned had a potency I had never experienced before. I imagined her smiling at me, holding out her narrow hands with the long sensitive fingers; her lying in my arms to be comforted from some night terror, her saying my name with some endearment attached to it, her teasing me in her high, clear voice, her eyes, like stars when she acknowledged my love . . . I lay awake for hours with all of this, until I was so on edge from excitement and lack of sleep that I had to revert to my first encounter with Lily, and her breasts.

The next morning, full of determination to behave as though nothing had happened, as though I had not kissed her feet or written the note, I walked to the cottage, being careful to arrive at exactly the usual time.

She seemed distant. She thanked me for the blanket and, as an afterthought, for the note, and I sensed that she, too, was determined to behave as though nothing had happened – as though my note was no more than a formal apology. I left her before lunch-time, but came back in the late afternoon in order to finish the planting. It was devilishly hot – humid and still – and I was glad when she called me in for some tea.

Then she asked me about the diary. Luckily for me I was washing my face at the time and I could think – fast. Of course I knew where the diary was, but did not she know that I must know that? Or had she not discovered yet where on the shelf it was? Then she said that it might have been in a large envelope, and then I knew that she was afraid I might have read it – either the diary or the contents of the envelope or both. I think I was pretty convincingly ignorant, and when I offered to look for the diary, she said don't bother, she would find it. So then I knew that she already had. We talked about shopping, but things didn't feel quite right between us and an apology seemed in order. (I seemed to have to keep doing it, but as it worked I didn't mind.) It did work, since her voice sounded quite different and friendlier. She had a headache. I said I'd stay with her if there was a storm and suggested Chekhov as a topic of conversation, but she said she was going to bed early. I asked if I could borrow a book, and saw that the place where the diary had been was empty. I said good night to her, and went back to the boat. There was a storm and the hatch leaked on to my bunk and I had a rotten time trying to clear it up and there wasn't a drop left to drink.

Although the rain had stopped, it didn't look as though it would be for long, and there was no sun in which to dry my bedding. I put the tarpaulin over the hatch that had leaked and then, while I was boiling water for shaving, there was a real cloudburst – it came down like knives, as my father used to say. It was a good thing that she had said she wanted to go shopping, otherwise I would have had no excuse to go to the cottage until the weather cleared.

The rain did stop, as suddenly as it had begun. Bits of blue appeared as the clouds shifted to reveal the sun. I had to bail out the canoe before I could use it, and one way and another I was running behind my usual time for arriving at the cottage.

I saw her before I even reached the gate because it was open. She was lying on the path, one leg with the knee bent awkwardly under her and the other stretched straight. For one second, I thought she was dead. I knelt by her and felt for her heart. She was soaked, and under the heavy drenched dress her flesh was damp and very cold, but beneath her left breast I could feel her heartbeat. She was unconscious, but she was alive. Half of her face was hidden and when I lifted it I saw the stone rust-coloured with her blood. She had cut her head open beneath the hairline. Drops from her hair, which was black with rain, ran down her neck. Very cautiously, I eased her on to her back and straightened out the bent leg. It was badly grazed. She did not seem to have broken anything, but I could not be certain of this. I was about to put her in the recovery position, when she opened her eyes and looked at me with such fear – or, rather, terror – that I threw all caution to the wind, took her in my arms and poured out every comforting endearment that I knew. As I carried her into the cottage, she murmured something and I stopped to listen.

'Not hospital,' was what she had said, and now said again.

'Promise you.'

She shut her eyes then – I think she passed out.

8

HENRY

That was the real beginning of the most exciting, most absorbing, and – to me – extraordinary time of my life. It began, prosaically enough, with my efforts and success in summoning a doctor, semi-retired, who lived in the village. I knew that he was an occasional locum for the medical practice in the town, but that he also kept on a few of the old patients who had been in his care for years. He was the old-fashioned visiting sort, and he came at once to see Daisy.

I had laid her upon the sofa and covered her with the same blanket before I called the doctor, who said he would be along at once. 'Keep her warm, and don't move her,' he had said. When I went back to her her eyes were open, but she did not seem much aware of what was going on. Her dress, which was made of heavy denim, was going to make warmth impossible. Fortunately, it buttoned all the way down the front and I cut the armholes open (it was sleeveless) and eased it from under her. Under it she wore only a brassière and white cotton knickers. No time now to look at her pretty body; I wanted the doctor to see that I was a thoroughly practical person who would therefore be able to look after her. I fetched a spare bath towel, laid it over her and then replaced the blanket. I had boiled water and filled her hot-water bottle, which I

255

wrapped in a tea-towel and placed under her feet when I heard his car and went out of the cottage to meet him.

I explained that I found her fallen on the path, that she had cut her head but did not seem otherwise to have broken any bones.

He grunted, 'Is she alone here?'

'At the moment, yes. But of course I'm here as much as she wants me.'

'You a relation?'

'No. I'm her gardener and general handyman. She's very anxious not to go to hospital.'

'A sensible anxiety, these days.'

We had reached the door of the cottage. 'She's on the sofa. I'll be in her kitchen, if you want anything.'

'You might boil some water – put it in a pudding basin or something like that.'

When he came out to the kitchen to fetch the water, he asked whether there was a lavatory downstairs, and when I said that there was, he said she'd be better off on the sofa for the night anyway: 'Perhaps you would fetch some bedding for her and night things.'

He spent a long time with her after I had brought down the bedding. I went back into the kitchen and boiled the kettle again. When I had made myself a cup of Nescafé, I took a quick swig of vodka from her bottle in the cupboard followed by a scalding sip of coffee. I managed this just in time before he reappeared. He brought with him the basin now half full of sodden cotton wool in water that was pale red with her blood.

'I take it you're available to stay with her? Because if not, we must—'

'Oh, no. I'll stay with her as long as she needs me.'

He looked at me over his spectacles, and I seemed to

reassure him, as he then gave me businesslike instructions. She was still in shock; had been mildly concussed and should be kept very quiet. Even if *she* thought it was all right, she was to stay put except for going to the lavatory when I should accompany her. He then said that he'd cleaned up her abrasions and main wound in the head but that the latter required a couple of stitches and he hadn't brought the apparatus for that, so he'd be back in an hour or so.

I waited until I could no longer hear his car, then I went to her.

He had bandaged her head slantingly so that her hair sprang from each side of the narrow strip, giving her a piratical appearance. She was propped up by the sofa cushion and the two pillows I had brought from her room, and she was wearing the white ruffled nightdress.

'Too ridiculous,' she said. 'I seem to fall about like a drunkard.'

'It was just very bad luck,' I said.

'The telephone was ringing and I'd been out for a walk because they told me to walk every day, and it rang and rang and I ran and I must have slipped because of the rain. I thought I had fallen again from the awful pyramid when it was so hot and in all the crowds there wasn't anyone I knew and it was all because I'm so bad at heights. I can't look down because then I would fall from wherever I was, let alone half-way up a pyramid, and then I thought someone—' She stopped, and said rapidly, 'Just dreams – or nightmares. Sometimes you dream something awful and wake up and find it wasn't true – sometimes you dream something not awful and wake up. And that's not true either.' Without any warning, tears began pouring out of her eyes and she began to shake.

I wanted to take her in my arms, but instinct prevailed, and I did not. I knew she was badly shocked and I did not want her – when it wore off – to have any memory of my taking advantage of her. Instead, I drew up a chair, sat beside her and gently took one of her hands in both of my own. She did not resist this – indeed, I am not sure that she noticed; she simply continued the downpour of tears.

I don't know how long we stayed thus; it might have been five minutes, it might have been twenty. I had observed that when women cry for any length of time, it is not for one thing but, rather, a painful chain of deprivation and actual loss. It is as though some contemporary shock opens the door upon a store-cupboard where earlier griefs had been preserved. I know this because I have been present during a number of these explosions of pent-up unhappiness, which seem to be so much of women's lot. For myself, tears have never been part of my emotional makeup, and having had as little as possible to do with other men I imagine that they are – in that respect, perhaps, only – like myself. I can recall a boy at school blubbing because some member of his family had died and feeling for him nothing but a mild aversion and contempt.

No, tears are women's province, arising as they so often do from mistreatment by men. I knew enough about Daisy to understand that she had had much to weep for, the infamous behaviour of Jason Redfearn being the most recent. So I waited until the tracks down her face were no longer glistening with movement, and then I lifted the hand I had been holding to my lips and laid it back upon the blanket with a little pat, as though the kiss had been no more than a small gesture of sympathy. I would get her some tea, or any other drink she might prefer, and she nodded and said that she would like tea.

By the time the doctor returned she had fallen asleep. I had lit the fire because she complained of feeling cold. Her tears had further exhausted her and it was I who suggested that sleep might be a good idea. I drew the curtain above the sofa so that the light would not fall on her face. Then I went and sat in the kitchen. I realized that although Daisy's fall might be the means of my spending far more time with her, it might also mean that this marvellous opportunity would be scotched if she or the doctor thought she should have some woman looking after her. Even if it was not either Miss Blackstone or her daughter, it could still present a serious challenge and prevent the development of any real intimacy. Somehow this had to be avoided. Immediately I had to convince the doctor of my suitability, but in the long run it was Daisy who must feel that she could trust me as housekeeper-nurse.

So when the doctor had finished with Daisy and came into the kitchen with a small bottle of pills and instructions about when they were to be dispensed, I launched into the briefest possible account of my experiences with Helen – the Helen Burns who had died after I married her. Naturally I did not go into any detail at all, simply said that for this reason I was accustomed to looking after an invalid of the opposite sex and had decided that it was essential to stay overnight in the cottage in case Miss Langrish suffered any complications. I assumed that he would be looking in on her tomorrow? That was his intention. He went on to say that he gathered she had been in hospital for some time after an accident. She was going to feel rather ropy for the next few days – a lot of bruising

– and she'd have a pretty bad headache apart from the cuts and grazes.

He'd left her with something to help her sleep tonight, and I could give her two of these every four hours if she was in pain. No more than that. He was handing them over to me because, in her present state, he wasn't sure that she'd remember when she'd taken them. He'd stitched the wound in her head. Leave the dressing – he'd come and look at it tomorrow.

As he picked up his bag to leave, he added, 'I gather she has a daughter. Perhaps she should be informed.'

'Of course. I could do that for her as well.'

He looked at me over his spectacles for the second time and seemed to take in my steadfast open frankness.

'Lucky you were around.'

He was gone, at last. When I went back to her, she was half sitting up, propped by her pillows: the bruise from her head wound was beginning to show down the side of her face – a blackish purple.

'What was he talking to you about?'

'You, of course.'

'He wasn't trying to plan with you to get me into hospital?'

'Well, that came up, but I assured him that I'm quite capable of looking after you. I think I convinced him. I think the best thing would be simply to *assume* that I'm your carer and not mention hospital to him at all. Do you agree?'

'Oh, I *do*. It's the last thing I want.'

'Would you like something to eat?'

'I made some soup – a boiled egg! That's what I would like.'

'You shall have it.'

But when I brought it she ate only half of it, said her head ached and she wanted to lie down. I gave her two of the painkillers and she slept.

That first twenty-four hours was more or less like that. I heated soup for her, made toast, took her to the lavatory. Getting to her feet was extremely painful – she used her stick, and I was her crutch. I sensed her embarrassment at this particular dependence, but by explaining that because of her delicate disposition I had often had to nurse Charley, I allayed at least some of her discomfort.

'But you were married to Charley.'

'That's a minor difference. I loved her, that was the point.'

She was back on the sofa. I was looking down at her when I said this. There was a short silence while she stared up at me: then, very gently, I moved her ruffled collar so that it did not obscure any of her face. This seemed to be the moment. 'I love you. I would do anything for you. I love you, but there is no weight attached to it. I don't expect anything back.' Then, because I could see her expression change – her poised-for-flight look, as I was later to call it – I said, 'There is nothing to be afraid of. You need never be afraid of me. I simply want to look after you, get you well.' She turned her face away from me and I saw on the unbruised side of it a faint blush. Then, almost as though to herself, she said, 'You can't possibly *love* me. You don't know me – at all.'

I did not reply to this – told her I would be in the kitchen if she wanted me. I had used the moment and that was enough.

For a week, my declaration lay between us like a piece of no man's land. During it, I looked after her (the nursing contracted to that after the first day or two, when Dr

Blake ceased his daily visits). He had shown me how to change the dressing on her head; had shaved some of her beautiful hair round the stitched wound and the bruise faded from blue-black to grape colours, purple and then green. She became accustomed to me, and I, in turn, was punctilious about her privacy.

I would bring her a basin of hot water and her washing things, then tell her that I would be in the kitchen and come only if I was called. She had grazed and cut her right hand so badly that she was unable to use it at all that first week, and I also took off the plasters and swabbed and cleaned the wound; a good deal of dirt had got into it and it was slow to heal. I took care to talk of impersonal matters when I was ministering to her, whether it was brushing her hair or touching any part of her in my capacity as nurse. None the less, I was now so finely tuned to her reactions (and sometimes apparently contrary responses) that I could sense and sometimes even see her regarding me with a kind of tentative speculation. I knew then that she wanted me to reiterate my feelings for her in order that she could further dismiss them – could convince me and intrigue herself. She was both distrustful and enticed.

The first intimation that I was making progress occurred when Anna rang her to ask how she was getting on. I had been on a shopping expedition (we were now living largely on cold or ready prepared food from the supermarket), and as I went through the back door to the kitchen I could hear her on the telephone.

'. . . not serious at all. Henry got a very nice local doctor who patched me up in no time. No, honestly not, I'm just a bit stiff, that's all. I've been very well looked after. What? It was the path – you know, the one Henry made. There was a lot of rain and I slipped trying to run in because the telephone was ringing. It's sweet of you, but really I'd much rather wait a week or two until I'm completely mobile. Then we can go out and do things. Well, I haven't sent it because when I read it I could see things that need rewriting. No, only one copy here. Of course I will. I'll ring you in a day or two.'

She had heard me return and the tone of her voice had not changed – there had been no confidences that she would not have wanted me to hear. But I also gathered that she clearly did not *want* her friend to come to the cottage – now, at once, or even for some time. This was a very good sign. It must mean that she wanted to be alone with me to find out – what? What I felt for her? Certainly, but also something of what she felt for me. For she felt *something*, I was sure of that. Her gratitude for my support had graduated from formality to small jokes about the ritual that had evolved. For instance, on one occasion when I took her to the lavatory I had remarked how this everyday and normal practice got left out of fiction. 'And not simply left out,' she had said, 'but characters are frequently put into situations where it would be literally impossible.' After that, it got called 'doing something never done in books'.

'I don't think,' she had said, 'that it in the least matters people *not* writing about it happening. What they shouldn't do is not take it into account when their heroine is left alone in a cave for days unable to move, that sort of thing. They don't need to *dwell* on it, simply take it into account.'

One evening, after she had had her first shower and was going to spend her first night in her bedroom, she said, 'By the way, you'd better call me Daisy. If you'd actually been a nurse, you would have been calling me that on sight.'

I said nothing.

'Why are you smiling?'

'Was I?'

'Yes. You know you were.'

'Pure pleasure. Well, I think, Daisy, it's time you went to bed.'

She agreed. I noticed that she was still in a good deal of pain, and that movement was difficult for her. She also had intermittent headaches, although she claimed that they were getting better. She never complained, and always seemed surprised when I knew.

'I notice everything about you.'

'Why do you? Perhaps I mean how?'

'You know that. I told you days ago.'

'What?'

She was determined to get me to repeat myself. How fascinating the most innocent vanity can be!

We had reached her bedroom and I released her arm as she sat on the edge of the bed.

'Love,' I said. 'Love is *not* blind. It reveals everything, if you look. I *look* at you: it's all I have to do.'

She was sitting on the bed feeling for her hairbrush in the dressing-gown pocket. She began, clumsily, to brush her hair with her left hand, then stopped and said, without any expression at all, 'I've told you – you can't possibly love me. You don't know me.'

'Last time you said "at all". "You don't know me at all." So something has changed.'

Her silence seemed to acknowledge this. 'In any case, my knowing you does not make me dangerous.'

Before she could stop herself, she said, 'It *could*. It

might.' Then she frowned. 'I really don't want to talk about any of this at all. I'm very grateful to you for all your help. Good night.'

Of course I left her at once. We had reached an extremely tricky stage; she was – I knew – in some sort attracted to me. Tender attention had achieved much there; second to making a woman laugh it is the surest way to touch her. Daisy, I knew, from all I had read that she had written (and in particular, her diary), was starved of this and therefore, unconsciously perhaps, unable to resist it. On the other hand, her recovery had reached the stage when, at any minute, she might say that she no longer needed me to sleep in the cottage, and she might in other ways assert her independence, none of which would be good news for me. Somehow I had to get her to acknowledge that something was happening between us, some brink, at least. I went down to the kitchen, uncorked the half-bottle of wine left from supper and wrote her a letter.

I sat at the kitchen table for what turned out to have been nearly two hours composing it.

It was not to be long, nor in any way accusatory, but it was necessary to make clear to her that I understood certain things about her that in no way affected my feelings beyond engendering extreme patience. We had been talking about trust last night (for that was what it would be), or rather *she* had been talking about *dis*trust. She did not trust me and, while this was painful, it did not alter anything I felt for her. Rather, it enhanced my love. Distrust did not come out of the air, it was born of painful experience, which I sensed had been hers.

I knew what it was like to be betrayed – none better – but one thing that I had learned from my – certainly unsuccessful – life was that while any experience must affect me, no one of them should absolutely determine how I lived after it. If that were to be so, one's life would contract to the nutshell that Hamlet had been so airy about. Infinite space was nonsense in this context: one would never go out, one would never allow any new sensation, one would end up with the emotional structure of a moth ('I am no entomologist, so this may be an inaccurate analogy.').

In short, I was asking that she look at me with a fresh eye; that she consider the possibility – even likelihood – of my meaning what I had said to her. Most people have told lies in their lives, and I was no exception, but I would never lie to her, and I had never lied to anyone about love. I was not asking for anything more than that she should consider that I might be honest. Was that too much to ask? In any case, even if it was, it would not alter my desire to be of service to her (back to sonnet number 57). I signed it simply, 'Henry'.

The chief reason why I knew that it was worth risking this note was her repeated reaction to my telling her I loved her. On both occasions she had said that I could not because I did not know her. If she had not been in the least interested in me, she would not have bothered with that, would simply have replied that she did not feel the same – did not care for me. But I was also unsure whether she was aware of her interest and this note would make her have to consider that. Or *might* make her do so.

What is more exciting in life than this kind of pursuit – with the delicious frisson of attendant uncertainty (we have all failed from time to time)? I do not think it is true that people abstain from conquest for love or money, rather that they court for love and *then* money. If we know how to order our lives, most of us settle for comfort after romance, or in many cases after sex; romance utterly escapes many people. I folded the paper and put it on her breakfast tray.

It was nearly one o'clock by the time I got to bed and I fell asleep at once.

9

DAISY

She woke in the night – suddenly – from a dreamless stupor, she was intensely alert. 'Love,' he was saying, 'love is *not* blind. I *look* at you: it's all I have to do.' She was not only exactly recalling the intonation of his voice, she could see him; his eyes that would both darken and glow – which, she now remembered, had happened several times before when he spoke of what he felt, or rather how he felt for *her*. When he said anything revealing about his past, his eyes would simply darken – there was no glow at all; they became almost opaque. Love, then, still seemed important to him. She was touched by his candour and his courage. Here she stopped. Was she not *more* than touched, more than grateful? For over two weeks now he had tended her with a delicacy and kindness that was surely unusual in any man, only credible, indeed, if some kind of love was involved. Perhaps he did love her, actually *love* her. The possibility, the faintest chance, that this might be so, might actually be real . . .

Here she had to stop – the enormous simplicity of such an idea struck her like a freak wave, winding her, making her incapable of any thought until her breath came unsteadily back, and she was able to make attempts at consideration, only to be confronted by a rabble of conflicting notions. He was an incurable romantic; he was isolated and lonely, parched for intimacy, for companionship, probably for sexual excitement or comfort or both – in one sense there might be nothing personal to her about his obvious needs. He was an attractive man with, clearly, considerable experience of these things. What was unusual about him was that deprivation had not destroyed his belief, or seemed not to have done. Seemed – how much did he seem and what else was he? And then, so suddenly that it made her laugh at herself, she thought, And where am I in all this? How do *I* feel? I am behaving as though I do not exist except as an observer of someone else. It is ridiculous at my age to let even the idea of someone loving me make me invisible.

She was hungry – no, ravenous. Not ravenous for romance but simply for something to eat. She put on the lights. It was nearly four o'clock, but she longed for digestive biscuits, or cheese, or toast and Marmite. She got out of bed, slipped on her dressing-gown and crept silently, carefully, in her bare feet down the stairs. It was not until she had found the packet of biscuits and the wedge of Stilton in the larder, and poured herself a mug of milk from the fridge, that she noticed the letter propped against the empty toast rack on the breakfast tray he had laid. She had been going to take her food back to bed; now she sat at the table and read the letter.

She read it twice; the first time at the speed that intense curiosity engenders; the second time very slowly and with frequent interruptions as she recalled things that he had said and the way he had said them to her. 'In any case, my knowing you does not make me dangerous . . .' and her replying, before she could stop herself, that it might. Of course it might. For years now she had kept herself emotionally anonymous for safety's sake. She no longer yearned over Jass, but she had determined never to let anyone else get so near. She had not liked being alone, but the alternative threatened her with the possibility – likelihood, even – of unendurable pain that would still have to be endured. Those months and months after she had last been with Jass when she had woken each morning not knowing how to get through the hours and hours of interminable day, when she had lived on cigarettes and sleeping pills and wild agonising fancies that none of it was real – that one day he would turn up and she would fall easily back into his arms, his heart, his life. In the end, she had had to accept that this would never happen. Marietta had a child; there were pictures in newspapers, scraps in gossip columns and posters all over London. She had become used to these huge, blown-up crude versions of his face, and body, attired variously in evening dress, animal skins, a naval uniform, a raincoat and a slouched black Homburg depending upon the film. What she eventually came to *know* was that their last encounter had occurred entirely from his feelings of guilt and pity. He had not loved her – probably he had never loved her, any more than Stach. She had loved him, but that is never enough: unrequited love is as though the two people exist in a different element and one of them is stifled by the richness of the air.

Oh, well. Why should all this come back – *again* – so long after it had seemed laid to rest? Because this man was saying that he loved her, understood her, knew she had been betrayed . . . Well, of course he might have deduced that from newspapers. But, then, he was saying the same thing – almost – that Anna had said. That if one succumbed to bad or sad experience and resolved never to be exposed to a repetition, one would not cross a road for fear of being run over. 'I would never lie about love.'

Oh, *that* resonated with her: it had been a single certainty – something that she knew she could not lie about. He was simply asking her to trust him; he could hardly know that this was no small plea. But, then, he *did* seem to know. She thought again of how he had cared for her during these weeks since her fall – how gentle, even tender he had been, how he had never encroached upon her privacy but had seemed always to anticipate her needs. And he had been a good companion. They had had many and varied conversations about books and poetry and plays. When she thought about what he had told her of his life, particularly his awful childhood in that dank cottage with an indifferent father and a stepmother who resented him, he *did* seem a most unusual and admirable man. Nothing seemed to have come easily to him, yet he had virtually educated himself, had retained principles and integrity that many people more fortunate than he were without. It seemed churlish not to say that she would trust him; she owed him at least that. She decided to put the note back on the tray: she did not want to have to talk about it first thing in the morning when she was in bed. She cleared up the remains of the food and rinsed the milk mug so that there would be no trace.

Trust, she thought, some time later as she lay awake in the dark, trust was not necessarily followed by love – of any kind. Or perhaps, at least, not love of a certain kind. But as she lay, trying to still her mind and sleep, pieces of things he had said recurred in his voice – the times when he had said them, his capable, gentle hands, cleaning the dirt out of her wound, massaging her feet one evening when they had been so cold . . . At this she experienced a sudden, astonishing jolt, as though there had been some collision at the bottom of her spine. For some time after it she lay rigidly still while the sensation ebbed slowly away, leaving her weak and, to her confusion, sick with longing.

She was asleep when he brought her breakfast and pretended to remain so while he put the tray on the table beside her, and drew the curtains. There was then a pause when she could hear no movement and knew that he was looking down on her. This made her feel uncomfortably vulnerable, so she went through the motions of waking.

'It is a beautiful morning,' he said. 'You should really be having your breakfast in the garden. Would you like that?'

'Tomorrow.'

'Right. I'm going to do some bedding out before it gets too hot. But I'll hear if you want anything. Just give me a shout from the window.' His tone was matter-of-fact. He smiled nicely at her and went.

She read the note again with her coffee. It seemed to her then that she had been making too much of the whole thing. He obviously cared for her, in a way, and after last night she had to admit that she found him an attractive man. No more than that. But what on earth did 'that' mean? She was not constantly finding men attractive – it was not usual. Well, everybody found some people attractive – that did not necessarily involve a passionate or heady affair. He could easily be courting her with an affair in view without caring for her in the least; in fact, that was most likely to be the case. And she, in common, she imagined, with most women, was familiar with that situation. The only differences were how convincing the men were – whether one fell for it hook, line and sinker or merely hook. Well, she had had experience of both kinds, she had fallen in love and thought it returned; she had experimented once or twice with men who wanted her to go to bed with them because she had felt she ought to want it too, and the fact that she seemed to have been more of a conquest to her lovers than a lifelong object of affection no doubt reflected as much upon her as it did upon them. She had wanted too much, and they too little. In those cases no harm – indeed, almost nothing – had been done. She had concluded that sex without love did not do much for her.

There was nothing extraordinary about that, but now, for the first time in her life, she wondered whether she had taken this romantic view for granted – that it might not invariably be true. How about sex and good companionship? Sex and affectionate friends? Surely a great many people in the world would be happier if they deliberately settled for that? Perhaps they were and they did, and perhaps *she* had landed up as she was because she had applied the same rigid standard to what had possibly been very different situations. It wasn't a question of romance with Henry – on her part, anyway. The things that he had said to her that in the night had seemed so overwhelming, now contracted to the commonplace behaviour of any man courting a woman he wanted to make.

These conclusions relieved her; she felt calmer and more resolute – able to be pleasant, kind and cool to him. It was really time, she reflected, as she picked her favourite yellow and red checked Madras cotton shirt from the drawer, that Henry went back to his boat: she did not need him caretaking at night any more.

10

HENRY

I had put out a box of night-scented stocks, a box of white cosmos and a box of 'Bowles' Black' pansies before she came into the garden, and for a minute I sat back on my heels and watched her. She wore a black linen skirt, a red and yellow shirt tucked into her waist and the yellow suede belt with a silver buckle. She had a red straw hat and her feet were bare. Her arms were full of her books and papers – her work. She walked over to her table not yet in the shade of the big tree.

'Would you like me to move it for you?'

'No, thanks, I rather like the sun.' Her tone had a kind of amiable distance about it and my heart sank. I collected my empty seed boxes and took them to the shed. It crossed my mind that she might tell me she no longer needed me to sleep in the cottage. It was a frightful idea, and the more likely the longer I thought about it. If she wanted to give me my *congé*, how on earth could I stop her? But I *had* to stop her: time was running out anyway, as she was getting better so quickly now that any minute she would be driving, having her friends to stay (she had talked of this once or twice already) and, worse, going to London and only appearing at the cottage at weekends. If she sent me away now, I might lose everything. I lit a fag – the last in my pack, which reminded me that we usually went shopping on Thursday afternoons. An idea

274

came to me – risky, by which I mean uncertain of success, but in the absence of anything else worth considering. I sat on the side of the wheelbarrow and thought.

Of course, I also thought, moments later, that I might simply be imagining her coolness. My letter might very well have made her feel shy, and an appearance of distance was one of her ways of dealing with that. I would feel my way, but as a means of pre-empting my being turned out, I resolved to show her the boat.

It had become a custom for her to take her lunch on a tray in the garden when she would invite me to share it with her. I always waited to be asked, and I was always asked. Supper was another matter. She usually ate it in the sitting room – until lately, by the fire – and I sensed that I was not wanted. She would read, or play music while she ate. I would usually go out then – for a walk, or to the village pub where I could please myself what I drank, and where I had lately become more popular since I had more money to spend. Daisy had insisted upon paying me very much more than she had as her part-time gardener, added to which I no longer had to buy my food. She had begun to cook, soups and salads or sandwiches for lunch and grills or casseroles for dinner. But what soups, what sandwiches, what casseroles! After years of Hazel's ill-cooked and dull, stodgy meals, and my limited repertoire on the boat, Daisy's food was a revelation. The various herbs and salad stuff I had planted for her – radishes, coriander, basil, spring onions, dill and various lettuces – were all doing quite nicely. It was another way of making myself less dispensable – those sorts of things need watering, thinning out, weeding and protecting from pests if they are to flourish. I spent the rest of the morning on that; my instinct was to keep away from Daisy until lunch-time. I did not want a casual injunction laid upon me from across the lawn; better a proper conversation at the garden table.

Accordingly, when I found her in the kitchen making sandwiches, I went and cleared her papers off the table, then carried her food out for her.

'You'd better bring yours out too,' she said. 'You want lunch, don't you?'

'Please.'

I saw that she had brought her list pad out with her on which she had already written.

'Shopping list?'

She nodded. 'Anything you want for the garden?'

'I'll think.' I had noticed by now that in spite of her apparent calm she was nervous and also that she thought she was concealing this. She remarked that she thought she would invest in a washing-machine. I agreed that it would save a lot of trouble.

There was a brief silence. Then we both spoke at once and both stopped. I indicated that she should speak first.

'About your letter. It isn't so much that I don't believe what you say as that I'm not sure that I want you to say it.'

She had given ground again, 'was not sure'.

'I only asked you to believe me. I will try not to say things that you're not sure you want me to say.'

'So what *were* you going to say? Just now.'

'To tell you the truth, I was worrying about my boat. It's not in a very good state. I was wondering what, if anything, I could do about it.'

'I know nothing about boats. What sort of things do you need? Because we could get things this afternoon, if you like.'

'I don't know. I'd have to go and have a look at it first. I've been neglecting it rather.'

'It's because you've been doing so much for me.'

'That's nothing. I've just been lazy about the boat. I don't like it enough, you see. There are people who simply love messing about, painting things, polishing things, even scrubbing things. They'd never do any of that in a house, but a boat is somehow – I don't know – different.'

'Is it one of those lovely painted boats – you know, roses and castles on doors and things?'

'Lord, no. It's just a thirty-five-foot motor launch, only the engine's never worked since I've been there. Like nearly everything else about it. All the same I should go and see what else has gone wrong.'

There was a pause, and then she said, 'I should rather like to see it. Perhaps it isn't as bad as you think. Perhaps I could help you clear it up a bit.'

'Oh! I think you'd be horrified. I don't think I could bear to expose you to such a shambles.'

'I wouldn't mind. No, I'd like to see it.'

I protested a bit more until I finally gave in with graceful gratitude. It was agreed that we would have a quick look before we went on the shopping expedition. I would have preferred more time to set the scene, but on the other hand it was better that she should see the boat before she made any suggestion of my leaving the cottage.

We went in the car as far as the bridge and parked on the towpath side of the canal. I explained about having to use the canoe and she seemed acquiescent, but when she saw the boat drunkenly moored on the opposite bank, she was suitably impressed.

'Yes,' I said, seeing her face, 'she's been taking in water

for weeks now – needs regular pumping out among other things. Sure you want to go through with this?'

'Sure.'

I helped her into the canoe, unearthed the paddle from its hiding place in the reeds and we set off. I held the canoe firm while she climbed aboard, and then got off and secured the painter. We stood in the cockpit, which was faintly awash, and then I unlocked the doors to the saloon and ushered her in.

'Mind your head.'

I knew that the place would be in a fair old state, since I had left it pretty messy the morning I had found Daisy on the path, and I had only been back once to collect some clothes, but it exceeded my wildest dreams. Apart from the somewhat oily water seeping through the duckboards, the bunk was soaking since the roof of the cabin had long since ceased to resist rain, and we had had several quite heavy storms. The bedding (I had not made up the bunk) was mildewed; the stove, whose doors I had left open, was full of damp grey ash that had gushed on to the small piece of filthy carpet that I had always meant to take to the local tip. The remains of my breakfast that last morning, and, come to that, my supper of the night before, a hunk of bread covered with grey mould, a half-full bottle of milk that had congealed to an unearthly green. The portholes were opaque with condensation and grease, the whole place covered with dust in which one could write one's name, and smelling both stuffy and rank. The small sink was piled with pots and pans that I had used; the sink basket was a hotbed of fungus. I saw Daisy taking all this in – could see that she was appalled, even revolted.

'The trouble is, that quite apart from cleaning it up, it

will still leak like a sieve – from the hull as well as the cabin top.'

'Couldn't it be repaired?'

'It could, I suppose. But they'd have to take her out of the water, and God knows what they'd find when they did, and I guess that the cabin top has simply got to be renewed. The moment you have a boat out on a slip they can charge what they like.'

'But if it's your *home*—'

'It doesn't belong to me. Look, let's get out of here. I can tell you the story of the boat on nice clean dry land.'

I locked the cabin doors and got her into the canoe and paddled back to the towpath side.

When we were back in the car I told her about the Watsons and his getting a job abroad for three years and offering me their boat while they were away. 'They only used it for weekends and short holidays, otherwise they lived in London.'

'Couldn't you write to them and tell them what needs doing and then they could tell you what they wanted to have done about it?'

'It may seem extraordinary, but the fact is that they didn't give me their address, and it didn't occur to me to ask for it until after they'd left.'

There was a short silence, and then she said, 'I suppose you could get the cabin roof repaired, and take it out of whatever rent you pay.'

This floored me. If I told her that I didn't pay any rent, she might expect me to pay for the repairs myself: if I agreed to her idea, I would be faced with paying for them anyway. I had, in fact, taken the boat on the understanding that there was to be no rent in exchange for my looking after it – 'maintaining' was the word used.

'Actually, although I *do* pay a peppercorn rent, I gave it to them as a lump sum as they needed it for their journey. Anyway, it wouldn't begin to mount up to these sort of repairs. I'm appalled at the domestic mess I left it in. I'll set about cleaning all that up, and see if I can fix a tarpaulin over the cabin roof to keep out the worst of the rain. But the hull has always been dicky. At one point they wanted to sell the boat, but when the prospective buyers turned up and saw how much water she made – and I was forever pumping her out – they all backed off. I'm sorry I subjected you to such squalor.'

'I wanted to see it.'

Much later, when we had finished our shopping, I said, 'So, you see, my looking after you has not been a one-sided business at all. Thanks to you I've enjoyed a warm dry bed, not to mention delicious meals, for weeks now. It will be quite a shock returning to my old way of life.'

'You can't go back to the boat in that state.'

Relief surged through me and I felt the sweat break out on my forehead. 'Thank you. That's very kind. But you must chuck me out whenever you want to.'

I had gained my point.

When we had loaded the car to go home, she said, 'I think I'd like to see what driving would be like. Whether my leg works or not.'

'Fine.' What else could I say? But it was another little thrust towards independence. 'If it's painful, let me take over, won't you?'

'I will.'

All went well for the first few miles, but then, when we reached the corner before the turning to our lane, she suddenly exclaimed, and braked hard; and I, who had been attending to her profile rather than to the road, looked ahead to find us skidding into the verge where there was a ditch. We stopped just before we would have gone into it. I still didn't know what was going on. She was getting out of the car, so I did the same. On the road behind us was a dark bundle of fur.

'I hit it,' she said. 'I didn't see it in time.' She was very distressed. She crouched down and touched its body – it was a young cat. 'It isn't dead,' she said. 'Do you think . . .'

I got down to look at it. It was clearly dying. 'You go back to the car,' I said. 'I'll deal with it.'

'Couldn't we take it to a vet? Save it?'

'No. You go back to the car. Daisy, *please*.'

The wretched creature was still alive; its amber eyes wide and staring, mouth agape, lips drawn back from the little white pointed teeth. As I took hold of it, it gave one weak wail of agony. I put one hand over its head and the other round its neck, gave one strong twist and felt the vertebrae snap. When I let go of it, its head fell back on the road with an unearthly quickness. There was no blood. I picked it up and laid it in the cow parsley on the verge. I was used, from my poaching days, to finishing off any damaged creature, but I knew that Daisy was not.

She was huddled in the passenger seat. I got in beside her.

'Is it dead?'

'Yes.'

'You drive. I'm not fit to. I killed it.' And she burst into tears.

I turned to her, put my arms round her shoulders and pulled her towards me until her face lay against mine. A faint resistance and then she let go. I held her until the convulsions of sobbing became less, then I tilted her head so that I could kiss her. I simply laid my mouth against hers and there was a kind of breathless pause, and then I became aware that the kiss was returned. I was careful to take no advantage from this: if some wild creature approaches and you remain perfectly still and quiet they are more likely to come nearer. This was the light in which I had early seen Daisy, someone whose experience had taught her distrust and fear of others, and subsequent information (from the diaries and letters) had confirmed this. So I remained still – not quite unresponsive, but passive.

She did not kiss me for very long, and when she withdrew, I sensed that she was at a loss, uncertain, indeed extremely shy about how to be with me. I released her at once.

'I will drive home, if you like. But it was not your fault. It could just as easily have happened to me – or to anyone. All right?'

She shot me a quick, nervous look.

'Yes – you drive.'

She was silent all the way back, and I was content to savour the salt of her tears from her mouth. I was light-headed with the exhilaration of that first kiss – are not all first kisses unlike any others? – and the certainty that I was on the brink of achieving all that I had schemed and dreamed about for so long.

This was right. That night, she invited me into her bed.

11

DAISY

I am not in love – I am *not*. So what is it that is happening – in me, to me, about me? I am confused, incapable of thought . . . Or if I have thoughts, they contradict one another as fast as they come. So I resort to my old habit of trying to write myself into clarity, or acceptance or comprehension – whatever is needed. He has gone to pump out the wretched boat, so I have some hours to myself that I need to sort things out. Already I seem to have two selves, two parallel lives, and I have no control over whether they will merge into one, or divide more and more widely until one is outdistanced by the other.

For instance, it was not he who asked if he might spend the night with me last night, I asked *him*. The moment that I said it I felt afraid, and the other part of me jeered and gabbled; what was the point of holding love dear, allotting it such significance, mourning its loss so greatly (as, indeed, I have done) if the slightest indication of its presence puts me to flight? It makes me nothing but words, a craven creature devoted merely to attitudes. You would not say, 'Life is supremely valuable to me, but I don't think I'll have it now.' That is poorly put. I suppose I mean that opportunity, like chance, is not necessarily a fine thing, but sometimes it is there. If I never trust anyone, there

283

will be no one to trust. I might endure that, but how could I want it?

He seems to have no conflict at all. Ever since I have known him he has shown me nothing but the most gentle kindness. Last night he was the same. When he got into bed with me I was shaking so much that I was embarrassed by my own fear. He took me in his arms and said, 'I'm not going to fuck you. I'm simply going to be with you.'

And that is what happened. He put the lamp on the floor so that the room was full of shadows and subdued light. I said that I had not been to bed with anyone for nearly ten years (this was some sort of apology for shaking so much). Much later, when I was naked, I heard myself trying to excuse my body – the stripes and blue veins on my breasts from feeding Katya, and he said that I was inside my stripes and that it was me he loved. 'If you were marked all over, like a zebra, I should love you.' All through the night he told me that he loved me – kissed me and touched me with real tenderness. Some time after the dawn chorus when I discovered, waking, that I had fallen asleep, I found him propped on one elbow looking down at me, and as I saw him, he smiled and as he began to kiss me again he covered my left breast with his hand and at once I started to tremble, but not from fear. But when I told him that I wanted him, he stroked my face and said, 'You're not ready yet.'

I felt such an amazing, such a sweet sense of relief, that there was time and that I could take it and that he understood my need, that I could have wept, but he sensed that too, and diverted me.

It was some hours later during that timeless night

that I recognized and could accept his unconditional love, and then, for the first time in my life, I felt free to be nothing but myself. Years slipped away from me until I was ageless, without shame or my lifelong anxieties that I was not giving enough, pulling my weight, doing or being what might be expected of me, all the armour I had always used when someone was going through the motions of intimacy with what I now realized had always been a stranger. I did not feel a stranger to him, and the extent of his strangeness to me was simply as much a pleasure as a mystery.

When it was light, he went downstairs to make tea and he sat on the side of the bed while we drank it, and we talked, exchanging small desultory facts about ourselves. I asked him how he had come to have such a passion for reading, and he said that he supposed it was an escape. When I said it was clear that he didn't read escapist literature, he said that escape didn't equate with unreality, it was simply different. 'Often,' he said, 'it seems more real than my own life. And far more variable.'

Then he said, 'We must think of a way to celebrate this day.'

'Haven't you got to do the boat?'

'Oh. Have I got to? Well, supposing I spend a couple of hours and then come back and, if you will allow me to, bath and shave and *then* take you out to lunch? Will that do?'

I agreed. I did not think that he ought to afford to take me to lunch, but I didn't want to hurt his feelings, so I said a pub by the canal somewhere would be nice.

Now he has gone to the boat, and I have bathed

and dressed and here I am in the garden with my diary.

That awful boat! I had no idea what it was like and I certainly had not realized that he did not even own it. Poor man! It is hard to imagine how someone so sensitive and intelligent could stand such a life – the discomfort, the isolation, the squalor! I suppose that, until he gets his divorce, that wife will continue to sit in their house and he will have no money to buy anywhere else. And yet I don't see how he can get the work that he is clearly so good at remaining where he is. No wonder he wanted to do my garden so much, although he has earned very little money from it. Perhaps, when I offered him more money for all that he has done for me during these past weeks, it was not nearly enough. If I had had nurses, or a house-keeper or, indeed, anyone living in, as he has been doing, it would have cost three times as much. Perhaps I should . . .

But here she stopped; somehow, after the last night, it would be invidious to offer him more money. It would seem as though – she felt herself blushing, some-thing that seldom happened when she was alone. No, a man – anyone – who was poor and honourable must have pride, and not to respect that would be patronising and altogether offensive. He had never complained about his life, and what he had told her of it, coupled with what she now knew about him, engendered a kind of admir-ation for him that was new to her. In spite of neglect and cruelty in childhood, and then a series of dreadful – in the case of his Charley, tragic – events, he had somehow managed to keep his freshness of heart, almost a kind of innocence that touched her.

Whatever happens, I must not hurt him: he has surely had enough of that. I must be clear and honest, never lead him to think I care more for him than is true. But what is that? Well, if I don't know, I should tell him so.

But then she thought that any kind of uncertainty about degrees of involvement – or love – seemed only to make the other person infer what they wished. So she must keep her uncertainty to herself.

What I *do* know, she thought later, as she shut up the diary, is that last night I wanted him. Pure lust, I suppose, something that I don't think I have ever felt before in my life (I *thought* I loved Stach; I *knew* I loved Jass) but that is what it was. And while she could acknowledge that to herself, the idea of telling him made her . . . But she *did* tell him! She said she wanted him. And he could easily have translated that into her falling in love with him.

The trouble with you, she told herself angrily, is that, due to being sixty, you have old-fashioned schoolgirl notions about this kind of thing. You manage to be too old and too young in the same breath. And then she remembered how she had felt in the night when he had given her time; how she seemed to become no age at all. All those sensations and memories were but a few hours old and perhaps suited only to the privacy and nakedness of night.

At any rate, she suddenly felt extremely shy of meeting him when he came back from the boat, and took refuge in household chores, ironing her shirts in the kitchen with the back door open for it was going to be a very hot day. She ironed to music, a Mozart piano concerto – one of the late ones – but when she reached the slow movement she stopped ironing and abandoned herself to its slow, gentle insistence, had never noticed before how erotic this particular movement was. But perhaps it was not Mozart, it was her perception that had changed. Any minute now, she mocked, the slow, gentle insistence of the iron on your nightdress will have much the same effect.

The telephone rang, and she went to the sitting room to answer it.

It was Anna, asking her if she wanted to do some programme.

'Hang on, have to subdue Mozart.'

'It's a series. They want you to make six programmes in pairs back to back.'

'Sorry. I didn't hear what it was about.'

'Oh. It's one of those guess-who's-written-this jobs. They want you as a team captain. You have two different people on your team for each programme and you play against the other lot. It's a live audience, going out at six p.m. You'd need to stay the night, I should think. But if Anthony has a friend staying with him in your flat you could always stay with me.'

'Can I think about it?'

'You can. But I know that that means you don't want to do it. Easier to say now, wouldn't it be? They don't pay much,' she added. 'I'll say you're working. Which is true, isn't it?'

'A bit – yes.'

'How *are* you, anyway? When shall I come and see you?'

'Oh, soon. Let me finish the new play treatment first. Then you can read it and we can talk. You know how that gets me going.' She could hear herself gabbling and she guessed that Anna could hear it too.

'Is your faithful serf still looking after you?'

'He's working on his boat, but he still does a good deal for me. He's not a serf,' she added: the notion made her feel angry.

'Can you drive yet?'

'I tried yesterday. But it was awful.' And she told Anna about the cat. It was a relief to have something of this kind to tell her – something where she was not with-holding anything. But after she'd told about not actually killing the poor cat, and Henry having to finish it off, she fell silent.

'How very upsetting. But it probably wasn't your *fault*, Daisy, just awful bad luck. It might have happened to anyone.'

'That's what Henry said.'

'It must be true, then, mustn't it? Nearly forgot. Anthony was asking about you.'

'What about me?'

'How you were. How you were getting on in the country. Whether you were ever coming back. He sent his love and said that, in spite of his loathing for rural life, he would brave it one weekend to see you.'

'Oh. Good. Give him my love. As soon as I've finished this treatment, I'll have a weekend party.' Then she could hear Anna's other line ringing, and Anna saying she must answer it.

It was an uncomfortable relief when she rang off. Daisy was not accustomed to withholding anything from Anna, but she knew she didn't want to talk about Henry with her at all. Anna would not understand. Anna might take – probably would take – the view that Henry was not good enough for her. And we all know what that means, she told herself grimly. It was snobbery barely concealed by a kind of nannyish concern. She did not want to expose Henry to any of that. He was quite intelligent and sensitive enough to be acutely aware of any patronage from people who fancied themselves better born. Look what he'd endured from the mother of the first girl he had been in love with. She certainly didn't want to put herself into a position with Anna, Anthony, etc., where even being defensive could appear as patronage.

What was the matter with her? Neither Anna nor Anthony were snobs – of course they weren't. Anthony, particularly, was one of those people who was at home anywhere or nowhere, depending upon the observer's point of view. He described himself as 'a colonial gay', had left South Africa when he was eighteen and never gone back. She had met him in his set-designing days when he had mounted her first television play and they had at once become friends, although his appearances in her life were widely spaced due to his roving nature: 'My autobiography will be called *Up Sticks*'; he had once, when reminding her of it, added gloomily that at the rate things were going (his life was regularly punctuated by emotional crises) it could well end up as *Up the Styx*.

Anyway, shortly after the play he had gone to Paris because of a new love, and there he had taken to photography at which he became very good. When she met him some years later, he greeted her as though they had been meeting every day for weeks, with a kind of buoyant intimacy and delight that was infectious, and she felt as suddenly delighted to see him. He never seemed to have regular work, and had long since given up the camera for painting; had got into an art school and actually stuck it for two years. He was larky and graceful and always seemed to have very expensive clothes in spite of his earnings being spasmodic and dicey. 'I incite generosity, darling,' he had once remarked, when she had admired a particularly beautiful Versace jacket.

She would have to explain him a bit to Henry, if he did come. Would she have to explain Henry to him? Less likely, she thought, with affection. Anthony was very good at liking people, at *harping*, as he put it, on their finer points.

Anna's call made her realize how thoroughly she had cut herself off from her London working world. It also made her wonder what was happening in Katya's life. She had rung three times now and left messages. The first time somebody she did not recognize had said that Katya wasn't back yet. The second time one of the children had answered and said that Mummy had gone to see a friend. The third time – in the evening – she had simply got an answering-machine. Now it occurred to her that Katya must have got at least one of the messages, and it was odd that she had not responded. She dialled the number and got the machine again. She thought then of ringing Edwin, but she didn't even know the name of his practice. She set about Directory Enquiries – there could not be many medical practices in Dorchester – but when she finally got the right number she was told that Dr Moreland was visiting and would not be back until two when he would be taking surgery. She left a message asking him to ring his mother-in-law any time after six.

All this was a far cry from what was happening to her

here – now – with Henry. Quite soon he would be back from his boat and she did not know how to meet him, how they would be, what they would talk about – ordinary things, as though nothing had happened between them? They had been naked and she had accepted his love without returning it – what could that mean to him? What could she say to him in recompense that would also be true? How could she pretend that everything was as it had been before she had tried to drive her car and killed the poor little cat? She was conscious of an unfamiliar simmering excitement, but it was encased in dread. She heard the gate click and looked wildly round for some immediate escape.

12

HENRY

It took about an hour to pump the boat out, and while I was doing that there was plenty of time for thought. I was far from complaisant. It was one thing to get invited to her bed, quite another to have the right to be there. If she agreed to marry me, I could afford to cut down my claims on Hazel's imminent pension, and simply agree to take half the price of the house she now occupied. This would facilitate divorce proceedings, but I did not want to do that without some surety where Daisy was concerned. I knew that this would not happen quickly. Apart from her nervous disposition, she had two failed marriages behind her. I reflected, not for the first time, how my dislike of men was actually a mite unreasonable. If they were not such rotten, adolescent, insensitive lovers, everything would be very much harder for me. The women I wanted would have standards that I would be expected to meet, instead of the pathetic fears from their experiences that I could easily dispel.

How she had responded – in those few hours! She had moved from fear and trembling to trembling of a very different kind. I could have taken her, but it was far better to make her wait. It was better for me as well: after weeks, months, of imagining my possession, the actuality (not unnaturally) fell short. The body of a sixty-year-old woman, while it may be good for her age, is hardly as seductive as it had once been in youth. Daisy's long limbs, her pretty neck, still smooth and unblemished, her slender hands and feet, were all good lasting points, but her breasts – small for my taste – were also marked by the veins and stripes that are the consequence of breastfeeding, and her nipples – small, also – had that rather desolate, compacted appearance I associate with lack of attention. She has no waist to speak of. Her face is arresting, because it is so expressive of everything she feels, and her hair, all gossamer luxuriance, is ravishing. She has a beautiful skin, utterly smooth and fine: stroking all parts of her body – excepting that most private part, which I have carefully avoided – is truly a delightful pleasure. It will not be difficult to be in love with her; what I have to do is to become indispensable, and sex and affection are the keys to that. And trust most of all. She must continue to trust me.

When I had done with the pumping, I lay on the bunk to consider practical matters. I must reinforce my foothold in the cottage and I must rid myself of the boat. This meant clearing things on board, so that when I wrote to the owners, saying that I no longer intended occupation and was sorry that it had not sold, it was in a reasonable state and I had transferred my possessions, such as they were, to the cottage. I could hardly put them in the bedroom that I had been occupying until last night. I knew, from various things she had said, that Daisy intended having people to stay, and I had supposed that this would mean my return to the wretched boat. I decided to ask whether I might not put my books and papers – the latter carefully packed in carrier-bags that I would tape closed – into her garage or the small workshop that was attached to it. I would produce these things unobtrusively, two bags at a time, and the plea would be that I wanted to protect them from damp. It would be easier to clean the boat if I emptied it of clutter first.

I fell asleep at this point, having had so little sleep the previous night, and when I woke it was noon and very hot in the cabin in spite of the doors being open. I locked up and took to the canoe. That, I reflected, would have to be returned soon because its owners would be down for the summer holidays.

I knew that she would be shy at meeting me, that indeed this first day of our affair would require constant tact and care, but such finesse was, after all, my forte, and I trudged back with a sense of mounting excitement at the challenge, running the last few yards, as I wanted to look suitably hot and sweaty from my labours.

She was not in the kitchen, but the back door was open and from it I heard a car door slam. The thought that she might be running away gave me a momentary shock, which passed as quickly as it came: the car keys still hung on their hook on the larder door. Then I saw her getting out of the car, standing by its door facing me. She *had* been attempting a runner. She saw me, and started moving – very slowly – towards me.

'Better not come too near me – I should think I stink of the bilges, et cetera. If it's all right by you, I'll have a quick shower – Daisy? What is it?'

'I thought I'd left something in the car.' She didn't look at me. I could see that her shyness was agony for her. She made an attempt to meet my eye and then she said, 'Actually, I suddenly wanted—'

'To run away from me?'

'I forgot the car keys.'

'I'm very glad you did that. Forgot them, I mean.' She had reached me now, and I stood aside to let her through the door. 'I *know* you feel shy. I know it because I feel like that too.'

This seemed to surprise her. 'Do you?'

'We're both a bit out of practice. We haven't got the confidence of the young. You know what they say about lovers' conversation consisting largely of reassurances?'

'I thought that *was* the young.'

'I think it's true for any age. But don't run away from me, darling – don't. I beseech you not to do that.'

That made her smile. 'Beseech.'

I knew that she felt more at ease and that I could safely leave her while I cleaned up.

We did go out. Sat in a pub garden and ate prawn salad and drank a bottle of wine, which she liked better than I did.

There were other people in the garden, so we did not talk about ourselves, which was good because I wanted to make her feel thoroughly at ease. I asked her if I might put a few parcels of my papers in the garage since they got damp in the boat, and she said of course. She said she had been thinking of enlarging the cottage somewhat; building a second room at the back on the ground floor and a second bathroom, and supposed she would have to get permission. 'I don't mean to do it now,' she said. 'Next winter, perhaps. When I'm back in London.'

'Is that your plan?'

'I haven't really got one. It's possible. It depends a bit on work – on what turns up.'

'Isn't it good working here?'

'For writing, yes. But I have to do other things as well. I have to earn my living.'

This baffled me. I had thought that with two places to live in and a very expensive car, not to mention sojourns in Los Angeles working on films, she must either have, or be making, a good deal of money.

As I poured out the end of the wine, I said carelessly, 'I'm just like the mob. I imagined that anyone doing films could have anything they wanted.'

'Most writers are far from rich. It is simply the few bestselling ones that even people who hardly ever read books have heard of that make people think that.'

Someone came with the bill which she tried to pay but I would not let her.

After lunch we went for a walk, a footpath beside a large meadow that led to the river. Apart from a few fishermen on the opposite bank, we had the place to ourselves. We walked hand in hand without speaking beside the river that was blue from the clear reflection of the sky, the air scented with cow parsley and the sun-warmed reeds by the riverbank. Then we came upon a cart-track that had once had a gate to mark its entrance, now rotted to one post still standing and the rest of the timber embedded in the long grass. Ahead lay the deeply ridged track bordered on each side by hedge. 'The road less travelled,' Daisy said.

'Shall we travel it?'

'Why not? Do you think it will make all the difference?'

'I'm not with you. What do you mean?'

'Robert Frost's poem. About the two roads in a wood. I'll find it when we go home.'

When we go home. There was something charmingly encouraging about the way she said that. I wondered whether to tell her so, but decided not to.

The track crossed a meadow, then ran beside a coppice and then declined into a small dell in the middle of which stood a most curious little building, about eight feet high. It had a gently domed roof, and at its entrance was a pair of wooden doors flanked by an absurdly large portico. There was ground about the size of a tennis court railed off round it.

'What is it for? It can't be an ice-house, surely?'

'No. It's too much above ground.'

'It looks rather like a dwarfs' temple – a kind of miniature church.'

We tried the doors, but they were locked. We walked round it, but it contained no windows so we were none the wiser. But then we saw a stone set at a drunken attitude in the long grass. It was just possible to see the inscription: 'Bonzo. A faithful friend to his sad end. 1888–1901'.

It was a dogs' or possibly pets' cemetery, since some of the monuments were very small indeed, and we suspected that 'dear pretty Polly' was a parrot.

'Do you think they all come from the same family?'

'Most likely. This must all have been part of some large estate.'

'It may still be. We're probably trespassing.'

'Don't worry. From the look of it, nobody cares about it. Shall we have a rest?'

She agreed to this and we sat on the steps outside the doors as the portico afforded some shade. I reflected how odd it was that when one was walking with somebody, you had either to know them very well indeed to talk, or they had to be a complete stranger. Anything in between was inhibiting. When I said this, she replied, 'Is that why you wanted to sit down?'

'No. I thought you looked a bit tired.'

She shook her head, and then said, 'Yes, I was. I am.'

It was a silent place – so quiet that the ticking and buzzing of insects seemed loud. She put her hands behind her neck and leaned her head against the door. Her shirt was fastened just below the hollow of her throat.

'We could have brought that poor cat here and buried it.'

'We didn't know about this place.'

She shrugged. 'And we haven't got a spade with us. I know.'

'May I kiss you?'

I saw her become unnaturally still. Then, with what seemed almost a gallant attempt at nonchalance, she said, 'Why not?'

I kissed her for a long time. I did not stop kissing her until I was certain that she wanted me to go on. When I drew away from her I could see from her eyes how little she wanted me to.

I unfastened her shirt until her breasts were exposed. I could see her heart beating beneath the white satin and lace that enclosed them and when I took a nipple between two fingers it was at once erect. Very slowly, and watching her, I slipped a shoulder strap from her shoulder and released her breast. Her eyes were fastened upon mine with a passionate intensity: she was no longer afraid; she wanted me to touch her too much to care about fear. I don't think that anything turns me on more than getting a woman into this condition. I love it, and love too the delay that I can then impose for as long as I care to. A certain amount of frustration can be invaluable in the long run, and Daisy, although she did not, I think, know it, had a long way to go yet. Now, I put my mouth on her breast and as I began to suck her, she shuddered and made a sound denoting exquisite pleasure. I stopped almost at once. Her head was turned to one side and her eyes were shut. She looked bereft and I could see that she was about to speak, so I put my fingers over her mouth, and said, 'I adore you.'

Then I returned her breast to its lacy prison and fastened her shirt.

'Is it really ten years since anyone made love to you?'

'I expect I'm behaving like a starved spinster.' She tried to smile and I saw that her pride had been touched. I had been kneeling by her and now I took her in my arms for a reassuring unsexual cuddle. I put her head against my shoulder and stroked her lovely hair and crooned, '"Daisy, Daisy, I'm half crazy, all for the love of you. It won't be a stylish marriage, I can't afford a carriage, but you'll look sweet—"'

She lifted her head and looked at me, half smiling. 'I don't want to marry you. I don't want to marry anyone – ever again.'

Oh, I thought. I might have known that there would be rocks ahead. I smiled back. 'Darling, it's only a song. I don't know why it came into my head. Shall we go home and get some tea? After all this sun I must do the watering.'

So we went back to the car, and thence to the cottage, and then I drew a plan for her of the additional room that she wanted. I am good at that sort of thing, having had to do it for gardens. She wanted a double room with a bathroom leading off it, and I suggested that while she was about it, she might add a small room for the washing-machine (which had been ordered) and a deep freeze so that less shopping would be needed. She got quite excited at the plans. Did I think she would have to get permission to carry them out, and how much did I think it would cost?

I thought it unlikely that the cottage was listed and therefore if she did need permission it would almost certainly be granted. As to the cost, I read somewhere that each room added to a house cost about ten thousand pounds, and this was more than that.

'Fifteen thousand?' I said this as much to see whether she was fazed by such a sum as to encourage her to think that I knew about such things. She did not seem surprised by the cost. 'But we can get an estimate,' she said.

It was a beautiful evening. She cooked supper while I watered the garden. It had not rained at all for nearly two weeks, and the new roses and other shrubs were suffering, as the soil was light and drained very quickly. I picked her a small bunch of roses, but when I went into the cottage – full of the delicious aroma of tomato and garlic – I heard the bath water running. I had bought myself a bottle of vodka the day we went shopping and now I decanted it into an empty Perrier water bottle. Drinking wine every evening had the effect of making me crave a real drink, but I did not want her to be in a position to monitor me about how much. So I gave myself a hefty swig then took the bottle up to my bedroom where it could be safely concealed by my winter jersey. Then I sat on my bed and wrote her a little note, which I took downstairs to put beside the roses. The telephone rang – a most unwelcome interruption. By the time I picked up the receiver in the sitting room, Daisy had reached the one in her bedroom.

A man's voice was saying, 'Daisy? I gather you rang me.'

It was too late now to put the receiver down without it being noticed, so I listened – poised to replace it at the precise moment that Daisy rang off.

'Oh, Edwin. Thank you for calling. I was trying to get hold of Katya, but she always seems to be out. Is she all right?'

'She's fine, as far as I know. She's gone off for a fort-night's holiday.'

'Oh, I didn't know.'

'France. With one of her university friends. She was getting rather fed up because I couldn't find a locum until September and she needed a change. I thought she would have told you.'

'What about the children?'

'They're both at school, and of course Thomas is away so there's only Caroline. My sister has come to look after her – came yesterday, in fact, so all is well.'

'Is Caroline there?'

'She's out with her pony, I'm afraid. But I could get her to call you later, if you like.'

'Only if she feels like it.'

They went on and on. I sensed that in reality they had very little to say to one another and were struggling with the tedium of abstract goodwill, which made them both dull. When they finally reached the reiteration that Katya – away for a fortnight – would be back on Saturday week, and that Caroline was not to ring her grandmother unless she felt like it, they were able to exchange farewells. I replaced the receiver with exact timing, and some anxiety. It was plain to me that I had a limited time marooned, as it were, with Daisy, before outsiders, in the shape of her friends and family, presented themselves. Alone with Daisy, I had only her to consider, to please, to interest. With other company I might face a critical, likely hostile audience that would certainly cramp my style. I knew now that she wanted me in bed; she had also to fall in love with me before I could count on her to defend and champion me against outsiders.

When Daisy came down, I was opening a bottle of red

wine. She was wearing a long cotton – I don't know whether it was a dress or a robe – garment of soft raspberry pink, with a low rounded neckline and wide but very short sleeves that made her thin white arms seem even more delicate. I told her how lovely she looked, put my arms round her, kissed her forehead and – very lightly – her mouth, and told her how much I loved her. 'I hope I don't say that too often.'

'Oh, no!' There was a second's pause, and then she said, 'It's very nice to be loved.' I gave her the roses with their stalks wrapped in the note. 'I hadn't seen you for some time, so I had to write.'

She read it with a little smile curling her mouth. She seemed altogether lighter, gayer, than I had ever seen her. All the evening she sparkled, she glowed – she was conscious of my admiration and she loved it. After supper she produced the remains of a bottle of a Turkish liqueur. 'It's called *ghul*; it tastes of roses.'

It was too sweet for me, but I loved to drink it with her. She told me all about the telephone call that I had heard, and said that she was worried that Katya was not happy, and more worried that she would not confide it if she were.

'I have not been a good mother. And she really didn't have a father.'

'Bedtime story,' I said. 'I propose that each night we take turns to tell a story of our life and, as it is my idea, I choose that you go first.'

'What do you want to know?'

'I'll tell you when we are in bed. If I may share your bed?'

'You may.' She did not look at me. Bed meant sex, and the idea of sex still frightened her.

So I was very careful, very gentle, full of homage to her beauty and care for her comfort. I made no attempt to arouse her. I wanted her to feel safe with me, to recognize that I was unlike other men she had known and to love me for it. I could feel that I was succeeding in this; her eyes when they met mine, now rested on me with a softness, a frankness that betokened, at the very least, affection.

When we were propped up in her bed (I had brought my pillows to augment hers), I said, 'I should like it if you would tell me about Katya's father. Was he the first man in your life?'

She told me – a mixture of things that I already knew and things that I did not. She said his being Polish had meant, in a way, that she had not expected to understand him. So she would make all kinds of assumptions ranging from what she felt was due to a battle-scarred hero, to his meaning every word that he said to her. 'And, of course, I was terribly flattered that he liked me.'

'He must have felt rather more than liking.'

'He said he adored me,' she said sadly. 'But, again, he was given to superlatives. The things he didn't talk much about were true – and the things he talked about all the time mostly were not. For instance,' she said a moment later, 'he never talked about his life as a pilot. But he was apparently amazingly brave. He got his plane back on one occasion with one engine blazing, and landed it and when they got him out, just before it blew up, they realized his neck was broken. He never told me, and he never complained of all the ghastly pain he had ever after. He never talked about his family until after Katya was born, and when he did, I realized how desperate he must always have felt about not knowing, and then knowing what

had happened to them. He talked a lot about how rich he
would become, but his jobs never lasted and he was hopeless with money. And, of course, other things.'

'It must have been awful for you if you loved him. Did
you? Was he a good lover?'

'Of course I thought I did – which is nearly the same
thing to begin with; it's only later that you see it wasn't.
I was flattered by so much intense attention. I was nineteen and I'd led a very quiet life with Jess – she was my
aunt who brought me up.' She fell silent again.

I took her hand and held it.

'But then, you see, it became clear that he didn't love
me – any more than he loved a good many other women
he met. We were all the same to him. A distraction. I think
he regarded most of his life as a game, a gamble whose
risks he got attached to. When he wasn't playing at being
madly in love with someone, he played at being a husband
and father.'

I was pretty certain of the answer, but I needed to
know for sure.

'But when he *was* being a husband, was it good for
you?'

She had withdrawn her hand, and now she drew up
her knees and put her arms round them.

'Oh, I suppose the first time one does something quiet
and private with someone, you don't really know. You
don't know what it's *meant* to be like. So you sort of –
string along with it. Or you think if you aren't – weren't
– enjoying it, it's something wrong with *you*. Sometimes
I just felt that I was failing him, and that was probably
why he went off with other people. And there was nobody
to talk to, of course.'

'Your aunt?'

305

For the first time she smiled. 'Jess! Oh, no. Jess always said that she knew nothing about sex because it had never interested her. She had inherited me, and that was marvellous, because she'd always wanted to be a mother. And when I asked her what she thought about my marrying Stach, she said, "You know best, dear, but always remember that that may not be much." She adored Katya – simply loved her. And she took us both back when I left Stach.'

'Do you ever see him?'

'Not any more. The last time was when Katya got married. By then, she didn't even want him to come. She'd been through everything about him – missing him, getting her friends to be sorry for her because he wasn't there, visiting him in his flat in Ealing, which always contained a strange, different woman every time she went. In the end, she didn't want to go – or see him at all. But for years and years and years she resented me for leaving him.'

There was a long silence.

'And then Jess died. Everything was much worse after that.'

I was looking at her face, so close to mine, seeing that the skin beneath her eyes had become transparent as it did when she was tired – and that she was brimming with tears. 'She loved me and I loved her so much. It was really *equal* love. I suppose everybody wants that?'

'Sure they do.' I took her in my arms. 'You're tired out, darling. You need sleep.'

I rocked and soothed and comforted her until she lay back on her pillow with her hand in mine, shut her eyes and – like a child – immediately slept. I lay and watched her for some time. It was clear that her aunt mattered far more to her than that first husband and I wondered how on earth anyone could be more upset about an old woman than anyone else. It was beyond me, and because it was that, it left me cold, but discomforted. Yet I too was short of sleep. I turned out the lamp.

In the early morning, when it was just light, I made more love to her – much as I had the previous afternoon, but this time for far longer. I did everything to her except take her. My experience of virgins came in handy here. I knew that penetration, after so long an abstinence and the age that she was, might easily be painful and I did not want to hurt her. I wanted her to be frantic for me (which was easy), and for her to know that I was as much aroused (more difficult), but I had only to imagine taking her by force – pain or no pain – to get an erection. My abstinence I intended her to interpret as my extreme love for her, and this was entirely successful; indeed, I had every kind of success and it was a sweet triumph to see her at ease, looking up at me with a kind of grateful radiance. I told her that she was beautiful and that I loved her (one cannot do this too often), and she answered that I made her *feel* beautiful. I knew then that I had accomplished much; was more than half-way to her becoming mine.

13

DAISY

28 June 1989

Am I in love? It is three weeks now since we went to bed; we have been lovers for twenty-one days and nights. He has continued to love me with the same wholehearted emotion and kindness and I have graduated from what I, somewhat defensively, described as some sort of old virgin to what he has described as a normal sensual woman for whom sex has become a joyous necessity. Indeed, I think I have become more sexual than he, but when I said this to him, he laughed and said it was because I had been starved for so long. 'Not just of sex,' he had added, 'but of everything that goes with it. My greatest pleasure is giving you pleasure.'

I am afraid that I do not give him enough back, but I have noticed that he often makes me want him and then withholds his favours – teases me – and that he certainly enjoys that. Sometimes he starts that game in the afternoon and then we go upstairs, but more often he deliberately excites me hours before he will take me to bed. I have begun to enjoy this game. It is wonderful to want him and to have no shame, no self-conscious reservations at all. 'You trust me now, don't you?' he said yesterday. And I do. Even when he hurt me a little at the beginning, he was so aware of it and so tender . . . Those are the moments when I do feel love for him.

We still have what he calls bedtime stories and I

have learned much more about him, and when I tell him stories, more about myself.

The second night it was his turn and he told me about his very first love – when he was still a boy at school – for a beautiful little girl called Lily. He said it was a case of worship from afar: she was the daughter of the local doctor, older than he. He used to pick bunches of flowers for her, and once he sent her a chocolate biscuit (a birthday biscuit, he hardly ever had them) wrapped up in a note with a poem he had written to her. She never answered and quite soon after that she went away. He said he watched her leaving the house with her parents – she was going to a boarding-school – and then he went into the woods and sobbed his heart out. Poor Henry! He was so isolated, so lonely, and then his father refusing to let him stay on at school but making him work as a gardener's boy. Still, I suppose it grounded him with skills to become a garden designer, which he did entirely self-taught. He has made the most detailed and careful drawing of the extensions, and we have discovered that we do not need planning permission for them, so we took the drawing and had it photocopied and sent it to two builders who are local – one very near, the other near enough.

I am utterly lazy. I do no work at all. The weather has been the best that June can offer, which is so ravishing that all I want is to be out in the country or the garden. I do read for my Brontë idea and he encourages me. 'I would never want to stop you working,' he said, several times. One evening, we went to a cinema in the town, and ate popcorn and held hands in the dark, and afterwards we went to a curry restaurant that had hard seats and hot flock paper. It was almost empty. Henry said he would pay, but he had paid for the cinema seats, so I said he must let me do my share. The bill had vodka on it – a double one – and I said that it was wrong because we had only drunk lager, but he said that he had had a quick drink while I was in the loo.

On the way home he suddenly said, 'When we're married, I'll take you to India, give you a ride on an elephant.'

I said that we were not going to be married.

He leaned over and put a hand on my breast. 'Have you not come round to the idea? Just a little?'

I don't know why (and it was the only time in these weeks) but I felt a tremor – a chill. I said I had told him that I did not want to marry anyone. I had had enough of marriage.

'That is because they weren't the right men for you.'

I said nothing. We did not say anything at all after that all the way home.

When we were back in the cottage he came up to me and put his arms round me. 'Darling, we'll do whatever you want.'

That night he asked me to tell him about Jass. I had avoided this particular story, because I was not sure that I could bear to talk about it – and also because it now seemed so *different*. I could no longer remember the good times with Jass – had come to distrust them, to think that I had invented them at the time, and that now, trying to unravel the truth about him to Henry might destroy this happiness that I have found with him, and turn me back into the frozen, mistrustful creature that I seem to have been for so long.

But he got it out of me. He asked the right questions, he listened, he made no judgements, and when telling him made me weep it was because it felt like such a weight off me or, rather, it shrank to a size that meant there was no weight. I loved him then. Confidence is such heady stuff; I felt like Othello.

But I no longer love him simply when we are making love. I love him at quite ordinary moments – or I have begun to – particularly when we sit in the evenings each reading. He is reading the Brontës alongside me; at least he is reading the novels – with the exception of *Jane Eyre* – for the first time and I love his perception, his sharp appreciation and his willingness to discuss what he reads. I cannot talk about the play that I want to write since the idea is too new and uncertain for exposure to anyone at all, but to talk of their lives and their work is a wonderful stimulus and I am fascinated by how – coming so fresh to them as he does – he is so quick to pick on salient points of mystery and interest. The distinctions between their 'family' voice and the unique originality of each sister, for instance.

He knows that I keep a diary from time to time, and that it is a piece of writing that is entirely private to me. He said that he understood this the more because he had often written what he described as notes about his life that he would not want to show to people.

He has told me a good deal more about his present wife. He seems to dislike her intensely, but most of what he has to say about her makes her sound merely dull. She works as a physiotherapist in a large hospital, I think in Northampton, but he seemed vague about that – said she had moved or had been thinking of moving. When I asked about his house, and what would happen to it if she moved, he said that he had bought it in her name and therefore it was legally hers. He added that she had burned everything that had personally belonged to him after he left. He discovered this when he had gone back to collect more things – 'clothes, books'. He said they ended with nothing to talk about, and that she resented people coming to the house as 'they always made so much work'. He said that she disliked sex and had never wanted children. Before I could ask (and I'm not sure whether I would have done) he said that he married her on the rebound, to assuage the awful loneliness after Charley died. I suppose that this is a much-used answer to what is, after all, an impertinent question, but it does not really *answer* it. It only answers the general without giving any reason for the particular. Why did he choose Hazel? There must have been something about her, but I did not feel that I should ask what. He had said at another time that she was cold and mercenary, and surely some of those traits must have been apparent? Even if she tried to conceal them, I would have thought that somebody with his perceptions would have divined their presence. He said that the whole affair had shown him so clearly that it was against his nature to marry for any kind of expediency. 'People with romantic natures, like you and me, should only marry our own kind, and there are fewer of us about.' When I asked what distinguished the romantic from anyone else, he went into a list that began with us being risk-takers and ended with our having hard centres like some chocolates; 'compared to romantics, the others are like a bunch of violet cream'.

When I asked whether all his women had been
romantics, he said no – and that that was how he'd
learned his need for them. 'You get a lot of sentimental
people posing as romantics,' he said. I said I didn't
think that they were necessarily posing; they might
really think that they were or, more likely, not consider
the matter at all.

She stopped writing there because of toothache. It was
the middle of the morning and Henry had gone to his
boat, which he had not done for some days. She realized,
as she made a cup of tea to drink with her paracetamol,
that in fact a tooth had been troubling her for some time.
She had had twinges with hot or cold drinks, and once
when she had tried to bite an apple. But now it seemed
to need no such excuses, settled into a dull, throbbing ache
that subsided briefly from the painkillers, but returned
with renewed vigour three hours later. Henry had returned
while she was asleep on the sofa, and was sitting reading
in the chair by the fireplace when she awoke.

'I can see you have,' he had replied when she told him
of her toothache. 'Your poor face is all swollen on the left
side. Shall I ring up that doctor and ask where the nearest
dentist is to be found?'

But she had a fear of strange dentists. She rang Mr
Ponsonby in London, who actually answered the telephone,
as he said his secretary had 'flu. 'Come round now, if you
like. You might have to wait a bit, but I'll fit you in.'

She explained that she was in the country. It would
take her about three hours to get to him.

'Oh. Well, try and make it before six thirty if you can.'

'Oh, I can. I *will*. Thank you so much.'

It was half past two. She didn't feel like driving. 'I'll go by train.'

'Good idea,' he said.

'And I think I'll stay the night with Anna if she's free.'

'Right,' he said, less heartily.

An hour later, she was sitting in the train. She had rung Anna, who *was* free and delighted to have her for the night; she had packed a rucksack and taken more paracetamol and tied a silk scarf over her head to shield her face. It was an abscess, she was fairly sure, and she dreaded the possibility of losing the tooth far more than the pain.

Henry had – of course – driven her to the station. He had been concerned and helped her in every way he could think of.

'I shall miss you this evening,' he said in the car. 'That's not exactly true. I shall miss you from the moment I can no longer see the train until I see the train tomorrow arriving with you in it. What time will you come?'

'Oh – I don't know. I'll ring you in the morning.'

On the platform he kissed her very carefully on the good side of her face. 'Oh, darling! I hate to see you in pain. I wish I was coming with you.'

But in the train she felt a sudden lightness – a relief at being alone, a state that she was used to and had been without for weeks now. It was lovely to be so watched, so responded to, so appreciated, but it was also remarkably peaceful to – as it were – stand at ease, to be anonymous and unobserved. It was simply that having an affair, living with, beginning to love another person, shifted everything else about life, and change, of any kind, while it was exhilarating, had also a certain amount of fatigue attached. My age, she thought – rather sadly. Once it would simply have been exhilarating.

None the less, in a taxi on her way to Anna's, after a successful session with Mr Ponsonby ('I don't see any reason for you to lose this tooth'), who drained her abscess and administered some far more effective pills, she thought of Henry, alone in the cottage, heating up the shepherd's pie she had made. She thought of how quietly he moved, how expressive were his eyes that seemed instantly to mirror her mood, the way he talked to her when they were making love, his unselfishness in every-day matters ('You have it', 'I didn't want to wake you', 'I thought you might prefer the shade'), and affection – desire for him – melded into something very like love. Shall I tell Anna? she thought. No, she would wait a bit before that.

But she did tell her.

It wasn't until after two stiff Ricard *en tomate* – Anna's new summer drink – and a rather dilatory and unfinished talk on her Brontë play, refusing Anna's offer to take her out to dinner and settling for cold lamb and a green salad at home, that a comfortable silence prevailed, and they lay back in their respective battered old armchairs eyeing one another with discerning affection. She thought that Anna looked tired.

'In spite of your tooth, you look remarkably well.'

'Do I?' She felt herself beginning to blush.

'About ten years younger than when I last saw you.'

'The country suits me. I'm going to enlarge the cottage.'

'Ah. Well, don't get rid of your London flat until you've spent a winter there.'

'Is Anthony looking after it?'

'I don't know about that, but he *is* paying the rent.'

'Anna, it's so kind of you to deal with all that. You do look after me.'

'There's something about you that cries out to be looked after.'

'No, there isn't.'

'Oh, yes. And there's something about me that cries out for people to look after.'

'Is that all there is to us?'

'Don't be silly. Will you come to Greece with me this autumn?'

'I don't know. When?'

'Well, it has to be before or after Frankfurt, but otherwise anytime.'

'I don't know. I'd like to – I don't know.'

'Daisy? What's up? You look beautiful and happy, and I've only known you look like that when you are working really well, or when you are in love.'

There was a pause, during which she realized how much she wanted to tell Anna.

'I'm not working – much – at all.'

'I realized that.'

'I think I may be falling in love.'

'With Mr Kent?'

She nodded. Her throat was suddenly dry and she swallowed.

Anna immediately pushed the bottle of wine towards her and there was silence while she concentrated upon pouring some. But when she had finished and taken a swig there was nothing for it but to meet Anna's watchful eye.

'He is in love with me.'

'Darling, I'm sure he is. I expect he wants to marry you.'

'As a matter of fact he does. But I don't want to. I don't want to marry anyone – else.'

'Good! That's something, anyway.'

'You sound very disapproving – against him.'

'I don't know anything about him.'

'Exactly! Well, I do. I know a very great deal. He's not just a simple gardener's son, you know.'

There was an uncomfortable pause, while Anna lit a cigarette.

'Daisy, darling, I'm not being a snob about him. I'm probably being one about you. I don't care a damn who his father was. I care about whether he's good enough for you. You are too like Jane Bennet. Of whom do you ever think ill? I'm the opposite: I think ill until otherwise convinced. So – tell me all about him.'

'I don't know where to start.'

'Start with the most important things and work out from there.'

She had been going to begin with a biography, the wretched childhood, the childhood friendship that developed into his first love, but now she dropped all that. Anna could read the letter some time. She said: 'The most important thing about Henry is his capacity to love. He's the first person in my life who seems to love me whatever I am – ill or well. He couldn't have done more for me after that fall, and he never presumed upon my helplessness. I mean he didn't try to be with me all the time – you know, meals, et cetera. He stayed in the cottage because I needed someone there. He got the doctor, he dressed my wounds, he used to take me to the lavatory, but somehow it was all easy and all right.'

She looked at Anna, to see if she was being understood, but all she could tell was that Anna was listening.

'The second thing – important thing – is that although he really has had a most difficult, sad life, he seems to be utterly without resentment. I know that if some of the things that have happened to him, had happened to me, I should be a mass of bitterness. He isn't that at all.'

'What sort of things?'

'Oh, he discovered that the girl he loved first – Daphne – was actually his half-sister. He wasn't even given the chance to say goodbye to her. Daphne's mother simply packed him off to another job with the blackmail that if he didn't take it he would get no other reference from her.'

'Do you mean that the girl's mother had had an affair with Mr Kent's father?'

'I know it sounds like a nineteenth-century novel—'

'More like a twentieth-century one.'

'Well, whatever you think it is, it's what happened.'

'And then what?'

'Oh, then he went to a place near Tonbridge in Kent.'

There was a pause. Anna lit another cigarette.

'That's not *all*?'

'Heavens, no! There's masses more. By then the war had started, and when he was eighteen, he was called up. The old couple who owned the place had no money, he said, to keep it up. The head gardener was well past retiring age, but they were never going to afford another one. He went back there to get a reference from them but they'd gone. The husband had died and the widow had sold the place to a couple from London. It had all been done up, and he went to see if they'd give him a job and they did, and this time he was the head gardener, with a cottage and a boy to help him. He said they were the opposite of the last owners, had a lot of money – the man was a banker and they wanted to turn the house and garden into a showplace. They put in a huge S-shaped swimming pool and —'

'But what *happened*?'

'Oh, what happened was that he fell in love with their daughter. She – her name was Charley – was already married to a colleague of the father, who more or less bludgeoned her into it when she was too young to face up to him. Henry said she was paralysingly shy and her father had always bullied her and the man married her because she was an heiress. He was horrible to her, and she used to come home for weekends when he went abroad. Henry got to know her that way. He came across her crying in the swimming pool very early in the morning and he said that, although she never talked about it, he had the distinct impression that she was trying to get up the courage to drown herself. He took her back to his cottage and fried her a breakfast and got her to tell him about herself. That was how it began. Eighteen months later she ran away with him. Her husband refused to divorce her, and her father cut her off – would have nothing to do with her. Henry said they were always short of money, but that they were so happy it didn't matter in the least. They had a tiny basement flat in Camden Town, and he worked as a jobbing gardener and started designing people's small London gardens. She died very suddenly, a heart-attack. They had only been together for a few months, not quite a year. He wrote to the parents, but they did not even come to the funeral. That's what happened.'

'Goodness!'

'He adored her. He said the only comfort he could take was that he *knew* she had been so happy during those months.'

'This was all a long time ago.' Anna's voice was gentle; she was well aware of Daisy's tender heart.

'Yes. I suppose it was. But he said it was the most awful thing in his life.'

'Here's a nasty old paper handkerchief.'

'Anyway,' Daisy said, when she had finished blowing her nose, 'he did marry someone else in the end. I don't know how long after Charley but he said it was some kind of rebound. It was a complete flop. They're supposed to be having a divorce. I don't think that's making him particularly sad. He just sort of wrote it off. But you see what I mean about not being resentful.'

'Mm. Like some coffee?'

'I would. Let me wash up.'

'No. You can bring things out to me.' This was all ritual. Anna's kitchen would hold only one person at a time.

When they were back in the two battered armchairs with coffee, Daisy said, 'So now I've told you.'

'Yes.'

'You sound as though you disapprove.'

'No. I mean I don't.'

'But – what?'

'I just want things to be all right for you.'

'They are. I don't think I've ever felt like this before.'

'But you don't want to marry him.'

'I told you I didn't.'

'So what do you envisage?'

'I don't – much. I'm just enjoying each day. And night,' she added, and felt herself start to blush.

'May I come some time and meet him? Not as your gardener, I mean.'

'Soon – yes. We haven't been with people at all.'

'You haven't met any of his friends?'

'No. I don't think he has any where we are. I do want you to meet him,' she added, 'I didn't mean to sound meagre about it.'

Afterwards, in bed in Anna's little spare room, she wondered why the idea of other people meeting Henry made her feel so defensive. Was she afraid that Anna would not like him? Or wouldn't like him for the wrong reasons? She sensed that Henry was of the kind who was at his best when he was alone with one other person: she could not easily imagine him in company.

'You've had your hair cut!'

'Yes.'

'And you've been shopping, I see.' He took the carrier-bags from her as they walked along the platform.

'It seemed silly not to. The sales have begun. I couldn't resist them.'

'And there's no sign of the tooth?' he said, when they were in the car.

'If I bare my teeth, there is. He didn't have to take it out. Such a relief!'

'May I kiss you?'

She turned towards him.

'Oh, my darling love! I tortured myself last night with the idea you might not return.'

'I would never do that! Just *disappear*.' She was faintly shocked that he could fear such a thing.

'Oh, well. One gets to imagining things on one's own. Shall we stop for a drink at that pub near the river?'

'Isn't it rather early?'

'It's after six. A celebration: your homecoming.'

They sat at what had become their table because this

was their third visit. The garden was nearly empty, although the long table was laid for a dinner. Fairy-lights – unlit – were strung through the lower branches of the trees or pinned to the top of the trellis that edged the garden. Apart from a few unspeakable roses (Henry's description), nothing much was grown, and the grass was worn rather than mown. It was the kind of place that needed furnishing with people, but apart from themselves and the pub's cat – an opulent ginger who was walking petulantly on a long table laid for supper – there was only one other couple with a baby in a pram.

They sat silently for a while. She was very much aware that he was watching her, and her pleasure at seeing him was blurred by some sudden anxiety about how she should tell him that Anna was coming to stay.

'What's up, sweetheart?'

She turned to find him regarding her intently.

'You've told your friend Anna about us, yes?'

'Yes. I was going to tell you all about that when we got home.'

'Is it bad news, then?'

'Of course not. She was a bit surprised – that's all.'

'I expect she's against me. I'm not good enough for you, something of that kind.'

He was so on the mark that she felt herself starting to blush.

'It's not that, exactly,' she began, and then – surprisingly – heard herself saying, 'but it's not easy to explain how one is in love.'

His expression changed. He took her hand and kissed it. 'Oh, my dearest love! Of course we'll wait until we're home.'

When they were back he led her, her suitcase in one

of his hands, her hand in the other, straight upstairs where he pushed her back on to the bed and, holding her shoulders so hard that she could not move her arms, he began to kiss her, stopping twice to say, 'Can you tell *me* how you love me, my darling? Can you?' But when she tried to speak he stopped her.

He made love to her until she was too weak to move or to speak – past all urgency, all streaming, until she felt like an empty seashell, as though if he gathered her up and listened to her he would hear the echoes of past loving, the ceaseless waves with their peaks and their troughs that were now imprinted in her. Then there was one last time and even in the stupor of exhaustion she sensed that he had at last got what he wanted.

She must have fallen instantly asleep, because the next thing she was aware of was the room full of warm grey dusk, turned to a darker violet where the window reflected the sky. He was not there, but she could hear him moving below. She got out of bed – she was still tired and her limbs felt stiff – and crept quietly to the bathroom; she did not want him to see her naked, for some reason. Indeed, she thought, as she pulled her dressing-gown round her, she was afraid to see him at all – felt much as she had that first morning when she had tried to take the car and escape from having to face him. And yet this had nothing to do with the absence of love; rather, it felt as though she was so much in thrall to him now that she would not know how to find any separate self. How could she live this violently satiating life with him and be with other people?

But it would not always be like that, she thought; familiarity would breed something more companionable, or of a gentler nature, more acceptable to outsiders. His

company, his averred and practised love for her, had made
for a delicious intimacy. But intimacy *à deux* was very
different from intimacy in front of other people – even
friends: or perhaps especially friends. As she laved her
face in very hot water, touching her bruised lips with a
light finger, and was continuing this comforting appraisal,
she was brought up sharp by the recognition of his lust
– hitherto held within comparatively stringent bounds.
He had always, until now, wanted her because he loved
her so much. But that last time had seemed different – she
had felt anonymous. When he called her from the kitchen,
and she nerved herself to go down to him, there he was,
bustling about, as gentle, as practical, as tender as before.
He had warmed the pie (which he had not eaten the night
before, he said, because he had been to the pub), and he
had made her a special drink. The kitchen table was laid
for supper.

'Sit down, darling, and try this.'

'I'd like some water first.'

He set the glass down beside her and then touched
the back of her neck with fingers cold from the ice in the
glass.

'I know you feel shy,' he said, 'but you're quite safe.
Nothing has changed.' And she saw that he was smiling
at her, almost with benevolence.

She said how good the drink was – a vodkatini,
perfectly made – and he replied that he had worked in a
bar for three months, on a cruise ship.

He was full of small surprises of this nature that
cropped up often during their bedtime stories as he called
them. Now, because she didn't want to talk about Anna
coming to stay, she asked him about the ship.

'Have you ever been on a cruise?'

She hadn't.

'Well, some of them are wonderful holidays, especially for the older passengers, and some of them are probably OK for the crew as well. But this was a downmarket affair: the ship was really too old for the job. She was filthy, overcrowded with as many passengers as they could squeeze into the small cabins. The tourist class had communal washing facilities, and as the toilets were almost always blocked, the floor was awash with sewage. The crew's quarters were bug-ridden and the food was – well, if you saw the kitchens you wouldn't have wanted the *passengers'* food and we got what they couldn't stomach, plus a lot of potatoes and macaroni. The captain was drunk a good deal of the time and left everything to his first officer, who was much younger and a real bastard. I knew nothing about cruise ships when I signed on, or I'd have chosen better.'

'Where did you go?'

'The Mediterranean. I thought I'd see a bit of the world, but of course I didn't. You don't get shore leave on a three-months' stint. Don't look so worried, darling, it did me no harm. Working one of the bars was a soft option, anyway, compared to being a steward or a waiter.'

There was a pause during which he took one of her hands and gently chafed it.

'One of the worst things about that time was the desperate divorcees – sometimes widows – who had expected a cruise would open up a whole new romantic life. When they couldn't find it among the passengers, they turned on the crew. There they were, with their newly dyed hair, and their tight bright clothes and their banked-up anger – like the pancake makeup over their scalding sunburn, and their charm bracelets and nothing to do.

ELIZABETH JANE HOWARD

They would hang about the bars for hours at a time –
everyone drank too much anyway – and ten to one they
would lie in wait for you when you came off duty.
Fortunately most of the cabins were twin-bedded, but
the ones who'd taken a càbin to themselves were a real
menace.'

'When did you do this trip?'

'Oh! After Charley died.' He looked at her and she noticed
again how his eyes became opaque when he mentioned
Charley. 'I had to get away, you see.'

'Yes.'

Soon after that they went to bed. 'You're worn out,' he
said. 'I'm going to sleep in the other room tonight, and
let you have a proper night's rest.'

Nothing was said about Anna.

14

HENRY

Of course I had always known that the isolated idyll was finite. Sooner or later, her friends would have impinged, but the sudden toothache was a stroke of bad luck. Going to London meant staying the night with Anna, and that in turn meant confidences about me – indeed, if she had withheld them, I might have had even more cause for anxiety. It would mean that she was afraid that Anna (and presumably others) would not accept me. It didn't seem to be quite like that, but clearly Anna wished to come down to inspect me, and somehow or other I had to pass that test.

As soon as I had seen Daisy on to her train, I drove back and stopped at a boatyard that lay about seven miles up the canal from my mooring. I had not visited it before. I explained that I had been looking after a boat for friends, but was now leaving the vicinity and would pay to have her towed to the yard. I wrote down the owners' name and address in London, and gave my name as Kenyon – not, I said, that it would be much use to them as I was going abroad. They asked for a month's rent for the mooring in advance, plus the cost of the tow: the whole business cost me the best part of fifty pounds, but I reckoned that to be shot of the boat it was worth it, having made sure that I had left nothing personal in it. Then I drove back and returned the canoe to its owners who were still fortunately absent. My papers and other bags of stuff were already stowed unobtrusively in the hut adjoining the garage.

It was a relief to have disposed of the boat: to have burned it, so to speak, as a refuge. It was after seven by the time I got back to the cottage and I did not feel like warming the shepherd's pie and eating it with the half-bottle of wine from the night before, so I went to the pub with *The Times* crossword and drank vodka in quantities that would have made it cheaper to buy a bottle and drink it at home. I'd had the sense not to take her car, and trudging back, I passed out in the ditch Daisy didn't drive into when she ran over the cat. I woke early with the sun glaring at my hangover. It was far too early for her to ring me, but I hurried back to take a long hot and cold shower followed by a large breakfast of eggs and bread. This vanquished the hangover, and by the time Daisy rang me to tell me what train she was coming down on, I felt ready for anything.

I knew at once that she had been confiding in Anna, but I waited until I'd got us to the pub and a drink in our hands. It was clear at once that Anna had not given her unqualified approval, and that Daisy was nervous about telling me, but then when she blushed and said something about loving me, I knew what to do. We were not going to talk about it until after a long, and to date the most exacting, session in bed. The odd thing was that in the process of manipulating and overwhelming her I got carried away – she really turned me on, as the vulgar saying goes, although I managed to wait for my own final gratification until after I knew she could entertain no more. By the time I finally took her she was long past wanting me but far too exhausted to resist – a combination that I found peculiarly exciting.

I left her sleeping and went down to get a drink, which I took out into the garden with a smoke to keep the midges away. It was dusk, and the white rose round the door of the cottage was luminous. The sun had disappeared behind the wood, but the moon – the colour of worn silver gilt – was rising in the opposite sky. The stocks I had planted were reeking sweetly for the moths, and two or three bats were feasting on the midges in a hectic silent frenzy.

I sat for a while in this scented silence.

This was a good place to be – better still when the cottage was enlarged. I did not want much, I reflected: the company and body of an attractive woman, and Daisy was becoming more attractive to me by the day; enough money not to have to work (which she undoubtedly had), a few treats, perhaps some travelling. Somehow or other I had to get shot of my wife, because it was necessary to get Daisy to marry me, as then I would not have to worry about anything at all. I knew for certain now that sexually she was completely in my power – could enjoy, endure, be made abject as I pleased. But I still had a few cards that could turn out to be jokers if I wasn't careful enough. Anna *had* to approve of me; this might also apply to the daughter, but somehow I felt that if Anna's trust could be gained, the daughter's would follow. I went back into the cottage, started heating the pie and gave myself another drink. The vodka level had sunk in the bottle. I decided to make a vodka drink for both of us to account for it.

She came down earlier than I thought she would, dishevelled, glowing, and every bit as shy as I had known she would be. This made everything easy. I knew just how to reassure her, to make her feel that the violent lovemaking came out of the deepest affection and love, and I had no intention of broaching the Anna business that evening, which turned out also to be easy. She asked me how I made such good drinks, so I told her something about the cruise ship. Not by any means all: the main reason that I had signed on for *that* was the well-known, well-supported rumour that cruise ships were full of women longing to get laid. This turned out to be true. I never had so much sex in my life, and at first the only problem had been keeping Doreen from knowing anything about Edna. That problem was temporary, as the passengers were only on board for a fortnight, and after that, I took care to stick to one woman at a time.

Anyway, by the time we had eaten it was late enough to warrant going to bed. I was tired enough after my short, uncomfortable night in the ditch, and she made no demur about sleeping alone – took it as further evidence of my thoughtfulness (a very useful reputation to cultivate, since you can, once it is established, do pretty much as you please).

We had several conversations about Anna, the first of which occurred on the evening of the following day. I carefully did not broach the subject, and in the morning Daisy was intent upon her work. The first builder arrived after lunch to have a look at the job and she was keen that I should discuss with him the drawings I had made. He left promising an estimate as soon as possible.

At lunch-time I told her that the owners of the boat had taken her away.

'How could they, if the engine doesn't work?'

'Oh, they got her towed. It was all quite amiable. They apologized for giving me no notice, and I apologized for the state of the cabin roof, so we ended quits as it were.'

She said nothing more, but I saw her look thoughtful, and I guessed that my possibly sleeping in the boat when Anna came had occurred to her as an option.

When we did talk about it, it was very clear that she was anxious. I decided to go for being anxious as well, taking the line that obviously Anna would object to my working-class origins: somehow I knew that that was the area where Daisy would most strenuously defend me, and also, that if I could implant that particular objection to me strongly enough, any other could be put down to it. It certainly seemed to work. She began by saying that Anna was not at all like that, would take me strictly on my own merits, but I could see that she had her doubts about whether this was really so.

'Well, my darling, *I* know I love you, and *you* know I love you, so perhaps when she sees that, she will forget about my being a prole.'

She laughed and defended Anna, but she did not say anything about *her* love for *me*: that came later and when I least expected it. It was about a week after she had been to London. She had been much more determined about her morning work, saying that Anna had asked her about it and she had been ashamed at how little she had done. The second builder had been and gone away promising an estimate. She had made several efforts to get in touch with Katya, to be told in the end by the husband that Katya had decided to stay away for an extra week. This disturbed her. 'Something is the matter,' she said. 'I do wish I knew where Katya *is*.'

Then, on the Monday morning, she got a letter from her. She took it into the garden to read, and from the house I watched her reading it – twice. I didn't, of course, know then who the letter was from, but I could see that whoever it was, it had upset her.

She did not stay in the garden, she came in to tell me. Another sign of trust, I thought.

'It's Katya,' she said. 'She wants to leave Edwin. In fact, she *has* left him for the last three weeks.'

'Where is she now?'

'London, I think. She hasn't put an address. And Edwin said she was in France. Well, she may have been. She's coming to see me.'

'When?'

'She doesn't say.'

Bad news. Who knew what the wretched girl might do when she did appear here (with no warning)? She might want to stay here. Worse, she might import her children and Daisy would become immersed in being a mother and grandmother with no time for me.

I suppose some of these gloomy apprehensions must have been apparent from my face, for she suddenly came to me, and put her thin white arms round my neck.

'You mustn't worry so much about other people not liking you. Of course when they know you they will, but even if they didn't it would make no difference – to us. It wouldn't change how I feel. At all.'

'Oh, darling.'

'Apart from anything else, it isn't their *business*. It's our life – yours and mine.' She kissed me. She had become far more open and easy about gestures of that nature.

So then it was in order for me to commiserate with her, to have those speculative conversations about where Katya could possibly be ('I don't know of any of her friends who are still in London'), when she might turn up ('She always does things on the spur of the moment'), and, above all, *why* she had left Edwin – as I now called him. I suggested very carefully that perhaps she might have found someone else, but Daisy seemed shocked by the idea ('The two children. She's devoted to them. She'd never go off and leave them').

Katya rang that evening. Earlier, Daisy had rung Anna to tell her, and to say that if Katya rang *her*, please find out where she was. Anna knew nothing, but I suspect that Katya *did* get in touch with her later in the day and was told to bloody well get in touch with her mother.

'She's coming down tomorrow morning. That's something.'

'Is she driving?'

'No. Coming by train. She wouldn't say what was the matter. I think I'd better meet her on my own.'

'Look,' I said, 'how about I go out for the day? If you dropped me in the town, I can get a bus back to the village about five. Would that give you a decent amount of time alone?'

'Yes, it would.' She was grateful.

'What will you do all day?' she said. We were in bed and I had made the lengthy, teasing, gentle love to her that I knew she enjoyed more than anything else.

'Don't worry about that. I'll go to the second-hand book shop: you know I can spend hours there. And I'll have a pub lunch. Might go to the cinema. I shall think of you. I'm never bored.'

She went to sleep in my arms and I waited until she was really gone before I disengaged myself.

'Are you going to tell her about us?'

We were on our way to the town next day, and I felt

I needed to know what she intended before I met Katya again. 'I think she quite liked me when we met before,' I added.

'Yes, I shall – if possible. I mean, if she's not so distressed that it wouldn't be the right time.'

'Well, make it clear to me when I come back. I don't want to put my great foot in it.'

'I can't imagine you ever doing that – with anyone.'

She dropped me outside the book shop.

'Hope all goes well, darling. Hope it's nothing serious.'

I spent a pleasant day. It was a change to be alone in a town where I could look at other women with carefree interest about their possible attractions. I shopped, bought myself a second-hand copy of a novel by Benjamin Disraeli, a couple of shirts, and a bottle of vodka. I spent a happy half-hour in the back of a newsagent's shop where he kept what soft pornography there was to be had for the casual client, and selected one that specialized in breasts – from boyish to grotesque. This I was able to slip into the carrier-bag that I got with the shirts. It occurred to me – after a preliminary flip through it – that I might possibly get Daisy interested: I had by then considerably changed the appearance of her own. On second thoughts, I went back to the shop and bought a second magazine, a woman's glossy, full of daring hints about getting the man you wanted, or getting rid of the man you wished to finish with and leading a full life as a single woman – that kind of thing. I wrapped this round the soft-porn job, in case by any chance someone looked in the carrier-bag before I could stash it safely away in the garage. I bought myself some sandwiches and a can of beer in the supermarket and ate them in the small park with my back to a large ash tree where I could peruse my magazines at leisure.

I passed an hour or so thinking about sex, about Daisy and about sex with her. It was becoming clearer and clearer to me that somehow I would have to get her to marry me: there could be no real security for me until that was achieved. It meant, of course, that I must get on with getting divorced from Hazel, from whom I had heard nothing since it had been mutually agreed that matters would be put in hand by our respective solicitors. I had requested legal aid for my side of the affair; she, I knew, had employed, or was going to employ, the husband of a friend of hers at work. Of course I had not heard anything because for four weeks now I had not been to the post office in town to collect any letters. This was chiefly because until today I had always been with Daisy except for when I took her to the train and my mind was too full of getting rid of the boat in the short time that her absence made possible. I packed up my carrier-bag and walked back to the high street to the post office.

There was a letter from Hazel. It was quite short and consisted of the complaint that her solicitors had heard nothing from mine, with the consequence that nothing was happening. Would I kindly do something about this at my earliest convenience.

The letter was three weeks old. I tore it up and put it in the litter bin. Then I went in search of a telephone box to ring the solicitors. I asked to speak to Mr Noon, who was in court that day. Could I in that case have a word with Mr Knight? On being asked, I gave my name and after a long pause I was told that Mr Knight was not in the office and that Mr Mawning, who had dealt with the preliminaries of my application for legal aid, was on holiday. Perhaps I would leave a number and Mr Noon would call me back? I didn't want to do that, so I said I would ring again.

I could write another letter to them. It then occurred to me that I had been remiss about checking on the *poste restante* at the village post office. Hazel was the only person I had given the town post-office address to, as I did not want her to know my whereabouts in case she took it into her head to turn up and make trouble.

By the time I'd caught the five o'clock bus, I'd started to worry about what I was going to find when I got back to the cottage. Nothing, I decided, that I could not handle in the end. If Katya was having some crisis and Daisy got caught up in it, it was simply up to me to be the loyal, the faithful supporter. In spite of Daisy's denial, it seemed likely to me that Katya had left her husband for someone else, in which case she would want to be with them rather than here with Daisy and me.

There was a letter from the solicitors – from Mr Noon himself, enclosing a form that required detailed information about my income. This one was a mere week old. It was tiresome because I most certainly did not want to let the authorities know about the money I got from Daisy, particularly since it had increased twice since the original modest payment. But withholding this information meant that I would have to ask Daisy to bear me out if enquiries were made, and I did not want to do that either. I had an uncomfortable feeling that she would regard this as some kind of fraud, and be shocked. I put the letter in the carrier-bag and resolved, with the exceptions of the shirts and my book, to hide it away before going into the cottage.

I trudged the mile from the village imagining what exactly Daisy would have said to Katya about me.

'You've no idea how much I love him. He makes me feel so at *ease*.'

'You may think it is sudden, but it feels to me as though it has been happening slowly – ever since I met him. It is amazing to be so loved. Oh, darling, I hope [Tom, Dick, or Harry] is as good for you.'

'Henry thinks love is the most important thing in the world. A lot of people say that sort of thing, but with Henry it is real. He says that nothing else matters more. But, then, he is a very unusual person. I never realized how much one needs to *trust*. I'd stopped trusting nearly everyone until I met him.'

'I know you'll like him when you know him. He has so many qualities that most people probably never see. And he is the most wonderful lover.'

No – I did not think she would say the last. Her shyness would intervene. Just as well. The less anyone was privy to that part of her life with me, the greater would be my power. I did not want anyone to talk or shame her out of her lust for me, although naturally, I would never call it that to her. To her it was love.

15

DAISY

As soon as she saw her, she knew that Katya was in serious trouble. There was something defiantly breezy about the way in which she walked down the platform towards her, smiling, but when Katya got close she saw that she was simply trying to smile.

'Hello, Ma.'

Katya stopped in front of her – absolutely not wanting to kiss or touch her. Daisy tried to take one of her cases.

'No. I can easily manage.'

Daisy looked at Katya for only a moment before they started to walk together out of the station, but there were all the signs she'd ever known: her eyes, revealing nothing but a kind of feline glassiness, the skin beneath them smudged with lack of sleep, or tears, or both; her mouth – so charming when she was really smiling or simply happy – compressed into a sullen shape. Daisy had seen her thus at six, when they discovered her guinea pig mysteriously dead in his cage; at sixteen when she had come back from staying with her father and eventually told her that she had arrived at the Ealing flat to find him in bed with his current girlfriend; at twenty-six (or there-abouts) when she thought Edwin was going to marry somebody else. There is no age to grief, she thought: it makes its mark regardless of time, makes the young look old. She remembered so well when Katya was six, that same green glassiness of her eyes that seemed like the gallant sophistry of someone far older, but now, in that fleeting glance, she saw the wounded child of six.

'Have you come alone?'

'Yes. Henry has gone out for the day to leave us in peace.'

'Oh. Would he otherwise be about all the time?'

'Well, he has been staying at the cottage – looking after me. I had a bit of a fall on the garden path. I'm fine now.'

They had reached the car. Katya got into the front seat in silence. Then, as they drove out of the town and Daisy was wondering what was the best way of saying, 'Let's talk when we get home,' Katya said, 'He seemed to have rather a crush on you. A bit of a fan.'

'Did he? Well, he's a tremendous reader.' She didn't at all want to talk about Henry at this moment. 'I really want to know what's going on with you, darling, but I thought we might get home first. Or not?'

'There's nothing much to know, really. I've left Edwin and I told you that.'

'Yes, but you didn't tell me why.'

'Why? The usual reason.'

'You're in love with someone else?'

'Oh, Ma! You would think that!'

There was an uncomfortable silence, while the other usual reason occurred to Daisy.

'When I rang up he said you were in France – having a holiday.'

'True. But it's quite possible, you know, to go to France minus a lover. People do it all the time. Sorry, Ma. Sorry I said that. I'm feeling – a bit on edge, that's all.'

'That's all right.'

After that Katya asked her, without curiosity, what

she'd been doing, what she was writing and so forth. Daisy told her that she was doing research for a play, and then that she had not been doing very much since the fall. It had made her rather lazy.

'Are you all right now?'

'Absolutely.'

'That's something – anyway.'

She did not say it as though she thought it was very much. The rest of the journey was more or less silent, except when Katya asked her how far the cottage was from the railway station, and on being told ten miles, said what a long way.

It was not until they were settled in the sitting room – cooler with the doors and windows open than outside – and Katya had accepted a glass of iced coffee, which she put untasted on the floor beside her, that she seemed to be screwing herself up to talk.

'Have you got a cigarette?'

'I didn't know you'd taken up smoking.'

When she had lit it, Katya said, 'Well, I have, in the last few months. It helps to get through the day, doesn't it?' With her left hand she was pushing hairpins back into the precariously untidy coil on the top of her head. She still wouldn't look at Daisy.

'Katya – please tell me.'

Katya made an unsuccessful attempt at shrugging.

'You might as well know: everyone will in the end anyway. Edwin is involved with someone else. There's nothing new about that. He always has been – ever since I had Caroline, anyway.' She gave a mirthless laugh. 'I've had all that for nearly seven years. But they've always been someone else's wife up till now. Now, he lighted on someone unmarried, ten years younger than me, and he's got her pregnant and they want to marry. Or – *she* wants to marry him. He *says* he doesn't want to marry her, but of course she's been a patient of his so there would be a hell of a row, and if he gets out of marrying her, she'll go for him and then he'll get struck off – or could be. He might be anyway, I suppose.'

Katya looked at her properly for the first time with unguarded misery.

'The point is I just don't – I *can't* love him any more. He's just a liar and a cheap, weak philanderer – like Dad. I couldn't believe anything he said to me ever again.'

At least, and at last, she was beginning to cry, or rather tears gushed in irregular little spurts from her eyes.

'I married him because he seemed the absolute opposite of Dad.' She took out a sodden handkerchief from the sleeve of her shirt and rubbed her eyes with it. 'I *so hate* not loving him! All these years I've loved someone – sometimes just put *up* with them because of loving – and they never really existed. You can't *imagine* how that feels.'

Daisy *could* imagine it, of course, but somehow, immediately to say so might sound to Katya like competition. She desperately wanted to be or do anything possible for her, and that meant feeling her way. Their relationship had always been an emotional see-saw. Much of the time, Daisy knew she felt guilty because she had never loved Katya in the way that Jess had loved *her* – had, indeed, loved Katya. Jess's love, for both of them, was like the sun: you did not need to look at it to know that it was there, lighting and warming every part of their lives. While Jess was alive, there had been no need for them to explore or test their relationship. Not that Jess ever usurped Daisy's position: it was simply that she loved both of them unconditionally. When Jess died, Daisy thought they discovered (though not necessarily at the same time) that they did not love one another like that. They were challenging, distrustful, critical and, with all this, desperately needy. Daisy could hear people saying that the responsibility for their relationship was far more hers than Katya's, and in a sense that was – or had been – true. But Katya was by then eighteen and for any relationship to continue with some reality there has to be a fulcrum of equality: dependence of one cannot be the order of the day. All the same, Daisy felt that she'd failed to be the person that Katya wanted and needed for most of her childhood. Katya blamed her for Stach's disappearance, and Daisy felt guilty of perhaps not so much depriving her of a father but of choosing the wrong father in the first place. She resented Katya not understanding how utterly bereaved she felt by Jess's death, or that the wrench of selling Jess's house in Brighton and much of what it contained was to send her to university. By then Katya had a carapace of almost wilful indifference to anything her mother did or said, which continued for five years until Daisy told her that she was going to marry Jason when, after an initial explosion of hostility, Katya turned up at Daisy's flat one day to make amends. She said she had begun to realize that her leaving Stach had been a necessity: that nobody could stand living with someone so childish and unpredictable (although long before Daisy left him he had seemed pretty predictable to her). Katya also said that her outburst about Jason had come out of worrying that he might be the same sort of person who would behave in the same way. 'Women are known to pick the same sort of men,' she had told Daisy, 'and you are such a *truster*.'

All those memories flooded back. 'Darling, it is awful for you, and I can imagine it.'

Katya came into Daisy's arms then, and cried until she could cry no more.

Finally, when Daisy made her a tomato sandwich – food that from her earliest days she would eat when she would eat nothing else – Katya said, 'I can remember telling you when I fell in love with Edwin – well, not then, but when he asked me to marry him. I remember saying how strong and certain he was, how honourable and trustworthy, and how much he loved me. How can I have been such a fool? So taken in?'

'I can remember telling you how much *Jass* loved me – how perfectly suited we were. And I'm sure both of us only said the half of it.'

'Both bad pickers,' Katya said, and her eyes began to fill again.

Daisy gave her a cigarette.

'Or,' Katya said a moment later, 'perhaps it isn't a question of choosing at all. Perhaps they're all the same.'

'No, they're not,' Daisy said, too quickly. She met Katya's enquiring eye just as she felt herself starting to blush. 'What about the children? We haven't talked about them at all.'

This was a completely successful deflection, not that Daisy regarded the poor little things as only that but it had felt necessary that Katya should unload some of her misery about Edwin before they got down to all the consequences.

'Oh, Ma, of course that's awful. Awful for them anyway, and awful because I honestly don't know what to do.'

They spent most of the afternoon discussing what she should do, about herself and about the children. She asked

Daisy if she could borrow the flat in London: the children's holidays were coming up and she thought that if she had them with her on her own, she would be able to explain things better to them. Edwin had apparently offered to keep them in the country and was adamant about Thomas continuing at his prep school where he was very homesick. 'I never wanted him to go in the first place, but there isn't a lot of choice where we are, and Caroline has only just started primary school. It would be easy to move her.'

'I'll have to get a job, Ma,' Katya said later. 'Edwin hasn't got any money. He owns the house, and I should think he'll sell it because he mightn't be able to stay in that practice after he's married. When he sells it, I'll get half of whatever it is. And he'll pay Thomas's school fees but I should think that would be about all.' Daisy noticed that Katya alternated, as very shocked unhappy people do, between periods of deadpan practicality and outbursts of wordless misery. Daisy rang Anthony at the flat, but there was no reply. She rang Anna, who said that Anthony kept going to Dublin about some film, but that she knew how to reach him. Meanwhile Katya was welcome to stay with her.

'How long does she want the flat for?'

'Well, for the children's holidays, anyway.'

'Best if I get Anthony to call you. He wants to make a plan with you anyway.'

Daisy made another sandwich for Katya to have with tea. She remembered how snacks seemed to go with grief. Real meals quickly became uneatable, but sandwiches, biscuits, even a hard-boiled egg or two do not seem to count as food.

They had tea in the garden. It was after five, and Daisy still had not said anything about Henry. If only the owners had not reclaimed the boat! The cottage was too small for secrets, and, in any case, she did not want to lie to Katya but, then, neither did she want to impose her happiness upon her daughter at this particular point in her life. She supposed there was also a third factor. She desperately wanted Katya to like and approve of Henry, to see him as he truly was, and telling her about him – or anyone else for that matter – would always have been a tricky business. Katya had a proprietorial sense about her that resented any outside intrusion. Daisy compromised, which she knew was almost always a mistake.

They had been discussing what work Katya might do, and Daisy had suggested that research might be a good idea. Before she married Katya had done some for someone writing an historical novel, but she imagined that literally thousands of undergraduates were looking for that sort of work. Daisy told her she would ask Anna if she had any contacts.

They were in the kitchen and Daisy was putting the tea leaves into the compost bin, when Katya said how serious she was about her compost.

'It's not really me. It's Henry. He takes compost very seriously.'

'And, of course, you must do what your gardener tells you.'

'Actually, darling, he's become much more of a friend than a gardener. I mean – he *is* the gardener, of course, but I don't treat him like one.'

'How *do* you treat him?'

But before Daisy could answer she saw him from the kitchen window coming from the garage up the path to the back door. Katya saw him too.

'Don't tell him about me,' she said. It was an urgent plea and there was no time to argue.

There ensued one of the most awkward evenings Daisy could remember. The fact that neither Katya nor Henry knew the salient facts about one another made for strained conversation in general and increasing discomfort for all three of them. Daisy managed to convey to Henry that Katya did not yet know about them: he was remarkably quick to pick that up, and of course he knew that Katya had left her husband but was in no position to tell her that he knew. Katya, for her part, resented his being there at all, since it prevented her – as she had decided – from any further confidence. And Daisy felt that she was, in some sense, betraying both of them. She was afraid that Henry would feel that she was ashamed of him. She saw him battling with Katya's hostility in the face of repeated snubs, and his gentleness, tact and unfailing courtesy kindled a love for him deeper and more complete, she thought, than she had ever felt. She loved him then for his virtue – for his loving kindness that could embrace her child however Katya behaved to him. There was a brief respite from tension when Katya went upstairs to wash. Daisy offered her a bath and she said she might – she'd see.

'You haven't told her, then?'

'I couldn't. I was about to when you came back. She's dreadfully unhappy.'

'I can see that. He's got someone else, has he?'

'Yes. Darling, you are being sweet to her. She's not usually like this. She doesn't mean to be rude. Well, I suppose she *does*. When she saw you coming up the path she asked me not to talk about her situation in front of you, and there simply wasn't time to argue.'

346

'Do you want me to go to the pub? Disappear for the evening? Would that help, my darling love? You look so anxious. How long is she staying?'

'I don't know. Just a night or two, I think. She wants to have my flat in London, and I've got to get hold of Anthony to ask him to go so that she can have it. She wants to take the children there.'

They could hear the water running upstairs. He put his arms round her.

'It's just – she hasn't the faintest idea about us.'

'I think she has.'

'I do love you.'

'I know you do.'

'It just seemed – somehow heartless to tell her when she was wanting to tell me how awful things are for her.'

'I don't want to leave you when you are so anxious.'

'Let's have supper, and see how things go. Make one of your wonderful drinks for us all.'

While he was doing this Daisy went up to the large spare room where she found Katya sitting on the end of the bed. She had borrowed Daisy's bathrobe and was combing out her newly washed hair, which hung in heavy dripping locks round her shoulders.

'Thought I might as well wash it as you had a shower.'

'I came up to see whether you want anything.'

'Well, I wouldn't mind a clean shirt, if you've one to spare.'

Daisy returned with her largest shirt.

'Darling, it really would be all right to talk about things in . . . front of Henry.'

'That means he's having supper with us, I suppose.'

'Yes. He lives here.'

'How long has that been going on? He wasn't when I saw him before.'

'Since I had my fall. The doctor said somebody must be here. He was extraordinarily good to me. Anyway, I promise you he would be sympathetic and discreet.'

'I don't want him to be anything. I feel so humiliated – you must see that I don't want to talk about it. In front of a perfect *stranger*.'

Daisy had to leave it at that.

They had the drink, and what Henry called a fill-up, which was really a second drink. And they had supper. The drinks had been in the garden, but Katya said she was getting bitten, so they moved indoors. Conversation was sticky. Katya behaved as though she was interviewing Henry for some unknown position or job, but he was unfailingly patient and courteous in his replies.

'How's your garden designing going? I shouldn't have thought that there were many clients rich enough to employ you in these parts.'

'Well – no. I usually have to go further afield. But I have been more or less fully occupied here lately.'

'Have you been trained as a nurse as well?'

'No,' Henry replied evenly. 'It just comes naturally to me at my age.'

'Your age?'

'I told you last time. Sixty-five. I was caretaking a boat on the canal for friends—'

'Oh, yes. And you've always been interested in writers, and you were trying to get a divorce and you were a gardener's boy at Rackham.'

'Rackham?' Daisy had never heard him say that.

'That hideous elongated castle in Wiltshire. It was famous for its gardens, and the park—'

Here the telephone rang and Daisy escaped to answer it.

It was Anthony.

'Anna tells me that you need your flat back. The thing is, could you be your usual kind, wonderful self and let me *camp* in a corner of it for just one more week – or possibly two? My film's behind schedule, but the *second* they have no need of me I shall vanish. Anna said it was Katya – well, she's a dear *friend* – I'm sure we wouldn't be in each other's hair . . .'

'I think ten days would be all right. Her children are going to join her, but that isn't until the twenty-first. She's here now – can I ring you back? Where are you?'

He was in Dublin, just for the day.

'She's having rather a horrible time. If she agrees, you must be very nice to her. Edwin has gone off.'

'How *silly* of him! Mark you, he always seemed like a piece of reproduction furniture to me.'

'Anthony, please don't say that sort of thing to her.'

'Oh dear! How I am misunderstood! I am probably the most intelligently tactful person you have ever met. I shall commiserate, I shall cheer, I shall think of a new way for her to do her hair – don't go off in a rage. Anna says that if I want to see you I shall have to brave the country. So I might just pop down with her for a day – and possibly a night *she* says, but I think a day will suffice. *That* will have to be within the next two weeks, because I am off to Rio at the end of the month. A little hol. You see how I love you? For nobody else would I brave the ghastly country. Do you remember Rodrigo? Bandy legs, but a marvellous bone structure . . .'

'Do stop talking about so many things. Give me your

Dublin number. But you are being nice about the flat. I *am* grateful. Now, number, please.'

In the kitchen, Henry had cleared the table and was making coffee. Katya was not there.

'She's gone for a walk round the garden.'

'Oh.'

'I think the best thing is for me to go to the pub. When I come back, I'll just doss down in the little spare room.'

'Perhaps that would be best. Oh, darling, I'm *sorry* it is all so difficult. But she's going to have my flat – for the summer, anyway.'

'Ah. If you get the right chance, it might be easier if you did tell her about me. I feel a bit of a – well, you know – fraud.'

'So do I. It doesn't suit either of us, does it? Telling lies.'

'Darling! I would never tell you a lie.'

He was gazing at Daisy so earnestly that she wanted to kiss him.

'I know. I meant we were sort of telling her one.'

'Well, see what you can do,' he said. He had just put the coffee things on a tray when Katya came back into the kitchen.

'Are you off?'

'Yes. I'll say goodnight to you, as you may have shut up shop by the time I'm back.'

'Goodnight. Are you by any chance going to a pub?'

'I am. Do you want me to get you cigarettes?'

'I'll give you the money.'

'Don't bother about that. You can pay me in the morning.'

'Thanks. Twenty Silk Cut.'

When he had gone, Katya said, 'That was tactful of him.'

'He is that. He realized you were unhappy, and thought we'd rather be on our own.'

'He's right there.'

As they went, with the coffee tray, into the sitting room, Daisy said, 'Why are you so disagreeable about him?' She might have added, 'and rude to him', but she did not.

'I don't honestly know, Ma. I quite liked him when I came here when you were still in the States.' She accepted a cigarette. 'Sorry I keep bumming them. I didn't buy enough at the station. That wasn't Edwin ringing, by any chance, was it?'

'No. Are you expecting him to?'

'No.'

'It was Anthony,' she said, and told Katya about all that. 'He's out most of the time, and in Dublin some nights, and he'll be gone before the children's school holidays.'

'I don't mind *him*! He pretends to be heartless and funny, but he cried like anything when we went to the cinema. And when you married Jason. Sorry, I didn't mean to talk about that.'

'I don't mind. I'm over him. You see? One does get over things – in the end.' But this elicited a fresh burst of tears.

'I do see now what it must have been like for you,' Katya said, when Daisy had found her some paper hand-kerchiefs.

'I had Jess.'

'Not when Jason left you.'

'No. But I had work. We ought to talk about that for you.'

'I've saved a thousand pounds,' she said: this clearly

seemed to her a very great deal of money. 'I saved it from the allowance Edwin gave me, and I sold some bits of jewellery he gave me. That would be enough, wouldn't it, to pay for the flat and the children until the end of their holidays?'

'You don't have to pay for the flat, darling. Any of it. And I should think Edwin will give you some money for them, but if he doesn't we'll work something out.'

'I don't think he will, because he disapproves of them being in London. When we talked about it, he said it was bad for them and they'd be much better off in the country.'

Daisy stopped herself from saying that they'd be a lot better off if he didn't abandon them for someone else.

They spent the rest of the evening thinking of work, jobs, careers, during which time Daisy realized that there was an element of unworldliness about Katya that nearly twelve years of marriage had simply enhanced. Edwin had paid all the household bills with the consequence that Katya had only the haziest idea about what things cost. She also had very little idea of what she might earn, although she did realize that a 2:1 in history did not in itself guarantee her any particular wage or salary. There was also the problem of who would look after Caroline while she was earning enough money to keep her. And then there were the holidays – when there would be two of them. 'How do people like me manage? What do they *do*?' Katya was exhausted, and Daisy could see that she was beginning to be frightened. 'I'm nearly thirty-eight – nobody will want to employ me. I'm not *trained* for anything.'

At this moment Daisy remembered that she had not called Anthony back. She said this and added that perhaps

Katya would like to talk to him, and then they could arrange about the flat together. Katya agreed to this.

While she was telephoning, Daisy slipped into the garden to smell the stocks. The silence and the darkness – the moon was obscured – and being alone were a relief, and she realized how exhausted she was. And if she felt like that, how much more must poor Katya! When she had finished talking to Anthony, Daisy would make her a hot drink and give her a sleeping pill. She walked slowly round the cottage, past the sitting-room windows where she could see and almost hear Katya in animated conversation. When she turned the corner towards the herb bed she came up against a firm, still figure standing motionless in the dark. A fleeting moment of pure terror, and then she knew it was Henry. He had put a hand over her mouth and was whispering, 'It's only me – Henry.' She was in his arms and he was kissing her – kissing her as though they had not met for weeks, and indeed she felt as famished for him.

'You've told her?'

'No. I will tomorrow. After she has had a good night's sleep.'

'Whatever happens, remember *how* I love you.'

But she did not tell Katya the next day, because she left. Anthony was returning from Dublin that morning, and they had made a plan to meet at the flat and he would take her out to lunch. She seemed almost excited at the prospect. A good night's sleep had done wonders; she was full of plans, of what she might do with the children that summer, of how she might find work that she could do at home, how she might even take some postal course that would qualify her in some direction. She would find a solicitor and find out what her rights were about the house and money for the children. She spoke of Edwin as though he was nothing more than a financial impediment. She was terribly grateful for the flat; she would keep in close touch with Daisy. One of her ways of showing how grateful she was was that she became far nicer to Henry than before. At breakfast, she even thanked him for looking after Daisy so well. She suggested herself that he should take her to the station in order not to interrupt Daisy's morning's work. Daisy agreed to this, feeling that Katya might get to know Henry better if they were on their own.

Daisy had slept very badly. She took her work out into the garden, but she had hardly settled there when the sun clouded over, and the dense grey sky seemed to be pressing down on her head, and soon after that her vision became jagged and dazzling – the herald of a migraine. There was nothing for it but to take the pills and lie down in the dark.

She woke to find Henry bending over her. For some reason this frightened her. She supposed she did not at first realize that it was he, thought she was dreaming and some unknown man was menacing her. She threw herself away from him with a hopeless cry of terror – hopeless because even in her half-awakened state she could see no escape.

Then his voice, reassuring her, stroking her forehead when she said that she had had a migraine.

'And then you had a bad dream,' he said. 'What was it, sweetheart?'

But she could not remember any part of it at all.

The rest of the day was very quiet. Daisy did not want any lunch, and Henry made himself a sandwich. She spent the afternoon lying in the garden while he pottered among the flower beds – dead-heading, tying up. She told him about Katya, and he said that she had told him a good deal when he took her to the station. Later, when they were in bed, he said that he had told Katya that he was devoted to Daisy.

'What did she say?'

'She said, did I mean I was in love with you.'

'And you said—'

'I said that I had been in love with you from the moment I saw you.'

'Did you say we were lovers?'

'No. I thought my loyal devotion was quite enough for her to be going along with.'

'Amazingly tactful. What did she say then?'

'She said that if I ever made you unhappy, she would want to kill me.'

'Oh, darling, that was a bit much.'

'No, it wasn't. I told her that *I* would feel much the same. If anyone at all did that to you.'

Then they stopped using words.

16

HENRY

I had been pretty certain that as soon as Katya was alone with me she would drop her hostility and succumb to confidences. We had scarcely gone a mile before she was telling me everything – about Edwin and his infidelities and how she had resolved to endure them until this last flagrant determination of his to go off with his latest fancy. She began by telling me as though she was over it, but in no time she was smoking and crying, and I decided to stop the car and, as it were, kiss her better. Naturally I did not literally kiss her: I played the part of Big Daddy, a character it was clear to me she had been short of all her life, put her head on my shoulder and found a nice large handkerchief. And I flattered her. It is amazing how people who are not used to flattery will absorb as though starving the merest crumb, the slightest hint, and who, after a few minutes of that, are good and ready for the stuff laid on with a trowel.

I said what a hard time she must have had; mentioned her dignity and then her courage – went on to express astonishment that *anyone* (meaning Edwin) could possibly contemplate someone else. I told her she was beautiful. The poor creature looked merely pathetic – eyes red, eyelids puffed up, complexion muddy with lack of sleep and inadequate food – but I used the word beautiful as though it was a sudden and wonderful discovery I had made about her. I could see her hesitate, then she actually blushed – like her mother – before it was shakily accepted. But I did not pursue that line. I was not courting her after all, and the last thing I wanted was for her to start fancying me, which in her vulnerable state she might well have been prone to do, or indeed any kind gentleman who chatted her up.

I said we must catch her train, gently detached myself and started to drive again. Then, to deflect her, I asked about her children and she talked much of them and I had only to murmur a few encouraging things, like how nice and intelligent they sounded and how much I hoped one day to meet them. I also said that Daisy (I called her that) had been very worried when she, Katya, had been out of touch.

As we neared the station she started fumbling in her bag. 'I never paid you for the cigarettes.'

'Oh, please. Let that be a very small token of my regard.'

She thanked me very nicely, and then, as I was parking the car, she suddenly said, 'Do you call her Daisy? My mother?'

'Yes. I do. She asked me to, of course.' I stopped the engine. 'Perhaps I should tell you one thing. I have been utterly devoted to your mother ever since I first saw her. Utterly.'

'Does she know?'

I shrugged – almost shook my head. 'That doesn't matter. All it means is that I am happy and proud to be able to serve her, look after her – like after her fall on the path.'

Our eyes met then, and I saw hers soften: the romance of secret lifelong servitude had touched her.

'Please,' I said, 'don't ever tell her I told you that. In

fact, I'd rather you didn't tell anyone.' I gave what I knew would look like a courageous, small smile. 'I'm very well as I am.'

I took her luggage to the platform for her. The train was arriving – we had only just caught it. She stood on the steps, then she leaned down and kissed me lightly on the cheek. I returned the kiss in like manner, and she smiled.

'Last time, you kissed my hand.'

Then the train began to move: she really looked most attractive when she smiled.

I waited politely until the train was out of sight, in case she should look out of a window and wave, but she didn't.

I had thought of confiding in Daisy about the problems of the form I had to fill in for the lawyer, but when I got back she was in bed with a migraine, and for the rest of that day she looked so rotten (strange how migraines make people's faces crumble; Charley was just the same although in her case it didn't produce such a marked contrast as it did with Daisy) that it seemed better to defer that.

I decided that it would be best to tell Daisy that I had declared my devotion for her to Katya. It was interesting that she did not ask whether I had said that she, Daisy, loved me. She only asked whether I had said we were lovers. I stopped prolonged discussion about all that by making love to her.

All the rest of that week and the following weekend, Daisy took to working indoors, which was cooler than anywhere outside. There was not much to do in the garden, but I pottered there, and what with that and Daisy's far higher standards than mine about keeping the house clean, there was more than enough to do for one whose inclination was not to do very much of anything. I did the shopping and it was usually when I was out that she rang Katya. She was quite open about that, but I sensed that she preferred talking to her when I wasn't there. She announced that Katya and Anthony seemed to have hit it off very well.

The builders sent in their estimates within two days of one another. It had begun to strike me that enlarging the cottage was not necessarily a good idea – at least not until I was married to Daisy, and that could not possibly be for some time. A larger cottage might mean that Katya would bring her children down, possibly for weeks in the summer. Anyway the project was going to cost between eighteen and twenty-one thousand pounds, money that might well be better spent, although it was comforting to note that Daisy did not seem to blench at the various costs.

'I could always sell the flat in London,' she said. This gave me my cue.

'I don't think you should consider that for a moment. Katya might turn out to need it. Wouldn't it be better to wait a bit before you let yourself in for such an expense?'

She smiled. 'You sound just like Anna.' And later: 'Anyway, we don't want builders with all that noise and dirt to spoil this beautiful summer. And they'd wake us up terribly early in the morning.'

'I'm the person to wake you up, then.'

'I know.'

We were sitting opposite each other at the kitchen table. She had looked away from me as she said that.

'Look at me, Daisy. Look at me, darling. Aren't we

lucky? To be so much in love? To have one another at last?'

She did look at me then. I don't think that anyone – not even Charley – had ever looked at me like that before.

'I can hardly believe it.'

Her eyes were full of tears.

Those halcyon days! The heat continued, the dew early devoured by the sun that shone with a pale intensity bleaching the sky, and the roses, making mirages on the lane, gilding the leaves of the large oak at the edge of the wood, touching the delicate tendrils of her fairy hair with coppery incident. The air each day became drenched with aromatic scent: of rosemary that I had planted by the front door, the thyme and camomile in cracks of the path, the lavender in beds each side of the door. Butterflies provided the silent, finishing touches.

We ate tomato salads that she made with chives or basil, and raspberries, and amazing cold soups that she could concoct of seemingly any vegetable.

Daisy bought a large-scale map of our district: she loved to find footpaths and explore them. We would go in the evenings after tea (I was even getting to like the Earl Grey that she was so fond of). Sometimes I would make her have a siesta. I bought her a hammock – as a present – and set it up between two convenient apple trees at the side of the house. She gave me presents: three shirts and a beautiful dressing-gown that she ordered from London. When we came back from our walk, she would prepare supper and I would make drinks for us. The lawn became full of daisies – something had gone wrong with the mower and it was too hot to get it into the car to take it to be mended. She taught me to play

Scrabble and we did *The Times* crossword together throughout the day, usually completing it between us.

The news from Katya seemed satisfactory. The children were to arrive as soon as the boy's holidays began – about a week hence. She did talk about them coming down, saying that they could sleep in the sitting room. 'I don't think we could share a room if they come,' she said. I said that we should practise making soundless love. I have come to adore making her blush.

'Oh, Henry, I'm not sure that I could—'

'Could what?'

'Manage it.'

I said I could evolve a system that would deal with that. 'I make love to you, you make a single sound, and I don't make love to you for two days.'

'Wouldn't that be – punishing both of us?'

'Of course it would,' I said. This was becoming true. I was far more taken with her sexually than I had expected to be. This was partly because I enjoyed the fact that she was undoubtedly addicted to me. She was thoroughly awakened now – all fears gone. She could be naked and shameless and completely at ease in her hunger, and her appearance was transformed: the myriad tiny lines of tension and strain had mostly vanished; her skin bloomed with sensuous health; her eyes were always clear and alive with whatever she was seeing and feeling about what she saw, and her body released from the taut fragility that I had first encountered was now that of a much younger woman. (All my own work, though I say it myself.)

Then, on the Monday morning, Anna rang to say that she and Anthony would like to come down to the cottage for the following weekend. Anthony would be going abroad soon after that, and she, Anna, could only manage weekends away.

Daisy was pleased, I could see that. She at once began making plans about what food she would buy and cook for them. Wine must be bought, and fish ('Anthony loves fish'), and she would make a large hors d'oeuvre, a favourite of Anna's. She discovered all kinds of things that she must buy for their visit: more sheets and towels, a fish kettle (she would buy a salmon), more ice trays, a larger coffee pot – the list went on and on.

I asked about Anthony. Somehow I knew that he in no way constituted any threat: he was homosexual, for a start. I knew that somehow, even before she told me. Had she known him long? No, she'd met him some time before Jason had left (it was interesting how she could now speak of this without any apparent pain), and they had got on at once. 'But I don't think it was anything to do with me. I think Anthony gets on with everyone. He has a real gift for friendship.' And for love? I asked. She didn't know. He was always mysterious, evasive, about his love life.

'He tends to tell me about it after it has finished,' she said. 'He's very sharp: he notices people.'

'You mean he's spiteful.'

'No! I mean he sees what they are. He's often funny, but he's never malicious – or anything like that. I'm sure you'll like him,' she finished, saying what people always say when they are more hopeful than certain.

Daisy became more and more excited (and, I think, nervous) as the weekend became nearer. On Thursday we went to the town because she suddenly wanted to buy two more deckchairs ('so that we can all eat in the garden if we want'). It was a breathless day, no movement of air to ease the heat. Children in prams were crying because they were too hot; everybody in the shops remarked on the length of the heatwave and hoped it would stop soon. Daisy chose the chairs and when we had packed them into the boot said she wanted to buy soft fruit to make a summer pudding. If I would drive the car to the green-grocer, she would just pop out and buy the fruit.

The car park winked and glittered and stank of exhaust fumes. Dogs who had been left in cars leaned their heads out of the open windows panting. Daisy got worried about them, but I hurried her on – just looking at the dogs made me thirsty.

There was a queue at the greengrocer's and a traffic warden waiting to pounce so I had to drive twice round the elaborate one-way system. When I finally stopped Daisy was waiting, laden with carrier-bags and an armful of delphiniums.

'Sorry to be so long,' she said, as she loaded the back of the car. 'I got one or two other things as well as I was there. I've completely run out of money, but we don't need any so that doesn't matter.'

'What about the pub?'

'Are we going to the pub?'

'Not if we've got no money. I'm afraid I didn't bring any.'

'Let's go home and have a drink there. It will be much nicer. I don't want to leave all the salad things and the flowers in the car.'

I started the car without saying anything.

'Oh dear. You wanted to go. I could cash some at a bank if I've got my card.'

But she hadn't got it, which, for some reason, made me crosser. I knew it was a mistake at this point to make any kind of scene, so I laughed. 'I'm just parched, dehydrated

– you know how it is. I expect they'd cash a cheque at the pub: they know us well enough by now.'

'All right.' She sounded resigned.

We had the drink, but I didn't enjoy it because I sensed that she was itching to get back. Nothing was said by either of us, but I felt that she knew I couldn't enjoy the drink so the feeling of faint tension prevailed. These gestures, or the motions of them, are the devil and how they characterize married life! I determined, with some grimness, that ours was not going to be a marriage like that.

Worse was to come. When we finally got back to the cottage and had unloaded the chairs and the shopping from the car and she was putting the delphiniums into a tall jug, she suggested that I should take the chairs outside to join the other two by the table. While I was doing this, she came to the open front door and called, 'And, Henry, you'll *have* to mow the lawn before they come. It looks so ragged.'

'Darling, I can't. The mower's bust.'

'Oh, I forgot. If only you'd thought of it, we could have taken it in to be mended.'

'Even if we had, it wouldn't have been done in time.'

'They might lend us one.'

When I was back in the kitchen, she said, 'We should have taken it two weeks ago when it broke.'

'Yes. I'm sorry.'

'You couldn't scythe it? If you can scythe, I mean.'

'Yes, I can scythe all right.' Backbreaking memories of scything in the orchard at Rackham under my father's merciless discipline came and went. 'But the lawn's too short for scything.'

'Well, then, we'll just have to ring up Hunter's and rent a mower. You could do it this afternoon.'

It was the first time for weeks, months even, that I felt she was behaving like an employer. The thought of lugging that bloody machine into the car and driving it the ten miles all the way back where we'd spent the morning, and then trying to coax a machine out of Hunter's, and all in the midday to afternoon heat made me feel really mutinous. And *then*, ten to one, they'd want their machine back at least by the following morning. As I could see no way out of it, I resolved to make her pay one way or another. Without a word, I stumped out of the back door. I knew she would come after me, or at least call out, and she did.

'Henry! Don't you want to have some lunch first?'

'No, thanks. I don't feel like lunch.'

'At least it would be better to call Hunter's before you go. To make sure they can lend you a machine.' She had reached me as I got to the car.

'What good would that do? If I can't get one there, I'll have to get one somewhere else. I promise you, I won't come back without one.'

I had opened the door and was wheeling the machine towards it.

'Do you want me to help you?'

'No. Just leave me to get on with it.'

She turned and left me then, and I felt some satisfaction to know that she knew I was angry.

I didn't go to the town. What I did was to get the garage in the village to agree to take it in for me when next they went there. Then I went to Mrs Patel's little supermarket where I had been a good customer for months before I'd begun living with Daisy, and coaxed/

bribed her into lending me the little hand mower that her husband used for their back garden. I promised to return it the following morning; then I cashed a cheque with her and gave her five pounds. Then I went to the pub, which was nearly closing so I bought a half-bottle of vodka and a large bottle of lemonade and a packet of fags and then I drove off past the cottage over the canal bridge and past the wood that joined the one beside the cottage garden, and continued for about half a mile where there was a cart-track on the right at its edge. Here I parked, and slipped into the shade among the bluebell leaves and clumps of bracken until I found a suitable tree to lean against. I drank as much as I pleased, smoked two or three cigarettes and then fell asleep.

When I awoke it was nearly five: I would have been gone nearly four hours. I buried the empty vodka bottle deep in the leaf mould, washed my mouth out with a swig of the lemonade – now unpleasantly warm – and drove back to the cottage, stopping at a bit of verge where grew some large clumps of ox-eye daisies which I picked.

I knew that Daisy would be anxious about my long absence, and I also guessed that, with her nature, anxiety would take the form of guilt rather than anger. In this I was entirely right. She came running out of the cottage as I parked the car.

'Oh, darling, I'm sorry! You must have had an awful afternoon. It's all my fault fussing about the lawn. I did so want everything to be perfect for the weekend.'

'I know you did.' I picked up the bunch of daisies as I got out of the car. 'This is just to show you that I love every single daisy I meet. Partly why we've got them all over the lawn.' I gave her the bunch and she flung her other arm round me.

'I was afraid something awful had happened to you.'

When I said nothing, she glanced at me and said, so quietly I could hardly hear her, 'Then I was afraid you were angry with me.'

'Oh, darling! I would never be angry with you – never!'

I told her that I had been all over the place trying to borrow a mower, and then, when I had despaired of finding anywhere in the town, had thought of Mrs Patel, whose mower we now had. 'It's not a motor mower, but better than nothing.'

'It was good of you to take so much trouble.' I could see that she had reverted to feeling shy. We went into the house for supper. The kitchen still smelt of the seething fruits for the summer pudding, which sat in the larder with the doorstop wrapped in tinfoil on a plate weighing it down in its basin. She showed it to me. 'Jess used to make them,' she said. 'I've never done one before.'

I admired it. All evening I was very gentle with her, and watched the way she regained her confidence: she was becoming like an instrument on which I could play any tune I pleased. But I wanted this to be a memorable evening (and night) for her to cement our relationship and protect it from any outside threat.

'Do you always take so much trouble over guests?' I asked at one point.

'I've never really had any before. One doesn't – much – in London. The occasional person for the night, but I didn't go in for that. So, yes, I am excited. But they are both such friends . . .'

'I hope they'll like me.'

'Of course they will. Of course.'

We went outside before going to bed – to smell the tobacco and stocks, to look at the moon, a deep rich golden harvest moon rising majestically in a sky pricked with stars. Moths blundered into us, with the lightest of papery thuds, the light from the open doorway attracting and dazzling them. The daisies on the lawn were all shut for the night and the dew had begun. It was a night for romance, for lovers – a night made for us, I told her, and saw her face, pale in the dark dusk, her eyes glittering with tears as she came into my arms.

'Henry, I love you so much. So *much*,' she repeated. I kissed her and wondered then what she felt, felt like.

17

DAISY

She knew that he was nervous about the weekend: he did not say so but she could feel it. Or perhaps it was simply that *she* felt nervous and attributed it to him. What would it matter, after all, if Anthony did not like him? (She did not say this to him; she was afraid of hurting his feelings.) But she thought it more than once, and the last time she realized that it was far more important to her that Anna should like him. She had done one thing that she didn't want him ever to know; she had sent Anna some of his letters – not many of them, but the ones describing his life. He wrote so well about it, she thought, that if Anna read them she would understand him better. In some ways she felt treacherous at showing anyone else what he had written privately to her, but if it resulted in Anna seeing more clearly her reasons for loving him, then it would have been worth it. He need never know. She had asked Anna to bring the letters back when she came.

Yesterday, when he was away for hours, she had begun to be afraid that he was staying away on purpose because he was angry with her. But when he did come back with his account of how difficult it had been to find a mower, he had been so sweet, so gentle to her, and he'd brought daisies that he had picked and that had touched her very much.

In the morning he had gone off to fetch the salmon

and she got the bedrooms ready. He had cleared all his stuff out of the small room where he'd put it when Katya came, and they had had to put most of it into a suitcase as there was no room in her bedroom for any more clothes.

When she was making mayonnaise for the fish, she suddenly thought, What about *Henry* liking *them*? It was odd that she had only just thought of it that way round.

In the afternoon, Henry mowed and clipped the edges of the lawn and she cooked; the sun disappeared but the heat was almost suffocating. There would be a storm, he said, and she was divided between longing for the refreshment it would bring, and wanting good weather for her friends. There was lightning, and very distant thunder, and no birds were to be heard or seen.

They arrived at six, came staggering up the front path with quantities of things that she knew would be Anthony's – Anna always travelled light.

He had brought her six bottles of champagne, a side of smoked salmon, a bottle of Fracas – her favourite scent – and a pot in which a delicate white orchid was flowering. He also had two suitcases – things he might want to wear, he said. His coppery hair was cut *en brosse*, and he wore trousers with enormous checks and an iris-coloured shirt.

'I do so love giving presents. I like them to be overwhelming. Are they, darling?'

'Utterly.'

He hugged her and Anna stood, smiling at them. 'I'll just go and fetch the rest of my stuff.'

'What sort of rest?' she asked Anna.

'Mostly games, I think.' She'd put her small bag down and they embraced.

'Henry's having a shower. I had the first one so as to be ready for you.'

Anthony reappeared with a canvas holdall that seemed to be full of boxes.

'These are not presents. They are indoor ploys to while away the rural hours. Shall I just pop two bottles into the fridge? You *have* a fridge, I suppose? Or do you just have a marble shelf with fly-papers and bowls of antique food?'

'I have both, of course.'

'I'll do it,' Anna said. 'I know where things are.'

'I suppose there's a distinct danger of my getting lost in a place like this. *Good* colours in your sitting room, darling Daisy. And you look lovely. More like a Hilliard than ever.' He put his hands on her shoulders and she met his penetrating pale blue stare. 'Sweet, happy Daisy.' He gave her shoulders a small shake.

'There's something different about you.'

'There is. Guess what?'

'You look different,' she began slowly. 'Oh – it's your nose!'

'I had a nose job last year.' He'd always had a rather large nose, but it certainly didn't look either smaller or a different shape.

'No, I had it made *larger*. I know some women like to have their breasts enhanced to be more sexy. Well, large noses denote character, and I decided I wanted more of that.'

As she was laughing, Henry appeared on the stairs. He came almost bustling down: he was smiling, in a sort of general, undirected way.

She introduced him.

'Hello, Henry. I ought to say Hooray Henry, ought I?'

Anna reappeared, greeted Henry, and said could she take her things up and have a shower?

'Of course. I'll come up with you.'

When they were upstairs, Anna said, 'I think it would be easier if Anthony had the larger room.'

'Because of his nose?'

'Because of his nose,' Anna said solemnly. 'He's mad, isn't he? But I always forget what marvellous company he is. He's brought so much stuff, and I don't mind in the least; you know I don't.'

'Have you told him about Henry?'

'A bit. Barest outline. I won't be long. Join you in the garden.'

So they sat, in the chairs near the big tree, with glasses of champagne.

'Madly green,' Anthony said, looking round the small, bosky place. 'Wonderfully hot, though. It's like abroad. Do you like heat?' he asked Henry.

'Within reason.'

'You don't like it.'

'I don't love it,' Henry said firmly.

'What do you love?'

Henry looked at Daisy and continued as he answered. 'Books, writing, writers . . .' He fell silent.

She knew that he wanted to say that he loved her, but did not quite dare.

Anna said, 'What about the second bottle?' and Henry at once said he'd fetch it.

'Potty about you.'

'Don't tease him. He's feeling a bit out of it.'

Anna helped her lay out the supper, which it was decided they would have inside. The rumbles of thunder were coming far sooner after the sheets of lightning. It was getting like the last act of *Rigoletto*, Anthony said. 'I do hope nobody turns up with a dead soprano in a sack.' She could see Henry smiling at this as though he knew what Anthony meant, but somehow she also knew that he didn't.

When they had finished with the salmon and were eating the summer pudding, Anthony whipped out a camera and started taking pictures of them, in ones and twos and finally all together.

By then they had all had a good deal to drink. Anthony had talked most; in fact he had talked nearly all the time, needing only to be prompted by herself or Anna with the simplest question. 'What did I do *then*? I simply waited until a man who looked as rich as he was going to be kind turned up and then I practically *assaulted* him and then we went to the Ritz.'

'But you said you hadn't a stitch on?'

'Daisy, dear, blankets don't have stitches. I was wearing a blanket – one of those little grey jobs you get on long-distance flights. I had been using it as a *shawl*, but by then it had become something of a *sarong* . . .'

'The lovely thing is that we don't have to believe a word you say—'

'My dear Anna, I should hope not. I can't tell you how boring it would be if I told you the unvarnished truth. Don't you find that?' He turned suddenly to Henry.

'Oh, well—' He was looking at Daisy again. 'The truth is often more strange than any invention. In my opinion.'

'Lucky you.' Anthony said it with careless amity, but she could see that Henry didn't take it like that.

Anna suggested that two of them should clear up. 'There isn't room for all of us in the kitchen. Daisy, you cooked, so take Anthony next door. You can do it tomorrow.'

'All right, bossy boots. Come on, darling. Yes, and I can tell you about Katya.'

Which he did. He was clearly being extremely kind to her.

'She's stopped crying so much. You're not exactly a dry-eyed family, are you? So it isn't simply her Polish blood. Anyway, we've talked a lot about what she might do, and we've been making the flat nice for the children. She says they regard coming to London as an enormous treat, so we've thought of lots of *excursions* she can make with them that won't be too costly. She said you were giving her the flat. She was thrilled about you doing that. Anna thinks that Edwin will have to come up with a bit more than the school fees.'

'Yes, but I don't think Katya will be very good at asking for it. She's very proud – stubborn, really. And she hates him at the moment.'

'Naturally. Well – actually, I've offered to go down with her and kind of be around while they talk about that sort of thing. If she leaves it to lawyers, it will take months and bitterness will prevail.'

'Goodness!' She tried to imagine Edwin's reaction to Anthony, and failed.

'It's just because I'm such an *unlikely* person that it will be all right. I'm frightfully good at making people think they've thought of kind things to do. I shall butter him up and be full of treacherous understanding for him and his adulterous plight. Anyway, Katya trusts me, so I do hope you will too. I don't *think* I could make matters worse. They must get on somehow, because of the kiddy-winks.'

'Dearest Anthony, of course I trust you. I'm so awfully grateful. He wouldn't listen to me – I know that.'

'Your lovely eyes are filling with tears of gratitude. It's

really not good for them. I can see you are in a very emotional state. Is that due to your friend Henry?'

She nodded. 'Do you like him?'

He looked at her thoughtfully. 'That is a hopeless question, darling, as you well know. Is he one of those people who has a heart of gold?'

'You mean you find him boring?'

'I haven't found anything.' He took one of her hands and gave it a squeeze. 'But I will, if you like. And meanwhile, if he makes you happy, of course I like him.'

'He makes me happy.'

'It's so marvellous when people do that, isn't it? And so *rare*. I'm awfully keen on it myself. Shall I show you my games I've brought? See what you'd like to play with?'

By the time they all went to bed, the storm had begun. Lightning and huge grumbling claps of thunder and, eventually, rain. She could hear it tapping on the leaves in the wood. She went to sleep to the pouring sibilant sound while the thunder lurched uncertainly back and forth above them, and with Henry's arms round her. They whispered; it was easy to hear any sounds in the cottage.

When they awoke the next morning, it was still raining. Henry seemed so fast asleep that even when she got up and dressed, he did not stir.

Downstairs she found Anna making tea.

'I always get up early,' she said.

When she had cut some bread and put it into the toaster, she wandered to the front door and opened it. The air was marvellously fresh, but the path was a chain of puddles, and the lawn – now miraculously a brilliant green – was studded with birds prising worms out of the damp earth.

'Oh, dear. What shall we do with Anthony in this

dreadful weather? It will simply confirm his worst views of the country.'

'I shouldn't worry,' Anna said comfortably. 'He prefers being indoors anyway, and he's brought an enormous jigsaw he's dying to do.'

'Did you read the letters?' Daisy asked, when they had begun their breakfast.

'Yes, I did.'

'What did you think of them?'

'You're certainly right about his writing good letters.' She waited. 'And then he seems to have had more than his share of misfortune,' she paused, 'and he does seem to be far more intelligent on paper than he does when one meets him.'

'Well, he doesn't know you, and he's shy. He's afraid you won't like him. I think he's one of those people who are only themselves when you're alone with them.' Then they heard sounds from above and stopped talking about him.

Later in the morning, she drove with Anna to the village because they hadn't enough lemons for the smoked salmon, and Anna suddenly asked, 'Have you met any of his friends?'

'Henry's? No – no, I haven't. You see, when he left his wife he left where he was living. He doesn't know people round here.'

'Where was he living?'

'Northampton, I think. He never talks about it. I think he does feel bad about the last wife: he really doesn't like her.'

'And she's still there?'

'Yes. She's kept their house, and she has some kind of job at the hospital.' After a moment, she added, 'I don't ask him about these things because I think he finds them very painful. Katya liked him, you know. She wasn't at all sure of him at first, but she told me on the telephone that she thought he was really a very nice and unusual man. *She* could see the point of him.'

'Daisy, I'm not against him, truly—'

'You sound it!'

'I'm really sorry if I do. I'm so used to finding the flies in ointment – you know how I nitpick over contracts, and I've seen you made so very unhappy. That's it, really.'

'You're not fussing about his being working class, or anything like that?'

'Nothing like that. Nothing at all like that.'

When they got back, they found that Anthony had cleared the middle of the sitting-room floor and emptied the pieces of his jigsaw puzzle on to a white tablecloth. He was busily engaged in putting all the pieces the right way up. He was wearing white trousers and a bitter chocolate-coloured shirt, and his feet were bare.

'You must look – it's the most wonderful piece of Victorian sentiment. *The Soldier's Return*. He's got his arm in a sling, and a bandage round his head, and she's dressed in a sort of *Wuthering Heights* costume standing outside a thatched ruin with ever such a bonny baby in her arms. And there's a huge faithful dog of uncertain origin. Heaven, don't you think? Fifteen hundred pieces. What about a little drinky-winky as my mother used to say before her infinitesimal glass of disgusting sherry? Henry kindly put some more fizz in the fridge for us. We were simply waiting for you.'

'Where's Henry?'

'Darling, *I* don't know. I offered him work on this jigsaw but he didn't seem interested.'

Anna, who was in the kitchen, called, 'He's outside, Daisy. Coming round from the back of the garage.'

She went out to meet him.

'How I first saw you,' he said, 'in that large black hat and your long mac. I've been cleaning up Mrs Patel's mower for her. It was in a rather dilapidated state.'

She put her arm in his and he gave it a squeeze.

'Is it going to stop raining?'

'Some time in the afternoon by the look of it. Mind you, I don't think it will last.'

He was right about that. At lunch she announced that she was going to take them on a small excursion.

'Where, darling? There isn't a fair anywhere about, is there? I simply adore them.'

'Afraid not. An amazing garden Henry and I found, and if you can face a little walk, there's a pets' cemetery on the estate.'

'Only if it stops raining. Do you want to go, Anna?'

'I'd like some fresh air – yes, I do want to.'

'You can get plenty of fresh air indoors. It's called draughts. I'm far from sure that I shall enjoy myself,' Anthony grumbled.

The rain did stop, and the sun came out and the sky was blue between the small white clouds. They had to go in two cars, as neither was built for more than one passenger.

They had not gone to the garden before; had tried once on a weekday in spring and it had been closed.

She had hoped that going round a large and beautiful garden would show Henry off to the others to his best advantage, but here she was wrong. He wandered round with them, displaying very little interest, although he answered any question she or Anna put to him. There were two walled gardens, one with old-fashioned roses now well past their best, and one with large herbaceous borders that had clearly suffered from the drought, and an elaborate parterre in its centre filled with pinks, whose scent after the rain was striking. There was a lime avenue that led to a water garden surrounded by a tapestry hedge with niches for statues. Anthony liked those, and took pictures of them.

'But I do want to see the animals' cemetery.' She felt bossy saying it, but she also felt anxious about straight society in the cottage. And tomorrow it might be raining again.

So they took the cars, and parked by the river, just as she and Henry had, and followed the track until they reached the small domed building. Fortunately, Anthony was enchanted by it. '*What* a find!' He examined the graves most thoroughly, and photographed them as well as the building. 'Now I'll take a picture of you sitting on the steps outside it,' he said, and obediently, they sat in a row, with her in the middle and Anna and Henry each side of her. Henry gently squeezed her arm and when she looked at him, she could see he was reminding her of the last time that they had been there. They smiled at each other and she felt much better. It was all right: it was simply that he did not have much – if any – general conversation.

She drove back with Henry in her car. He was curious about Anna, asked whether she had anyone in her life, asked whether she was a lesbian, and she answered that Anna did not talk much if at all about her past, and that now she devoted herself to her work. And no, she wasn't a lesbian; she was a very good godmother to the daughter of one of her writers, and she had many friends among them, but tended to keep them apart.

'She looks after everything for me – makes the hard decisions for me, helps me about my money – I'm not very good at that and writers' money is always rather a dicey business.'

'You don't live as though it is.'

'Don't I? Well, Anna would probably agree with you.'

He was silent for a while, and then he said, 'Your friend, Anthony, I can't make him out at all. Is he acting or is he always like that?'

'He's always extreme. No, he doesn't exactly *act*, but he likes to entertain people.'

'I'm afraid he doesn't find me very entertaining. I can't talk about the sort of things your friends talk about. I don't move in those circles.'

'I know you don't. But people don't have to be the same for one to like them.'

'I see that.'

'They loved the garden. And you were awfully good at knowing the names of everything.'

'Well, they would expect that, wouldn't they, from a gardener?'

She could not get the chip off his shoulder, and gave up.

'Are they following us?'

'Oh, yes.'

'What it is,' he said, moments later, 'is that I'm suffering from withdrawal symptoms. I want you to myself. I want to undress you very slowly and put you on the bed and do all the things I know you like.'

'Oh, darling! They're going tomorrow.'

'Are they?'

'After lunch.'

This seemed to cheer him considerably.

As they got out of the car, he said, 'I will try. I will try not to be such a bore.'

At dinner, Anna tried as well. She asked him more about the garden they had seen; wanted to know how long it would have taken to make, and whether it had been designed by one person, or was the consequence of generations of gardeners.

'Oh, I should think that originally a good deal of it was laid out by one person. But the second walled garden – the one with the roses – came later. You could tell that by the different brick.'

'Would you like to design something of that size?'

'It would be a challenge. But I've mostly done quite small places, where the scope is limited. You can't plant trees with any grand design in a small place.'

'Is that what your book was about?'

'What book?' Daisy looked from Anna, who had asked the question, to Henry, who did not immediately answer it.

'Henry told me about the book he was doing that got destroyed.'

'Who—'

Henry looked at her and mouthed, 'Hazel.'

'Oh, that one.' Daisy had never heard of it before, but she realized that Henry did not want to talk about it.

'It just came up,' he said, when they were going to bed. 'Anna asked me if I'd ever done any writing, so I told her. It was when I took her to the station, last time she was here.'

'You never told *me*.'

'Didn't I? I thought I had. But it upset me so much at the time, I suppose I've kind of buried it.'

There was another storm that night and the next morning they woke up to heavy rain.

'There's nothing for it,' Anthony said. He had wandered downstairs in a scarlet silk dressing-gown. 'No Sunday papers and all that weather outside. You'll all have to buckle down to my jigsaw.'

So they did, spent hours on hands and knees fitting and not fitting pieces. The atmosphere became much easier. Henry joined in: he collected the pieces of the cottage with its thatched roof, and this pleased Anthony. Daisy was given the sky to do, and Anna the rather muddy indeterminate foreground. Anthony did the people.

'Far the easiest,' Anna complained, 'and much the most fun.'

'Darling, it *is* my jigsaw. And I have done all the edges for all of you.'

Daisy had made a lamb stew for lunch and they had it very late, because of finishing the jigsaw. Anna and Anthony had both been very nice to Henry, praising him when he got something right, commiserating when he didn't.

When lunch was over Anthony said they really ought to go because he'd promised to take Katya to a movie, so Anna told him to go and pack, and Henry offered to pack away the jigsaw, the Scrabble, etc.

Anna helped her clear away the lunch and they talked a little about the play.

'I meant to give you the rough structure of it.'

'Could I take it and make a copy and send you back the original?'

'You could. There's not an awful lot of it, but enough

for you to see the way I have in mind to do it. Only I'm not sure yet whether it's going to make a good shape. Anyway, I'd really like to know what you think.' Then, dropping her voice, she said, 'Did you bring the other papers back?'

'What papers? Oh – *those*. I'm so sorry, I clean forgot. I put them out to bring and then somehow I forgot.'

'You could send them back with the treatment.'

'I will.'

They looked at each other, and then Anna embraced her. 'You do look well and happy, and I am glad,' she said. 'Don't forget you're a writer, will you? And come and stay with me sometimes if your flat is full of family.'

'Here I am with just what I stand up in,' announced Anthony. 'Dearest Daisy, it has been marvellous seeing you. If I were you, as people say when they're so glad that they aren't, I should paint your walls with *slightly* less blue in the red. It will make them that much prettier. I'll send you some pics. Let you know before I leave for Rio. Where's Henry?'

'He's probably taken all your toys to the car.'

He peered out of the door.

'How kind of him. Still raining, I see. How you can *stand* everything being so wet and so green is utterly beyond me.'

'I'm going to drive,' said Anna. 'I haven't had a drop to drink since last night.'

'And I've had thousands of drops. Lend me that carrier-bag, darling, to put over my head.'

'It's only a few yards—'

'I know, dearest Daisy, but at the slightest excuse my hair goes into silly curls. I like it to stand on *end* – all the time.'

He stooped to kiss her and she put up her hand to touch his hair. It was as rich and thick as an otter's.

They all went out to the car, with Anthony carrying the remains of his luggage. Everybody said goodbye again. Henry kissed Anna, which surprised Daisy as well as Anna.

Then they got into the car, and were gone. She stood for a moment, looking then listening to the car until she could not hear it at all. She felt curiously flat, which seemed odd. She was conscious of missing these two special friends, and yet during the whole weekend, she had seldom felt at ease with them, and fleetingly, she wondered whether it would always be like this. Then she felt her hand taken and she followed him back into the cottage.

18
HENRY AND DAISY

The sense of relief at seeing them go was enormous. I realized then what a strain I had been under since Friday evening – less than forty-eight hours, but by God, it seemed longer. I've never liked queers – too clever by half, most of them, but except for when I was in the Navy, when I could hardly choose my shipmates, I have had very little to do with them. I came early to the conclusion that the trouble with Anna Blackstone was that she was jealous of me. She didn't want anyone coming between her and her precious Daisy. She was probably a repressed lesbian. I remembered Daisy telling me that it was she who blew the gaff on Jason – Jass, as she called him. Jass and Stach – when things were very easy I had teased her and said that she would soon be calling me Hash.

Looking at her face listening to the departing car, I knew that she felt in some sort sad that they had gone. I must make it up to her. I took her hand and led her into the kitchen where there was all the debris of lunch.

'You have very good friends.'

'You liked them?'

'Of course I liked them. The question is – did they like me?'

'Of course they did.'

I can recognize a lie when I hear one – nobody quicker.

'I know we ought to clear up.'

'Yes?'

'But what I want to do is to take you to bed. Two nights of abstinence is something of a strain.' And later: 'And the same applies to you, doesn't it, my sweet and only love?'

We were on the stairs and I was leading her. She did not answer, but her hand trembled in mine.

We had a delightful time. By now I had the map of her body by heart. I knew exactly how to rouse her, please her, torment and finally satisfy her. I had thoroughly taught her to need me. The fleeting thought, when we had reached somewhere near the half-way mark, when she had come several times and I not at all (how age interferes with performance! Once I would, not have matched her, but certainly had my share; now it is necessary to save it – to wait until the last possible moment) it did occur to me that sexual boredom was always lying in wait. Once one knew all there was to be known, one was left with repetition, which could become dangerously dull. I could even envisage the time when familiarity might breed impotence. But this lay far ahead. I could for some time enjoy her eagerness, her pleasure, her dependence. They say a good lover gets more pleasure from pleasing his love than pleasing himself, and I had no false modesty about my capacity as a lover.

When they were gone, he took me upstairs to bed. It almost frightens me to want him so much. But it was wonderful to lie there not needing to whisper – we felt like children let out of school. At least, I did. When I said that to him, he laughed. 'We are not children,' he said. 'We are old, old people, supposed by many to be well past this sort of thing.' And then he came out with an extraordinary piece of information. Did I know that a woman's vagina was the only part of her that never betrayed age? You could look, he said, at dozens of photographs of them and be unable to distinguish between a girl of sixteen, and a woman of sixty. How did he know this? He'd read it somewhere; he'd seen the photographs that illustrated the point.

When we got up, the rain had stopped, the afternoon sun had come waveringly out, not bright enough for shadows – it was more as though it chose what it had the strength to light. He showed me how to gently shake the heavy sodden heads of phlox that were bowed down by the weight of rain. We went to pick parsley and chives from the herb bed. I made a fish salad from the remains of the salmon. At supper we talked mostly about Anthony and Anna – 'The rock I shall founder on,' he said, 'is intellectual. I shan't be able to keep up with your clever friends. I shall always be at a loss when they make musical allusions.' He looked sad, and I told him that I did not think this was true, or needed to be true. They would not know the Latin names for plants.

That evening we drank some brandy (I drink far more with Henry than I usually do), and I played him the first act of *Rigoletto*. I think he was surprised at how much he enjoyed it. I felt selfish then: up until now I have played what music I have wanted, I have not thought what he might like to encounter or learn. I was so relaxed and tired, I fell asleep on the sofa. Going to bed as loving friends was lovely.

I woke in the night because the moon was shining across the bed. Henry, asleep beside me, did not stir.

I propped myself up on one elbow to look at him. His face was in shadow, but there was enough light for me to see it. I touched the lock of hair that always fell over the side of his forehead. He lay on his side, turned away from me. His mouth in repose is pre-Raphaelite, a sculpted mouth, with a full, clearly delineated upper lip. It is interesting to look at a face when the eyes are shut: it makes the whole thing look more like a mask; you cannot tell what the person *is*. They could look noble and be stupid; look peaceful and be militant; look saintly and be a villain. Henry does not look his age when he is awake, and asleep he seems to be no determinate age at all. I amuse myself for a few minutes imagining a very different person from the one I know: a hectoring bore; a man who talks of nothing but killing things and making money; a man who has an innate contempt for women (and fear of them too). Then I think, supposing I was in bed with a genius? What kind of genius would he have? A writer, I decide: he writes so well that I am sure he could write good fiction – particularly as he knows so much about women. His men might be rather weak, though. He was out of his depth with Anthony; I think he was afraid of him. And Anna . . . He does not understand Anna at all. But all that will get better. I think of how he was with Katya, how he won her round in that drive to the station.

The moon has reached his face, and he stirs. He turns towards me and I take him in my arms. I love him and I long for him to know it – really to *know* it.

A beautiful morning; no more storms lurking and everything freshened by the rain. She is full of plans. Wants to repaint the sitting room – simply a slightly different shade of red. It seems dotty to me. She also thinks she would like to make the best spare room 'prettier'. I shall enjoy this, as it will involve going to local auctions and I like picking over old things, finding bargains among the rubbish. She has changed her mind again about the builders – wants to start all that. I suggest that we go away while they are doing it – Ireland, perhaps, or the Channel Islands. I've always wanted to go there, but she says we cannot possibly go away while the builders are here, they will do everything wrong. But I noticed that she did not seem to rule out going away altogether, and this cheered me. It is sometimes frustrating to be so much under her orders, so to speak. However, I draw my money every week and stash it away in a biscuit tin hidden in my plastic bags with my papers in the shed. If we *did* go anywhere I would bury it for greater safety.

Days pass. They are punctured by small events. Katya rings to say she and Anthony are going to see her husband. The garage rings to say the mower is back. Unluckily, Daisy answered the telephone, and of course she wanted to know why the village garage would have it when I had taken it to the machine shop in town. I had to think quickly there. I said that the machine shop had suggested that it could be taken to the village if anyone was going that way. An unlikely tale, but she seemed to believe it. *I* fetched it myself to stop them giving the game away. What a nuisance all that kind of thing can be! I was only trying to save myself trouble, after all.

Last night, she asked me what happened to my father. I told her that he had stayed in his cottage after his retirement until his death; it seemed the most likely thing to have happened to him, but I never went back there, and spoke to him only once when he telephoned me just before I was called up, I really have no idea. I said that my stepmother had effectively cut me off, and that I had ceased to care. Daisy was most concerned: I saw her eyes fill with tears. She is such a soft-hearted creature that she would cry for anyone.

We went to some auction rooms in the town yesterday, and she put in a bid for a small fruitwood table that she wanted for the kitchen. When she rang up the next day, they said she'd got it, so I offered to fetch it for her in the morning while she worked (which she did every day).

After I had got the table, I saw two dealers sorting out a tray of oddments, salt spoons, a couple of watches, fountain pens and an assortment of rings, and I suddenly had an idea, so I went and asked them if I could look at the rings and if they were not too expensive, buy one, and they said I could have a look if I liked. I chose a small gold ring with a red stone in the middle and white ones either side of it. Eighty pounds, the older man said; it was nine-carat gold. He didn't say anything about the stones. I said I wanted something far cheaper; it was for my daughter's birthday and she was just a teenager – I didn't want anything valuable. 'What's not valuable, then?' the younger man said. Five to ten quid? The younger man snorted; the older said I could have the silver ring for that. It was a plain band about a quarter of an inch wide with a scroll of what looked like strawberry leaves etched upon it. I offered a fiver; they wanted ten, and we settled for eight. It would rub up nice; it was real silver. They put it in a weak brown envelope – no, they hadn't got a box.

I didn't give it to her immediately; I wanted to make an occasion of it.

*

Last night, we had our first row. It seemed to come from nowhere. He had been especially sweet to me all day; he even helped me in the afternoon with painting the sitting-room walls. I am doing them one at a time, since we cannot stop using the room, but this entails moving bookcases and furniture and spreading newspaper all over the floor. We have done two of the four walls now and Anthony was quite right – it all looks far warmer and wonderful with my pink curtains. We played the rest of *Rigoletto* and Henry said that for ever more he would smell paint when he heard the opera.

We stopped at six, and had showers, and then he made one of those amazing vodka drinks – only this time he put Angostura and elderflower syrup in it with ice and soda water, and I was very thirsty and drank two of them without noticing. So when he started pouring me a third drink, I said I didn't want any more.

'Oh, come on,' he said, 'it's far weaker than the vodka drink I usually make.' So I had a third one; it is quite difficult to tell how much vodka there is in a mixed drink. Anyway, we both got quite jolly and had dinner rather late. Henry had opened a bottle of wine but he had to drink most of it – I'd really had enough.

We left the supper things because he wanted to go up. He came into the room after I was in bed, and I could see that he was very pleased about something. He took my left hand, told me to shut my eyes and when I opened them there was a silver ring on my finger. His eyes were sparkling, and he was so pleased and excited: I was touched, it was the first present he had given me. The ring was too big for my third finger, so I put it on the second one, and when he protested, said I should lose it if I did not. He would have it made smaller, he said: it had to be on my third finger, it was my engagement ring. That was the first bad moment. I looked at him and said that I had told him – several times now – that I did not want to marry him, did not want to marry anybody.

'You *must* have changed your mind by now.'

I shook my head.

'We'll go to some wonderful exotic place for our honeymoon; somewhere that you have never been.'

'No.' I said that I loved him but that I wouldn't marry him.

'For *Christ's sake*! You know *nothing* about love!'

And then he hit me. I can hardly believe that – even now, the next day, when I am sitting in the train going to Katya. But he hit the side of my head, one heavy blow. It was so unexpected and awful that my heart stops when I think of it. I fell back and hit my head against the wall.

'I can't be with you when you are like this!' He almost shouted it, and stormed out of the room. I heard him going downstairs, and then silence.

It was dark. We had put out all the lights. It was dark and perfectly silent. I could feel my heart banging away, but that made no sound either and suddenly I felt very frightened. I was frightened because I did not know where he was, or what else he might do to me. I got up and stood by the open door, trying to hear where he was. Nothing. He could move very silently, I knew that, and he had once told me that he felt utterly at home in the dark – it made no difference to him at all. I shut my door very quietly, then realized that I could not lock it – I could not stop him coming back.

In the end, I put a chair so that its back was jammed against the door latch. It did not feel much safer, but it was something. I realized that I was shivering violently. I could neither hide nor run away although those were the only coherent thoughts that I had. Part of me could not believe what had happened. I had to put my hand to my head where he had struck me and feel the bruise to believe it. I wanted to go to the window to listen and hear if he was somewhere outside the cottage, but I could not bear to put out the lamp and if I did not and he was there he would see me. And what? Thoughts, imagination of further violence – or murder, even – came and went. It was as though I had a high fever and could make no sense of anything at all, but had to endure again and again his shouting and the blow. I sat on the bed for a long time, trying to listen, trying not to think, waiting for it not to be dark.

In the end, I lay down because my head ached. I remember taking off the ring and putting it on the table by the lamp and a kind of stupor set in when I seemed neither asleep nor awake.

I became aware that it was light; an amazing relief. I turned off the lamp and dressed – in my jeans and a shirt and my track shoes, and immediately felt less vulnerable. I undid the door and went, very quietly, to look at the other two bedrooms to see if he was in either of them. He was not. I went to the bathroom. I longed for a hot shower, but I didn't want to undress until I knew he was not anywhere in the cottage. He wasn't anywhere. I even looked in the car and the shed behind the garage, but there was no sign of him. So I locked the cottage doors and did have a very long, very hot shower. All my bones seemed to ache, and the hot water relieved some of the stiffness. It was six o'clock. I made a pot of coffee and drank it while I cleared up the supper from the night before. Activity was good; and I even felt that perhaps I was making too much of the whole thing. He loved me, wanted to marry me, he had drunk too much and when I turned him down he couldn't take it. How did that sound? In a way, it sounded quite reasonable – the *un*reason came with the chilling quantity of fear that I had felt about it. My head still ached, and I got some Panadol and made more coffee.

At eight the telephone rang. It was Anna.

'I don't suppose that you are alone,' she began.

'I am as a matter of fact.'

'I'm ringing you for Katya.'

'What about her? Nothing awful has happened?'

'No, she's fine.'

'Is it the children, then?' Anna did not sound all right.

'No. Nothing like that. It's just that she wants you to come up to see her – rather urgently. Well, *today*.'

'Why isn't *she* ringing me?'

'She asked me to. Really, Daisy, you must come. Catch the train I caught before. Nine thirty, wasn't it?'

'Anna, what *is* going on?'

'She wants to tell you herself. Where is Henry?'

'Out at the moment.'

'Has he taken your car?'

'No. Why do you ask?'

'You can drive to the station then. Daisy, it's important that you come. I wouldn't be asking you like this if it wasn't.'

'All right, I'll come, just for the day, or does she want me to stay?'

'I should come prepared to stay. Will you catch the nine thirty, then?'

'Yes.'

'Good.' And she rang off.

I went and packed a bag and changed into a skirt. I looked awful. I put some colour on my cheekbones, but it looked worse and I rubbed it off. It felt odd that I had wanted so much to flee last night and was now doing it for an entirely different reason. I took my bag downstairs, and was writing a note to Henry simply telling him that Katya wanted me and I might be away for the night, when he knocked on the door. I let him in and picked the note off the table to throw away. I felt quite calm at that moment: the sight of him did not frighten me at all.

I don't know what came over me. Too much to drink – and then, if things don't go my way, sometimes I lose control. I really thought that the ring would do it, that I had en-trapped her at last – that she was mine. Anyway, I got out before too much damage was done – I have learned to do that. Or discovered last night that I have learned. I went to the shed where I kept an emergency supply of vodka in an orange squash bottle and then I just went off into the woods and found a place to have a fag and a nightcap and then sleep it off.

In the morning I knew that I must eat humble pie. She had locked up the cottage. I tried both doors before I knocked at the back. She let me in at once. I hadn't reck-oned on two things – how awful she looked, and the suitcase on the kitchen floor.

'I don't know what to say to you.'

She stood quite still – looking at me. She seemed quite calm which surprised me. She wasn't wearing my ring. I began to feel really anxious.

'Oh, darling – please, please forgive me. I can't think of any reason why on earth you should. The fact is – I had too much to drink. I'm not used to heavy drinking and I overdid it. And then I so wanted you to be pleased about the ring – oh, I don't know. I can't – were you going away? Running from me? Oh, Daisy, my darling love, what have I done? You don't know – I don't think you can imagine – what you mean to me.'

Standing there, looking at me, she started to sob. I put my arms round her and felt her lean to me as she wept. It was a painful, piteous sound. For minutes we stood there. I knew she must get it out, whatever she was feeling, and that I must wait. I did this, and gradually, she stopped.

'I have to go,' she said at last.

'No. One thing I promise you. Nothing like this will ever happen again. Will you trust me, darling? I would do anything for you. I'm so dreadfully ashamed. I wouldn't blame you for not taking me back, but you are – you have become – my life. So I beg you, don't go.'

Then she told me that Katya wanted her and she didn't know why but that it sounded so urgent that she had no choice.

A kind of relief, mixed with irritation, came over me. At least she was not running away from me, but she was going, when I badly needed to repair the damage that had been done. The best course, it seemed, was to affect concern over Katya, to co-operate, to use affection, to which I knew she was remarkably sensitive. I would drive her to the station, I said. Of course she must go, and I understood that she must feel anxious.

She had to go at once, she said. She had promised to catch the nine thirty train.

So, I drove her. When we got to the station, I said, 'Please remember that I love you. This doesn't make me any better or more in the right. I simply want you to know it.'

And she answered, so quietly that I could hardly hear her. 'I love you. That is what made it so—' Then, and I could see it was an effort of trust, she said, 'I was frightened. You frightened me.'

There was silence, and then she said, 'Why did you do it? How could you – hit me – if you loved me?'

'When you come back, I'll tell you. You never escape damage, really. Damage means damage. I've been hit a good deal. I suppose you could say it became a kind of marker for feeling.'

I picked up one of her hands and kissed it. 'But it's not like Wilde. I love you – I shan't ever kill that. May I kiss you before you go?'

She turned her face to me: her lips were cold, but her eyes, when we drew apart, revealed what I needed to know.

I saw her into the train, of course.

'You'll ring me about coming back?' I looked at her with the most beseeching affection and she said yes. Then the train was starting and I had to go. I stood looking at her, and as the train moved, I blew her a kiss, but I am not sure whether she saw it.

As I drove back via the town post office I began to wonder what on earth could have happened to Katya to bring about this sudden journey to her side. All I could think of was that she had found she was pregnant (by Edwin, presumably) and did not want the child. It was certainly hard on Daisy – who had been subdued by exhaustion as much as anything else. I knew from the dark circles under her eyes that she had not slept, and sleepless nights don't suit women of her age.

And then I thought that I should have offered to go with her, but it was too late for that now.

19

DAISY

Finally, after the endless ride in the cab with Anthony who had met her at the station, after the climb up Anna's stairs ('Katya is with Anna,' he had said when she asked why they were going there – it was the only question he answered), she was sitting in one of Anna's battered armchairs opposite the three of them. There was coffee on the table but nobody was drinking it.

'What *is* it? It's clearly something awful – *what is it?*'

Anna said, 'It's about Henry. I'm afraid it's very bad news about Henry.'

'Has he had an accident? He drove me to the station—' She stopped because they had asked her to come before he could possibly have had an accident.

'No. He's not what you think at all.. He's a con man. He's a liar, he's a fraud, and he's dangerously violent.'

There was a stunned silence. Then she said, 'You'd better tell me why you think that.' She felt furiously angry with all of them, sitting there, treating her like a child or a fool. 'Go on. Don't spare me. Tell me everything you know that makes you think he's so bad.'

Anthony said, 'When Katya and I went down to see Edwin, we went on to Rackham. We saw Lady Carteret, Daphne's mother.'

'And?'

'Anna showed us the letters he wrote before we went,'

Katya said. 'Oh, Ma, I didn't want to do this, but the others said we must. He lied to you about Daphne.'

'For God's sake, tell me exactly what *happened*. Don't leave anything out. Stop just accusing him.'

'She's quite right,' Anna said. 'Tell her the whole story. What it was like when you went there.'

'We didn't even know if she was there, or even if she was still alive. We stopped at the lodge at one of the entrances. It all looked so seedy – the drive was just weeds and there was a woman hanging up washing outside it. She said old Lady Carteret did live there, in one corner at the back of the place. The house, when we got to it, looked completely shut up but we drove round to the back and there were two or three windows without shutters and a black door with most of the paint off. We pulled a kind of iron bell pull and heard it jangling, and then we heard someone coming. It was a very old lady, with short, untidy white hair, who said, "I thought you were Thomas, or I wouldn't have opened the door," and began shutting it.

'I asked if she was Lady Carteret. She was wearing trousers and a jersey with food spilled on it and I thought she was probably a faithful old servant. But she said she was. Anthony said that it would be very kind of her if she would spare a few minutes to talk to us about Henry Kent. She said, "I don't want to hear that name in this house!" and banged her stick on the stone floor. I said, please would she, because my mother had got entangled with him and I was extremely anxious.

'"I should think you would be," she said.

'Anthony said he was sure it wasn't good for her to stand, and couldn't we sit somewhere just for a few minutes, and he took her arm very gently and smiled at her, and she liked it.

'She took us to a very small room that had a kitchen range in it and other kitchen things, and an upright canvas chair which she sat in and we sat at the table. Then she said that Henry Kent was an "infamous villain". Those were her words.

'I told her we knew that he'd been in love with her daughter, and she said, "Oh, you do, do you? And what else do you know?"

'Anthony said, "I'm sure this is not true, but he alleges that you stopped them marrying because in fact they were related."

'"Related? *Related?*" she repeated. "In what way related?"

'He told her Henry had said they both had the same father.

'She stared at us for a moment and then said, "That is the most monstrous lie. He was an accomplished liar, but that is, is – utterly monstrous! *I* did not stop them marrying. But by then he had long ceased to pull the wool over my eyes. He was simply on the make. He thought Daphne, as the only child, would inherit a great deal of money – *that* was what he wanted. When I told him that she would not, not a penny, you could not see him for dust.

'"He left his father's cottage that same night. I did not turn the father out. He had been with us for years and it was not his fault. But I told him not to allow the boy back. And that was that." There was a silence, while she hunted in an old shopping-bag and found cigarettes, one of which she fitted into a surprisingly elegant green and gold holder.

'Anthony produced a lighter. She bent her head towards

him, and he said, "How awful for you. That was the end of the story?"

'"No, it was not. He left my Daphne pregnant and, of course, devastated, as anyone would be when their first love turns out to be a mere money-grabber who had never loved her." Another silence. "He broke her heart. She did marry someone else in the end. *Faute de mieux*: she simply could not manage on her own. It's not much of a marriage. She lives in Australia now. I never see her. I'm too old for that journey, and she could never bear this place after what happened to her."

'Then I burst out in my usual tactless way, "You could have given her money! After Mr Kent left." And she said, "Mr Kent indeed! We called him Hal and his father was Kent."

'Then she said, "There is one more thing that perhaps you should know. My husband, who was always frail – his health was wrecked on the Somme – died of a heart-attack. I found him. He recovered enough to . . ." and she said we couldn't imagine how hard for him it was to face *her* with the question of Daphne's parentage. She'd never told him about Hal's conduct, you see. She thought it might kill him to know. She sent Daphne away to have the baby and it was adopted, but he never knew about any of that. But he told her then he had had an anonymous note. She never saw the note; he had burned it. It simply alleged that Daphne was the result of her liaison with the gardener. The writer thought he ought to know. She looked hard at us for a moment after this, and then with a huge effort at control, she said, "I don't even know whether Reggie, my husband, believed or even heard what I said. He died minutes later. He was very distressed." Her voice had become unsteady and she frowned. Her

402

own distress was miserably evident. When she'd recovered a bit, she told us that the joke, of course, was that there was no money anyway. Reggie had been too unwell to pay attention to his investments; there were death duties. Nobody wanted to buy the house: there was no money at all except for a legacy left her by a godfather and they couldn't touch that. All that unhappiness, that anguish, even, was for nothing. "I rot here," she said, "and the house rots round me." Then she said, "I am telling you all this and I do not even know your names. Or do I know them?"

'We said no, and told her. She said something about hoping that we were Thomas who was mending her wireless . . . Then, without any warning, she began to cry – not making any sound, just tears. She fumbled in her trouser pocket and brought out a much-used handkerchief. She said, "My dog died, you see. It is very hard to be without him. I'm sorry I can't offer you tea." So we went.'

All three of them were silent.

'So that's it? That's what you found out.'

Anna said, 'Only some of it. I found out about Charley, too.'

'How on earth did you do that?'

'I'm afraid I'd got suspicious of Henry. I asked him where he had worked in Kent. I asked quite casually, because I said I knew some people who had a wonderful garden there, and I wondered whether he'd heard of it. And he said, yes, but his place was the other side of Tonbridge – people called Mead.

'After I read the letters, I went to St Catherine's House. There was no death certificate for a Charley or Charlotte Mead or Kesler that remotely fitted with his dates. Then I knew something was wrong. You remember he described the garden, and the huge swimming pool shaped like an S? That was a starting point.'

'Did *you* do all this sleuthing?'

'No, I didn't, Daisy. I paid someone to do it. But when they'd found the house, and the Mrs Mead who lived there, then I rang her up and asked if I might see her. She seemed nervous and kept asking what it was about, and in the end I said it was about Henry Kent who wanted to marry my oldest friend and that I was worried, and she agreed.'

'And what did *she* tell you? What's the next story?' Even Daisy could not recognize her own voice.

'Well, she was a woman in her sixties, very carefully dressed as a country lady. The house was posh nineteen twenties; a lot of pink and fumed oak inside. She gave me tea in what she called her morning room, although it faced the wrong way to be that.

'I began by telling her that Henry had told you that Charley was dead, had died trying to open a window. She wanted to know why on earth he'd said that. I said that as he'd been married to Charley and presumably not divorced, and he wanted to marry someone else, he had to say she was dead. Mrs Mead was amazed at this and said he was never married to her! Not *married*. Apparently her father wanted Charley to marry one of his City friends – he was very hard on Charley about it and she'd always been afraid of him. She wasn't the pretty little daughter he'd wanted, so he was always hard on her – a bit of a bully. He was obviously a man who liked to get his own way. Anyway, without any warning, she found one day that Charley had gone. She left her a note. She'd taken all her jewellery that they'd given her to Come Out, and one or two other things, and she said that she wanted to marry "Harry" Kent, who was the gardener there. She'd left no address – they'd no idea where she was. Mrs Mead wanted to get people to find Charley – the police or someone – but her husband (she said she thought he was going to have a stroke) was so angry he wanted to "let her stew in her own juice". He never wanted to see her again. He called her a tart! She said excuse her using the word but that was what he'd said – about his own daughter! Nobody would ever want to marry her now, he said. He washed his hands of her, and told his wife to have nothing to do with her if she came whining back.

'She said a lot more about him; it was clear that he was a monster and that she was frightened of him.

'I asked where Charley was now, and she said that after Derek died she was able to help her, and now Charley had a safe place to live. I asked her what she meant by safe, and she burst out, "You can't imagine what that poor child went through!" She said Charley had been "very naughty", but she was head over heels in love with "that man". It was he who made her write to her father, and when that wasn't answered, to her. That started about three months after she'd left. By the end of the year she sounded desperate. She said she was going to have a baby and that Harry wouldn't marry her unless she was reconciled to her parents. Charley told her she was feeling very ill, poor child, and she went to see her. She never told her husband, and begged Charley not to tell him. Apparently it was a horrible place, a very nasty, damp basement flat – "Only two rooms and my Charley used to the best of everything," she said. They'd been living off selling her jewellery. Harry was out a lot but he didn't seem to earn much money and Charley was desperately hard up. Of course she gave her what she had, but it wasn't much – only about twenty-five pounds. Harry wasn't there, and she asked Charley not to say she'd been there, was afraid he'd write to Derek. A few weeks later, she rang her mother from a call-box, asked her to ring back as she had no money. She arranged to meet her under the clock at Charing Cross. She was so shocked when she saw her, said that Charley looked awful and seemed unable to stop crying. She'd had a miscarriage – had been taken by Harry in an ambulance to hospital, and that was the last she saw of him. When she came out, and went back to the flat, it was empty: he'd taken his things and gone, and she couldn't stay there because there was a lot of back rent to pay.

'Her mother had thought she was in such a state because Harry had left her, but it hadn't been like that at all. She was terrified of him. It was then that it all came out about how he used to beat her up: she'd been twice to hospital saying she'd fallen downstairs, walked into a door – all those things. But when she told him she was pregnant, thinking that this would change everything, he made her go up a step-ladder and then knocked her off it. So she lost the baby. That was what she really minded. She'd wanted to have children all her life, but after that they said she couldn't have any more. She got a council flat in a big block, but she didn't know anyone and she was afraid to go out. Of course she had to go out to buy her food and that was when the real trouble started. She used to see these prams with babies in them and the mothers would sometimes leave them while they filled their trolleys. At first she used just to look at them, she said, but then, one day, she simply took a baby and walked home with it. Of course it didn't last; she knew she was wicked and she took it back and there was a fuss and she had to go to court and was given a warning. But she did it again, and that time she went to prison. She wasn't herself at all, you see: she was demented and she had nobody to turn to except her mother, who was too much under her father's thumb to be of much use. She used to go and visit her, Mrs Mead said, but it was very difficult. It all changed, she said, when she found out about Derek having an affair with his secretary. It had been going on for years.

'That, Mrs Mead said, was the end of his bullying either of them. She divorced him and got a large settlement, including the house, and at last she could look after Charley.

'I asked whether Charley was in the house, and whether I might see her, but Mrs Mead said, oh, no. Nothing would induce Charley to live in the house. She didn't feel safe. She was obsessed with the idea that Harry would come back one day and kill her. So Mrs Mead bought her a little house quite near and that suited Charley. She had ever so many cats, her mother said. They were always having kittens, and Charley loved kittens. It being a small house, she could make it quite safe. It was a job ever to get in or out of it – the place was like Fort Knox.

'Apparently Charley doesn't go out. She has all the animals' food delivered and she doesn't eat much. Which was funny, because she'd become quite heavy, her mother said. She ended by saying that she'd gone to see the prison doctor about Charley. He was a psychotherapist, and he said something shocking about Harry, which she had been unable to get out of her mind. "He said that men like Harry Kent had nothing between the head and the genitals." Again, she said, "Excuse the expression, but that is what he said. Your friend shouldn't let him into the house."'

'Could I have a glass of water?'

When she had drunk a little – she found it difficult to swallow – she said, 'And I suppose you tracked down Hazel, who is supposed to be his wife. Or isn't she?'

'Yes, we have, and yes, she is. She's a physiotherapist at a hospital in Northampton. She's been married to him for nearly fourteen years. She's a bit older than he is, and she met him soon after her parents died. They left her a bungalow and about twenty-five thousand pounds. She let the bungalow and they moved to a rented flat for her to be nearer the hospital. He took charge of her legacy, and eighteen months ago she discovered that it was all gone. He tried to make her sell the bungalow, but she refused and they had such rows about it that they split up. She wants a divorce, but his terms are half of every-thing she has got and she's struck at that. So – yes, they are still married. She didn't know where he had gone: he gave her a *poste restante* address.' Anna paused, drank some of the cold coffee before she added: 'She's afraid of him too. He went to a place to dry out – she still loved him then – but he left it almost at once and began drinking on his way home. She's been afraid of him ever since he backed their car suddenly into the garage doors when she was opening them. He said he thought he was putting his foot on the brake, but she never felt sure.'

'Did she think he was trying to *kill* her?'

'She said,' Anna spoke carefully, 'she said that she thought he was trying to hurt her. It made her have to accept that he didn't like her at all. She had a bad time because she said he was the only man she'd ever loved: she'd never looked, or even been looked at, by anyone else. She said she still felt that somewhere inside him there was a good man trying to get out. Oh, Daisy darling, that's enough, isn't it? He's got no moral brakes at all. He's a psychopath. He can never see any reason for not doing what he wants to do.'

Daisy felt, rather than saw, that they looked at her and then looked away.

'Oh, there was one more thing that Hazel said. She did manage to turn him out of the flat by threatening to get the police. She says he's always been afraid of the police.'

'I should think with good reason,' Anthony said grimly.

'Is that all? The lot?'

'Oh, Ma! Surely it's more than enough!'

'So, he never actually loved – cared for me at all?' She sounded as though she was trying to remember or sum up something very difficult.

Katya, who for some time had been trying quite hard to suppress tears, said, 'Ma, I'm sure he was – very fond of you!'

Anthony put a hand on her arm; she glanced at him and was silent. 'But – why *me*? I'm not young and I'm not an heiress.'

'You were there,' Anna said. 'You had the appalling misfortune to be there.'

'Thank you for taking so very much trouble.'

'We love you very much.' But the moment he'd said it, Anthony saw that it was too much for her. 'Anna! Didn't you say you had some soup?'

Anna went to get it, and Katya followed her. Anthony stayed.

'I expect it sounds mad to you, but I find it very difficult to take all this *in*! I mean, it seems so . . . *against* how

409

he is – was – with me. How could I be so easily taken in?'

'It wasn't a question of easy at all. He's a con man, and he wouldn't be one if he couldn't do that. They go about like other people, only slightly better. He really worked on you.'

'And the others!' She looked up with streaming eyes. 'Those poor girls, and that tragic old lady.'

'And there are probably others – in fact, almost certainly. One of the curious things,' he was continuing in an ordinary voice; she was in too much pain for sympathy, 'about that kind of person is that they not only lie to everyone they meet, but they lie to themselves, and a good deal of the time they take themselves in as well. They live in a kind of desert of deceit, their landscape dotted with mirages. The first person I fell in love with was one of them. A too, too charming man who made a living out of finding people like me for clients. One gets over it, you know,' he said gently. 'One can get over absolutely anything. And you are a survivor.'

'It's very difficult to stop loving somebody – quickly – just like that.' She reached for a box of tissues that suddenly was on the table.

'It's impossible.'

Anna and Katya returned with trays.

'I think Daisy might like a drink. Have you got any brandy?'

Anna opened a cupboard under one of the bulging bookcases. 'There's some left in this.'

Anthony poured it out. 'Want a fag with it?'

'I've run out.'

None of the others smoked. 'I'll get some,' Katya said: 'Gauloise, isn't it?'

'Don't bother.'

'No bother at all,' and she almost ran out of the room.

'She wants to do something,' Anna said. 'She's terribly upset for you. She even thought that if she was here, you might blame her for all the detective work.'

'Of course I wouldn't. No!'

'Well, tell her that.'

The brandy was doing her good, they both noticed. She'd looked pretty ill when she'd arrived, but the news had really knocked her out. At one moment, Anna had thought that she was going to faint.

Time passed. Anthony opened a bottle of wine; Anna produced the soup. She sat, pressing her fingers through her hair at the side of her head. Katya returned with the cigarettes. She opened the packet, took one out, then put it on the table in front of her.

'Have some soup,' Anna said. 'You probably didn't have time for breakfast.'

She shook her head.

'Have some, Ma. It will do you good.'

'Don't be too kind to me.'

But she did have some of the soup. Anna said that there was cheese, and Katya said she would get it.

'Finish the brandy,' Anthony said, 'and then I can pour you out a glass of wine.'

She did as she was told: she still seemed stunned. When Anna was clearing away the soup bowls, she said, 'I suppose I ought to have known—'

'You would have, in the end. Better to know now.'

She watched them eat the cheese. Katya said smoke, and she did. Nobody said anything while they were eating. She became aware that her head ached and that she felt sick and went to Anna's little bathroom in case she was. She retched once or twice but it only brought tears to her eyes. Very faint, repetitive thoughts churned slowly round. It couldn't be true: how could he – how could *anyone* – continuously, successfully lie? There must be a mistake somewhere: he had done awful things, but people could change. But she felt the bruise again on the side of her head and knew he could not.

She heard the murmur of them talking, but when she went back they fell silent.

'I must do something.'

'Yes, we must.' It was Anthony who spoke. 'Let's talk about it.'

'Go back there, I suppose, and face him.' She realized, as she said it, that the thought terrified her in several, quite different ways.

'No, I don't think so. I don't think you need to see him at all.'

'Just – ring him up?'

'No,' Katya said, 'that'll warn him. He'll ransack the place or set fire to it or something.'

Anna said, 'Anthony – well, all of us, really – thought it would be best if he went down, with someone else, and turned him out. Put him on a train and changed the locks on the cottage and asked the police to keep an eye on it. And you stay away from the cottage for a bit.'

She picked up the glass of water and drank some. Her mouth had felt full of ash, and the water left a bitter taste.

'I don't want to go back there at all.'

Then she said, 'It's my mess. I ought to deal with it. There are things I should say to him!' And seeing no agreement to this: 'I need to *ask* him *why*?'

'But nothing he said to you would mean anything. It would be more lies.'

'You mean – nothing he has *ever* said meant anything?'

Before Anna could answer, Anthony said, 'We can't know that. What we do know is that he has lied so much of his life that nothing he said now would have any value. Dearest Daisy, you're not the kind of person who takes to accepting the worst in anyone, but this time that's how it is. There's something wrong with him. You remember what that doctor said to Charley's mother? "Nothing between the head and the genitals." A total absence of heart. That's not for you.'

This made her able to cry.

20

DAISY

She slept heavily in the afternoons – the long, hot siesta time when everything was stilled. They had been there in Anna's little house on the island for three days now, but each time she woke it was as though she was lost in some unknown place: there were those mysterious moments when she had no memory, either – was nobody, a lightness, a kind of bliss. And then who she was, what had happened, came rolling over her with the speed of molten lava down a mountainside. An ageing woman who had actually believed that a man had loved her when he had done nothing of the kind. A common enough situation, perhaps, but what difference did that make to any particular recipient? Awake, she had to think about it: jagged little pieces of memory and information crowded in, no one piece fitting with any other, no sense that could be made of what she had experienced and had thought she'd understood.

They filled her days for her, her kind friends: they took her swimming in the clear warm sea, they made picnics which were eaten in the shade of rocks at one side of the bay with the retsina slung on a rope in the water, after which they would climb the hill slowly in the burning heat, up the white dusty track to the cool of the house that had a terrace each side of it – one for breakfast and one for watching the sunset. They would all sleep: she

414

would cast herself on the small hard bed and almost at once become mercifully unconscious.

And they let her talk, ask questions, go over things, discuss: they never showed impatience or tried to divert her. The hardest thing had been just writing the brief note to him saying that it was the end, she did not wish either to see or hear from him again. Anthony had taken the note with him. He had driven down with a friend. They had taken her key. She had wanted to know what happened – everything about it – and they told her.

'We arrived about eleven, and let ourselves in. He was still in bed.'

'In my room?'

'Yes.'

'And you gave him my letter?'

'Not then. I told him to get up, put his clothes on and there was a letter from you in the kitchen. He came down pretty fast. We watched him open it. He read it twice and said what on earth had happened, he couldn't understand it. I have to hand it to him, he looked the picture of shocked innocence. Then he said that something must have happened to you, that you must have been *made* to write such a letter – he could think of no earthly reason . . . He started to work up some indignation, said that we were all snobs, didn't think he was good enough for you, it was all a class plot. You loved him, he knew it, whatever we might think.'

There was a pause, and then he said, 'Do you really want me to go on?'

'I need to know.'

'Well, then it seemed the time to tell him his cover was blown – that we knew that Charley was not dead, and several other things. He went completely silent. He was looking at Giles and I could see that he reckoned it wasn't worth going for me. So then I said he was to pack up and we would put him on a train: he'd got twenty minutes to get his stuff together. I introduced Giles then – as Detective Inspector Cairns. That was a good move – it really shook him. You remember Hazel said he was afraid of the police? She was dead right. He said he hadn't got anything to pack his things *into*. I found a big blue canvas thing and said he could take it, but we'd be watching what he put into it. He said most of his stuff was in the shed outside except for some clothes in your room. I cleared them out, while Giles went with him to the shed. That was it.'

'You took him to the station? Where did he go?'

'That was quite funny. He said he hadn't got enough cash for a ticket, so I bought him a one-way ticket to Edinburgh. He was going to have to change to get on to the express, but he wasn't going to be able to change the ticket. We saw him on to the first train. "I hope you're pleased with yourself," he said, as he climbed on, but he was frightened of Giles – he didn't say a word all the way to the station. That was it, Daisy darling. That's how it was.'

'Do you think he'll go back there – to the cottage?'

'I think it very unlikely. We went back and packed up your things and found your passport, which wasn't where you said it was, but we had to wait anyway for the builder to change the locks – just in case. I got his keys off him, by the way. No, I don't think he'll go back. But I think you might as well keep away for a while. We did ask the local police to keep an eye on the place.'

'I don't want to go back.'

'Sell it,' Anna said. 'That would be the best thing. People like Henry are unpredictable. They've got no moral brakes: they can't see why they shouldn't do exactly what they feel like doing at any time. I wouldn't like to think of you alone there. Katya hopes you'll come back to the flat with her – help her get sorted out.'

That seemed mildly sensible – something to do.

There were many conversations: after the practical narrative there were other things she had to resolve. She needed these facts of the matter – the manner – of his going, to help her feel that it was over. For, on another level, it was very hard *not* to have confronted him, hear what he had to say, not to have asked him *why* it had seemed worth all the trouble he had taken to bamboozle, to con her, why he had told so many lies that did not even seem necessary. 'It's what I can't understand,' she kept saying to Anna. 'He didn't *have* to say that Charley was dead. He didn't have to say that Daphne was his half-sister. And so many other things.'

'He wanted your attention. He wanted you to be sorry for him.'

'But why me? I'm not an innocent young girl of the kind he seemed to go for. And he can't have thought that *I* was an heiress or anything like that.'

Anna said, 'I don't think it was simply money he was after. He wanted that, of course, enough anyway for him to be idle, but I think he was also pretty set on sexual power: that's what all the tales we uncovered had in common.' She added, almost tentatively, 'You said he was very good at sex.'

'Yes.'

There was a silence while each of them thought about that in different ways.

417

'I think also,' Anna said, when they were walking down to the taverna to eat, 'that he had ceased to *know* what was true. I think Anthony was quite right about that.'

'You mean, it's not his fault?'

'That's an interesting speculation, isn't it?' Anthony, who'd been walking behind them on the narrow path, now joined them. 'I mean, in one way everything that a person is or does is *them*, and basically they have to take responsibility for whatever happens. Fault is usually just an accusation from someone at the receiving end who hasn't got what they wanted. But, on the other hand, if someone really has a fault running through them – in the geological sense – then people talk about anything from madness to diminished responsibility. I think with the Henrys it is a bit of both. They could indulge their fault, or resist it – lay off it – be aware. Two things that seem common to psychopathic personalities are indolence and not having any friends. We couldn't find evidence that Henry had a single friend.'

The nights were the worst. She would lie down, and try to read herself to sleep, would find almost at once that she had not known what she had been reading; would take a sleeping pill and turn off the light and try to play some familiar piece of music through her mind. But the music would be soon drowned out by a fearful jungle of memories and the sensations that had accompanied them – times with him like small pieces of film that would freeze at the salient point: his kissing her for the first time in the car after the cat was killed; his gentleness to her that first night; his hand on her breast.

'You are beautiful, do you know that?' and she *did* know it then completely, for the first time in her life. His stream of endearments when he picked her up from the path; his face asleep beside her in the moonlight – how she had wanted him, how she ached now for things to be as they were. How could she still feel this?

But she did. Knowing that it had all been a fraud, a sham, did not quench or vanquish what she had felt. If she tried to imagine what his private thoughts of her must have been while he was making love to her she was overwhelmed with shame. He had made a vain fool of her, which must at times have amused him. She could not help imagining the coarse and cynical generalisations that he must have made, as people do generalize when they dislike or have contempt for the particular ('women are always like that – etc.'). Then she would be rescued from humiliation by the reflection that trusting someone – something that had never come easily to her since Jess had died – must make for vulnerability. It had to be a risk, and if one wanted something very much, commensurate risks had to be taken. He had made her recognize afresh how desperately she had wanted not to live the rest of her life alone, to be first in somebody's affections, to have a last chance to grow into the loving friendship that can flourish from chronic intimacy. Marriage: but she had not wanted to marry him; why was that? Was it some dimly felt but deep warning that somehow all was not well? No, part of the shock was that she had had no inkling: she had not wanted to marry anyone, but again, yes, she could recall the faint chill when he pressed her to marry him. So somewhere, however deeply buried and unconsciously expressed, there was an instinct for self-preservation.

All this could flood through her and only minutes would have passed, and then the jagged fragments of film would resume, lingering now on painful detail, till it was as though he was in the room with her, had just spoken; she could turn her head and there would be his arm reaching out for her. The idyll had not become a mirage – it was before the lies and she had been alive, so much alive and well. And then she had to weep – cry until her throat ached and her eyes had become dry and burning and she could feel nothing but an anonymous despair. Then sometimes she could sleep, but more often she would get up, go on to the terrace, drink water, smoke a cigarette, stare out at the rocks dark above the sea that was sometimes illuminated, sometimes simply a different dark. She would try then to prepare herself for the resumption of loneliness, the discipline of work, the making-the-most, the small pleasures, the satisfaction of having the secondary wants to compensate her primary need.

When she thought of Anthony and Anna, her gratitude for their loving kindness would make her cry again, simpler tears, and it was good to think of them. They could so easily have not taken her seriously, have not taken the trouble, have been impatient with her sensibility, have not listened or given so much of their time. Anthony had mysteriously cancelled his travelling plans; Anna had suddenly brought her holiday forward. They had arranged everything – a different scene hedged by their protection and care. She thought how much she loved them, and although any feeling beyond a very small degree brought tears, there was comfort; with so much affection it was not an airless desert.

Often, in those nights, she thought of Katya. It was odd how Katya seemed to occupy a separate part of her mind, but that had always been so. They had been through so many of the familiar stages; of guilt, of inadequacy, of incomprehension, of distrust, yes, and on Katya's part, anyway, of disapproval, that it was a wonder they had survived together as they had.

Katya's efforts on her behalf had been far more than she had any right to expect. She had bothered to see if the cottage was suitable; she had gone with Anthony to see Daphne's mother; she had endured the awful day in Anna's flat when they told her everything. And all this when her own life was in crisis; when she had been betrayed and faced a bleak and uncertain future; when, in fact, she was in much the position that *she* had been in with Katya's father. Only she had had Jess. I must become Jess for Katya, she thought now. To hell with the mother/daughter relationship, I must become her steady friend. A small spark of resolution – if she'll have me. We are very different . . . I am by nature cautious and distrustful; Katya is a passionate, impulsive creature – a dramatic person, her sensitivity often concealed by a breeziness that is deceiving, and her warmth can go undetected. Then she thought of her daughter's face in the flat when Anthony and Anna had been telling her everything; she had known then that Katya's impulse had been to throw her arms round her, sob with her, revile him, attempt any comfort she could give, and she had done none of it, because then it would not have helped at all. She had gone to buy the cigarettes instead. If she could make that effort for me, there must be things I can do for her.

These thoughts, notions, ideas did not all come at once: they developed over those weeks of insomnia; they became something that she could work – through loss and shock – towards. When she was cried out, exhausted by the repetition of misery, there was Katya. She had fantasies about her and Katya: they would live in the flat together; they would share their lives, share the children; she would help Katya to find something interesting and rewarding to do – it would all be wonderful. And then, in the daytime, she would know that it would not be at all like that: they would share the flat while it was expedient, etc. They would quarrel. Katya would make scenes – no, she would *induce* Katya to make scenes; there was collusion about incompatibility. If she was unresponsive, Katya would sulk; she would pretend not to notice and Katya would shoutingly sulk, would bang about until she got some change out of the situation. But it would be Katya who would do the making up; the hugs, the cups of tea in bed in the morning, the little jugs of well-chosen flowers on her desk . . .

But it wouldn't be like that either. She thought of Jess yet again, and how Jess had always been to her. Accepting: she had been accepted for what and who she was without judgement or questioning. She never went further in correction than making the pertinent suggestion. 'Daisy, pet, how would you like to be that little boy?' when Daisy threw some sand into (what was his name?) Christopher Watson's eyes. And she had suddenly become Christopher, rubbing his eyes and crying and she knew she would hate it, and that was the end of sand-throwing. She had no parents that she could remember; Jess had been everything, and she had never felt conscious of loss, whereas Katya had had to contend with a father who abandoned her, and a mother who was certainly no Jess.

She had many thoughts of this nature during those long nights; landmarks of childhood, treats, illnesses, holidays, loved and hated teachers, rainy days, learning to cook, toffee and pancakes, playing Old Maid and Racing Demon with Jess, Jess teaching her to clean silver, to knit, to make a glass ring by rubbing her finger round the rim, to make lace on a cotton reel with pins, to ride her first bicycle, to grow mustard and cress on a piece of flannel, to watercolour the black-and-white pictures in her Andrew Lang fairy books. Then there were absorbing hours of helping – Jess was always repairing things she bought cheaply at auctions or sales: gluing the spines back on to books, making good the stucco on gilt frames, putting back little pieces of veneer on to workboxes and the like, cleaning old canvases with soap and water and sometimes a touch of turps, mending pieces of china, sanding down tiny chips in glass. She was always allowed to help, to feel that she was helping, and of course in the end she learned to be useful. She had not managed to give Katya that sort of childhood at all. Katya had gone – admittedly at her own request – to boarding-school: that had been largely because life alone with her mother in the small, cramped flat had been dull and exclusive of friends or fun. She herself, she now recognized, had been too exhausted by a failed marriage and Jess's death, and the quest for how to earn her living, to have much over for poor Katya. She had *paid* for her and tried to keep things going and no more. Hence her feelings of guilt and inadequacy, for both of which there was reason. But however much water flowed under the bridge, one was still left with the bridge.

Sometimes she thought, almost with terror, about the cottage; empty and deserted but full of him with her, of her excitement and joy at being able to trust that she was so loved, and now full too of some unknown evil undercurrent of his plans. Sometimes she thought that if he had succeeded in getting her to marry him, he would then have murdered her – for whatever she owned or had – and gone on to the next woman: an exaggeration, possibly, but one that she could not absolutely dismiss. She said something about it to Anna, who had agreed – quite calmly – that indeed it could have been his option. Being able to talk about him in that way became a step away from mindless pain. She would not go back to the cottage. Knowing that, she could allow herself to look at it, to see it as it had been when she discovered it: the slates on the roof blue from a recent shower, the white walls streaked with livid green where a drainpipe had leaked; the cobwebs on the window in the kitchen; the mossy smell of airless damp, the unkempt ragged garden – a desolation of weeds. And then its transformation, the cleaning and the painting, the very simple furnishing that turned it quickly into somewhere that she longed to return to. She remembered lying in her hospital bed in Los Angeles, imagining herself there, sitting by her fire in the long, low-ceilinged room with its pale red walls and its white bookcases waiting to be filled. She would garden and cook and write: it was to be a new life and she would not mind being alone there at all. And then, because of his first letters, she had begun to imagine the garden that he wrote about, the charming scented place that she was to enjoy.

It was half-way through the second week before she felt able to consider work – the play – the idea for which was so embryonic that it could not stand much sustained attention. Possibilities, details so small as to appear useless, pieces of bone structure that did not seem to fit with one another, and – more than anything – what it was all *for*, occurred and vanished like gnats in summer air, or the tiny indeterminate specks that come from holes in the cornea, gone before she could record their erratic mazy movement.

When she said something of this to Anna and asked what she had thought of the treatment, Anna had simply said, 'I don't think you were ready to write it. I think your attention was otherwise engaged.' She smiled with an ironic sweetness that left the truth with no sting in it. It was perfectly true.

And eventually, she began to notice where she was – the climate, warm, scented air, the clear Greek light, the dazzling whites of the houses and the low walls that surrounded them, the chequered shade afforded by the dusty plane trees in the village square, the vine-covered terrace of the restaurant, and the pure, clear, beautiful sea that changed throughout the day from colours of verdigris and jade to the richest ink blue and slowly darkened as the sun sank until the random glitter of crocus lights from the fishing boats decorated its blackness.

The evening before they were to leave she tried to thank both of them for the time they had given her. They had returned from the restaurant, were settling on the sunset terrace, but there was a little light coming from the open kitchen window – she felt concealed enough to say such things that brought tears to her eyes which they would not see.

'You have made the whole difference . . . I cannot imagine . . . I am so . . . fortunate to have either of you, let alone both . . .'

'Yes, we are rather marvellous,' Anthony said, 'but it is good of you to say so. Darling Daisy, if you don't know how much we treasure you by now you never will.'

'But I do.'

'She does,' Anna said.

'I do rather dread going back.'

'Of course you do. This isn't ordinary life – it's been an interlude. It's always nasty having to stop being in them.'

'Katya will be pleased to have you back: she so wanted to come – to be here with you. But she'd promised the children their London treat.'

'You'd think they'd rather come here than be stuck in London.'

'No, *no*. They want to go on the Underground, and have hamburgers at McDonald's and go to that swimming pool that's got a wave machine and a water chute. Oh, yes, and have tea in an hotel. I don't know why they thought of that, but Caroline was mad for it. I staked Katya for that.'

'You have been a fairy godfather to her.'

'Careful what you say. Not a bad fairy, anyway.' He passed his hand lightly over the top of her head.

'You have got the most staggering hair. You'll get over that horrid old shit, you'll see.'

'Yes.' His demotion was curiously comforting: he shrank in significance.

'Yes. I can even imagine,' she said uncertainly, because it was not quite true, 'even imagine really knowing that he never loved me at all. Not for a second.' She looked at them. Maddeningly, her eyes filled. It was not yet true, but she did know then that it *would* be – both true and, eventually, acceptable.

21

HENRY

She has left me. This last, most terrible blow has knocked me out. Everything going so well, more or less according to plan, you might say, and then she slips off to London on some excuse about her daughter. Obviously a ruse, I can see that now, but I would never have suspected her of dishonesty. The shock! I am peacefully asleep, and that queer is standing over me telling me to get up – there's a letter for me in the kitchen.

'I have learned a lot about your past that you did not tell me, as a result of which I never want to see or hear from you again . . .' *What* had she learned? That was my first thought, although I gave nothing of that away to the two standing over me at the table. He'd brought a pal with him – wouldn't have the guts to face me alone. He'd have been right about that: for a moment I was filled with such rage that I could have strangled him with my bare hands.

I tried argument, of course, but I knew really that, somehow or other, the game was up. Then it turned out that the other one was a policeman, and that did put the wind up me. I know I don't stand a chance against them. Twenty minutes to pack. The policeman followed me out to the shed; it was lucky that I had everything in carrier-bags – my writing, my magazines, my money, all paper and stuffed in a tin so he couldn't know what

427

anything was. I stowed it all away in the bag she'd brought down with her files, and then, without so much as a cup of tea, they bundled me off to the station. I'd thought of going back to the cottage when I'd made sure that they'd left it, but they got my key off me. The policeman warned me not to go back and it seemed best not to say anything. I told them I had no money for a ticket – at that point I had no desire to go anywhere – and the queer fished a bunch of notes out of his jeans' pocket and bought me one. 'A one-way ticket to Edinburgh,' he said, with a nasty smile. That lot are always spiteful, if they get the chance.

Then I was in the train on its way north. They said I'd have to change for Edinburgh and I didn't answer them. What was the point of going there? Or anywhere else, for that matter?

What can have possessed her to go like that, giving me no chance at all to find out what she knew, what she minded, how I could mend the fences? She was in love with me – I'm sure of that – or was she simply sexually infatuated? But infatuation should have done; it has served before, for as long as I have wanted it to.

They must have told her I wasn't good enough for her, not middle class enough, didn't have enough money or a nice car, the things women are supposed to go for.

I just don't have any luck, that's what it is. In spite of all my efforts, the time and trouble and, yes, intelligence I put into getting my life right, it goes wrong. People are so selfish, so concerned for their own welfare that they can't look at anything excepting from their own point of view.

She'll miss me in bed. She'll remember that for a long time. I hope she aches for it: it would serve her right. A woman of her age isn't going to find it easy to get a man to want her enough to do it. I'm not usual there. In fact, she probably hasn't realized what she has missed out on.

What to do now? I thought of returning to Northampton, having another go at Hazel – turn over a new leaf and see if I could persuade her to change her mind about selling her parents' bungalow, and we'd go off to Wales or somewhere and I'd grow organic vegetables. I'd taken the ring, which Daisy had left by the bed; it would do as a peace-offering . . . But I discarded the notion. I hadn't the heart for it. It would be a heavy, unrewarding slog to bring Hazel round.

I realized that I badly needed a drink, and went along the train to the buffet car where I bought four small bottles of tonic to go with eight minute bottles of vodka. I helped myself to four plastic cups. 'That'll keep them happy,' I said to the barman. I wanted to be able to return for more without comment.

The drink helped. I was able to think a bit more clearly. How on earth had they found out about Charley? And what *else* had they found out? There have, naturally (I have lived a long time), been incidents I hadn't mentioned to Daisy: the short but disastrous affair with Carol, which had forced me to leave Bristol, and then that divorcee I picked up on the boat. What was her name? Jackie something or other. She'd pursued me in person and then through some agency because she'd left her credit card about and blamed me for what happened with it. I didn't think much of any of that would have come to light. But Rackham – I had made a serious mistake in mentioning Rackham, and maybe they'd gone poking about there. Not being able to smoke on these trains is monstrous. My nerves were still on edge. I went to the lavatory and had a quick fag, but quite soon someone rattled the door so I had to get rid of it.

When it comes to the point, people are just out for themselves. It doesn't matter what you try to do for them, it's never enough and you get no gratitude.

I finished the vodka.

What was *she* doing now? I tried to imagine her, sitting in some smart restaurant in London with her daughter and that woman I've never trusted. She'd gone to London in her denim skirt and red and yellow shirt. They'd probably take her shopping: women are material creatures and spending money always seems to cheer them up, but really, given what she'd done to me, I need not care too much what she felt like then, or ever. Water under the bridge – that was the way to look at it.

As I went along the train to get 'a second round' from the barman, he pointed out that the train was stopping shortly and it would be all change. So I took the drink and went back to get my stuff off the luggage rack.

The train for Edinburgh was on a platform the other side of the station: it was not due for some minutes so I bought a ham roll and a packet of cigarettes from the station buffet.

Platforms are desolate places. Not many people were waiting for the train. I was still in two minds about catching it, but no alternative presented itself. When it came in, I simply got on to it without thought.

It was a very long train, of the kind that has long, open carriages, interspersed with closed compartments and a corridor. As the train drew out of the station I started to walk forward through the coaches in search of a closed compartment that was not full of children or garrulous businessmen. Eventually, right at the far end, I came across a first-class compartment that contained only one passenger. She wore a grey linen suit and her shoes and bag were black, real lizard skin, and she had very fine, grape-coloured stockings. There was a book on her lap and she looked up from it as I slid open the door, peering at me over her small, smart spectacles.

'Is this seat taken?'

'Not as far as I know.'

'I hoped that it wasn't.' I sat down opposite her. She glanced at me and then continued to read. My magazines were not suitable for railway reading, so I stared out of the window – at the dull north-Midlands countryside. Time had to go by, but during it I had the chance to observe that she was somewhere in her late forties, that she bleached her hair and that she was making conscious efforts to ignore me.

The train entered a tunnel and the compartment was dark except for my companion's reading light, which shone down on her book leaving the rest of her in shadow, and I almost invisible to her.

For the last time, I considered the blow that Daisy had dealt me – the poor return it made for all my trouble. She had left me and the shock of it was still appalling. Then I decided to think of it no more, or perhaps to think of it merely as an incident – an unfortunate incident, which really, when one came to think about it, could have turned out very much worse.

The train emerged into grey daylight, and I caught her eye and smiled, but I said nothing. One should never seem to rush anything on these occasions: I would wait because I knew that in the end she would be the first to speak.

picador.com

blog
videos
interviews
extracts